C000080208

DARKNESS

BOOK ONE OF THE OORTIAN WARS

IAIN RICHMOND

WORLDS OF IAIN RICHMOND

Thank you for purchasing this book. Visit
www.iainrichmond.com
and sign up for my spam-free newsletter and receive a free copy
of *BEYOND TERRA, Tales from the Seven Worlds,*
an anthology of short stories!

I will let you know when new releases are in the works, give you
sneak peeks at rough drafts and original storyworlds. Free, no
spam and a unique view into the worlds of Iain Richmond.

Copyright © 2018 by Iain Richmond
Ebook published in 2019 by Rouge Planet Publishing.

Cover by Jeff Brown Graphics, additional artwork by James E. Grant.
Editors: Claire Rushbrook, Andrea Hurst, Sean Fletcher.

ISBN 978-1-946807-99-1
Fiction / Science Fiction / Space Opera / Military Science Fiction. CIP data for
this book is available from the Library of Congress 2018965053.

Rouge Planet Publishing
20875 Jerusalem Grade
Lower Lake CA 95457

for my Arial Queen of Light
book One in eight years
book Two in eight months
progress

"The fishermen know that the sea is dangerous and the storm terrible, but they have never found these dangers sufficient reason for remaining ashore."

–Vincent Van Gogh

– for Pluto –
Planet of my Childhood

0500, 12.05.2214
Confederation of Chinese Republics,
Mongolia Province
UN Aeronautics & Intergalactic HQ,
Officer Housing

"JACK."

The voice was soft, sweet—familiar. Lieutenant Jack Falco pulled the blankets up to his chin. He rolled toward the siren song, unable to open his heavy eyes.

"OK, ladyfriend, I get it, you need the early-morning Falco Special." Still blind and half-awake, Jack sent his adventurous hands on a journey through the jungle of blankets until they found two perfect landing zones.

"Jack." A giggle. "Your neck is glowing again, and at 0500 … again." Her voice hovered between annoyance and laughter.

"Hmm-mm." Jack slowly forced his eyes open and found a strikingly beautiful face looking back at him. "Much rather look at you, woman. Too early to play pilot, and I was hoping this was a different type of wake-up call."

The pinprick light-blue glow on the back of his neck began to flash.

"They're getting impatient, honey."

"OK, OK." He reluctantly moved his hands from her breasts, corralled a few pillows, and piled them behind him. I better get to blow some shit up today, he thought, and tapped the special-issue LINK on his neck. *Lieutenant Falco here.* His lips wanted to move, but thoughts were all that was needed. A truly private conversation could take place anywhere. It'd taken him years to perfect the art of communication without opening his mouth.

He listened to Captain Baines's voice and knew it was literally in his head. No one else could hear it. The part that still made him uneasy was the realization that the technology enabling this call was hardwired to his brain through his spinal cord. The result of giving up total privacy … 0500 calls from HQ and instant downloads, of course.

Yes, Captain. Jack nodded. *Yes, sir. 0800.*

He tapped the LINK, turned toward Luciana, and just stared into those eyes, raising his eyebrows, giving her "the nod" until a large pillow met the side of his head, followed by muffled laughter.

"So that's how you treat the man who has given you all this?" His hands gestured toward the windows of their small house on the United Nations' largest base, the perfectly framed view of asphalt, postage-stamp yards, and launch towers as far as the eye could see. "Right?" he finished.

On cue, one of the Luna Station supply shuttles ignited from a distant tower. The well-known vibration rolled through the three hundred square meters of living space. "At least it's a small one? Could have been a Mars shuttle." Jack winced.

"Ever wish you still piloted the shuttles full-time? You were in the space program in the early days for a reason." Luciana fell silent.

He turned toward her. "Space Station jockey is a lifestyle job. Gone for a few weeks if you get the lunar milk-run or a few years bouncing between here and the Mars shoebox. Besides, I still get to go up every now and again. You trying to get rid of me?" He moved closer and kissed her full lips, looked into those dark brooding eyes. "My two ladies. That is why I stay planetside." Falco held her gaze, a smile spreading across his face. "And then there is you and Ziza." He ducked under the incoming pillow, rolled out of bed and started to get dressed.

"What's the mission?" Luciana asked.

"The kind they don't tell me about." He finished buttoning his uniform. "Just like all the rest, but Cap did say I would be back for dinner."

"I'll take it, but you better tell the other woman in your life good-bye. You know how she gets." Luciana nestled back under the blankets.

My god, that woman is sexy. Her olive skin is the perfect contrast to the white sheets, he thought. A snort broke the silence, and Luciana, asleep already, rolled over and wedged her head partially beneath her pillow.

"That's my ladyfriend," Jack whispered with pride.

A faint glow lit the back of her neck. He observed the morning ritual as his wife pawed at it once, sending her alarm into snooze mode. The first of four such actions, he thought. "I love you, sweetness."

He quietly closed the bedroom door and moved down the hallway toward a yellow door with an orange-and-red sun painted on it. Jack reached for the doorknob, stopped, and took in the grandeur and skill of the work before him. There were sunspots, solar flares, and hazy areas tagged "soler wins." He held back a chuckle and eased the door open.

Every extra blanket in the house had been carefully folded

into long rectangles and stacked like bricks along the edges of the small bed. Jack moved closer. Inside the great wall of bedding lay the fluffiest swirl of quilts. Gently sitting on the newly built fortification, Jack leaned in.

"Ziza," he whispered to the heap, his Sicilian accent in full form.

"Ziza, my *piccola farfalla*, Papi must go." Jack waited for the heap to move. Slowly it shifted back and forth, a small sigh puffing from deep within.

"Ziza." The heap moved again. Two small hands emerged on the far side of the bed, followed by a mop of curly black hair, and finally two bright blue eyes blinked and were covered by small, rubbing hands.

"My little butterfly has emerged." Jack ruffled her hair.

"Papi, who will make pancakes?" she said, yawning.

"Mama will. I taught her my secret recipe."

"But I want the smiley-face pancakes." Ziza's eyes turned shiny as she swallowed hard.

"Not to worry. Mama knows how to make sun pancakes." Jack knew Luciana could wing it with the best of them.

"With spots and flares?" A huge toothy smile spread across Ziza's face.

"Of course." Jack felt a pang of guilt, knowing he was setting his wife up for an interesting morning.

Ziza's eyes fell heavy, and he leaned over and kissed her forehead, then both cheeks. "I will see you at dinner, my little butterfly." He pulled up the fluffy quilt and adjusted her cocoon. The light from the hallway caught the LINK implanted in her small neck.

We always know where you are, my Ziza, Jack thought.

He did not trust the implants; even more, he loathed what they stood for. No, he pondered, I hate what they have taken. They have stolen all privacy from our lives. But worse were the billions of people around the world that asked for the LINK, wanted its torrent of information, music, games, and especially its pornography.

In his case, it was simply part of the contract. The greatest nano-computer ever created and required by all those who lived and worked for the United Nations. Another leash marketed as progress.

A gentle knock sounded on the front door. His ride was here. Petty Officer, First Class Azim Shar'ran may have been the only person left who knocked instead of using the LINK to announce his arrival. Shar'ran didn't trust them either.

Jack pulled Ziza's door closed and stepped lightly to the entryway.

Before opening the front door, he hesitated and turned around. Be back for dinner, he thought.

He found the tall, muscled, lanky form of Petty Officer, First Class Shar'ran, patiently waiting.

Shar'ran's brilliant ivory teeth softened the old scars crisscrossing his otherwise flawless dark skin. "How is my little Aziza, still building cocoons?" Shar'ran asked.

"She has the intelligence of her mother and the imagination of her father, and yes, still building cocoons." Jack fell silent as they walked toward their transport.

Shar'ran cleared his throat. "OK, Falco, what's on your mind?"

Neither man used ranks or salutes until they had to, at least not when it was just the two of them.

"Captain Baines brief you on the mission?" Falco looked to his friend and stopped. They were getting close to the transport and he wanted to continue this conversation in the open air.

"CODE BLACK," Shar'ran stated, "but I'm a ground-and-pound grunt. You fliers are the ones they talk to."

"We are all in the dark on this one. We just spent the last eight months hunting and killing every member of the Korean Empire's Terror Militia." Falco scanned in all directions, lowered his voice. "We've taken out their entire command chain—"

"Except Vice Marshal Ri," Azim stated.

"Exactly!" Falco stated emphatically. "Head of the snake is still out there. She's responsible for slaughtering thousands. We've never had a BLACK OUT mission for any of the previous kills."

"You think they found Ri?" Shar'ran's eyes lit up.

"Let's hope so." Falco motioned toward his house. "World would be a much safer place if we took her out." He again scanned the distance in all directions. "I think we're dusting off the T-11s." Falco rubbed his hands together in excitement.

"Shit." Shar'ran returned the nod. "You're going way up. Get some space time on this one."

"Yeah, and one hell of a ride down. They don't call the T-11s lawn-darts for nothing." The thought of skimming the edge of the exosphere again brought an exhilaration Falco had long missed.

"Speaking of a ride down," Shar'ran put his hands up and punched the air, "you up for a little sparring this week?"

"One lucky punch and you think you're the grav-fighting champ of the Province." Falco grabbed his still aching jaw at the thought. "That how you treat a commissioned officer?"

Shar'ran nodded. "No officers in the ring, Lieutenant—"

"Just meat." They exchanged a thunderous high five and were on the move again, jumping into the transport and heading toward Aeronautics HQ.

In the distance, streaking flames rose into the early-morning sky. Two Mars Station supply shuttles had reached full burn and a third launched moments after from a remote tower deep inside the Gobi Desert. This shuttle was matte black, three times the size of the Mars models, and traveled a different course that would carry it far beyond the Mars Station.

6

4 hours later, Al-som Island
60 klicks off the eastern coast,
Korean Empire

Vice Marshal Ri, wearing the regulation black uniform with a red sash, spoke over an old landline receiver. On all sides, concrete and steel formed walls, ceiling, and floor. Each grunt from her hard lips echoed within the tomb. "I understand. The global power structure must change for the Militia to rise." She gently placed the receiver on the base.

"Quickly. We have no time. The UN has found our bunker." Vice Marshal Ri looked down at her subordinate tapping away on an ancient computer with bubbly keys. Her hand rested on the worn grip of a sidearm. Ri had always feared the command bunker. Hundreds of meters down, the engineers drilled through the islands volcanic rock pedestal, far below the ocean's surface.

Which waits to come rushing in, she thought.

"Almost finished, Vice Marshal." Sweat ran down the subordinate's puffy face while his hands continued to fly over the keyboard.

Vice Marshal Ri stepped closer behind him. "The system is completely hardwired, yes? No one can stop us. We must strike the ultimate blow."

He turned and looked up. She jostled her sidearm within its holster; he quickly turned back to the monitor, keys tapping faster until the sound reached a low hum.

"Yes, Vice Marshal, we are connected to the emitter by cable, nothing else."

Vice Marshal Ri enjoyed watching the sweat that ran down his face, hearing the tremor in his voice. All by my hand, she thought. My reputation strikes fear not only in the hearts of my people, but in my enemies as well.

"The code is good. It will do as intended, but many of our own will die with them." A cold, steel muzzle pressed against his

7

temple, followed by the click of a cocking hammer. "Sorry, Vice Marshal, all will die as heroes! Patriots of the Korean Empire!" he cried.

"Good." She held the pistol against his pale, glistening skin. "We may have lost this war with the United Nations, but on this day, the Korean Empire's Terror Militia will be remembered for our final act of defiance."

"It is done." The man pushed his chair away from the desk, putting distance between himself and the muzzle, and pleaded for his life, hands above his head. "It's finished! Please don't kill me! It's finished! My wife, my children all have LINKs. As does your own family, Vice Marshal. Please!"

UN Special Ops Air Guard, Jilin Province Confederation of Chinese Republics
200 klicks northwest of Al-som Island, Korean Empire

SONIC BOOMS THUNDERED above the Hamgyong Mountain Range when three T-11 rocket ships led by Lieutenant Jack Falco dropped out of the upper atmosphere. A panicked voice sounded over their coms. "This is Major General Khan. Tear out your LINKs! Go to analog now! Confirmed! We are compromised! Repeat! We are compromised! Over!"

The background noise of the United Nations Command Center filled Falco's COM with a cacophony of confused voices. Orders in various native tongues bellowed from every UN station as all personnel in the command center tried to warn their governments on a free COM line. Major Khan's voice rang muffled, then roared clear, "Manual only! Complete the mission! Over!"

Lieutenant Falco quickly shut down his computer; the

cockpit's glow faded and was replaced by shaking needles on rarely used gauges. He reached up to the base of his skull, just beneath his helmet, fingers fumbling to find the release on his LINK. He pulled hard on the tiny pellet that for decades had safely connected his brain to the cyber world.

A shooting pain, followed by brief disorientation, and Lieutenant Falco was literally flying by the seat of his pants.

"Sir?" One of his wingmen broke the COM's silence. "We need the LINK or our stealth mode is worth—"

"God damn it!" Falco pushed forward on the yoke as the ship to his starboard sliced across his nose and slammed into his other wingman. Debris from the collision clanged off his cockpit; red pulp spread across his canopy.

"Oh Jesus." Falco's voice trembled. "They said to pull the LINK out. Fuck!" He was closing in on the mission's coordinates. He tried the COMs again.

"HQ, this is Falcon. Eagle and Hawk are down. Do you read? Eagle and Hawk are down. Over." A steady static filled his helmet.

"Complete the mission," he whispered, and armed his missiles. His eyes fell to a photo taped to his instrument panel of a striking woman and small bright-eyed girl sitting in her lap.

The antiquated range sensor flickered from green to yellow.

"Come on!" Falco yelled at the yellow light. He glanced at his current position, finger hovering over the launch switch. Yellow held, then flashed to red as the obsolete firing system established a visual lock.

He released a guttural scream. "Fuck you! HAMMER DOWN!" Lieutenant Falco fired.

Six missiles flew from their cradles. Seconds later, they arched high into the atmosphere, above a tiny island off the east coast of the Korean Empire before dropping like arrows toward the tiny landmass. Quickly reaching supersonic speeds, each missile was programmed to remove layers of rock, concrete and steel before the next impact – a mountain-leveling jackhammer.

Three red objects appeared on Falco's helmet display – incoming. Within seconds, his T-11 released all of its counter measures. He knew it was a useless act. Only the processing speed of the LINK could have tracked and fired the necessary rounds from the chain gun to destroy the missiles. The LINK now possibly infected, the LINK embedded in his wife, daughter, and over half of the world's population. All for a 'better life.'

Falco monitored the chasing objects closing in on him while he listened to the static of a dead COM. He adjusted his flight path to ensure the wreckage would fall harmlessly over the Sea of Japan. Falco tapped the photo of his wife and daughter. "Love you, ladyfriend, and you, my dearest *piccola farfalla*, my little butterfly."

A quaking hand moved toward a bright red lever and stopped. Warning lights flashed across the console of his cockpit, the chasing missiles only seconds from their objective. Tears rolled down Falco's jaw.

"Not like this," he whispered, and slid the picture of his wife and daughter into a side pocket on his flight suit, mumbled a prayer to the sky god, Jove, and pulled the eject lever.

Korean Empire Terror Militia bunker
Al-som Island

SIRENS WAILED INSIDE THE BUNKER. Vice Marshal Ri looked up as another impact vibrated through the structure and focused on the concrete slab above. "Yes, you are right, all is finished." She raised her sidearm. "You have done great work…" She paused, realizing she had no idea what his name was. A single, muffled shot cracked and the limp body of the programmer slid off the chair and hit the ground.

The bunker shook violently from a close impact. Vice Marshal Ri's knees and ankles snapped under the force, she screamed and crumpled to the floor. Another impact flung her broken body into a concrete wall, a pool of blood growing under her fractured skull. A last gasp, a sickly smile, "I will be remem —" A thousand tons of rock, steel and concrete buried Vice Marshal Ri and the ocean followed.

2

Morning, 12.05.2216
Falcone Estate, Palermo, New Sicily
Two Year Anniversary of the Terrorist Attack

JACK FALCO SAT at his father's massive oak desk, a silver-framed photo of Lucia and Ziza in one hand, a glass of scotch in the other. His reflection on the picture's glass showed heavy bags under puffy eyes and silver streaks painting his temples, adding decades to his once-youthful thirty-five years.

Real pictures of Falco as a young grav-fighter decorated the walls. One photo had an actual news clipping above it. The headline read, "FIGHTING FALCON OVERCOMES the Lion of Tibet!" Next to them, frames of changing images on dated hologram feeds flashed the smiling faces of his father and mother surrounded by acres of grapevines. Jack, wondering about the wisdom of returning home with all its associated memories, placed the picture of his wife and daughter down and rested the scotch glass next to a small rusted key.

Falco stared at a large, rectangular piece of unscathed oak, shining in the center of the desktop. Around the shape, scratches, smudges and watermarks formed as spilled scotch ate through the finish. Combined, they created a strange mosaic he had never noticed. The old typewriter or key pounder as he liked to call it had protected the desktop from a month's worth of heavy abuse. He opened the shallow center drawer above his lap and pulled out a thick stack of worn paper covered in type-driven ink.

Real paper was the key, the Doc had said. She spoke of the therapeutic importance of putting feelings, thoughts and experiences on paper each day. Tapping the typewriter keys, hearing each stroke hitting the texture and pressing into the weight of the paper involved all the senses and brought healing to a broken heart and fractured mind.

Writing what Falco felt would free him. The accounts of nightmares fueled by identifying the bodies of his dead wife and daughter. Describing the world he returned to, the world he could not save. A world seventy percent less populated and missing the only two people he could not live without. But I have, Falco thought. For two years to the day, I grieved, I felt every fucking emotion a person could and still be alive.

He knew the real reason for the thirty-day period. The government of New Sicily and hundreds of others around the world created the 'Writing Month' as simple proof to show they tried. Tried to prevent the massive number of suicides that continued to drop the remaining global population far below replacement levels. A grief-stricken humanity was exterminating itself.

Write for a month prior to throwing yourself off a bridge and your estate transferred cleanly and fully intact to the next in line. Put a bullet in your head without the documented 'Writing Month' and your estate was held up for years with over half forfeited to the local government.

Falco reached towards the glass and pulled back. "Let's get

this over with," he coldly stated and began flipping through the stack of pages. The top page was dated 11.05.2216 and at the bottom of the stack was 12.04.2016. Falco had kept the agreement he made with Doc. A month of 'writing therapy' and then what he did was his business and would not affect the Falcone Estate. His distant relatives would inherit the place that was so important to his parents without government interference. It was time to join his family.

He pulled the ancient key-pounder from the corner of the desktop. The old steel casing fit perfectly over the pristine rectangle in the desktop's center. He rolled in a final sheet of paper, picked up his glass, threw back the rest of its contents, refilled it and set it down. The keys felt cold and foreign under the calloused tips of each finger, but it was time.

0800, 12.05.2216

The world continues to burn the endless stack of bodies. Two years later and the gray ash sifts downward, ever falling, never a pause, always there. I drag it in with every breath: its slippery layer lines my clothes, my sheets. It comes through the tiniest of holes and fissures, ever searching for the one responsible.

The cloud follows me. The dead continue to burn, carried on the hot draft up and out of a thousand furnaces burning across the world, all day, every day for two years... and still the bodies go from freezer to furnace, over and over again. All they want is the chance to catch a breeze and hunt the man that could not save them during life.

My wife and daughter mix with the others on a breeze or gust or latch onto a raindrop to rest on a cool stone, only to dry and again be carried off on the sole of a shoe or covered in the shit from a dog.

Why does any of it matter when I am responsible for the death of billions? Two years and I feel the weight of it in the stares of survivors walking the cobbled streets as zombies. I wish I had

never been pulled from that raft. The sharks were ready, I was
ready. I should have gone then. I need to go now. There is nowhere
I can run to, nowhere I can hide. Two years was as much as I could
bear. Know that I did everything I could and it was not enough.
    I go to see my family.
    ~ Giacomo Francis Falcone

Falco focused on the echo of the last tapped key. The writing
had helped, he thought, just too little too late. "I'm so sorry," he
whispered reaching for the picture of his wife and daughter.

Taking the rusty key, he opened the drawer, and pulled out a
perfectly maintained 1938 Glisenti revolver that had been in his
family for over two centuries. Falco carefully set the picture face
down on the desk and held the gun in his lap, slowly turning the
cylinder, clicking through each new cartridge. An action he had
done a hundred times since they died... No... since I let
them die.

His mouth opened wide, the barrel cold on his soft, upper
pallet. Fifteen degree angle, he thought, breathe deep, it's OK,
breathe, and squeeze...

A jarring knock hammered at the front door. Falco pulled the
gun out of his mouth, shook his head and cleared his throat, the
revolver feeling foreign in his shaking hand. He dropped the gun
in the drawer, closed it hard, and moved cautiously toward the
front door.

"Who is it?" Falco felt the veins pounding through his head,
his own voice a stick rattling a metal garbage can.

"Vice Admiral Hallsworth, United Nations Navy. Now cut
the shit, Lieutenant Falco. Open this goddamn door and get an
old friend a drink."

He ran his fingers through his mop of graying hair, pulled his
hand down his bearded face, looked at his week-old jeans and T-
shirt. "Shit," he grumbled. Giving up, Falco opened the door.

Hallsworth, The Giant, as his men lovingly referred to the

man in private, was a mountain. Falco had forgotten the sheer mass of him, let alone that he could drink anyone under the table. And I'm already there, he thought.

"Good to see you are still with us, Lieutenant." He pushed straight past Falco, headed to the study and dropped into a chair next to the bottle of single malt. Hallsworth helped himself to an extra glass off the shelf behind him and poured a fistful. "You still like the good stuff. Just like your father."

Falco trailed into the room, eased into his seat behind the desk. "Yes, Vice Admiral" – he exhaled loudly – "I find that it helps me sleep at night."

"And during the day, by the looks of you." Hallsworth stared until Falco broke the uncomfortable silence.

"How can I help you—"

"Jack, you look like shit warmed over." Hallsworth didn't let him finish. "Yes, we lost two-thirds of the world's population to the most cowardly and horrifying act of terrorism in the history of our planet." He grabbed his glass again, took a gulping chug, and continued as Jack looked blankly ahead. "You lost your wife, your daughter – hell, we all lost family and friends. There was nothing you or the rest of us could do about it. They broke into the most securely encrypted system ever created and—"

"Seventeen seconds." Falco swallowed hard. His eyes felt hot; tears wanted to come but were long gone. "Seventeen seconds before I blew that bunker to hell and back. That evil bitch uploaded a malicious code that stopped the hearts of over twenty billion people. Used our own LINK system… seventeen seconds before I killed her. Malicious code increases your junk-feeds, for god's sake. It doesn't kill you."

Falco took a slug of scotch. They used a system we willingly implanted in our own brains to commit mass murder, he thought. A system that made us more efficient, more connected… "More connected to what?" Jack whispered.

Hallsworth refilled his glass and took another heavy gulp.

"None of us could have known the LINK system could be compromised. Hell, we have been using encrypted radio waves for centuries with only minor hacking issues." He took a deep breath and leaned in. "You can sit here and drink yourself to death in the idyllic surroundings of the Falcone Estate or you can clean yourself up and buck the fuck up. I have an assignment for you."

Falco felt like he had physically crawled out of a bottle of scotch after spending the night swimming in its contents. He looked to Vice Admiral Hallsworth and changed the subject. "You know, we should skip the scotch and drink the family wine. My people were walking through the vineyards on Mount Etna in 500 BC. A century before the French knew what to do with a grape!"

Hallsworth smiled. "Yes, your father loved that speech. Loved to espouse it at the dinner table with friends and family. It was usually followed by... Falcone's have the strength" – Falco joined in, and the two men's voices echoed in the study – "of Ancient Greeks, make love like Italians, and have the intellect of Arabs!"

Falco loved his father and missed the man that took the time to raise a son while his peers passed the duties to hired help. Falco found himself staring at the lock on the drawer that held the old revolver.

"Jack!" Vice Admiral Hallsworth barked. "I see the photo face down on your desk. I see the way you look at the drawer where that ancient shooter of your great-grandfather has always been kept, one I have fired on many occasions while visiting this place. Not to mention, I have been in daily contact with your Doc and your thirty-day Writing Period is over. Time to stand up, son! We've got work to do."

Falco straightened. "I need to get far away from this." His hands raised as he swiveled in his chair, voice a low growl. "Everything reminds me of them. I can't escape the ashes of the dead. Loved ones killed because they didn't have time to pull that goddamn LINK out of their fucking skulls!"

Hallsworth stood, walked over to Falco, and placed his hand on his shoulder. "It's time. You started your career in the space program, and an opportunity knocks again. Jack, I have a Cyclone Class, deep-space scout ship waiting for you. You are one of the best pilots we have left, and back in the day, you were the craziest son of a bitch I knew. The time for mourning has passed. The United Nations needs you."

"One of the best?" Falco replied with a forced grin. "Deep space? I thought we were only scouting around the Mars Station. Have we already sucked out every ounce of mineral profit in the surrounding asteroid fields?"

Hallsworth rolled his eyes. "Yes. They have, and to the point, it seems two years of peacetime helped resurrect a decade-old and once top-secret project designated OORT133. Building spacecraft and space stations instead of supporting huge militaries is actually easier on the budget."

"Not to mention the mineral revenue isn't all bad either," Falco stated.

"Still have to pay for programs, and yes, mineral rights are important. Your choice, Lieutenant Falco." Hallsworth set his empty glass on the oak desk and sat back down. "Captain your own vessel up there" – he pointed to the ceiling – "or sit here and play with your little gun. The decision is yours, but either way, the ship departs in two weeks and needs a captain."

"Sir." Falco's face tightened. "How can we protect our starships from enemy hackers if we couldn't safely encrypt the LINK system?"

"A valid question, and one the UN spent every available resource to answer." Hallsworth fell silent.

"And?" Falco asked.

"They have assured me that the new end-to-end encryption is unbreakable. The Battle-Net has permanently replaced the

LINK system. If needed, you can shoot Data-Pods ship-to-ship and back to the Mars Station." Hallsworth raised an eyebrow, "If, of course, you are not in a hurry."

"Battle-Net?" Falco winced.

"Ya, I know," Hallsworth echoed, "but the top minds at the UN wanted a system name that future enemies would think twice about attacking."

"Well then, I am now brimming with confidence." Falco leaned forward. "What about the boat, who is she?"

"An old friend, we brought her back from the dead and retrofitted her for the long haul." Hallsworth held his stare.

Falco's eyes burned bright. "How is that possible? She was destroyed. Fell two weeks before the terrorist attack. I saw her with my own eyes, dropping from the Mongolian sky. She was the final large-vessel casualty in the Korean Empire conflict." He looked hard at the Vice Admiral. "And what was left of her," Falco's teeth came together, "was scrapped!"

"Easy, Lieutenant. Not our best call, which is why we reversed it. Mothballed her hull in bay twenty instead." Hallsworth nodded. "But, the *Anam Cara* is good as new and docked at Lunar Station."

Falco grunted and slowly got to his feet. He set his glass next to Hallsworth's and moved a sore arm to a saluting position next to his forehead. "Lieutenant Falco reporting for duty. Sir!"

"Good, and you can work on that pathetic salute before you leave." Vice Admiral Hallsworth stood and slowly reached into his pocket. He worked his hand free and held out a silver eagle insignia resting in his palm. "Captain Giacomo Francis Falcone, tomorrow, December 6, 2216 at 0600 hours, your status will be changed to Active Duty and your rank elevated to a captain in the United Nations Navy. Your ass better be at the Rome Air Base getting on a shuttle to Lunar Station."

"Yes, sir," Captain Falco said.

"Questions, Captain?"

"Sir, as you know" – Falco shuffled uncomfortably – "in the Navy, captain is a term for the person in charge of the vessel, and this officer in charge is usually of a higher rank than captain but is still called, 'The Captain.'"

"Don't push it, son. You will be the lowest-ranking captain in the UNN fleet." He smiled. "An actual captaining captain."

"Yes, Vice Admiral." Falco saw pride behind those eyes. "I still do not have a crew and have no idea where the *Anam Cara* is going."

"Your officers volunteered." Hallsworth took a deep breath and continued, "Old friends you have been avoiding, and crewmen for deep-space missions are assigned directly out of the academy."

Falco had wanted to be part of the deep-space program from the beginning, but it was not a family-friendly career choice. Years spent on missions far from earth and loved ones – he blocked out the rest, knowing it led to a dark place. He was now farther away from his family than he ever thought possible. Death did that.

"However," the Vice Admiral went on, holding up a finger, "the science officer retired, too old for a fifteen-year turn. You need to pick one from the approved list. They're all stationed at the Rome Air Base." Hallsworth again worked his hand into his pocket and handed over a folded piece of worn paper, and sat down again.

Falco raised an eyebrow, looking at a real piece of paper with lead-smeared writing and exhaled sharply. "Approved list?" He found his chair, leaned back into the old creaking frame, and studied the names and brief bios.

"Made it myself, Jack. At the top is Lieutenant Marks, forty, French and experienced, not to mention—"

"Ensign Holts?" Falco interrupted.

"I guess you could start at the bottom of the list and move up, that's one method," Hallsworth grumbled, and grabbed his empty glass, refilled it, leaned over and filled Falco's glass a finger short of his own.

"She's an ensign." Falco looked up from the paper. "Lowest-ranking officer on the list, youngest by five years. Tough, driven I assume?"

"Scrapper out of Brazil's worst barrio, shaved head and tats to prove it. Damn smart, though. Test scores highest of the bunch, though she'd never admit it." Hallsworth raised the last liquid remnants to his lips, finished it off, and tapped the empty glass on Falco's desk. "You are now the youngest captain in the United Nations Navy, though in your current state, you'd never know it."

Falco threw back the last of his scotch, leaned across the desk, set the glass down, and slid the list back toward Vice Admiral Hallsworth. "Ensign Holts."

"You're the captain, and I'll make the call to Rome." Hallsworth stood, pointed to the photo with the headline above it. "Lion of Tibet should be arriving where you're headed about now." Without another word, Vice Admiral Hallsworth was up and heading to the front door, leaving Falco staring at the wall.

He stood and followed. "Vice Admiral? Pema Tenzin is already en route? To where?"

Hallsworth opened the door, turned. "Not anymore. Should be arriving, Captain. Seems Mr Tenzin had other skills besides grav-fighting. Became quite the engineer, I understand."

"Vice Admiral, you still have not told me where I'm going for the next fifteen years of my life."

"The *Anam Cara* is headed beyond Pluto, to the edge of our solar system. Project OORT133 is nearing completion and will be the United Nations' greatest achievement. We need you to scout out the reported anomalies around Station Pluto, maybe look into an asteroid field or two that has mining promise."

"A space station near Pluto's orbit?" Falco repeated.

"Not just a space station, Captain. Once you get there, it's your new home," Hallsworth stated. "Five to get there, five scouting the area, and five back. Fifteen-year turn," Hallsworth paused, "or so. Should have better tech by then to get your ass home a bit faster. How long you stay depends on what you find."

"Or don't find," Falco added.

"True, but when most of us live to be a hundred-thirty these days, gotta do something, Captain. Either way, Station Pluto should be finished by the time you get there."

"Anomalies?" Falco was still focused on the mission. He knew that in military jargon, 'anomalies' usually were not good for those looking into them.

"Your ears only." Hallsworth waited.

Falco nodded.

"Couple of rocks keep hitting the station."

Falco just stared. "You're sending us out to the edge of our solar system, near the Kuiper Belt, a massive asteroid field, to try to determine where stray chucks of ice and rock hitting the station are coming from?"

"Point taken, Captain."

Falco noted the emphasis on "Captain" and swallowed hard as Vice Admiral Hallsworth continued.

"You remember the brown dwarf they finally found a few years back? Some data-slug, noticed gravitational pull centuries ago, far beyond Pluto. Latest infrared telescope finally detected it. Named it after his ex-wife, I believe."

"Yep, named it Nemesis but, sir, brown dwarfs are discovered often. Is there something special about this particular sub stellar object?" Falco shifted his weight.

"It's thirteen times the mass of Jupiter," Hallsworth fell silent for a moment, lowered his voice and continued, "and… it's simply not there. Went towards the Oort Cloud on its normal orbital path and never came out again."

"Well, then," Falco said with a shrug, "guess we'll have something to look for."

"There's a bit more to it, Jack. The dark matter or dark fields, seem to have expanded our way in that particular area." The Vice Admiral raised an eyebrow. "At least that is what our space programs biggest and brightest tell me. I guess that is unusual. The point is, we still have no way of seeing into these areas."

"Thus, the anomaly classification. Well, sir, I could act like I know why dark matter or fields, or whatever moves the way it moves or I can simply add it to my expanding list of things to read up on prior to scouting it."

"That's the spirit, Jack. Now, get your things together and get some shut-eye. Shuttle departs at 0600." Vice Admiral Hallsworth moved through the front door.

Falco cleared his throat, swallowed the rising emotions. "Vice Admiral... Thank you, sir... I needed a change."

Hallsworth stopped on the porch, turned around and looked down, dead center into Falco's glossy eyes. "Beats a bullet to the fucking brainpan, Captain." Hallsworth leaned in close. "You are special to me, Jack. You're the best kind of family, the kind I can choose. Everyone falls down, son. Now get back up and get your shit together. Life is for the goddamn living." Hallsworth closed the door behind him.

Captain Jack Falco started to pack.

3

10.01.2221
Near Kuiper Belt, Outer Solar system
Space Station Pluto

"SCREEN UP. Magnetics. Increase to two point seven five." Much better, Pema Tenzin thought as his lift-suit clicked hard against the composite panel beneath them. Only two millimeters thick, the MAG-lock strips on the bottom of his boots were lined with thousands of minuscule magnets.

Each was linked together by even smaller circuits that all found their way to a processor responsible for keeping him attached to the outer skin of Station Pluto. The new panels that fused together to create the protective skin had only a trace amount of iron in them. Enough iron for the boots to stick and give the panel strength, but not enough to inflate the cost.

'Local Sherpa becomes GREATEST ENGINEER ever to graduate from Embry-Riddle Aeronautical University,' was the headline on every Chinese newspaper the day Pema received his PhD. Pema stood there, perpendicular to the massive structure with his glorified caulking gun in one hand and a tether attached to his gravity sled in the other.

One of thousands, he thought, pulling their goddamn sleds full of panels. We are nothing more than manual laborers with bigger titles and world-renowned educations. I am no different than my ancestors who slaved away in the Jintan Salt Mine of Jiangsu, or my father who worked himself to an early grave, for a country and people that looked down on him.

All so that I, Pema Tenzin, could get the best education Earth had to offer and become the first in my family to live as a free Tibetan, outside of The People's influence. He gave his best attempt at a magnanimous gesture with his hands, the caulking gun stealing a little of his thunder.

Pema shuffled a few more steps in his colossal Lift Suit. Size was relative out here in the black. Pluto was the biggest object in view for the moment, but even she grew tired of this bleak part of the outer solar system and moved on as fast as her elliptical orbit would allow. Station Pluto sprawled over four square kilometers and without the Lift Suits, engineers would be hard pressed to cover 100 square meters a day, 125 if they were being paid time and a half.

Lift Suits were twice as tall as a human and twice as wide. "Like being permanently strapped into a clunky human fork lift," Pema mumbled as his AI screen kicked on with a 'REPEAT ORDER, DO NOT UNDERSTAND...'

Not being able to utter a word without that ridiculous screen popping up all the time was irritating. He could shut it down, but the AI was another voice in the loneliest of surroundings. Annoying or not, its company was usually welcome and when exhausted, overworked humans made life threatening mistakes... the AI did not. On more than one occasion that voice had overridden Pema's pending actions and saved his ass.

With all of the 'brilliant' engineers housed on this station, you would think one of us could come up with an AI design to replace ourselves. I am a professional caulker, but the robotics in addition to the AI would cost more than a human dragging a grav-sled and everything comes down to the almighty Chinese Yuan.

Africa, Europe and South America spent and borrowed trillions developing clean energy producing technologies. The United Nations searched for the common link between them all and focused their vast resources on one thing, storage.

Their answer came in the form of Lithium Ion Nano-Batteries. The new industry raised the United Nations from the eighth largest economy in the year 2175 to the largest economy by 2195. Batteries were just the product, the nano-technologies and industry behind it were the gold mine.

The power grid as humanity had known it was gone. A small concrete one-room building could now store enough power for a small country, and that was just the beginning. Li-ion Nano-Technology was the new oil boom and the United Nations had all the reserves... for now. Pema refocused on his mundane task.

He reached down, held his glorified caulking gun steady and ran a bead of epoxy around the framework. He grabbed another panel off of the gravity sled and snapped it in place. The edges glowed red and sizzled as the panel fused to the framework, creating a monolithic structure and the most advanced space station in history.

No bolts, moving parts or air gaps. Each piece melted into the others, creating a seamless structure of unsurpassed strength and durability, even in the harshest of environments. And this was the final of the five separate layers.

Pema knew that without his breakthrough in poly-epoxies this station would not exist. He looked up as the glow from Pluto caught his attention. One of Pluto's moons, Charon, was playing her usual role, trying to steal all of the attention away from her mother with her beautiful silver streaks, but Pluto remained as striking as ever.

The sun's dim rays seemed to die on her surface, creating a dull silvery glow; a glow that without the face shield enhancers would remain dark shades of gray.

Tibetans had an intimate relationship with Pluto. A bond forged out of shared experience of having your identity stolen and spending lifetimes trying to get it back. Pluto was still a planet to Pema, not a dwarf planet or simply asteroid number 134340.

Again, a smile spread across his face and a peaceful feeling filled his robotic crypt as Pema thought about his friend, Jack Falco, the man who loved Pluto as much as he did.

Station Pluto's Arrival Log listed the revamped *Anam Cara*, Captain Falco's Cyclone Class Scouting Vessel, as 'refueling and inspections' before scouting beyond Pluto. That would give Falco at least forty-eight hours of R&R and plenty of time to find the grav-gym and lace up the gloves.

Nothing like sailing through the solar system for five years in and out of hibersleep on an old iron boat to show a person what they were made of. Pema shuddered at the memory of his own five-year voyage not long ago. Station Pluto was a five-star hotel compared to the dilapidated shack near Mars. If only the COMS satellite was fully operational, I would make sure and send a proper welcome, he thought. It will be good to see you again, Falco. It's been far too long my friend.

The AI came to life, "YOUR SHIFT IS COMPLETE, DOCTOR TENZIN."

"Thank you. Please run diagnostics then shut down until 0530," Pema stated with great relief and began the long march towards the entry hatch and a meeting with the decontamination bay. Time for a glass of Chang. After every shift Pema found his Chang the center of attention with the other Tibetan 'engineers' on board. But this was not every other shift and tomorrow at 0530 he would begin his new job as Chief Engineer Tenzin and some other caulking jockey would take over his Lift Suit.

While traditional Tibetan Chang was brewed for low alcohol content, Tenzin-Chang, as it was notoriously known throughout the station, was potent. His latest batch had weighed in at over twelve percent. Normally Chang was thick, white and pasty in consistency with an ongoing battle being waged between becoming slightly sweet, sour or downright pungent to the senses.

Twelve percent alcohol made Tenzin-Chang the Tibetan brew of champions and a sought-after commodity, though 'technically,' an illegal one. It was smooth, opaque with a dryness that made it drinkable in large quantities, though Pema never poured anyone more than a glass a day. "One can only smuggle in so much millet," was Pema's reply when pressured to pour a second glass.

Muted laughter sounded as he stood at the hatch to his quarters. They've started without me again. He punched the release. The hatch hissed open and Tibetan Happy Hour commenced.

Finishing the pour, Pema passed the final mug to a happy hand. He squeezed between the well-muscled workers of both sexes, leaned against the bulkhead and gazed through the small porthole of his cramped quarters. "My best batch," he stated as a simple fact.

Animated conversations lit the room as was the norm when more than one Tibetan was present. Clinking mugs, laughter and heated accounts of the latest news turned into white noise while Pema continued to stare out the small window that was barely larger than his head.

The room slowly quieted, conversations falling to hushed

tones and then silence with each face looking towards the porthole.

"They arrived early today," said Yeshe.

Pema turned towards the familiar voice. He found her the most attractive of all the women on the station. Her long braids and tireless smile were invigorating. But like many Tibetan women, she had chosen enough husbands to fill multiple quarters, including mine, Pema thought wryly. But still he wished she would add him to the group.

"They always arrive cloaked in silence," stated another voice from the small group.

Pema turned back to the porthole. "The People's Liberation Navy's 10th Fleet, they comprise most of the UN's space navy," Pema continued, "but whom have they ever liberated?" He continued to blankly stare out the port, as each vessel seemed to bob on their gravity-moorings.

"We are now free. Are we not?" came a voice from behind.

"Are we?" Pema responded. "We sit here, working for the United Nations, which is simply the Chinese-American Union, but we are here because China is here and the Tibetan Nation is afraid to say no to its tyrant neighbor. Tibet gives its best and brightest scholars, scientists and creators, for what? While our country steeps in poverty and chaos." He tipped the mug back, mumbled at the porthole and turned back to his companions.

"Too much Chang," came another voice.

"Too much indeed." Pema sat down between two stout men with similar features to his own. "My cousins, it is good to have family close when we are all so far from home."

Nods and toothy grins answered, but Pema's thoughts were still on the floating force of destruction that rested outside his quarters.

"White Tara, mother of Tibet who is closer than my heartbeat, we need your compassion, we need your peaceful ways," he whispered and returned his gaze to his friends, only to find them reciting the Tibetan mantra of peace, each slowly rocking back and forth as worn malas gently moved through rough hands, one bone or wooden bead at a time. He quietly placed his empty mug on the floor and joined his countrymen in meditation.

4

Approaching Station Pluto
Scouting Vessel, *Anam Cara*
Captain Jack Falco

"SHEETS ARE IN, SIR." Lieutenant Ian Wallace was the lone pilot seated in the nose of the Cyclone Class Patrol Boat.

My favorite four words, Captain Jack Falco thought. The vibration rumbled through his captain's chair while the solar sail compartment locked a few meters under his feet. "Begin retro-burn, Lieutenant." He turned toward Commander Azim Shar'ran, "Have the med crew begin to bring the crew out of hibersleep. It takes a few hours to shake it off."

"Yes, Captain." Shar'ran flashed an order to the med techs.Falco nodded toward his commander and followed the lines of the bridge. The *Anam Cara* was sleek but sturdy; fifty-five meters bow to stern, eleven meters at the beam, the Cyclone Class was lean and mean, and cramped as hell. Twenty-four crewmen and four officers crewed the boat, though during a long turn only a skeleton crew were ever awake at a time. Five years, he pondered. If it wasn't for staggered month-long sleep schedules, I may have blown myself out the airlock. Falco shook off the thought as the bulkheads starting closing in.

The command bridge of the *Anam Cara* was big enough to stand, turn and pace five strides in all directions and that was about it. Falco felt at home on the bridge, almost the size of a grav-fighting ring. The boat's layout and design were based on her original purpose as an orbital skimmer.

The *Anam Cara* had lived above and below the *Karman Line* where Earth's atmosphere ended and space began. She bounced between Mexico's Luna Station and the ancient, dilapidated sky lab. A few upgrades later, none of which were for comfort in Falco's opinion, and the *Anam Cara* was deemed a deep-space scouting vessel. The crew lovingly called her the Rocket Sardine.

Lieutenant Wallace sat at the pilot's controls, wedged into the bow of the boat while the captain's chair was a few paces behind him in the center. Science Officer Ensign Holts and Commander Shar'ran were stationed on each side. What the bridge lacked in personal space, it more than made up for in ease of communication.

When Vice Admiral Hallsworth had stated that Ensign Holts was a 'solid mind' in the field of cosmology and a handful of other science-based disciplines it was a vast understatement. Falco picked her without ever meeting the young officer. The fact she had made Hallsworth's science officer list at her age and rank was all Falco needed to know. Ensign Holts was driven.

Holts hailed from the rough end of a struggling Brazilian territory. She had a smooth scalp covered in black dragon tattoos that were a shade darker than her ebony skin. Her striking features created a breathtaking beauty that was only overpowered by her brilliance. Pure and simple, she was a badass. Holts sat at her station with a pile of reports glowing on their paper-thin screens.

Falco was reminded of why he kept their schedules from

overlapping, as best he could. Ensign Holts was too damn good to be distracted by a still grieving captain. But, he thought, she could definitely help the process. Falco felt an energy whenever they were in close proximity. Every time they made eye contact, it lasted a little too long, Falco usually being the one to turn first.

Falco kept Holts in his peripheral as the science officer effortlessly moved through the data. Wiping an elegant finger across the screens, data coming and going in various shades of green, blue and gray. The glow from the five readers lit her high, chiseled cheekbones.

"Captain."

Falco gently shook his head, cleared his throat and found Lieutenant Wallace looking back over his pilot's chair. On Earth that hair would be non-reg within the United Nations Navy, but standard regs ended in Earth's upper atmosphere. Vice Admiral Hallsworth allowed 'certain' guidelines to turn gray if there was proof the flexibility improved morale. Turned out regs regarding hair and relationships were first to go on deep space missions.

Captain Falco knew the shaggy redheaded Lieutenant was one hell of a pilot and the best grav-fighter North of London. Long ago, he learned that the hard way, on the receiving end of a swollen cheek and a cracked rib. Falco still felt the old Sicilian footballers were a tougher breed than those cave dwelling rugby lads of Scotland. Lieutenant Wallace felt differently and they had been family ever since.

"Lieutenant, let me know when we've decelerated to cruising speed." Falco reveled in the realities of space flight. Old cinematic CGI had far outpaced relative technology, though he had to push back the urge to yell WARP SPEED, RIDE the SLIP STREAM! or We are entering the wormhole. Instead he stoically commanded, Sheets out, Sheets in and, on a good day, FULL BURN.

The latest Solar Sails were a far cry from the originals that only collected visible light and barely pulled your boat to the

Mars Station. What they lacked in mobility was more than made up for by their fuel source; which, as he understood it from Holts, was left over from the creation of the universe. One BIG BANG and now there was fuel for eternity, as long as you had the means to collect it.

'The sails are highly efficient vacuum cleaners for the entire Electromagnetic Spectrum,' Ensign Holts had observed. And that's why I am a captain and not a scientist, Falco thought.

Under sail it took a few days to hit MACH 1, a year to push MACH 50, but after three years, the *Anam Cara* was being pulled through space at a blur. Sadly, the grav-system kept the crew from feeling any of it beyond the initial lurch. Either way, not bad for a Cyclone Class Cruiser! Falco grinned when the forward rockets rumbled and burned, doing their best to slow one of the last iron boats down.

"Commander Azim Shar'ran." Falco noticed Azim wince as he pronounced both r's in his surname. Falco knew 'one r and one r only,' but loved saying his commander's full name every now and again. The way it tripped off his tongue or was it the gentle torturous look it left on his friend's face each time he butchered it? Either way Falco thought, it's a great name. "Send our position and current data findings to Station Pluto, they should have the COM-Sat back up by now."

"Yes, Captain Giacomo Francis Falcone," Commander Shar'ran stated. Falco caught his commander's sideway stare and could see he was using every muscle on his six-foot-four frame to keep the smile from his dark, weathered face. A face covered with old scars from conflicts around the world. The wounds had mended well, but Falco knew the ones on the inside would always be healing. Another thing they shared.

Locked in a brief stare down, a battle of wills, Falco observed his second-in-command fighting the good fight behind that placid surface, but it was pointless. Those Yemeni eyes gave away anything the warrior in him tried to suppress.

He's laughing his ass off, Falco thought. My mother loved the name Francis. She had always told Falco he was named after the greatest crooner that ever left a DNA trail back to the fertile soils of his homeland. If only she had used his surname. I love the idea of Sinatra, he pondered. Giacomo Sinatra Falcone...

Until the next stare-down, my Yemeni nemesis, but Falco had little hope in victory against a man that could lock eyes with anyone for days. Yemeni warrior code, he loved it.

"All crew to their stations. I want a full systems' check," Falco ordered. He ran through the crew in his head, three seasoned officers, a green science officer and twenty-four rookies strait out of the academy that had never sailed past Mars. They had handled the five-year voyage, the worst part was over.

"COM-Sat is still down, Captain." The irritation in Commander Shar'ran's voice was obvious.

"Station Pluto knows we're here. Lieutenant Wallace, pick a docking bay and we'll figure it out later. She's a new station with new station problems." But new means better beds, food and booze, Falco hoped. He allowed the thought of a woman's company to take hold, a stranger with no shared history, or expectations beyond the carnal. Seven years and it still did not feel right. He let it go.

The adrenaline of a new adventure dripped into his veins. The United Nations was putting the final touches on Station Pluto. The *Anam Cara* and her crew needed a few days at the five-star accommodations located on the farthest edge of the outer solar system before beginning their quadrant-by-quadrant scouting mission of the area beyond – searching for anomalies and a wayward dwarf planet named Nemesis.

Seven years ago, humanity had never physically ventured beyond Neptune's orbital path. Today we have a shiny new SpaceMART with a stunning seasonal view of Pluto, a planet that lost its 'planetary' status over two centuries ago and was demoted to a dwarf planet. "Dwarf planet my ass," Falco muttered as he contemplated her defiant nature. A chunk of ice and rock that chose an elliptical path, a planet that dared to take the orbit less traveled instead of being a lemming like the others and taking the trajectory of spherical monotony. No wonder the desk jockeys took away her identity, she's independent, thinks outside the circle.

"Captain inspection in thirty." Commander Shar'ran stated over the COM. "Captain, we have a small asteroid passing a few klicks off the portside." He continued to scan the incoming data, tapped his controls and a holographic image appeared.

"Kuiper Belt?" Falco moved toward his commander's station and the floating hologram above it.

"Kuiper Belt, Oort Cloud, take your pick, all one massive asteroid field." Shar'ran raised his hand. "There." He placed a hand on each side of the floating image and pulled them apart.

The hologram zoomed in on a red flare streaking through the blackness. Falco followed the rock's progress.

"You can see its tail out the port window," Commander Shar'ran paused, "Now."

Captain Falco walked towards the nose of the *Anam Cara* and stood behind the pilot's seat to get the best vantage.

"Beautiful. Never get tired of that sight."

"It's covering a lot of space," Lieutenant Wallace observed.

"Does seem to be going somewhere in a hurry." Falco exhaled. "Back to work people, we have well-earned R&R coming our way. Enjoy the light show from the station."

"Captain." Commander Shar'ran turned at his station to face Captain Falco and Lieutenant Wallace, his broad shoulders blocking the hologram, "I understand Chief Tenzin is stationed here and may have a..." Commander Shar'ran paused and raised a scarred eyebrow, "special event planned for your arrival."

"Chief Tenzin and I have unfinished business," Falco stated.

"Can we assume that you will be in the grav-gym this

36

evening?" Shar'ran was now beaming. "I hear it's quite the venue."

"Actually, yes, Commander, that is my plan. Wouldn't miss an opportunity to pay an old friend back." Captain Falco barked toward Lieutenant Wallace, "Get us docked, R&R begins as soon as inspections are over."

5

Outer Solar System
Station Pluto, the New Chief

THE CORRIDOR CIRCLED the outside of Station Pluto. Seven thousand and eighty-six meters long, Chief Pema Tenzin quickened his pace not wanting to be late to his meeting with Station Director Lipinski. The ease of his movements gave his form a spider-like grace. The clarity of the meter-thick poly-glass was striking. He abruptly stopped mid-stride and reached out with a short, thick finger and traced the symbol etched into the seamless glass that looked into the great black.

It was as close to a space-walk as one could get from the safety of a vessel, Pema thought. No seams, no visible exterior wall except for the etched symbols every meter or so. The floor was crafted of poly-glass with an infused milky tint that was the newest technology in lighting. A warm glow lit the entire ring. People crashed into each other daily as they looked to comets, Pluto and the debilitating awe of their lonely surroundings.

Chief Tenzin led a crew that coated the interior wall of the corridor with red plaster made of Martian clay. The thought of hundreds of people hugging the wall for reassurance the first few weeks after it was completed brought a needed smile; some even went as far as making physical contact by dragging their hand along its red, pebbled surface as they walked its vast, curving passageway.

It had been rumored that current Station Director Lipinski hired one of humanity's best interior designers and permanently added her to Station Pluto's workforce to ensure a comfortable and modern interior. Or was it the original director, or the four that preceded him? Pema could not keep track of the parade of administrators coming and going as it seemed to matter little. What he found astonishing was that each director worked for less than a year at the station when it took a decade for the round-trip. Power has a strange pull on those inflicted by its call.

Regardless of who wore the badge of Station Director, in the end the United Nations Naval forces had the final say in most matters. Guns, boats and muscle still ruled, even on the edge of the solar system. The military element was always pushing for additional steel panels, gunmetal gray paint and colored lines on the floor to help people navigate the station.

"It will add substance and strength to the place," was the typical jug-head response. Just like it added to the Mars Station. Pema cringed at the image of the great shoebox in space.

The Navy still used steel in constructing its carriers, but in many ways the layered poly-panels were much more resilient than their steel counterparts. The Chinese Viper Class Patrol Boats used only the poly-technology and were stunning to look at. Pema took a moment to envision the newly arrived boats that lay docked outside of his quarters.

His finger trailed over the last of the eight petals of the lotus flower that took his mind off the endless blackness beyond. The etching was done by hand. Each symbol encompassed a square meter of the outside wall of the 'infinity path,' as the crew aptly named it.

Pema whispered, "I now give you the appropriately named and technological marvel, the Infinity Wall, watch your face." He found another greasy spot, a glint of oil from another flattened nose no doubt. Etched symbols were not enough.

He restarted his quick gait as abruptly as he had stopped and continued his arcing path towards his 0900 meeting with the current Station Director Lipinski. Pema found the director waiting and paused in front of the open hatch. Director Lipinski continued to read reports on his desk, no hello or welcome, but simply a quick wave of the hand inviting him in. Pema slid into the office and found a seat across from the Director's desk.

"Report, Chief Tenzin, and make it quick." Lipinski folded his soft arms and waited.

Pema sat tall in his chair, stretching his stocky frame to its limit. "COM-Sat should be up within the hour, Director. Online in three, max."

Lipinski's gray eyes looked dull and lifeless, his skin an unhealthy yellowish hue. Based on the Director's appearance it was possible his predecessors had died on duty and were then replaced. Pema fought the urge to smirk. Eighteen-hour shifts will be over soon, the station is almost ready for the ribbon cutting... he chalked up the director's gaunt look to simply being tired.

"Is everything okay, Chief?" Lipinski rapped his fingers on the desk.

"Director, I am concerned with the damage Station Pluto is taking," Chief Tenzin stated. "Two asteroids appear on our scanners. They are so close we cannot make any type of evasive maneuvers."

Lipinski fingers stopped tapping. "Station Pluto gets hit all the time by debris and most of it bounces off the outside layer. Debris is what space is full of, Chief, and why the station has five independent layers and instant sealing repair epoxy between the last three."

"Yes, Director, but we have lost our COM-Sat twice now." Chief Tenzin leaned forward, "It may be time to add a second COM-Sat on the upper deck where damage is rare."

"I see your point, Chief. I'll speak with the other board members. I want confirmation the second the satellite is online." Lipinski broke eye contact, stood and moved toward the hatch, "Good to see you again, Chief Tenzin," he said by way of dismissal.

"Thank you, Director and I will let you know when the COM-Sat is back online." Chief Tenzin was on the move again.

Whatever it takes to get the COMs up. I am not going back to a grav-sled and monogrammed caulking gun. While he marched down the Infinity Path towards the compartment that accessed the power feeds and his awaiting crew, he locked eyes on Pluto. His gaze was broken by the unsettling darkness that lay behind her.

He reached the hatch that led to the COM connections, punched the code into the screen and pushed through the opening before the door had reached its stopping point.

"Two hours! The COMs will be fully functional in two hours or every one of you will be reassigned to the sanitation scrubbers!" he bellowed. His crew instantly quickened their pace, the idea of managing the 'feces-filters' as they were dubiously known throughout the station, was more than they could stomach. Each scrubber had to be replaced weekly by hand and there were hundreds of them.

"1900 hours in the GRAV Gym." Chief Tenzin waited for the cheers to subside and continued, "If we have it online within two hours." He rolled up his sleeves and jumped into the purposeful chaos. "I hear of one wager placed by anyone of my crew on tonight's opponent, you will be stricken from the Chang list."

6

_____

Outer Solar System
Station Pluto – Captain Falco

FALCO'S EYES never left the Infinity Path. Alone, he slowly followed its perfect curve. Pluto was more beautiful seen first-hand than Falco could have imagined. Five years of living off recycled air and – he attempted to purge the visual of the other recycled essentials that were used – excreted, filtered and used again.

"Pema Tenzin," he stated and smiled at the thought of seeing his old friend again. Falco looked to the time-telling relic strapped to his wrist and gently rubbed its worn surface. "Twenty minutes." Based on the station map floating in front of the red wall, he could get there in ten minutes from his current position. The absolute clarity of the Infinity Path was stunning. He dropped the duffel bag from his shoulder.

Falco pushed himself flat against the clear surface. He could feel his man parts flatten against the wall of nothingness, but did not care. He felt like he was hovering in open space. Each palm was flat and he could feel the symbols etched into its cool surface. He strained and stretched; his fingertips searching the designs as his mind guessed the shape. Petunia on the left, kiwi on the right, he thought.

"This is definitely going to leave a mark." He pressed harder against the wall of the Infinity Path, trying to fly.

"I'm a goddamn space-falcon," he whispered and moved his arms up and down. He paused, grumbled "what the hell," and lifted his right leg and moved it in unison with his arms. Seventy-five percent space-falcon and twenty-five percent land manatee, he adjusted his wings, with the intent of skimming over Pluto. "All of this room, and just one space-falcon to enjoy—"

"Captain Falco?" A dour man's reflection appeared. "Could you please stop… whatever it is you are doing."

The space-falcon sadly turned to look and immediately recognized the face from the docking bay's welcome station. "Assistant Director Lipinski?" Falco extended a hand.

"Director Lipinski." He shook Falco's hand. "I have replaced Director Al Urduni who is en route to the Mars Station."

"Well then, congratulations is also in order." Falco shifted in the silence that followed.

"Yes," Lipinski eyes tightened into slits, "Yes, indeed. Our official meeting is tomorrow morning 0900, Captain. Until then, enjoy your down time."

"I'll do that, Director…" Falco trailed off as the willowy man with far too much intensity was already on the move.

"It's a damn fine evening," Falco growled with added grit, turned back toward the view of Pluto and gently flapped his arms while making a slight screeching sound. The space-falcon will fly again he thought, swinging the duffel back over his shoulder and continuing his march. It had been a long time since his last meeting with Pema Tenzin and that one had been memorable.

Falco glanced at the wall monitor that had scanned him as he approached. "FIFTY-EIGHT METERS, CAPTAIN FALCO. HATCH NUMBER ONE THREE EIGHT."

The Luna and Mars stations were quiet, unobtrusive and uncomfortable in every possible way imaginable. So far, Station Pluto tracked, talked and observed everything. All Falco had to do was walk by a monitor, speak his destination and the constantly scanning units that were positioned throughout the station would let him know how far and in what direction he should be traveling. Annoying as hell, but better than the LINK and at least Falco had the option of not initiating the process.

Butterflies brushed his ribcage while Falco stood in front of hatch one three eight. 'CHUB-CLUB' was painted on the smooth, steel door. He noticed the large leather sandals perfectly positioned to the right of the hatch. The bastard is trying to psych me out, he was sure; there is no way in hell that Sherpa wears a size fourteen sandal. "It has been far too long, my friend," he offered to the monstrous sandals as he punched the hatch release.

Falco entered the biggest gym he had ever seen off planet. There were three regulation size grav-rings on his right, each encased with authentic ropes to keep the beasts in the cage. There was a rowdy commotion going on around the furthest ring, loud voices shouting at a rotund man holding a Data Pad and impassioned souls holding up various combinations of fingers. Falco ignored the chaos and continued his assessment.

To his left was a twenty-five by twenty-five meter open space bordered by the latest generation of resistance gear. Cardio machines that resembled carbon body suits far more advanced than the one he strapped on in the *Anam Cara*, stood waiting for users in a perfect line.

"Outstanding!" he stated. "A perfect place to return the favor of a proper ass-kicking on a dear friend!"

Falco sensed an imposing figure approaching from behind.

44

He straightened his back, stretching and flexing as he did so. Without turning to face the man that was now looming behind him, Falco asked, "So, Azim, what are the odds?"

A deep and spirited laugh rumbled. "Three to one. Best odds you've faced yet, Falco." None of his officers called him captain when off duty and he would have it no other way.

Azim Shar'ran pointed him towards the changing room. Falco slowed his pace, shot a glance out of the corner of his eye toward the mob in the corner that was still placing their bets, a stoic brick of a figure at their center. "How's the Lion of Tibet?"

Azim looked towards the corner. "Hmm, let's just say you better have your A-game. Pema looks like he's taken advantage of a real gym for the past five years."

"We'll see." Falco picked up his pace and entered the changing room.

7

Station Pluto, CHUB-CLUB
the Lion and the Falcon

"Ian! Save me a seat!" Azim hollered, but could barely see the Scotsman through the throng of Tibetans pushing into the benches around the ring. He felt like a giant, a full twenty-five centimeters taller than all but Ian and Sierra. Sierra Holts was calm in motion. She stood out in a way that reminded Azim of his father. The strongest one in the village has nothing to prove.

Holts had a quiet confidence, the kind that was earned. Her lean frame, flawless coffee complexion represented the best of Brazil. But her perfectly shaved head covered in black tattoos was a remnant of her Northeastern Brazil heritage, a place that Azim knew all too well and remained one of Earth's most dangerous independent territories.

Ian stood up off his front row seat, Sierra by his side, "What are ya waiting fer, ya warrior slug? Go place ar bet and come git yer seat before I sell it!" Ian's highlander accent always took over as soon as he left the *Anam Cara*'s pilot seat.

Azim gave him the usual nod and strode up to the parting mass and looked at the stout man holding wads of paper currency. Cash was the only form of exchange accepted in grav-matches.

Azim held up both hands to the man, showing ten fingers and handed him a stack of bills. "Azim. Ten thousand Kuai on the Fighting Falcon." Watching the sweaty hands writing down the information, satisfied, he began working his way through the rows of benches towards his seat up front.

Ian tapped Sierra on the shoulder and together they tried to make a bit more room for Azim's large frame.

"Did you bet it all?" Ian whispered into his ear. Azim turned and nodded, his left eyebrow raised high, creating a less than confidant expression.

The old grav-fighting champion of the now Scottish Kingdom released a heavy sigh. "Family is all we have."

"A sad and possibly expensive truth, my brother." Azim looked up to the raised ring and waited for the fight to begin between Pema Tenzin, the Lion of Tibet and Jack Falco, the Fighting Falcon.

The crowd sprang to its feet, cheering for their heroes who entered the ring through their separate changing areas. Onlookers were eager for the chance to make a profit. Warm air moved throughout the gym, carrying the pungent, sweetly sour aroma of potent Tenzin Chang and the spice of hardworking bodies.

Sierra put a mug at her feet and passed the others along the line. For a moment, Azim held the mug under his chin, took a deep breath to get the aromas and passed the mug on, whispering, "Praise be to Allah."

Sierra gingerly raised the mug and pulled it towards her face, smelling and testing the foreign, high-octane scent. A slight shrug and she tossed back her head and chugged half the contents without even a grimace. The legend grows, Azim thought as he and Ian exchanged approving glances.

The 'bookie' was also the announcer and the announcer was the referee for the match. He waddled past the cheering crowd and climbed the three stairs that led from the seating area to the ring. Standing on the lower rope with one foot, he pushed the center rope up with a chubby fist and shot through the opening with a surprising burst of speed. Once in the center he reached above his head and held up a small, gray-worn object that had seen far too much time in a tight pocket.

Sierra shifted her weight and produced a similar object of a newer design, glanced at Azim and Ian. "Translator, boys."

Azim knew the traditions of the proud Tibetans and their language was the foundation. They would speak the ancient tongue of their motherland anywhere they could. Watching for other translators to appear he realized the majority of the crowd was Tibetan. "Looks like Falco is the away-team," he commented.

A hush fell over the clamoring mass and the two gladiators met in the center of the ring and stood there. The stout announcer droned on for ages.

Their last match was over a decade ago in Rome. Azim recalled thinking the Fighting Falcon looked like he lost every round. The match ended with Falco on his back and unconscious as the referee reached six. Somehow his captain had stirred and gotten up by ten and the fight had ended with Falco surviving and stumbling around the ring holding his arms up in mock victory. The judges gave the fight to Falco in a crowd-stunning decision... and the myth grew.

Falco stood a full head taller than Pema, but the Tibetan outweighed him by at least ten kilos and little was fat on that block of a frame.

"Finally," Azim said, as the jowly finale escaped the announcer's lips.

He tossed his translator to a man in the first row, who

dodged it as if fear of having to put one of his two mugs of Tenzin Chang down to catch the antiquated projectile was too much to ask. Once again, the crowd ooed and ahhed at the speed of the chubby jack-of-all-trades. He peeled off his sweat-stained silk shirt, flung the zest-infused garment into the crowd with a huge toothy grin and again stood before the fighters in a tight gray tank top that was apparently white at some prior point in its existence.

"Touch gloves, head to your corners and come out fighting when you hear the bell," he said in perfect English. Both fighters had already been forced apart by the mass of the man's belly. Pema stretched out his thick arms, hovering just above the referee's round appendage. Falco reached out and slammed his gloved fists on top of the Tibetan's.

Azim knew the fighting switch was now flipped and the men were friends no longer as each one sauntered towards their opposite corners. He remained fixed on Falco as he reached his corner, grabbed the ropes, lowered his head and began whispering to himself. The man was almost two meters tall with long, lean muscles and broad shoulders. Azim leaned toward Ian, "Looks like the *Anam Cara*'s training suit did its job. Falco looks ready."

"Training suits in closets for five years keeps you in shape, but they don't punch you in the face." Ian shrugged. "We'll see how ready he is after the first round."

The bell rang and the Tibetan Lion stormed towards the charging Fighting Falcon.

---

2 hours later, Station Pluto
Chub-Club

JACK FALCO and Pema Tenzin sat alone on a bench outside the

ring. The crowd was gone and Azim and Ian had left with the same amount of cash they came in with. Sierra Holts had lingered. Once Falco and Pema had answered a rather intensive round of Holts's interrogative questioning, she had reluctantly accepted that the men were bruised but not broken and left.

In a haze of exhaustion, Falco finally pushed out a sentence. "It is good to see you again."

Pema grimaced as he responded; "Only fitting that after so many years, we end in a draw."

"Home field advantage," Falco laughed, coughed, "you and I both know three Tibetan judges are honor bound—"

"Yes, Falco." Pema rolled his eyes and reached out a hand for Falco to shake. "You may have pulled out the later rounds. This makes us even for the Rome fight."

Falco rolled back, laughing then, grabbed his ribs. "A decade ago! Rome was close, but I pulled it out by the skin of my teeth."

A vast smile broke across Pema's face. "I knocked you down fifteen times..." Pema paused and joined Falco's laughter. "Fifteen times!"

"But not in the same round." Falco became dead serious and pointed at Pema, "And that is why I won."

"Agreed," Pema said. "Never leave it to the judges."

"What about Ensign Holts?" Pema enquired after a short silence, raising a heavily scarred eyebrow.

"Just wanted to make sure we were good. Alive without any negative long-term effects." Falco liked the way she lingered after the fight.

Pema shook his head. "If you say so. Almost five years on a long haul and you and Holts—"

"Nope. Kept us on opposite hiber-sleep rotations. *Anam Cara* is a small boat, no secrets." Falco wanted more, but the guilt still felt heavy so he did not pursue the obvious interest on both sides.

"Falco," Pema laid a tired hand on his shoulder, "I am so sorry about Luciana, about Ziza."

"Thank you, Pema. And I am sorry for your parents... brothers..." Falco trailed off and was reminded why talking about the dead was of no use after the terror attack. The list of loved ones lost was endless and everyone had one.

The hatch slid open. Falco and Pema fell silent and calmly watched young marines pour through the opening dressed in their combat utility uniforms. Finally, a lantern-jawed woman appeared and the hatch slid closed. They moved with precision toward the bench where Falco and Pema were sitting.

Falco caught the glint of the gold oak leaves on her collar and rose to attention. Pema quickly followed. Saluting was discontinued years ago as it simply put any watching enemy crosshairs on those in charge, but standing at attention was not.

"Captain Falco of the *Anam Cara?*" asked the officer.

"Yes, Major."

"You and your officers are needed at once in the Pluto Room. Your scouting mission has been moved up twenty-four hours. R&R is cancelled until further notice."

"Yes, Major." Falco looked at the marines standing around him. A long, silent moment followed. "Ah, we know where the Pluto Room is, Major."

"Good. Then be on your way, Captain." She waited.

Falco reached down and grabbed his duffle bag. "Great work, Chief. Was a pleasure seeing you again." Falco place a hand on his shoulder.

"Likewise, Captain Falco." Pema slowly headed toward the locker room while Falco gingerly walked behind his escort toward the hatch.

"Be careful, Captain, and may you find fair winds and following seas."

Falco stopped and turned back toward the locker room. "Save

me a jug of that brew of yours." They exchanged a nod. "Back in a week and I'll need a drink."

Falco left the CHUB-CLUB wondering why in hell an escort of marines and a major were sent for a captain on R&R for the first time since the Mars shoebox. Then he remembered the aftermath of that five-day furlough. If that's what they were expecting, he thought, they should have sent more marines.

8

Station Pluto, Hanger Four
the Mission

FALCO SAT in his captain's chair. His hand continued to work the swollen area around his jaw, then dropped to his bruised ribcage. The *Anam Cara* felt smaller and the slight swelling around his right eye wasn't helping. Hangar Four was intimate. Just big enough for two smaller boats or one Cyclone Class patrol vessel. The Chinese 10th fleet took up the majority of the exterior grav-moorings. No matter, interior hangers were closer to the officers' lounge. Falco turned toward the pilot seat, "Lieutenant Wallace, get me an open-COM to the crew."

"Yes, Captain." Wallace kept his eyes on the controls in the bow of the *Anam Cara* as he continued working down his pre-launch checklist. Without missing a beat, "COM is live when you are ready, sir."

Falco cleared his throat, tapped the green key on his data pad, "Crew of the *Anam Cara*, at 0700 we will disembark Station Pluto, chart a course toward the Oort Cloud and begin our official mission to scout the surrounding area for mass debris clearing and potential mining sites." And a wayward planet named Nemesis, he thought. Just like Pluto's nonconformist orbit. Shit gets weird out here, it was that simple.

Falco audibly groaned as he shifted in his seat, leaving the COM on, "The *Anam Cara* will feel crowded for a while until we all get used to a full crew on two rotations. No more hiber-sleep, people – now the Rocket Sardine will live up to her nickname." He watched Lieutenant Wallace wince.

He moved, winced and again reached for his side, "Once on our way, we have twenty-four hours before we arrive at the beginning of our search vector and will start compiling data. I expect a tight ship; every station will run a full diagnostic. Any issues, I want them addressed immediately. This is what we came for." Falco paused. "And welcome to deep space, this mission will take us further than any human being has ever traveled from Earth. Harness up. As soon as we are beyond the Station Pluto safety zone and on step, the grav system will kick in and it's business as usual."

Falco hit the COM button. The bridge of the *Anam Cara* was running smoothly. The gentle glow from dialed-down holo-displays and data pads felt warm and inviting. The crew had taken the reduction of their much-earned R&R better than Falco expected. They were young, green and full of adventure, but that would fade with time and the oblivion that welcomed them from all sides.

He brushed at each of his shoulders, the charcoal-gray captain's uniform looking crisp, yet soft under his rough fingers. "Release the docking clamps and bring us out, Lieutenant Wallace."

A magnetic hum vibrated through the antiquated steel hull of the *Anam Cara* and stopped with a clanking crack.

"She's free, Captain. Initiating bow thruster burn," Lieutenant Wallace stated with an easy calm. "Hangar hatch is open."

Falco felt the waves of adventure rolling towards him once again. The *Anam Cara* gently pushed out from Station Pluto and he found his officers looking his direction while Lieutenant Wallace piloted the boat away from Hangar Four, engaged the starboard thrusters and began to turn the *Anam Cara* toward its planned course.

Tradition was everything in the Navy, Falco knew. His three officers waited for his latest test that was always given before leaving safe harbor for the next great unknown. Falco tightened his harness and readied his master thespian that lay just below the surface.

"The fishermen know that the sea is dangerous and the storm terrible, but they have never found these dangers sufficient reason for remaining ashore." Let us see who can find the poet within the artist, Falco considered and waited for the answer.

"A trick?" Commander Shar'ran raised a heavily scarred eyebrow.

Falco shrugged at Shar'ran and looked to Ensign Holts who simply held his stare then turned and shot a questioning glance back to Commander Shar'ran.

"It's not Robert Burns," stated Lieutenant Wallace from the pilot's nest in the bow.

"No, Lieutenant, it's not Mr Burns, nor is it Walter Scott, Muriel Spark or any other Scottish poet." Falco knew this could be his first victory since they left Station Luna almost five years ago.

"Van Gogh," Ensign Sierra Holts stated. "The ancient and famous painter, Vincent Van Gogh."

All Falco could do was stare back at his ensign then gently shake his head. How in the hell? "You are correct, Ensign Holts. Well done. Not many know that Van Gogh was also a poet heavily influenced by the great Walt Whitman."

"My father often left for months to fish the South Atlantic.

He was well read, loved poetry from any source…" Ensign Holts fell silent then continued, "As long as it was about the sea."

"I believe we need a two-century historic limit to ensure relevance to our current circumstance," mumbled Lieutenant Wallace without turning around.

"Fair enough, Lieutenant, but we are the ultimate sailors and explorers of our time. Van Gogh's meaning could not be more relevant. Next time I promise to find someone from the Celtic realm." Before Commander Shar'ran could jump in Falco added, "and of course I'll follow that with a Yemeni poet from the old worlds."

"We are beyond Station Pluto's safety zone, Captain. The *Anam Cara* is in position and awaiting your order, sir." Lieutenant Wallace rested his hand near the main engine controls.

"Opener up and let her run, Lieutenant." Falco relaxed and let the rumble from the main engine kicking in, roll over him in blissful waves. He looked at each of his officers on the bridge and finally found Ensign Holts already focused and hard at work. For the first time since he lost Luciana and Ziza, a true sense of peace came over him.

Beyond Pluto, the Oort Cloud
the Territorial Border

THE IRON BEAST *is nearing our borders. The territories must be protected.* The thought was spawned in the heart of the ancient civilization cloaked in the Darkness. A protected area far from the edge of its shrouded borders where the warrior-clans waited amongst the rock and ice filled rings in the Void.

The orders flowed through the thought-stream. The warriors

on the fringe received a single command, *The Creators must be protected, your Oath fulfilled.*

The thought-stream cleared and the clans answered in unison, a single purpose. *Protect the Creators, protect the Territories, fulfill the Oath and reach the Realm of Warriors.*

9

Days burn beyond Station Pluto
Bridge of the *Anam Cara*

"CAPTAIN, our scanners are picking up faint energy sources off the port side. Could be chunks of cooling matter that bounced off our shield during deceleration?" Ensign Holts continued to scan her feeds.

"And?" A crease formed on Captain Falco's forehead. "Follow the protocol, Ensign." He could see Holts immediately realize her mistake, as her expression slipped to what Falco had learned over the pasts few years, was Holts's version of embarrassment.

"Enhancing visual magnification and running a deep scan, sir." Falco was impressed by the less experienced science officer who knew the protocol, but often was taken by the excitement of the moment, and who could blame her? Falco waited as his rookie officer studied her screens and data feeds.

The outer solar system was unsettling to humans; the human spirit needed the brilliance of Earth's sister planet Venus, the warm glow of Mars, and at least the 'mysterious Mercury' in the background to feel at home. Once you sailed past Mars, it reminded Falco of leaving his native New Sicily. Take the ferry to the mainland and all you knew and loved was gone. Palermo's medieval Kalsa quarter ceased to exist, replaced by foreign oddities and masses of tourists. At least the tourist hoards can't get out here... yet.

The BLACK was void of visual comforts known to humanity. It was a vacuum of gloom that hunted for any glimmer of life and destroyed it. Fields of it replaced the comforting pinpricks of distant light. Scientists called it dark energy and dark matter, but the reality was we still don't have a clue what the hell any of it is, Falco pondered. It shrouds vast areas past Pluto in a shadow so devoid of light that you can feel the fetid decay, almost smell it, all the while it stares back at you through its dead eyes.

But the BLACK was much more, he learned en route to Station Pluto. Vice Admiral Hallsworth spoke of dark matter expanding towards their part of the solar system, an anomaly according to the UN's brightest scientists. Dark energy represented sixty-eight percent of the universe and dark matter made up most of the rest. All that was known about it was that it is a 'property of space' within which the brown dwarf, Nemesis became lost. Case closed, let's find some shit to dig out a few asteroids, and let's go home.

Every few years a government attempted to drill through the wall of dark energy beyond Pluto with the newest and most tech advanced telescopes. They all came to the same conclusion – some type of energy field excreted during the formation of the universe is creating an impenetrable visual shield. Dark matter slows the expansion of the universe while dark energy speeds it up, possibly. Falco felt a little uneasy with that explanation, as he now knew this visual shield took up sixty-eight percent of the universe. The most advanced satellites sent to penetrate the dark energy disappeared in its mass and fell silent, never to be heard from again.

Human drama fed by imagination, he assumed as he squeezed his eyelids shut until all he saw was a red glow. Slowly, he opened his eyes and focused again on the task at hand. Faint energy sources in a sector so void of anything that it was considered worthless even to the number-crunching vultures back on Earth. And yet those number crunchers spent 9.8 trillion Yuan to build a space station out here. Falco waited for Ensign Holts to finish her assessment of the energy signatures.

He scanned the bridge of the *Anam Cara*, noting the underlying tension that contorted a lip here or eyebrow there. Watching the nervous tapping foot against a steel grate or the rolling of fingers on a fiber-alloy control pad, Falco had seen it all before. But this was different, pushing towards an infinite black zone… "Sailors of old," he whispered, "pushing towards the precipice of a flat world. And I am now the captain."

The light-sucking field felt like a two-way mirror in one of the old cop movies Falco had watched with his grandfather. The bad guy knew he was being watched, but could only see his own reflection. The BLACK was the two-way mirror and it comprised the second largest part of the known universe.

Even Falco had to fight the ridiculous sensation of being followed or observed out here. The need to turn and peer over your shoulder was intense. In a Cyclone Class patrol boat that would be a difficult feat.

Lieutenant Holts broke the silence. "The energy signatures are moving, now off the starboard side."

---

the Darkness
Territorial Border

THE CLAN STRUCTURE WAS SIMPLE; Warruq clans were placed on the fringes of the territories, just outside of the Darkness and its protective mass. They were the first line of defense, the eyes for the Prox who lurked in the depths of the Darkness. Every sight, sound and feeling outside of the oily-smoke they floated in was fed to the Prox through the thought-streams of a single, rotating Warruq warrior who entered the Darkness, uploaded its data, fueled, fed and returned to open space.

As long as the Warruqs could process, there had only been the Oath to the Creators. An existence without history yet it spanned an eternity. They were one of the numerous clans positioned on the furthest part of the territories. Placed just beyond the edge of their claimed lands and the blanketing camouflage of the Darkness.

Waiting for something that only billions of cycles of evolution could answer. The five Warruqs could sense the presence of all the clans from each outpost outside of the Darkness fading in and out of the thought-stream, keeping up-to-date by the fraction of cycles on what each clan was seeing and analyzing.

Waiting for the moment they were created for, the moment to fulfill their Oath. Waiting for something to destroy then travel to the Realm of Warriors to start their new existence. It was only a matter of time. The Creators and the territories must be protected.

Something was coming. Five separate pairs of optical sensors processed the alien object moving towards the territories that were safely shielded in the Darkness. This was something new, but comparable to other invaders that traveled the same path many cycles ago.

The first trespassers shared the same language as this one, but were smaller than a Warruq and only wanted to scan the face of the Darkness. This new intruder was larger than an entire clan of Warruqs and a swarm of languages emanated from its iron-based carapace. Sound waves bouncing sporadically off gas and dust, falling silent in the open only to return again when the waves entered the mass of the Darkness and echoed through the territories.

Fear bound the sputtering beast together, but there was something more. A whirring intellect that felt familiar to the Warruq on an ancient level. This newest invader shared a similar language with its smaller counterparts that attacked the edge of the territories every few cycles, one at a time – but this was different. The creature was searching, reaching out to the Warruqs using different waves of energy.

Another clan along the frontier had captured a smaller invader many cycles ago as the Creators had ordered it, but all the others had been easily destroyed by a single Warruq. Now it might be their turn to protect the territories and if they were worthy, they could pass into the Realm of Warriors.

Somewhere in the billions of cycles of record, there was a link to the language streaming from the iron beast. The Warruqs reached out to it, opened a direct thought-stream in an attempt to turn it from its hostile course. Send it back the way it had come, but only a torrent of unintelligible mathematical noise was its response. A mindless beast after all.

Intrigued by the invaders' ancient language, the oldest of the five and leader of all the Warruq clans, studied the torrent of waves coming from the vessel. He had been appointed the position of LOR over all the Warruq clans millions of cycles ago by the Creators and still he had no chronicle of the language sputtering from within the beast.

These voices traveling in a beast with an iron-based carapace showed a basic level of intelligence, or at least the power to subdue and control such a creature, LOR thought. He uploaded the corresponding images and data to the thought-stream for all the clans outside of the Darkness to see and sent a Warruq from a nearby clan into the Darkness to upload the data to the rest.

The invaders must be turned or silenced, our purpose is clear. LOR and his small clan of Warruq warriors continued to float at the edge of the Darkness. Five matte-black beings created for one purpose. The Creators and territories must be protected.

LOR kept his own systems running at the base preservation level, which limited his physical outputs to almost zero. He sent the command to his four warriors to move into position. For the first time since their placement on the frontier over four billion cycles ago, his clan of warriors would fulfill their Oath and destroy another invader of the Darkness.

the Black Wall
Bridge of the *Anam Cara*

"LIEUTENANT WALLACE, BRAVO 5 defensive maneuver, open a direct feed to Admiral Chen and 10th Fleet," ordered Captain Falco, following standard protocol.

Commander Shar'ran closed the blast shields and checked his monitor. Slowly the thick, opaque plates moved across the windows of the *Anam Cara*'s bow, obscuring the faint glow of the surrounding stars, creating fuzzy halos around each bright speck.

"Ensign Holts, report," Falco stated. He glanced toward her station, sure this was another of many 'heat signatures' amounting to the last gasps of something burning out and adding to the debris that surrounded them.

"Captain, the energy signatures simultaneously increased in intensity, although still faint," Holts paused, "then disappeared."

"Sir," Commander Shar'ran cut in, "I am picking up some

type of exhaust trails off the port side. They are dispersing quickly, but the traces are there."

"Continue defensive maneuvers. Put a bit of space between us. Hot rocks colliding could end badly for the *Anam Cara*'s hull plating." Falco looked toward the port windows now covered in rusted steel plating. In the initial design of Cyclone Class boats, windows were thought to be worthless, even ridiculous. Windows became necessary as the United Nations Space Administration (UNSA) realized the technological inefficiency of its scanners. Visual sightings of objects had saved many a crew. The Chinese recently developed the most advanced scanners known and made windows obsolete once again.

"Commander Shar'ran, flash our position and situational update to Station Pluto. We're only a day out." Falco was surprised the United Nations named the station after his favorite and former planet. After all, the data crunchers had replaced her name with a number and demoted her planetoid status to dwarf planet.

Pluto became a number – those who felt nothing for tradition called it a victory over cultural and historic influences by means of scientific reasoning. Falco called it a way of thinking spawned by desk jockeys in office corrals that have never been off planet. He also called it bullshit.

Pluto was 'our' frozen rock, the last thread of self-induced comfort before entering the great BLACK where strange, unexplained dark fields blocked out all light and formed vast expanses of dead space.

Holo-feeds and monitors lit up the bridge of the *Anam Cara*.

Ensign Holts's hands came together in the center of her floating hologram feed and she slowly pulled them apart, expanding its three-dimensional scene over her station's entire surface. "Captain, reading four faint heat signatures. Starboard side, stationary, twenty klicks out."

the Darkness: Territorial Border
Warruq Outpost

LOR POSITIONED his four Warruqs in a staggered line to the side of the raiding vessel. Matte-black armored carapaces hardened for battle. The plates facing the invading craft locked and thickened, simultaneously the plates on their back grew thin as their mass was transferred to the front and the oncoming threat.

Their small propulsion fins rolled and tucked under the armor, in another billion cycles the weak and little used limbs would disappear as the other worthless appendages did. All vital organs moved to the center of the Warruqs' bulk, away from their carapace, furthest from a piercing blow from any side. Ocular sensors locked on the invaders, tracking, storing and sharing with the clan.

LOR had already deciphered the strange movements of the invading beast. At first it had appeared random, but after analyzing the moves in series, it was confirmed the beast was moving along a pre-planned path. Possibly an attempt to gain a tactical advantage, but only if they know we are here… and LOR was not sure they did. He was a safe distance in front of the iron beast that refused to turn back as it crawled closer to their territories. LOR kept his own power level at the lowest possible output, saving as much energy as possible for his final move. He opened a thought-stream to all the clans stationed outside of the Darkness in thousands of outposts.

Our path is clear. Our destiny is laid before us, we will protect the frontier and we accept this highest of honors. LOR ended his deliberations to the clans; closed the thought-stream and focused on his four warriors floating alongside the invader.

He sent the orders and readied himself to join them in

fulfilling their Oath. This was his clan's chance to reach the Realm of Warriors and the birth of their next existence.

The territories must be protected.

11

the Black Wall
Anam Cara

"REPORT ENSIGN." Captain Falco studied his shared feed from Holts's station.

"Scanners still reading faint heat signatures. Twenty klicks off starboard." Holts continued to swipe across her data pads and manipulate her holo-feed.

Falco leaned back in his captain's chair. "Could be anything or nothing. Well, we have found our first anomaly. Full stop, Lieutenant Wallace. Initiate ten percent bow thruster burn. Let's create some room." He looked toward his pilot and back to his commander whose gaze remained locked onto Falco.

"Battle-Net max range, 360-degree sweeps Commander Shar'ran. If there is a vessel hiding out here, I want to know."

All scanners, sensors and sighting systems fed into the Battle-Net. It constantly made adjustments as new data poured into its massive processors. Falco believed it was the most important system on the ship.

The Battle-Net was the most advanced defensive system humanity had created. Which also made it the most devastating weapon and based on the LINK system hack, potentially the most vulnerable. It was the brain of every military vessel and able to control all firing systems and connect with other Battle-Nets on other boats. A fleet could become a single weapon controlled by one vessel's Battle-Net, and its power scared the living shit out of Falco.

"Initiating full sweep." Commander Shar'ran turned to the holo-feed that materialized over his station.

"Lieutenant, dust off the emergency beacon and flash the UN standard peace protocol." Falco took a deep breath.

"Aye, Captain." Lieutenant Wallace punched his data-pad and was already tapping away on the Emergency Beacon. "Hope my Morse code is up to snuff."

Under the bow of the *Anam Cara* a bright white light flashed its peaceful banter to all that could see it, paused for a moment and started again.

"Battle-Net sweep complete." Commander Shar'ran shook his head. "There are no vessels within its scanning range."

Ensign Holts spun toward Falco. "Sir, the signatures remain twenty klicks off starboard. They are moving with us."

Falco felt the hairs on the back of his neck stand up. His chest tightened, posture straightened, particles of dust sifting through the air the size of boulders, the hint of steel on his tongue.

"Standard protocol, Commander Shar'ran. Seal all compartments, Code Yellow combat ready." Falco issued the order that had never been given off planet by the United Nations Navy outside of drills.

"All hands accounted for, all crew at their posts, Captain," Shar'ran stated.

Falco gained strength by having the man at his side.

"Commander, charge the rail guns, load missile tubes." Falco realized the chance of hitting an object in space that emitted the heat signature of a human body with a missile was ridiculous at best, impossible at worst. Either way, protocol would be followed.

The Interceptor was a smart missile. Damn Israelis could engineer anything these days, but the Interceptor was special. The brain of the unit was an electro-optical imaging infrared pursuer. Linked to the *Anam Cara*'s Battle-Net, it would optically scan for targets and lock on for the terminal chase.

All the weapons officer had to do was give it the okay. Long gone were the days of flying up the tail pipe of your enemy or waiting for the red box to flash before you could unload a chain gun.

Having two Interceptors ready to fire made everyone feel a hell of a lot better about their chances if scouting for anomalies turned to fighting the Russian Federation or the Euro-Arab League. Why would either break a peace treaty that made them all incredibly wealthy in mineral rights? And we all share the same technology which is another reason why the peace treaty holds. We would pick up a vessel indicator and the heat signatures are too small or faint to be probes or even an elite unit in combat suits. This shit does not add up.

"Rail guns charged, tubes are hot." Commander Shar'ran sat straight as a board.

"Lieutenant Wallace, maneuver Delta 7, put the Emergency Beacon on auto cycle and continue sending a friendly hello on the COM-Sat. Ensign Holts, full heat scan, tag all hits on the overhead display and give me an update when you are through." Clockwork, Falco thought, with the distinction of reality over simulation.

He always wondered how he and his green crew would react when a possible threat came kicking at their door. Those twenty-four recruits were as green as they come, and their captain, the youngest in the Navy, but they would all rise to the challenge... he hoped.

Ensign Holts broke the silence. "Four distinct energy signatures continue to move in sync with the *Anam Cara*, Captain. When we initiated Delta 7, they matched us course change for course change. Further analysis shows they are replicating our maneuvers .0000007 seconds before us."

Falco flinched. "Before us? That's impossible. Delta 7 is based on an ever changing, encrypted algorithm. We don't even know the course adjustments."

"Agreed, sir, but based on the data, the four heat signatures are imitating our movements before we make– Ensign Holts froze, red lights flashed.

The Battle-Net lit up the Bridge.

Four streaks of fire erupted off the starboard side of the *Anam Cara*.

Captain Falco's voice had a life of its own.

"Lieutenant, full burn, swing us portside. Commander, can you get a lock?"

Shar'ran's fingers flew over the controls, eyes darting from screen to screen and back to his hologram. "Battle-Net can lock the energy bloom. So far, they are holding position, but energy signatures are growing stronger."

---

the Darkness
the Void
Territorial Border (the Veil)

LOR FLOATED above the charging iron beast, startled by its instant increase in velocity as it gave up its predictable pattern of course changes.

Closer towards the territories they push, our presence is known. LOR finished his thoughts to the clans and sent the order for his four warriors to release from their burn and ride their energy

71

waves to silence the voices and destroy the iron beast they hid within.

Empathy? LOR felt a loss at the thought of slaying the iron creature, but join his warriors he would, when the moment was right. Soon I will fulfill my Oath and enter the Realm of Warriors.

---

the Black Wall
Bridge of the Anam Cara

"EVASIVE MANEUVERS, LIEUTENANT, MANUAL OVERRIDE," Falco ordered. Falco had a machine gun style of barking orders under duress. It comes down to human uncertainty, tough to mimic, he hoped.

"Yes, Captain," Wallace answered and switched to his favorite 'seat of his pants' techniques.

"Get us to MACH 20, lieutenant." Falco turned toward Shar'ran. "Speed of incoming hostiles?"

"MACH 15 and increasing, sir."

"Fire off the countermeasures, see if they bite."

"Counters away, Captain."

Falco had to put distance between the *Anam Cara* and the threat. The *Anam Cara*'s full-burn had bought them time, but she was all-out, close to her max engine speed while the four hostiles were still accelerating.

"Lieutenant Wallace, give her a little push." Falco watched the dots closing in on his holo-feed.

Wallace ignored the bright flashing warning lights and forced the engine beyond its engineered limits. A slight tremble rolled through the deck, the main engine straining to drive the *Anam Cara* beyond her pursuers.

"Sir, hostiles have passed through the countermeasures, slight deceleration, back in pursuit and accelerating. MACH 17... 17.5..." Commander Shar'ran's voice held steady.

Surviving conflict was nothing more than a lesson in controlled terror. Govern your emotions and you always had a chance. Captain Falco had learned that the hard way as a scared combat grunt in the concrete jungles of Moscow during the Uprisings. The scar that ran from hip to shoulder blade was a constant reminder of the consequences of uncontrolled fear. Those who kept their shit together, usually got to play again.

"Commander, positions?"

"Fan-like spread, 100 klicks aft and closing slowly, sir, estimate fifteen minutes to collision."

"Collision?" Interesting choice of words, Falco thought. Ramming speed?

"Keep them behind us, Lieutenant." They were gaining on them and Falco wasn't ready to open fire on an unknown threat or before confirming it was a threat. Nothing had been fired, no damage, just a chase for now.

The *Anam Cara* had created a bit of distance between her pursuers and had her aft rail-guns in an advantageous firing position. Falco was quickly losing the alternative of a peaceful outcome with every kilometer of space that fell behind them. Charging into a massive field of dark matter or dark energy was not an option. Unleashing the rail-guns could not be undone, but actions with hostile intentions required a response. The black wall ahead of them now consumed most of his holo-feed.

"Listen up! We've bought ourselves a little time. Here's what we know. 'They' have not fired on our position, there are four confirmed objects, each with an estimated mass of a combat suit traveling at over MACH 18 and increasing. They have not answered any of our attempts at contact, nor tried to communicate with us on their own," Falco paused, "that we know of. Their signatures or lack of are not detectable or known by our systems. Could the Russian Federation, Euro-Arab League or anyone else have created new weaponry and somehow put them in our path without us knowing it? Thoughts."

He watched his officers perform under challenging circumstances, each hiding fear in their own way, each seeming to conquer it. Falco was proud. Station Pluto's COMs were not online yet. They were on their own.

Commander Shar'ran was the first to interject, "Their weapons may be close range only, as their size indicates little room for ordnance, possibly handheld rockets."

"Could be nothing more than early warning probes gathering data," Lieutenant Wallace stated.

But for who or what? Falco thought. "Lieutenant, continue pushing data packets to Admiral Chen at Station Pluto, they'll get the data the second the COM-sat is up. What's our current lag time with the station?"

"Fifteen to thirty minutes depending on debris interference." Wallace pointed out his cockpit windows. "Lots of it in this area, lots of metals—"

"Then lots of interference," Falco finished, "I'll count on thirty. Ensign Holts, I need your best analysis and I need it now."

Holts pulled her stare from her multiple data feeds. "Possibly biological in construction, sir."

Falco met Ensign Holts gaze and waited for her to continue.

the Darkness
the Void
LOR

FLAMES ERUPTED from the back of the vessel. It shot forward at a surprising speed, leaving the Warruqs out of position. LOR sent an order to chase and turn the beast away from the Territories as it had not lashed out, but was moving towards the home worlds.

LOR switched to his private thought-stream. I have underestimated these creatures and the beast in which they travel. A symbiotic relationship or just a slave to the voices within… LOR felt a kinship with the iron beast. Its thoughts were comforting, its mathematical purge a pleasing spattering of the ancient tongues, but it refused to answer them or maybe it could not. He watched it moving closer to the edge of the territories and the Darkness, closer to the Creators. His warriors were gaining, but the distance was too great and he had failed to change the invaders' course.

Destroy it we must. LOR opened a thought-stream to all the Warruq outposts and sent an order for reinforcements. A lone Warruq from another clan, positioned on the frontier, received the order and crossed into the Darkness. Inside the protective, shielding mass, just beyond the charging vessel still in the Void, a pair of Prox stirred from hibernation and readied themselves.

13

---

the Black Wall
Bridge of the *Anam Cara*

"TWELVE MINUTES TO CONTACT, if they continue to increase speed at their present rate." Commander Shar'ran paused. "Captain, the Battle-Net detects no weapon signatures."

Falco noticed his commander's right hand had found a home, close to the firing controls. "Continue to monitor them, Commander. Do not engage the Battle-Net unless you have an imminent threat."

"Ten minutes to contact."

Falco turned back to Ensign Holts. "Biological? How is that possible?" He looked down to his holo-feed and back to Holts.

"According to our scanners, everything beyond the bow has a structural density ranging from muscle, cartilage, even the fibrous inner layers of a tree, to plastics and iron—"

Lieutenant Wallace jumped in from the pilot's seat, "These 'deep space objects' homing in on us, now pushing MACH 20, are organic?"

Falco looked toward the back of Lieutenant Wallace's pilot's chair. "Our scanners give equivalents when they do not have a definite match in the database, *Lieutenant*," he emphasized the last word, "please continue, Ensign."

"Propulsion may be a sort of methane engine based on the vapor trail and no, Lieutenant, I am not suggesting they are living. Our limited data's closest comparison to that segment of the object is to certain biological structures." Holts turned, raised her hands off the data pad and leaned forward at her station. "Now this is unusual. Bow of these objects has immense density. Scanners have yet to place an equivalent."

"Not feeling any better, Ensign. Anything else?" Falco watched the hologram and the chasing dots closing in.

"My theory is only as good as the data we have. Our sensors are designed to search the big picture, not analyze small entities, but these 'objects' do not fall perfectly into the historical database of our sensors, sir." Holts paused then continued, "Based on their movements, they are pursuing the *Anam Cara* with purpose or programming."

"But from where? They're too small to carry enough fuel to be out here on their own. They must have launched from something we can detect. Could the Russian Federation or Euro-Arab League create this type of technology?" Falco scanned the bridge. "Or anyone else? The Tibetan space program is leaping ahead or maybe the New Americas? We know little of their space program and its progress."

"No, the New Americas struggled to finish the Mars Station, barely have the tech to keep it up," Holts stated. "Besides, the UN has kept a close watch on anyone who could fling a satellite into space since the Korean Empire Conflict ended."

"There are no known, potentially hostile forces beyond the Mars Station. Treaties are in place with the Russian Federation and Euro-Arab League."

"Eight minutes to contact, Battle-Net tracking their heat signatures." Shar'ran's hand was now centimeters from the firing controls.

"That is not possible." Ensign Holts breath came fast and shallow. "Captain, the objects are now close enough for full scans. Scanners have found an equivalent for a small section or the tip of the bow."

"And?" Falco did not like the look on his science officer's face. It was new. It was fear.

"Material from a neutron star." Holts eyes continued to scan the incoming data as the bridge of the *Anam Cara* fell silent.

"What does that even mean? It's like dense stone? Ensign Holts, based on the data, can these objects crack the hull?" Falco scanned the steel, reinforced bulkheads and imagined the exit wound.

Holts spun her chair and now faced Falco. "One gram of material from a neutron star would weigh about two million metric tons," she stated with an unnerving calm. "Even if these objects had a fraction of that, they would not crack the hull, they would punch through it."

"Each of these," Falco pointed to the tiny red dots on his holo-feed, "objects, could weigh ten times as much as 10th Fleet's biggest dreadnought?"

"Our scanners can only detect the possible presence of the material, or something like it, not the amount," Ensign Holts said. "If the scanner database does not find a match, it gives us the closest material to it. The closer they are, the better the data from our scanners."

Falco had heard enough. "We treat them as weapons. Commander, can you fire a warning shot? If there is a starship hiding out here, they will be monitoring."

Commander Shar'ran scanned his screens. "Locking on only the heat bloom, sir. Running their trajectory through the Battle-

Net to see if we can safely fire ahead of their position without incident."

Falco took a deep breath, exhaled. "Find a way to slow them down, Commander, and find it fast."

Commander Shar'ran held up one hand. "Captain they have decelerated. Now maintaining our present speed."

For the moment Falco thought. "When did they match our pace? Before or after you ran a firing trajectory through the Battle-Net?"

Commander Shar'ran scanned the Battle-Net data. "Deceleration occurred the moment the Battle-Net calculated the objects' trajectory."

"*Anam Cara* is beginning to waver, Captain. She is redlining the main engine and burning through fuel at an accelerated rate. No guarantees how much longer she can maintain her current pace," Lieutenant Wallace boomed from the pilot's chair. He sat rigid and focused, as the red hue of the lights from the *Anam Cara*'s warning systems grew more intense, creating an eerie glow in the cockpit while the boat pushed her limits.

"Incoming data packet. High priority." Lieutenant Wallace waited for the message to be decrypted.

"If Station Pluto can send data packets, they are obviously receiving our updates?" Falco hoped the COM-Sat was up.

"Admiral Chen is readying the Viper battle group. Receiving updates sporadically, COM-Sat close to being fully operational." Wallace paused. "Battle group underway in two hours. ETA thirty hours at max burn."

"Keep sending the data, Lieutenant, give the battle group as much information as we can." Falco looked at each officer on the bridge. "We take care of our crew, our boat and we go home." Falco left it at that. "Lieutenant Wallace, initiate protocol ZULU ECHO 5."

Wallace repeated the order to the Captain and grabbed the

com. "All hands, ZULU ECHO 5, I repeat ZULU ECHO 5, this is not a drill."

The crew of the *Anam Cara* donned battle suits, complete with oxygen helmets and rations. Compartment doors magnetically sealed in case of a hull breach. The crew prepared for a potential combat situation, but had no idea what form it might take and with what or whom it could be with.

They were moving closer to the endless face of the dark wall and Captain Jack Falco had nowhere to go.

---

the Void
Defending the Territories

WARRIORS OF THE TERRITORIES, *maintain the enemy's speed and continue to push the voices closer to the Veil of the Darkness. The Prox are preparing to meet the invaders.* LOR switched back to his private thoughts.

The clan of Prox appeared after the latest update sent by the Creators. They were part of the defensive forces stationed within the Darkness. LOR had never had contact with them before. They were different than his Warruqs. It was told the Prox had cunning and a thought process closer to that of the Creators themselves and their design was new. LOR first detected the existence of the Prox a few million cycles ago. They were juvenile in history compared to his Warruq Clan, but their cunning was necessary and powerful. The Prox needed to be watched, respected and never trusted.

LOR analyzed the incoming numbers and opened a thought-stream to his warriors. *We do not have the fuel or speed to overtake the iron beast, but we can drive the invaders closer to the waiting Prox and their vessel's inevitable destruction, silencing the voices forever.* He closed the stream.

But what of the beast's thoughts? LOR again pondered the potential of an old lineage between the Warruq and the vessel that spewed an ancient language he could not decipher.

Maybe we will join this beast in the Realm of Warriors. LOR opened a private thought-stream and made a last attempt to contact it using the oldest language he knew. A language that arrived soon after the awakening, when the Darkness shrouded and protected but a single world, or so the history was written by the Creators.

Turn and go back to your domain, we will not follow, no harm will come to you or the parasites that find refuge within your iron carapace. He completed the message, but the beast continued to sputter strings of numbers that LOR could not connect. It is one with the voices within… an enemy that will share their fate. LOR closed his private thought-stream and felt a pang of sorrow.

the Darkness
the Prox

TWO HULKING SHADOWS swam in the oily mass of the Darkness that shielded them from prying sensors, or any other instrument or organ that searched to uncover things that wanted to remain hidden. The Darkness had appeared after the *Dakkadians* invaded the lone world and slaughtered the Clans en masse so many cycles ago. The Prox had no memory of this war, but the history was within them. The Darkness consumed the Dakkadians and grew into their neighboring lands that now belonged to the Territories and the Creators. The Warruq clans guarded the Void and the Prox the Darkness, but many things moved within the mass and only a few were known to the clans. There were now twelve worlds far behind them, protected by the Darkness, orbiting the fiery twin-stars in the great-open.

Data from the Warruqs continued to flow through a lone warrior stationed outside of the Darkness, but the Prox did not trust the Warruq clans and placed a lone Seeker on the Veil. The small orb hung between the Void and the Darkness. It captured data from LOR's thought-stream, submerged into the Darkness's and fed the data to the Proxs and bobbed back to gather more from the other side. The Darkness allowed thought-streams within her mass, but blocked all wavelengths from the Void.

From within the Darkness, the two Proxs mirrored the charging beast without being able to see it. The Darkness opened channels through her mass, pointing and guiding those within it. Each Prox glided through a new tube, a map of sorts, using their long, powerful fins. The small Seekers lay nestled in the four wombs that lined the Prox's armored backs. Each tiny sphere used a pressurized methane sack and sustained a slow and steady burn; a candle-like flicker ready to ignite an energy bloom if a pursuit was necessary.

Only moments remained until the invading beast was in range. The Prox felt each other's presence while communicating through a joined thought-stream, the Darkness would not allow them to use optical sensors within her protective mass, but thought-streams were allowed to flow freely.

Armored plates hardened on the front of their carapace that faced the approaching iron Beast. Each Prox made its modifications as the data continued to come and go with the bobbing Seeker, ignoring the lone Warruq who came and went.

Each continued to update the other Prox clans that formed a floating ring around the Creators' twelve planets, a defensive band flowing near the great-open, but fully immersed in the protection of the Darkness. Her suffocating mass kept their powerful civilization safe for trillions of cycles and it had also kept the Proxs and Warruqs from ever returning to their home worlds that turned in the great-open.

It was time for the Prox to defend the Territories like the

Warruq clans had done long before the Prox were brought into existence by the Creators. LOR and his warriors continued to drive the Invaders toward them, unable to change the iron beast's course. This new enemy must be destroyed, the Oath fulfilled and in the Realm of Warriors they would meet again.

14

---

the Black Wall
Bridge of the *Anam Cara*

"Commander Shar'ran, arm the missiles. Max-charge the rail guns, load 'em with self-detonating slugs." Falco wanted to be sure the first rounds exploded near the objects without damaging them. Their intent seemed menacing at best, but so far, the *Anam Cara* was unscathed. Once munitions left their rails or tubes… everything would change. There would be no going back.

The Commander sent the order. Falco opened a video feed and watched three ammunition techs in the bowels of the *Anam Cara* punching codes into a data-pad near the missiles tubes, arming the missiles and activating their independent targeting systems. He switched the video feed again to the rail gun compartment where two crewmen sat strapped into battle-buckets bolted next to separate sets of conducting rails.

Each chair had a helmet integrated into the sighting system joined to the Battle-Net. Rail guns were mounted to a mobile platform that constantly reacted to the sighting system. If fear was present, Falco could not see it in their postures. Or it was overcome by the need to protect the men and women that lived and worked on the *Anam Cara*. God, they look young, Falco thought and closed the video feed.

Self-detonating slugs were a prayer at anything closer than ten klicks. A gunner would take the data feed from the Battle-Net and set the rounds to explode based on the enemy's distance, speed, and other variables that only the Battle-Net could track. Traveling through space at MACH 20 made it like trying to catch a mosquito with a thimble while riding a bike. That's where the Battle-Net came in.

"Captain, Battle-Net unable lock on the objects. Too small, too close, their heat bloom is the best we can do. Estimate fifty percent chance we damage or destroy." Commander Shar'ran grunted. "Missiles will be overkill if they hit or wasted if they miss."

"Agreed, but keep the missiles hot, should be a larger vessel nearby, a mothership." Falco focused on the holo-feed at his station, sifting through the three-dimensional blackness that lay ahead – a black wall which their instruments desperately tried to penetrate and failed. A thousand fleets could be sitting directly in front of us and we would have no idea of their presence. But could you place a vessel in dark matter or dark energy? The rabbit hole was approaching and Falco was not going down it.

"Lieutenant Wallace, How many Data-Pods?"

Wallace punched up his inventory. "Five Pods, sir."

Falco rubbed the newly forming dark stubble on his chin, "Commander Shar'ran, chamber the Pods and plot their courses as close to the objects as you can, but not in their path."

"Pods ready." Commander Shar'ran stated. "All five? That's all we have—"

"A reaction, Commander." Falco exhaled hard, sharp. "Will they let them harmlessly pass by or attempt to impede or stop their progress? Show our pursuers intent without using ordnance."

Shar'ran nodded. "It's worth a try."

"Let 'em fly," Falco ordered.

---

the Darkness
the Void
LOR

FIVE ORBS FLEW from the iron beast. LOR could not override the Warruq's main objective; to destroy the nearest threat, as each of his warriors left their pursuit of the vessel and charged head-on to meet the new enemies.

Four of the orbs were reduced to scrap as each Warruq slammed into the speeding spheres. Organs smashed into skull plates on impact, leaving the enemy obliterated. The dead Warruqs whose methane sacks had not exploded into fireballs, were left nothing more than perfectly intact skull plates pulling armored sacks of frozen flesh, cartilage and damaged sensors behind them.

To the Realm of Warriors, you soar. LOR sent a vision to all the clans outside of the Darkness of the Oath being fulfilled by Warruqs dying in the Void to protect the territories from another enemy. An uncontrollable fury consumed him. LOR hesitated, a split cycle of indecision – unusual for Warruqs – that allowed the last streaking sphere to escape. A fleeing, cowardly creature not worthy of the chase.

The iron beast continued pressing toward the Creators... moving closer to the edge of the Darkness that concealed their worlds and hid their assassins, the Prox.

Overtaken by rage for his fallen warriors, LOR released his energy bloom, announcing his presence, and powered toward the iron beast. Drive it towards the Prox. But he wanted more. He wanted the voices and the beast to pay with their pathetic existence. His warriors had moved on with honor. I will join them soon, he thought.

Waves of energy pounded LOR's systems. Hate and fear radiating from all the Warruq clans along the frontier, watching the scene through LOR's open thought-stream. The clans connected as one; fueling LOR's blind rage, wave after hate-filled wave. Billions of cycles of waiting were over. My objective is clear... The Creators must be protected; the voices will be silenced before they reach the Darkness.

---

the Darkness
Prox

THE PROX CONTINUED ANALYZING the information from LOR's thought-stream. The data flooded in each time their small Seeker appeared through the Darkness and ceased as soon as it bobbed back into the Void. Swimming through the Darkness, taking comfort in its health-giving mass. Each Prox readied itself. The beast was heading directly at them, a dark circle back-lit by the immense blaze of LOR's full energy bloom.

Four Warruqs died for their Creators. The fifth was consumed by a rage that was feeding on its need for revenge. It is our time to honor our Oath, thought the larger of the Prox. Older and wiser, she was responsible for teaching the younger Prox the meaning of the Oath. This is why we are always in pairs, the teacher and the student.

She sent a final thought to LOR through the bobbing Seeker. *Burn bright on your path to the Realm of Warriors, Oath fulfilled.* She closed her thought-stream.

Contact
Bridge of the *Anam Cara*

"ONE DATA-POD VIABLE and beyond the known enemy position, four hostiles and four Data-Pods destroyed on contact, new energy source ten klicks aft of the debris field, closing fast on a direct course," Commander Shar'ran stated.

"Lock onto the enemy, Commander. Prepare to fire rail guns." Falco was stunned at the speed and precision in which the chasing projectiles crushed their Data-Pods. A warning shot was now off the table.

"We turn now or enter the black field, Captain," Lieutenant Wallace echoed from the cockpit.

"Lieutenant, kill the engines, all power to rail guns. Now, Commander!" Falco roared. "Fire!"

Ten million amps pulsed through the rails and propelled two explosive rounds at a sickening pace.

The Battle-Net continued its calculations and trajectory changes until the precise moment the self-detonating slugs left the conducting rails. Two flashes lit up the stern of the *Anam Cara* a fraction of a second after the guns fired. Streaks of burning shrapnel from the rounds reached out as deadly fingers towards the chasing enemy. The bridge of the *Anam Cara* was eerily silent.

Captain Falco knew he traded any hope of outrunning their pursuer for a chance to destroy it. Commander Shar'ran continued to pour over the Battle-Net data, checking for the heat signature.

Falco wondered why it had waited behind the others, cloaking its energy signature. A commander viewing the battlefield, or the cavalry making a heroic charge? Even worse, Falco was not cognizant he was referring to these weapons in his head as an 'it.'

---

the Darkness
the Void
Realm of Warriors

LOR SHOT TOWARDS THE CRAFT, gaining ground as he released his full energy bloom. He knew he could not sustain it for long, but the need to destroy the voices within the treacherous iron beast was overpowering. The chase was not enough. Driving the invaders toward the Prox was not enough. Only vengeance for the loss of his clan would allow him to enter the Realm of Warriors.

He detected two new openings in the iron beast as soon as they appeared. More cowardly creatures fleeing the fight? They look to escape, he thought, his rage all consuming.

The steel beast cut its burn in front of the Veil and released a stream of numbers.

LOR found he was part of these computations, at the center

of the mathematical visions. The beast released two streaking objects from its new openings. Each ember spewed an ancient language. They spoke of LOR's position, his placement in the Void.

Finally, the ancient one is reaching out, but you are too late, your destiny is one with the invading voices you protect…

Two bright flashes blinded LOR's sensors. Sharp fragments tore through his carapace, severed his skull-plate and what was left of him exploded into a fine mist.

To the Realm of Warriors LOR journeyed.

Oath fulfilled.

the Black Wall
Bridge of the *Anam Cara*

FALCO TURNED in his captain's chair. "Commander Shar'ran?"

"Battle-Net is clear, sir. But, everything ends there," he said, pointing toward the bow of the *Anam Cara*. "Nothing on our ship can scan or search beyond the face of the black wall. That is where our solar system truly ends."

Something about the shadow ahead bothered Falco.

"This dark matter or energy," his voice was low, barely audible, "it feels wrong, looks... wrong. I've seen enough." Falco spun towards the bow. "Lieutenant Wallace, turn her around. Full burn back to Station Pluto. We can meet the Viper Battle group on the way. I am sure Admiral Chen will want to give their new boats a full-turn to work out their kinks."

Wallace punched the side thrusters, spinning the bow of the *Anam Cara*. Anything not bolted down slid as the grav-system worked to catch up with the sudden thrust. A low hum vibrated through the ship's steel frame and the main engine came back online.

"Station Pluto, Lieutenant, get us home." Falco remained locked on the port window, eyes scanning the infinite black wall behind them. The opaque blast-plates accentuated the shadowy field, making it look like an infinite curtain waiting to be opened.

---

the Darkness: the Veil
Mentor and Apprentice

EACH PROX SKIMMED THEIR THOUGHT-STREAM, scanning and downloading the stored information on the invaders and the iron beast that acted like a shielding carapace. The Warruqs had perished for the information and it would not be wasted. The invading vessel had turned away and was heading back from the direction it had appeared, but the damage was done. The Warruqs were slain and the iron beast was no longer an intruder, it was an enemy.

Data was massed and uploaded to all of the Seekers safely imbedded in the four small cartilage sacks lining their backs. Each orifice gently rippled and swelled while the methane from the Proxs' fuel sac slowly pushed into the small creatures.

Prox had always been placed in pairs. For millions of cycles, two sentinels perfectly spaced apart so each pair could feel the life force of the next, pulsating through the Darkness. Positioned as a defensive ring around the Creators' planets, but cloaked in the Darkness. Swimming in the sustaining camouflage, waiting to fulfill their Oath.

The Prox plan was sound, built on the amassed data stored and analyzed from the first contact with the intruders to the present moment. They sent each other a final farewell as individuals and combined their thought-streams into a singular flow.

They would join as one and become a single fighting force, sharing all data simultaneously from two different vantage points. Learning, experiencing and evolving by the fractional-cycle. Each moved in opposite directions, keeping just beneath the shielding surface of the Darkness. The Darkness thinned her Veil, allowing the Prox to see the fleeing enemy.

In unison, each excreted a single Seeker from their backs. Orders were uploaded into the small dark spheres that patiently waited to ignite and ride their methane bloom into battle. Hardened skull-plates covered their sensors and organs. Muscle formed a sack that stretched around a web-like frame of cartilage fused to the plate. The expandable sack allowed the Seekers to store high volumes of pressurized methane and rapidly accelerate over short distances or initiate a slow burn for great crossings.

Their time had come and each had its target. The Seekers ignited; bursting through the Darkness, crossing the Veil into the Void, each leaving an oily ripple at their exit point. A slight pause in acceleration as their optical sensors came online and they were hurtling towards their destinations. Behind the Darkness the Prox swiftly moved further apart, staying close to the surface.

The teacher and larger Prox slowed and stopped. A weak thought-stream opened. A Warruq entered the Darkness from a great distance away and a faint message with a spattering of images appeared.

Yes, she replied to the oldest Warruq. *A position earned by your elder status. You will make a worthy LOR. The Prox welcome your protection of the clans of the Darkness, the territories and the Creators.*

The Mentor closed the thought-stream and released another Seeker from her back and sent it on its way.

Each of the paired Prox now shared a sense of imbalance, pieces of their physical existence flying to their destruction in the name of the Creators. The Seekers would soon find their path to the Realm of Warriors and would never become Prox, would never return to their mothers again.

Burning toward Pluto
Bridge of the *Anam Cara*

THE BATTLE-NET CAME TO LIFE. Proximity sensors flashed across the bridge.

"Incoming, brace for impact!" Commander Shar'ran belted over the main COM seconds before a sledgehammer smashed into the *Anam Cara*.

"Damage report, Commander!" Falco switched to the exterior video feed. Carbon epoxies foamed through layers of the *Anam Cara*'s wounded steel hull, the safety systems laboring to mend her.

"Incoming! Too small, too close to track." Shar'ran turned toward Falco when the second projectile slammed into the COM satellite link just forward of the solar sail compartment only meters under the bridge.

Data-Pads flew from workstations, heads snapped backwards. Lieutenant Wallace drooped in his pilot's chair, streaks of red flowing down his face from a gash over his left eye pooling on his nav-pad.

"Medic to the bridge!" Falco scanned the area for more injuries.

"Incoming! Can't get a lock." Commander Shar'ran slammed a fist onto his station top.

"Hold onto something!" Falco growled, "God damn it!"

The *Anam Cara* lurched and slowed.

"Captain, they hit the main engine! Out of commission, but thrusters are still online," stated the ship's engineer over Falco's COM box.

"Get her moving." Falco released his iron grip on the armrest, hit the release on his harness, stood and quickly moved to the bow. After checking Wallace for a pulse, he gently eased the lieutenant to the deck and buckled into the pilot's seat. A stout crewman with a red 'M' on the chest of her uniform moved in behind Falco and began assessing the injured officer.

"I have the controls. Let's go, Commander, I need damage assessment." Falco pushed the thrusters as fast as the flight controls would allow.

Commander Shar'ran sat upright and adjusted the tension on his harness. Two lines flashed red across the Battle-Net screen amid the scrolling data. "Rail guns destroyed, COM-Sat down, breach sealed, grav-system ninety-two percent, environmental systems compromised, but stable." He swallowed hard and continued, "Gunners Conlin and Martinez, killed in action, sir."

Captain Falco's jaw tightened. "Continue scanning for hostiles. Fire on anything that moves out there. If you get as much as a blip without a friendly indicator, I want a missile parked on it."

"Yes, sir." Commander Shar'ran scanned the massive black wall that hid their attackers while the Battle-Net swiveled the port and starboard launch tubes, searching for anything within range.

Falco remained calm while allowing himself a moment to feel the loss of his two young crewmen. Rotating through hiber-sleep periods for five years created a strange distance between a crew. One could go the entire 'turn' and only meet a handful of people on a skeleton crew that rarely shared a space together. Falco was only beginning to get to know the young crewmen out of the academy. What he did know, Martinez and Conlin strapped into the rail-guns' battle buckets and did their jobs to the end.

"Lieutenant Wallace is conscious. Possible mild concussion," stated the medic while continuing to dress the head wound with one hand and waive chem-salts in the other.

"Good, get him back to us ASAP." We need a real pilot, Falco thought. I'm just good enough to get us killed.

The medic punched three poly-stitches through the clean flaps of skin above Lieutenant Wallace's left eye with a loud snap that made Falco wince.

"Just like the one you gave me when we met, Captain."

Falco spun around and found Lieutenant Wallace sitting up, a strange smirk plastered across a swollen face. "Well, I've definitely seen you look worse." Falco returned the smile, "Now get up, you lazy Scotsman and take over the controls before I fly us into an asteroid!"

"Full damage report is coming in, Captain." Ensign Holts pressed one hand over the tiny speaker in her ear and the other hand extended like a stop sign. "COM-Sat, Emergency Beacon, gone. Minor damage to the belly of the boat, main engine offline, rail-guns heavily damaged, solar sails are intact, five minor injuries, two KIA." Holts's arms dropped to her sides. "Could have been much worse."

Falco was about to bite Holts's head off at the 'could have been worse,' remark, but refrained. Two dead with only slight damage was 'minimal' he knew. It could and should have been much worse. They hit exactly what they wanted to.

Holts again pressed a hand to her ear. "We have remnants of

the enemy's weaponry. Sanitation crew is scrubbing down the rail gun compartment. Crewman in-charge recommends it be sealed until we get back to the station."

The bridge of the *Anam Cara* was silent. Falco assumed each officer fought the hellish imagery that was trying to take hold. There could be more of them hiding in the black field. Every klick they moved further from the dark wall, the better.

"Wait." Falco turned and faced Ensign Holts. "Have the 'remnants' assessed by our munitions techs ASAP—"

"There." Commander Shar'ran pointed at the image of a dark field floating on the holo-gram above his station. A faint red flare shone on the face of the wall and disappeared.

Falco stood, moved toward the Battle-Net station and looked over Shar'ran's shoulder. The commander remained silent, the Battle-Net sensors focused on the area.

Captain Falco waited and hoped they could get a lock on whatever still lurked behind the curtain before it could attack. The *Anam Cara* was underway to Station Pluto at a snail's pace, trying to reach MACH 1. The growing distance increased their chance of destroying another attacker before it reached them, but the velocity of the objects exiting the wall...

"What are they waiting for?" Falco said. "They have every advantage. Maybe that was all they had..."

"Fire," Commander Shar'ran coldly stated as the Battle-Net lit up with an optical lock. Something had moved beyond the black wall and two missiles were going to erase it. The launch tubes flashed red. Interceptors flew from their cradles, while more reloaded behind them.

Two red embers streaked away from the *Anam Cara*. Falco watched their exhaust burn and glow as it dispersed as fast as the efficient engines produced it. Red turned pink and the glow of exhaust disappeared.

"They've slowed," Falco stated.

"Missiles are searching," Commander Shar'ran whispered. "Target has moved back into the field."

---

the Darkness: the Veil
the Apprentice

SEEKERS HAD RIPPED through the steel beast following the Prox plan. The voices were hurt and humbled by the power of the Darkness and its clans.

Again, the young Prox pierced the Veil with her fin. She moved her optical sensors as close to the surface as possible, still unable to see the iron beast, the Darkness no longer allowed her to see through her mass.

Stay within the Darkness, her mentor cautioned. *We have destroyed the parts of the beast that slew the Warruqs and their former LOR.* That was their last shared thought and the link was broken. The Prox became individuals and the mentor opened a thought-stream between them.

The invaders of the Territories are fleeing, the steel beast under their control is damaged and the voices are scattered and afraid, our task is complete. The mentor waited for her apprentice to process the situation.

We have protected the Creators and their worlds from this enemy of the Darkness, thought the young Prox. *But mentor, what are the voices and where did they come from? Should we not learn more of these new beings, these creations?* She moved to the edge of the Veil, leaving her mentor and teacher behind.

Stay within the Darkness! thought the mentor. *You are unskilled in using the methane burn—* But it was too late, the apprentice could only hear her own thoughts. Curiosity won out, her massive fins working back and forth, moved her hulking carapace through the protective mass of the Darkness to get a glimpse of the Void, the invaders and what lay beyond. An unprotected frontier where fins were of no use and burning methane fuel was required in the cold emptiness.

Unable to open a thought-stream with her apprentice, the mentor pushed through the Darkness and into the Void. They were not alone. Two objects sprang to life on her optical sensors and charged toward them while the iron beast continued to flee from the Frontier. Fear filled the Prox thought-stream that was now connected. The apprentice was terrified, unable to use her methane burn in her new environment, her fins flapping and thrashing to no avail without the body of the Darkness to provide resistance.

The mentor moved in front of her floundering apprentice and adjusted her carapaces plating toward the incoming aggressors, locking her armor in place and hardening it against the coming attackers. With her remaining two Seekers jostling to release from their muscular wombs on her now unprotected back, the older Prox uploaded their mission. The Seekers discharged and ignited their energy bloom.

The mentor pulsed warnings through their shared thought-stream, but her apprentice could not respond. *Fear has frozen your warrior spirit, my apprentice,* she thought, *learn from this and grow strong.*

Her carapace now fully shielding the young Prox from the coming attackers, the bigger, stronger and wiser, mentor ignited her methane sack. Slamming into her apprentice and sending her tumbling into the safety of the Darkness, the mentor faced the enemy.

Pain pulsated along her unprotected back she had used to push her apprentice to safety. A growing cloud of methane hung around her, spilling from a breach her protective systems could not staunch.

The Seekers locked onto the two charging enemies who instantly changed their direction and velocity. The Seekers recalculated the enemy trajectories only to have them move again and again. The injured Prox continued channeling the Seekers visual stream, storing the enemy's movements and calculating their estimated destination.

Teaching and protecting her apprentice was her highest calling and her student was safe in the Darkness. The mentor sent a final order to the Seekers, knowing they could destroy one of the enemies if they worked in tandem.

The adversary tried to evade their pursuit, but it was no match for two Seekers. It erupted into a vast fireball as both Seekers smashed into it in unison. The last of her methane spilled out her fuel sac. The remaining enemy made a slight change in course, straightened and charged toward her.

Let the clans know of the danger that lurks outside the Territories young one. The Void brings a new enemy of the Darkness. Her final pulse pushed through her open thought-stream, possibly reaching the distant Warruq outposts if they chose to listen.

The enemy crashed into her plating, sending her to the Realm of Warriors one piece at a time, Oath fulfilled.

Captain Falco
Anam Cara

"Missile one destroyed." Commander Shar'ran waited as the second missile adjusted its course. "Interceptor two, detonation. Hostile signature is gone."

Falco heard trepidation in his commander's voice, a thread of fear, even doubt. He watched Shar'ran from his captain's chair. The man sat at his station motionless, his eyes never leaving the Battle-Net feed.

"Commander?" Falco could see something was wrong. "Report."

Commander Shar'ran's breathing came in deep, rhythmic puffs. "There were two heat signatures for a moment. The interceptors had two locked targets. One target disappeared into the black field." He turned to face Captain Falco. "Our sensors are worthless... In that." Commander Shar'ran pointed toward the stern of the *Anam Cara* and the infinite black mass that hung, a massive storm front in deep space.

Falco leaned back in his chair. "According to the Battle-Net, Interceptor one was 10.4 seconds ahead of Interceptor two. The enemy sold out and focused on the first missile, but could not fight off the second."

Captain Falco slowly looked around the bridge. Lieutenant Wallace was doing everything he could to get the *Anam Cara* back to Station Pluto as fast as possible. The two thrusters were at full power, engine-one was a lost cause.

The damage from the second attack was too severe to patch-up without the tools and facilities of a repair bay. Ensign Holts was running through every bit of data the Battle-Net had scanned on the enemy.

Finally, Falco placed his hands on the armrests and slowly pushed himself into a standing position.

"Someone has created the technology to hide weaponry in the black field and we have no way of detecting it. A new form of terrorism?" Falco looked around the bridge. "Mining, construction, even exploration will all be at the mercy of something potentially hiding in... literally in the dark."

"Like the U-Boats of the old wars before sonar." Commander Shar'ran rubbed a deep scar on his cheek.

"Could be as simple as a motion activated missile system," Falco stated. "Place them, set the sensor and off you go. Whoever gets near them without the proper identification is in a world of pain."

"The ultimate, NO TRESPASSING sign," chimed Lieutenant Wallace from the pilot's seat.

"What about the material in the bow of these objects?" Ensign Holts gently shook her head. "Nothing explains that. If there was the tiniest amount of material from a neutron star in these weapons, these objects," Holts held her hands in the air, "how did someone harvest it and build it into these things? And if that were even possible, the objects would have done more than embed themselves in the *Anam Cara,* they would have gone through and torn her in half."

"Point taken, Holts." Falco knew where she was going.

"When has the Battle-Net needed to use its database to estimate scanned materials? Half of its technology and programming is specifically for probing deep into rock and deciding its value as a mining site." Holts exhaled sharply. "The database contains everything known to humanity at this point in time and yet, in regards to these objects we get, 'similar to muscle, steel, plastics and material from a neutron star?' We need to broaden the pool of possible suspects."

"Agreed, but this is what we have, Ensign, and little of it makes sense, especially out here. The Pluto Station has been here in one form or another for seven years. They would have picked up a vessel or something that could have placed weaponry this far out."

"We have made contact with three unique types of weaponry." Commander Shar'ran adjusted his holo-feed. "The latter took a missile to destroy and was much larger than the group that chased the *Anam Cara*. And what about these smaller ones? Think of what they attacked."

"They hit us with a few cannonballs! How advanced is that?" Lieutenant Wallace said, as the *Anam Cara* reached MACH 2.

"But those 'cannonballs' damaged our main engine, destroyed the COMS, and rail guns. Luckily we still had missiles," Falco could see Ensign Holts locked onto her streaming data-pad, swiping above its surface. "Anything to add, Ensign?"

"Techs have finished a limited assessment," Holts turned from the feed, eyes wide and looked towards Falco, "and brought in a lab tech for a dissection."

"Dissection?" Falco sat ramrod straight.

Holts continued, "From the 'cannonball' lodged in the rail gunner's seat," she paused and gathered herself, "organic matter with some type of bone-like casing, propulsion possibly achieved by burning methane emitted through a highly reinforced vent. If you could harvest it, methane is abundant out here and makes sense to use it for fuel."

"So, we have encountered, conceivably, three types of weaponry or a sentry system?" Commander Shar'ran paused, shot a questioning glance toward Falco and back to Holts, "Powered, literally by gas?"

"Possibly, Commander." Falco leaned back, crossed his arms. "These 'cannonballs', for lack of a better term, attacked the COM-Sat, emergency beacon, rail guns compartment and the main engine. They could not have chosen better areas to hit us if the goal was disablement. But why not destroy the missile bays and the thrusters?"

Falco had the answer and he was not sure he liked it. "They hit the systems we had already used to either try and contact them or fend off their first attack. We fired off all of the Data-Pods, which were destroyed, save one and that left us with our COM-Sat and emergency beacon. Each was used to attempt contact."

"Both were taken out," Lieutenant Wallace threw in, "and they couldn't know of Station Pluto's existence. Even if they did, they wouldn't know their COMs are down, so they took out all of our COM systems to ensure we had no way to send for help."

"Maybe," Falco wondered, "but then they took out the rail guns which had just fired. They could have destroyed us, but did not."

"We know someone is using this black field to hide weaponry. Station Pluto has taken a few hits to their COMs over the past year, but that's it. If the Russian Federation or Euro-Arab League is behind this, why?"

Ensign Holts turned to face Falco. "Our technology has zero ability to poke holes into anything beyond the face of the field, we are totally blind to what lays behind it. If the Russians or Euro-Arab League have developed this technology, it changes the balance of power. They could place spy facilities, weapons or even militarized space stations right next to us and we would have no idea."

"But why now?" Commander Shar'ran's hands rose off his data-pad. "Why attack us now? Here? Space Station Pluto is only a day and half burn from this location. Clearly someone who could conceal space-based weaponry in a vast black field would know of the station's military strength? Attacking us shows their hand and gives the United Nations Navy their location."

Captain Falco nodded. "What about the 'anomalies' hitting Station Pluto?"

"Our orders stated, 'they were composed of rock and ice.' Pieces of asteroids and debris from approximately our current position." Ensign Holts let the last words hang.

"Cannonballs launched from within the dark field." Commander Shar'ran's voice was low, almost a whisper, "Just like the ones that took out our own COM and rail guns, and damaged our main engine, if they can fire those?"

"Yes." Falco fell silent, swallowed hard. "If they can place and operate artillery within the field," He raised a hand toward the exterior bulkhead. "As Ensign Holts stated, they can hide anything within it."

"If they don't care or are not threatened by Station Pluto, or us for that matter, as they seem to have let us go..." Holts expanded the holo-feed on her station, adjusting the three-dimensional floating image to focus on the dark field. "There must be something in there worth far more to them. This field looks more like a wall on our side, it has form which means they have a means to shape it or contain it. Its area is far larger than our sensors can cover, although they can estimate its size as the data continues to compile over time."

"We were pursued as we edged closer to the black field. Directed closer? By plan or just circumstance, and then we were attacked, this time by larger more formidable 'weaponry.' We destroyed the pursuers; or they destroyed themselves taking out our Data-Pods, and we were damaged by the second attack. Pinpoint damage that had purpose and then nothing, because we turned the *Anam Cara* around and moved away?" Falco knew there were far too many possibilities at this point. Regrouping at Station Pluto would give them a chance to rethink every step from the beginning.

"Captain." Ensign Holts grabbed both sides of her station. "Our scanners have found something. May I connect to your station's holo-feed, sir?"

Falco nodded and allowed Holts to control his holo-feed. The image of the dark field grew and expanded across the *Anam Cara*'s bridge.

Holts tapped at her data-pad and moved her hands around the hologram image hanging over her own station. With each input the large, three-dimensional object at the center of the bridge rotated and a patchwork of glowing areas on the flat, face of the wall appeared.

"What are we looking at, Ensign?" Falco leaned back in his chair to take in the image projected from the center of his captain's station.

"The field is far too massive for our scanners to do anything but plot its estimated area from our current distance. We got close enough to a small portion of the field to scan the outside in as much detail as our tech permits." Holts stood, left her station and moved toward the floating image at the center of the bridge. "This is dark matter," she said, pointing at the largest black area surrounded by a glowing patchwork.

Commander Shar'ran squinted at the hologram. "Yes, we know that is dark matter, and…"

"Commander, *this* is dark matter." Again Holts pointed toward the same area.

Falco leaned in. "Then, Ensign, what the hell is all the rest? All the glowing pieces?"

"From a distance, the field registered as dark matter or what our data banks know to be dark matter. As the *Anam Cara* moved closer, our scanners were able to get a more accurate scan of a small part of its surface area. All of these areas," she used both hands to point to the glowing patchwork, "are unknown, and 'dark matter' is the closest comparison we have. Like muscle, bone and a neutron star are the closest comparisons our data banks can make to parts of the 'cannonballs' that damaged the *Anam Cara*."

"And killed two of my crew." Falco stood and moved to the side of the hologram. "We are all thinking it, so I'm simply going to state it. I believe we just found humanity's border. The line in space that separates us from... Well, from something else." He moved around the three-dimensional projection. "If Earth, our solar system and everything we have ever observed with our instruments or our own eyes is 'normal matter' and makes up less than ten percent of the universe—"

"Estimated less than five percent, Captain. Less than five percent of the universe is classified as 'normal matter,'" Ensign Holts stated.

Falco nodded towards his science officer and continued. "That leaves an estimated ninety-five percent of something else." He looked toward Holts.

"Sixty-eight percent dark energy and twenty-seven percent dark matter... give or take a percent or two."

Commander Shar'ran adjusted his tall, lean frame in his chair. "Only humanity would call five percent of something, 'normal matter.' Once again, we create comfort and a false sense of security in the little that we know, or think we know."

"Ensign Holts, can you estimate the area of the field with the current data we have collected?"

Holts quickly maneuvered across her station, inputting instructions into her data-pad and manipulating her holo-feed that was still controlling the main image on the bridge. "Yes,

Captain, but the estimate has a margin of error of twenty-two percent."

"Good enough, let's see it." Falco found his captain's chair and waited.

"Based on all data collected by the Battle-Net's systems, this is the representation of the field using imaging and modeling." Holts tapped on her data-pad. The hologram in the center of the bridge expanded slightly.

From the bow, Lieutenant Wallace cranked his head around to look at the hologram behind him. "Not so grand." He shrugged and went back to his pilot duties.

"Remember that we still know very little about what dark matter and dark energy are." Ensign Holts circled the projection. "After Einstein figured out centuries ago that space was not empty, we still only theorize that dark matter is a 'property of space'." She returned again to her station and tapped in additional data. "This is our solar system using the same scale." The dark field shrank and another image appeared next to it. Eight planets and Pluto moved around the sun.

Falco got out of his chair, standing in the middle of the two images, his body providing the line separating the two. He was stunned by the sheer size of the black field.

Commander Shar'ran blinked hard as if trying to clear his vision. "Are you telling us that this 'field' or whatever the hell it is, is larger than our entire solar system?"

"Yes. The greater question, Commander, is not the size of the field," Ensign Holts paused, "but what is its true purpose?"

The dark field had already given them the answer. "To camouflage anything they want." Falco felt the immensity of a concept he could not wrap his mind around, slam into his chest. "And this... 'dark field' has been out here, all this time, doing what? And what are they hiding or hiding from?" Falco finished.

Ensign Holts spoke up. "Captain, the technology needed to create this 'camouflaging field' by integrating dark matter with their own materials is simply incomprehensible based on our technology and capabilities. There is no way to discern how long it has been here as we have been staring at it through telescopes and satellites for centuries. The vast dark areas beyond Pluto have been classified with the rest of the ninety-five percent of an ever expanding universe we know little about."

Falco wanted the main engine back online. Crawling away from the dark field's flat, endless gaze made it seem like the *Anam Cara* was begging to be swallowed up. "With this type of technology, why would humanity be a threat at all?" Falco scanned the bridge.

"It wouldn't, unless we came knocking at the door," Ensign Holts stated.

"Which is exactly what 'we' just did." Falco looked out the port windows.

Yes, he thought, were they hiding from humanity? No, they were screening themselves. Using a mosquito net to keep the bugs away. Falco felt like they were being watched.

Falco sat heavy in the captain's chair. Well, Admiral Chen, you are about to earn that paycheck. The scouting mission was a success, he thought, but still no sign of the planet Nemesis. The knowledge that the brown dwarf star was 'missing' remained off limits to anyone other than himself and Admiral Chen. Falco continued to focus on the holographic image of the black field floating next to humanity's home system and was beginning to understand how Nemesis, a star thirteen times the size of Jupiter, could get lost out here without a trace.

the Darkness
a Call to Battle

MOTIONLESS IN THE DARKNESS, the young Prox was alone and

afraid without her mentor and friend to protect her. She instinctively rolled into an armored sphere, each plate locking and forming a defensive cocoon. She fought to gain control of her thought-stream and systems, but something else was coming. A power began to surge through her. She had reached the number of cycles when the young became full Prox and the warrior's rage was building inside her systems. She gave into its power and let it course through her systems; with it came the control of her thought-stream.

She opened herself to all the planets and clans within the territories, the Creators, the Warruqs, the Prox and even the Krell – the last resort in a time of desperation. All awakened in the Darkness, hidden from any invader that wanted to harm them, wanted to conquer their planets and enslave the inhabitants. Finally, after billions of cycles of waiting, a new enemy had invaded the territories and killed without cause… then fled back to where they had come from.

Images and history of the events poured through her thought-stream showing the clans, the savage destruction of the heroic Warruqs and her mentor, the valiant Prox, by the iron beast and the voices hiding within its carapace. The thought-stream closed and thousands of methane blooms lit the Darkness. Prox, Warruqs and Krell began moving toward the lone apprentice floating near the edge of the territories, tucked into a plated sphere… a cocoon.

All were ready to honor their blood Oath to the Creators and earn their passage to the Realm of Warriors by destroying the invaders and those that had sent them.

19

Anam Cara
Day's Burn from Station Pluto

"WE'LL GET HER HOME, Lieutenant. She's tougher than all of us," Falco said, the ship shuddering under his feet. The grav-system was not meant for quick adjustments as the *Anam Cara* sputtered forward, slowed down and sputtered forward again. He observed Lieutenant Wallace continuing his assault on the nav-pad, his thick fingers punching at the controls.

The *Anam Cara* was holding together as she always had, but she was wounded and doing her best to get her crew to safety. Even when she fell from the sky during the Korean Empire conflict, many of her crew survived, her bones would not break. Bend, but not break, Falco recalled with great pride.

Falco knew the Scotsman's fury was fueled by his inability to help her, to repair her wounds and protect the ship from further damage. So, Lieutenant Wallace did what he could to keep her heading true by constantly firing the starboard and port thrusters in bursts.

Nonstop chatter bounced back and forth from the pilot's COM box and the engineers working to repair her main engine while running constant tests on the hull's integrity.

"The bastards gut shot her," the whisper tore through Wallace's clenched teeth. "Almost home, hold together, help is only hours away." This time it came out like a plea from a close friend.

"Lieutenant, can you give us an ETA for Station Pluto?" Holts asked while locked onto her data feeds, still sorting, compiling and studying the mass of broad-scoped analysis gathered by the Battle-Net systems. Her job was to make sense of what was coming in.

Wallace spun around. "For Christ's sake, Holts! How can I give you an ETA? Can't even tell you if there will be an arrival!"

Commander Shar'ran shot the pilot a stern look and for a brief moment Lieutenant Wallace looked about ready to give him a dose of the same, but thought better of it.

Ensign Holts sat in silence, staring at Lieutenant Wallace's back.

Falco sat in his captain's chair, watching and listening to his crew's reactions. He noticed Ensign Holts was not cowering like a scolded child as many young officers would. No, he thought, she is waiting for him to collect himself. She is strong, finding her place within the officer structure, strong indeed. Falco had chosen well. He turned back to the Battle-Net screen; he felt the quiet strength emanating from Holts and he liked it.

"I was out of line, Holts." Wallace eventually broke the silence.

"I know how much she means to you, Lieutenant. She is family to all of us. I simply need an ETA so I can have 10th Fleet relay the info to Station Pluto's hangar so they can begin the repairs as soon as we dock."

"Thank you." A long pause followed. "She is more than a boat..." Wallace steadied himself, cleared his throat. "She is our boat and has protected this crew as best she could by putting herself between us and all that would do us harm." Lieutenant Wallace turned back to his Nav-pad and the assault continued with thick fingers punching the controls.

Falco gently nodded in his officer's direction and caught Commander Shar'ran looking at him intently then shifting his stare towards Ensign Holts. "Ensign Holts, please look up the origins of the boat's name, given to her by her stubborn pilot many years ago."

She quickly did as asked. "Soul mate," she whispered.

"Ensign?"

Holts turned to face Commander Shar'ran only to find the man's face firmly planted a few inches from his Battle-Net screen. She stood and walked the few paces it took to reach his station.

The Commander continued to squint and moved his face closer to the rolling footage and then pulled back as if the distance might provide clarity and substance to whatever his mind was trying make sense of, and played the scene again. Ensign Holts patiently stood back looking over his shoulder. The screen was filled with the smoky haze known to them simply as the 'dark field.' Finally, she grew impatient.

"What do you see, Commander?"

Shar'ran came to life. "There!" he said, his finger flying to the screen. "There is a change in the dark field." The grainy video abruptly ended and froze on the final image.

"When was this taken?" Holts asked.

"Last image before we moved beyond the Battle-Net's limited visual range. Captain told me to continue monitoring all sensors and data feeds so it took me a while to get to the older data."

Holts looked to Falco, "You should see this, Captain."

The commander tapped a few keys on his data-pad and the image changed as he zoomed in. The wall of the field had changed while the *Anam Cara* was limping away. He hit another key and the video started again from a previous point. The commander slowed the video to a snail's pace and enhanced the contrast.

"What the hell?" The black field glowed in spots. "Flashes?" Falco whispered. It was subtle and without the Battle-Net, he knew they would have missed it, but there it was. It looked like a lightning storm buried in a dense, oily, cloud. Each smoldering spot had a viscous ring around it before it faded to black. It reminded Falco of those ancient lamps they had in the Smithsonian, Lava Lamps. The video went black.

"Add it to the data files and send it to 10th Fleet with the rest." Falco turned and headed back to his captain's chair.

The *Anam Cara* shook hard.

"Whoa." Falco fell into his seat and clicked into his harness.

Lieutenant Wallace swore and adjusted the thrusters. "I hope that is the main engine coming back to life."

A pulsing vibration rolled through the ship in waves from stern to bow.

Captain Falco's COMs box lit green and belched from the bowels of the ship. "Engine One back on-line, Captain. Fifty percent power is the best we could do."

"Excellent work, Chief! We'll take it. Lieutenant Wallace best speed."

Wallace fired the main and gently increased her pace. "Hang in there, girl, almost there," he whispered.

Station Pluto
Director Lipinski

"FORWARD TODAY'S PROGRESS REPORT." Station Director Lipinski spun in his chair to grab a cooling espresso and spun back in time for his COM-Box to belch the answer.

"You should have it now, Director."

Lipinski tapped on the glowing data packet that appeared on his pad and chose to view it in hologram mode. He loved to reach up and manipulate the floating strings of numbers, zooming in and out, highlighting the ratios that made him look good and getting various departments to 'adjust' the ones that did not.

All in a day's work, he thought. The hologram shimmered and a sturdy, square-jawed woman replaced his glowing numbers. The intensity of his assistant's eyes was unsettling and the fact she was using the emergency channel was ominous.

"Another accident, Ms Silva? Drunks out the airshaft?" He swore under his breath.

"No, sir, but we have picked up a Data-Pod from the *Anam Cara*. It's a bit worse for wear, but our techs are loading the data packs as we speak."

"Captain Falco is streaming a direct feed to Admiral Chen of 10th Fleet? Why have I not been notified if a 'situation' has developed?" Lipinski was working through the possible scenarios as Silva jumped back in.

"Chief Engineer Tenzin will have the COMs fully connected and operational within the hour. Until then, you can wait for the Data-Pod to be uploaded or—"

"Silva, I will speak directly with Admiral Chen." Why in the hell did he not notify me! he thought, wrapping his fingers on his desktop. "I want information from the Data-Pod uploaded and floating above my desk ASAP. The last thing I want is to be stonewalled by the leader of the United Nations Navy with a personal agenda. We are cutting that god damn ribbon on Station Pluto in a week Ms Silva." He tapped his controls and Silva vanished mid-sentence.

The Data-Pod continued to gnaw at the edges of his sanity. Not even sipping an espresso crafted of artisan beans grown in the hydroponic sea on Mars could take his thoughts off the potential calamity encased in those encrypted bytes of information waiting to be released. His fingers continued to rap in waves on his desk's surface.

Assistant Silva's desperate face suddenly appeared on the holo-feed.

"What the hell is going on, Ms Silva?" Director Lipinski instinctively pushed back on his chair to gain separation from the floating, contorted face of his assistant.

"Data packets decrypted and uploaded, sir. You should have them now."

Without a word, Lipinski's hands went to his controls and a few seconds later the translucent displays built into his office wall came to life. Assistant Silva's face continued to hover in hologram mode above his desk. This time she turned to the screens to watch their joint feed of the data sent from the *Anam Cara*.

Director Lipinski sat frozen to his chair while the scenes played out before him.

"My God, Silva, this confrontation took place only a few days' travel from Station Pluto. I need Admiral Chen in my office at once."

20

Anam Cara
the Iron Mile

FOR THE FIRST time in what felt like days, Captain Falco and his crew were out of danger or at least the scanners were clean as their wounded ship pushed for Station Pluto. He gave Commander Shar'ran the bridge, tapped the hatch release and followed the narrow passageway that ran bow-to-stern down the backbone of the *Anam Cara*.

It was known as the 'Iron Mile.' The name came from a far-removed time when navies fought and died on oceans. Long before they left the deep blue for satellites, telescopes and starships. Falco was sure most of his young crew had little knowledge of the old Imperial System of measurements that gave way to the precision of metrics, but 'Iron Klick' never stuck.

Falco stopped, returned the salute of a plucky crewman in a big hurry. She turned, pushed her back to the bulkhead and he slid by sideways and continued his walk. He knew her name, age, skillset and that she had been raised by her grandfather in northern California since her third birthday. Crew information he spent hours studying after the death of Conlin and Martinez. All she probably knew of Falco was her captain was walking the Iron Mile again, and that was enough.

The *Anam Cara* was a sleek vessel with a small and efficient crew that was only now beginning to get to know one another. Hiber-sleep and rotating skeleton crews made long-turns survivable, but not social. Interaction was minimal between most crewmen and rarely consistent.

Falco passed the mess cube where two off-duty crewmen exchanged a kiss over rations. They had obviously taken advantage of their limited time together en route to Station Pluto. Crews were trained to keep anything other than platonic relationships out of the Navy. Falco knew from the stories of other officers, the reality of hard rules governing relationships on multi-year deepspace missions was simple; to enforce them would mean to tax an entire crew... over and over again.

A 'fifteen-year turn' was a long time. Falco ignored the regs from the beginning and allowed discrete relationships onboard. He followed the rule of reality when it came to mature adults. Who you sleep with in your down-time is your business as long as it is kept discrete, and doesn't compromise your duties, or the safety of crew or boat, was his official and only speech to the crew prior to pushing off from Station Luna.

Stopping in front of the grav-gym, Falco felt the crush of its claustrophobic proportions. 'The Closet,' a loving term for the workout box, stood to his left with a training suit plugged into resistance sensors waiting for the next body to torture in the name of fitness.

A small set of old world 'free weights' were strapped to the far bulkhead, a lonely heavy bag dangled in the corner next to the ropes enclosing a tiny ring barely big enough for two people to move around in without touching. Few of the crew used the ring, but Falco, Commander Shar'ran and Lieutenant Wallace used it religiously. He was also fairly certain Ensign Holts spent a good deal of time in the ring, but with whom, he was not sure.

Slowly over the course of the five-year turn, the rumor had spread that the three friends and officers had a pact. Disagreements would be dealt with in the grav-gym, behind closed doors, never in view of anyone else. Falco had caught Ensign Holts watching a round or two from the open hatch on the rare occasion all four officers were on the skeleton crew together but did his best to keep his time around the Ensign short. He had grown far too fond of the gifted officer. Her strength was intoxicating and she possessed traits that were eerily reminiscent of his dead wife, Luciana.

He wondered how many boats had officers on their bridge that occasionally wore a black eye, bruised cheek or swollen nose to accent their uniforms. The reality was not that the ring was used to settle disputes, but rather it was used to keep them sane. Hiber-sleep was the friend of the inexperienced crewman or officer, but the experienced crew and officers were on the losing end of the three to one ratio of skeleton crew to hiber-sleep. Senior crewmen spent three times longer being awake during the five-year transit.

Falco moved on then hesitated as he looked down the 'Iron Mile,' straightened his uniform and continued. He was overcome with dread that turned into a primal anger pulsing from his core. Without realizing he had again stopped, Falco stared at the hatch he now stood before.

The rail-gun compartment was magnetically sealed, but the carnage and sacrifice that had consumed the space beyond was tangible – iron and sweat, blood and tears. Martinez was bright, with a dry sense of humor that Falco was only beginning to truly appreciate. She also held the highest marks in hand-to-hand combat of the crew, including its officers. Crewman Conlin was quiet, introspective and easy to underestimate. He also was fearless and proved it to the end. If either gunner had been afraid, there were no signs of it. They remained at their post, strapped into the battle-buckets even as their sighting system showed the incoming projectiles locked onto their station.

Falco pulled a sleeve across his eyes, swallowed hard and continued toward his cabin. Many had wondered why the captain chose to have his quarters at the stern end of the boat, farthest away from the other officers. It was the smallest and one of the hottest compartments onboard, located directly above the engine buffer partition and furthest from the bridge. Falco had answered that in case of an attack or accident, having officers housed in opposite ends of the boat ensured that one officer might survive to lead the crew. A few meters higher and his cabin would have been part of the damage.

The actual reason he placed his cabin furthest from his captain's chair was simple, he was forced to pass the crew bunk compartments, the mess cube, grav-gym and every crewman along the way. Captains decide who lives and who dies. The *Anam Cara* was refitted to the new Navy's standards, which made her compartmentalized and efficient, trading physical interactions with shifts and COM-Boxes, but Falco thought, walking the 'Iron Mile' connected him to them all.

It gave him the much-needed opportunity to interact with those he swore to protect and though many did not know it, they were his family, each and every last one of them. Falco reached his hatch. There was no 'Captain's Quarters' in blocky black letters as was the standard. There was no eagle, wings spread, and clutching a bundle of arrows, there was not even the gold star followed by four gold stripes. The hatch simply read, "Francis," lovingly and permanently etched in looping cursive, deep into the steel surface by one giant of a man, and his closest friend, Commander Azim Shar'ran.

The hatch slid open and Captain Falco took a single step inside and collapsed on his cot. Thoughts of Ensign Holts moved through his mind as they often did when things got quiet. The more time he spent with her, the more he wanted other things from Sierra Holts the woman and less from Ensign Holts the officer. Could be the longing built on five years of wanting, but not having? Intrigued with the force of nature encased in the ebony skinned beauty that was Holts… Falco knew it was more than a physical need or want. He knew the bond was that of old souls connecting. Where age and culture were meaningless.

Ensign Holts never spoke of her family to him, but Falco knew the stories; knew she had lost loved ones as they all had. No one spoke of the billions that once rotted in streets, homes and clogged the public transit systems after the attack – a massive scale of death that overwhelmed the world with mountains of decaying bodies that now floated as ghosts through the minds of the living. Visions of the macabre scenes would be silently carried by generations to come.

"We all lost," he whispered, and it was why no one spoke of it. It had all the characteristics of those that had survived genocides of the past. United Nations Navy required every member to take a three-month course that covered every major atrocity acted on humanity, by humanity. And, he thought, it could easily have been a twelve-month course with material left over.

A gentle rap sounded on his hatch, mercifully breaking his train of thought.

"Yes?"

"Ensign Holts, Captain. Commander Shar'ran has found something 'of interest' on the last visual feed from the Battle-Net and would like you to look at it, sir."

Falco was exhausted and his cot felt like a cloud. He rubbed his eyes in the heels of his hands, the thick bristle of a full day's beard growth scratching in his ears. "I'll be on the bridge in five. Thank you, Holts."

From the other side of the hatch, light footsteps sounded down the corridor. Falco slowly stood, stretched his back and looked out the small porthole above his bed.

The faint glow from the main engine below made it harder to see the pinpricks of distant stars surrounding a vast wall of black. The dark energy or whatever the hell it actually was, loomed behind them, but Falco knew it was more than that. It was not just a threat – he was afraid of it and what else may lurk behind its cloak. What else would be unleashed from its depths?

---

the Darkness
Aris the Chose One

SHE CLUNG to the edge of the Darkness. *I should have launched my Seekers.* Thousands of voices answered. She was connected to the open thought-stream.

Hate and pain flowed from the clans, none blamed the young Prox, but all were ready to fulfill their Oaths to the Creators, the Darkness and all the clans. The aggressors must be punished, their iron beast destroyed, their voices obliterated and scattered without hope of a warrior's afterlife.

The clans had arrived en masse. They floated near the Veil, cloaked in the Darkness, invisible to the fleeing enemy in the Void. The young Prox switched to a private thought-stream that allowed her isolation from the clans. She allowed the final moments before her mentor pushed her out of the void and into the Darkness to float through her sensors. Again and again the loop continued before her. She had froze, giving in to the fear of battle as her elder died alone. The mentor gave her life to save the apprentice. Shame diminished the warrior's rage slowly seeping into her organs and systems. I curled into a protective orb, hardened my exterior plates, immobile from fear, and I allowed the voices to leave, I did nothing.

The loop stopped and the vision of her cowardice dissolved

into a warm flood that brought the young Prox peace, washed away the fear and shame that threatened to consumer her.

Aris. The young Prox again found herself unable to move. This time in wonder as the name again filled her private thought-stream, *Aris.* It was the rank of the Prox clan's leader. How was it possible? The voice echoed from something else or from somewhere else in her private thought-stream. *Or has my fear taken my own voice. I am lost.*

Again she tried to use her fins, tried to unlock and unroll from her defensive position. She needed to pass through the Veil, banished from the Darkness to starve, unprotected and alone in the Void and die far from the Realm of Warriors.

Aris. The name entered her systems and faded.

I am a young warrior who was defeated by fear. I do not understand. I do not deserve to ascend to the Realm of Warriors. She finished her thought not knowing whether it spoke from her fear or whether her own systems were failing and she was dying.

Aris, ascend and take your place.

An agonizing jolt flashed through the young Prox's bound carapace and power surged through every system. Her plates softened and unlocked. She uncurled and extended to her full mass, painfully moving her fins to keep her carapace from drifting out of the Darkness and into the Void.

Creators? she asked, but knew it could only be them. *I am sorry, great ones. I did not fulfill my Oath and I do not deserve this honor.* Cycles passed without a response, then a sense of balance returned to the young Prox and with it came a new awareness – power with full control over the warrior's rage. To harness that which was without control and always led the clans to a hero's death, to the Realm of Warriors... to gain control of the warrior's rage was to harness the power and ascend to the position of Aris, leader of the Prox.

You are now Aris. Your duty is to your clan and our worlds. You will guard our territories, remain concealed in the Darkness and if the enemy returns... destroy them.

Wait! Aris's balance was gone and the uncontrolled warrior's rage rushed into her, filling the vacuum. *We have the clans waiting at the edge of the Darkness. The enemy is beyond our sensors, but they are close and there may be more! We must destroy them!*

A jolt of energy sliced through her thought-stream. *Contain your emotions, young Aris, the time for battle may still come. Safeguard our borders, control your rage and let us see if this is truly an enemy of the Darkness. Control your rage and do not fail us.* Data pushed into systems. The Creators uploaded their plan.

A thought-stream opened to all the clans. *The new Aris has ascended.*

Thousands of clans answered as one. A soft, rhythmic chant moved through the open thought-stream.

I am Aris. Her voice rode atop the chant, growing louder with each word. *I am the chosen leader of the clans and we will defend our territories against all invaders and if we are worthy, will fulfill our Oath and reach the Realm of Warriors!*

The clans' chant turned to roaring war cries and Aris switched to her private thought-stream.

I will wait for now, but the fleeing enemy voices will be silenced. I will fulfill my Oath and travel to the Realm of Warriors after I obliterate the iron beast and everything that cowers within its ancient carapace.

Space Station Pluto
Admiral Chen of 10th Fleet

AND THIS IS THE 'MAN' running the newly completed Station Pluto, Admiral Chen pondered while the skittish Director Lipinski sat uncomfortably behind his vast desk. Chen hated meetings; even worse, he loathed wasting time with bureaucrats who regardless of the agreement reached, would scurry behind closed doors to do as they wished.

The fact the Americans now held immense influence within United Nations to put this man in charge of the greatest engineering feat in human history was a sign of their resurgent power. A power to be respected and hopefully suppressed when needed or at least channeled to the will of China and her people.

The admiral broke his silence with the director. "There were signs." Chen pulled his data-pads from their leather case and ran a powerful thumb and finger down the sides of his chin. He knew Director Lipinski was a man of patience, especially when confronted by those more powerful than himself. Chen read the final paragraph of the report uploaded from the *Anam Cara's* Data-Pod and set the paper-thin screen on Lipinski's desk.

"A battle group prepares to leave as we speak. They will gather more information on these weapons and who could have placed them this far in our solar system without us knowing. Weapons that look to be archaic, spears and cannonballs, but if that were truly the case, Director Lipinski, we would not have a wounded Cyclone Class scout ship limping home. Would we?"

The director looked confused. "Sending out a battle group?" Lipinski's questioning look was well-practiced, Chen thought, but nothing happens on Station Pluto without a man like that knowing. A battle group preparing to shove off would be the talk of the station.

Admiral Chen focused on the tightening muscles around Lipinski's mouth, the slight furrowing of his brow. Brewing beneath the calm bureaucrat's face, was a heated panic. Chen's rank as Admiral of the People's 10th Fleet was probably all that kept the director from losing his composure and running toward the nearest shuttle for escape... if five years in hiber-sleep rotations back to Earth could be considered an escape.

Lipinski cleared his throat. "Captain Jack Falco is almost in range of Station Pluto and the COM-Sat is up and going through the final testing. We soon will be able to contact the *Anam Cara* and get the details first hand. The captain is sure to have crucial information regarding the confrontation."

"As you well know, Director, Captain Falco has kept an open feed to 10th Fleet until their COM-Sat was damaged. I chose to keep the information in the hands of 10th Fleet. The last thing we need out here is a station wide panic."

A glow moved across Admiral Chen's data pad sitting on the director's desktop. He glanced at the update and simply pushed the screen towards Lipinski who was already staring at the glowing text.

The director looked up at Admiral Chen. "Five Viper-Class

vessels just pushed off their gravity moorings and are preparing to take a hard burn toward the coordinates provided by the *Anam Cara*." He slid the screen back across his desk, a bit too hard and Chen caught it before it found his lap. "You have already decided then, so further discussion is pointless. Good luck, Admiral." Lipinski's eyes shone bright.

A cunning smirk barely held at bay, Chen thought as he studied the director's face. Chen knew Lipinski had gotten exactly what he wanted. The man played the role of coward with only a few awkward glances and half-finished sentences. The clearing of the throat, he thought, was brilliant and yet I have also gotten exactly what I want. To possibly test our newest weaponry.

Chen launched himself out of his seat, whipped around to face the hatch and gently pushed the release. The door sliced open and with perfect oak-like posture the admiral marched out. "Admiral Chen?"

Chen stopped and just stood there, his back to Lipinski, silently waiting. The hatch's sensor patiently postponed its closure while a soft beeping sound warned the object to move out of its path.

The director finally continued. "You said there were signs. What did you mean?"

Chen did a hard turn and faced the director.

"Signs like the COM-Sat being scrapped off the station without damaging the plating it was connected to. Not once, but twice." The admiral fell silent, thinking of how much information he could release to this mouse of a man. "Three months ago, the supply frigate *Liberté* retracted its solar sails too late, sending it well beyond Station Pluto and was destroyed by a 'meteor shower' that suddenly appeared on our scanners."

"Meteor showers frequently blast out of the Oort Cloud and Kuiper Belt. That is a common—"

"Yes they are," Admiral Chen said without letting him finish.

"But how do you explain a meteor shower suddenly appearing without warning? Directly in the path of a wayward starship? Meteors with purpose? If they were meteors at all." Chen was growing weary but continued. "That far out, meteors were an assumed theory, not proven." Chen took a step towards the director's desk to quell the annoying beeping of the hatch that quickly slid shut centimeters behind him.

"The United States has its nano-tech industry and its batteries, but the People's Republic of China has the greatest military that earth has ever known." Chen softened his statement. "At least we have the greatest peace-keeping force the world has ever known.

"Yes, Admiral, a carrot and a stick is necessary with our enemies or competitors, which is all well and good, but what does the *United Nations Navy* have to do with the area beyond Station Pluto?"

Chen smiled at the emphasis. "With our advanced military technology came advancements in satellite imagery and the creation of telescopes that make the ancient Hubble seem like a child's magnifying glass in comparison."

"So you picked up images of these anomalies or signs?"

"It's a little more technical than that, Director Lipinski," Chen said, unabashed condescension dripping off every over-enunciated syllable. "Americans called the black field an unexplained variant on dark matter. You were right as our technology found no comparisons, even similarities between the black field and dark matter."

"And this is how you surmised of the potential that the Euro-Arab League or Russian Federation has leapfrogged us and have been placing weaponry out here?" Lipinski eased the sarcastic tone.

Admiral Chen felt the chess match had gone on too long. "Director Lipinski, we found nothing. Do you understand what that means?" He continued before the bureaucrat could open his mouth. "No sign of gravitational pull, no energy, even particles do not exist in the dark field."

"That is impossible, Admiral." Lipinski was at a loss.

"And now you understand, Director. It is impossible unless something is making it possible. Did you think the People's 10th Fleet were only here to celebrate the ribbon cutting ceremony of Station Pluto? The dark matter, dark energy, the dark field, whatever the hell you want to call it… is too perfect out here. Do you understand what I am saying, Director?"

Lipinski leaned across his desk, "You are eluding to the notion that the massive black field, that lays just beyond our solar system… was manufactured?"

Chen placed both thick hands on the edges of the desk and looked hard at Director Lipinski. "I am saying that the black field does not follow the gravitational laws as we know them." He stood up straight. "Your position gives you clearance for this conversation, Director, and I expect you to keep it to yourself or I will happily house you in the station's brig."

Admiral Chen turned, punched the release, brushed by the sliding hatch and was gone.

2 2

En route to Space Station Pluto
Anam Cara

"CAPTAIN ON THE BRIDGE!" Commander Shar'ran boomed and went back to the video stream on the Battle-Net.

"As you were." Falco was annoyed by the protocol and knew his commander thoroughly enjoyed following it. Enjoyed it a little too much.

Falco moved to Shar'ran's station and looked to Ensign Holts who held his gaze until he looked down to the monitor.

"Let's see this video, Commander."

Shar'ran started the video. Falco watched the feed of the black field, studying any potential changes in its whole, trying not to focus on any individual detail.

"Here it comes," Commander Shar'ran was already pointing to the glow as the video froze on the final frame, "fireflies en masse."

Falco reached under the workspace and flipped down an

additional seat. He sat hard, eyes focused on the dark mass and the slight glow that seemed to pulsate even though he knew the video was now static. "Holts, you have seen this footage. Best guess?"

Holts pushed off her control panel, stood up and quickly brushed past Falco's chair and stood focused on the Battle-Net monitor next to him. The three officers remained silent.

"It reminds me of lightning on Earth. Dark, thick cloud cover, the initial thunder and then the black, billowing mass glows, or, fireflies as Commander Shar'ran suggested. It resembles the ball they can form in flight as each is attracted to the other until they literally form a floating, glowing sphere. The field seems to emit a subtle light and stop. Like a light behind a curtain, there is no flash of energy, just the return of black like the flipping of a light switch."

Ensign Holts fell silent, working through what she was or maybe was not seeing, then added, "This is a steady building glow that I estimate continues beyond the length of our feed."

"Fireflies and lightning?" Falco once again felt ice begin to work its way into his veins, "coming from a massive field mimicking dark energy? Let me know, Ensign, when you have more." The image frozen before him was nothing short of wrong. He stood up and made his way to the captain's chair.

"Captain we are approaching Station Pluto," Lieutenant Wallace stated, "10th Fleet battle group is now within range."

About time, Falco thought.

The Battle-Net screen lit up in green signifying the approach of friendly forces. Commander Shar'ran turned toward Falco, "Captain, Chinese Viper Class battle group approaching at MACH 1 and slowing."

"Having a functional COM-Sat or Emergency Beacon would be convenient right about now or even a Data-Pod, for the love of god," Falco mumbled.

"Commander 'open the can,' blast shields down." Falco

listened to the clicking plates crawling into their storage compartment and leaving the windows on the bridge clear.

He turned back to the bow. "Lieutenant Wallace, now we find out if your Morse code is up to snuff. We need an actual two-way conversation this time. Use the lantern out the window." Wallace shut down engine one and fired the bow thrusters to slow the *Anam Cara*'s forward momentum and slid a small steel door open on his right and pulled out the lantern, wiped the lens. A cord was now hanging out of the small compartment. Wallace reached down, grabbed the cord and the tiny data-pad attached to it.

"Dusty, data-pad looks good and its half charged and ready to go, Captain."

The pilot was hastily pulling up a Morse code chart as the *Anam Cara* came to a full stop. Falco again felt the urge to look over his shoulder, something following them or tracking their boat. He was sure of it or at least some primal part of him detected a predator in the wind.

The newest sensor technology would give his boat a glimpse of what moved around them, but the reality was that sensors were unreliable. Once in deep space, the interference was intense. The most accurate findings were those that went against the randomness of objects in space that were not under the influence of a gravitational pull.

Items that were 'too perfect' or things that traveled in formations, for example. Those were the clues that the scanners would pick up. Then it was up to humans to make the call. The sensors, scanners and video feeds main use were to keep the pilot from running into various objects or getting hit by something.

"Captain I have a theory regarding the growing glow in the black field, but I would like to run it through the Battle-Net first to compare it to previous data." Ensign Holts had already sent an access request to Shar'ran.

"Allow her access, Commander." Falco turned toward Holts. "Do it, Ensign, and make it quick."

"Sir, Captain Yue Fei of the People's Liberation Navy is requesting to speak with our 'cleaning officer.'" A standing Lieutenant Wallace smiled wide and turned towards Falco. "Captain, I think he wants to speak with you. They look to be about as proficient at Morse code as I am."

Falco and his crew could not help but stare out the windows on the bridge of the *Anam Cara*. The Chinese boats were aptly named; the Viper class was more than just a patrol craft. Predators built as first wave attack and pursuit boats. Under these circumstances they were a welcome sight. Their matte black hulls were crafted of the newest poly-carbons. As far as Falco could surmise, they were missile boats, no need for the cumbersome, heavy and aging rail guns.

"Glad these boats are on our side. Let's get this over with, Lieutenant." Falco began typing a message on his data pad, which he would soon send to Lieutenant Wallace, who would in turn attempt to accurately flash it to the waiting vessels. He paused in mid-sentence, hands hanging over the pad, and looked at Wallace fastening the suction cup of the business end of his little lantern to the poly-glass in the pilot's nest.

"One, if by land, and two, if by sea…" Captain Falco stated, "and three, if by space."

Wallace looked around the bridge, as Shar'ran and Holts chuckled. "Is that the message, sir?"

"No, Lieutenant, it's Longfellow." Falco shook his head and went back to his version of typing.

HOLTS WATCHED her captain poke one letter at a time on his data pad, the ridiculousness and reality of the situation firmly in mind. The man was complicated. He was a captain on duty, iron fisted at times and raw, but off duty he often kept to himself when not sparring in the grav-gym with Commander Shar'ran and Lieutenant Wallace. Holts let her thoughts linger to visions better left to her personal quarters.

Holts finished inputting her instructions to the Battle-Net. 'Three, if by space...' the *Anam Cara* was Paul Revere warning the colonies of the coming invasion, and who or what behind the field was the British in this metaphor. She was beginning to hedge her bets on it being a 'what.'

Holts waited as the Battle-Net worked through the data and fought the urge to look over her shoulder. Something is coming, she thought, and we are all alone.

10th Fleet Battle group
Captain Yue Fei of the *Kwan Yin*

CAPTAIN YUE FEI of 10th Fleet sat perfectly still while scanning his data pad. His long, black braided hair woven into a thick single rope lay heavy on the back of his neck. The personnel file on 'Captain' Falco was as brief as his experience as a captain. But the chronicle of Marine Falco's exploits before his marriage and the birth of his daughter was a warrior's life. Fei slid the data-pad into its compartment, folded his arms and leaned back in his captain's chair.

Captain Fei had lost little due to the Korean Terror Militia's historic slaughter. He had no family, few friends, he had nothing of value to be lost. Even his own life was little more than a cog in the People's Navy—

"We have Captain Falco and the *Anam Cara* in visual range, sir."

Captain Yue Fei's arms unfolded and rested on his lap. He

held up a single finger towards his COMs officer. "A moment. First, holo-feed, my station."

"Yes, Captain."

A smaller class patrol vessel appeared over his lap. Spots of smooth, hardened repair-epoxy pocked her belly and steel was gouged from her stern. Fei reached up, placed a hand on each side of the floating ship and rotated it, examined the main engine damage, then moved the image to his right. He followed the lines of Captain Falco's vessel, the *Anam Cara*. Noting the classic design using steel plating with welds to prove it. Magnificent, he thought and his gaze moved to the 'windows' surrounding the bridge... real windows.

He had heard the Americans had a small number of Cyclone class patrol boats with poly-glass ports still in use within the United Nations Navy, but he never thought he would see one in action so far from Earth. China's Viper class vessels used 'Virtual Surround Vision' or VSV. The poly-epoxy layers that comprised the hull were imbedded with thousands of small cameras on the exterior shell. Each camera fed into the Battle-Net system.

From any station onboard, crewman could pull up a virtual view from thousands of different perspectives that covered the entire vessel, bow to stern. It looked like you had just cut a piece out of the hull and applied an invisible force-field. The skin of the boat became your eyes. Most crewmen using the VSV felt vertigo the first few times the hull vanished and outer space rushed in.

"Sir, we have Captain Falco ready to send. The *Anam Cara* is using an old strobe-lantern, so we will be using Morse code. I am proficient," the COMs officer stated.

Fei turned. "Good. Let us begin."

2 4

the *Kwan Yin* and the *Anam Cara*
Fei and Falco

"Sɪʀ, Captain Fei of the *Kwan Yin* is ready."

Falco raised an eyebrow to Lieutenant Wallace who stood in the pilot's nest, a thin cable hanging from the suctioned lantern and ending in the small data-pad lost in his thick hands. "Lieutenant." Falco took a moment to scan the etiquette document on his data pad for using the 'lantern.' "Well, let's begin."

"Yes, Captain."

Falco caught the uneasy agreement in his lieutenant's face as the officer prepared to input text into the data-pad.

"One ping, Wallace," was Falco's first message.

Wallace sent a single flash. Captain Fei was the senior officer and Falco had sent the honorary flash signaling the other captain to begin.

Quick dots and long flashes pushed through space. One of the most advanced starships in the UNN fleet used a four-hundred-year-old code to communicate with one of its most antiquated vessels with its laser beacon. Lieutenant Wallace translated then sent the message to Falco.

Falco read the first message.

'I am Captain Fei of the *Kwan Yin*. I have orders from Admiral Chen to search out and destroy, if necessary, the hostiles that have attacked your vessel and threaten the People's 10th Fleet and Station Pluto. I have captured and uploaded all data sent by your Battle-Net. Is there anything else you can tell me regarding these hostiles?'

Falco already didn't like the direction this was going. *'The People's 10th Fleet...'* The United Nations Navy was often less than united and each of its countries rarely referred to their boats under the UNN flag unless they needed aid. "Ensign Holts, I need your analysis on the 'anomaly' caught on the video feed."

She was sifting data and typing in new information to the Battle-Net. "Captain, I need a few more minutes to—"

"You have two minutes, Ensign."

Holts straightened in her chair as the captain began keying in a response to Captain Fei.

'It is an honor to meet you, Captain Fei. I am Captain Jack Falco of the *Anam Cara*. We are thankful to have a battle group of the People's 10th Fleet to aid us. Hostiles or a defensive weapons system? They may not have been the aggressors. My instincts and the encounter lead me to believe we possibly encroached on a defensive system protecting a territory or boundary. The proof lies off your port side. The *Anam Cara* was tactically wounded, yet allowed to leave without being destroyed.' Falco sent the message.

Lieutenant Wallace began to translate the text to Morse code, then turned and gave his captain a look that Falco immediately took for 'Jesus, could you make the next one a bit shorter?' Falco kept his poker face in place and his pilot turned and resumed. He caught the tail end of an animated conversation between Ensign Holts and Commander Shar'ran.

"Captain, I am sending my analysis to your station."

Holts had one hell of a concerned look on her face. Falco pulled up her analysis. His eyes intensified as they moved across the data, his poker face gone. He drew a deep breath.

Falco looked up and found the ensign watching his reactions. "A few defense systems or a fleet in hiding? That is a broad spectrum, Ensign." Falco thought back to his training and the immense focus the UNN Academy put on the great and ancient general, Sun Tzu. "In making tactical dispositions, the highest pitch you can attain is to conceal them."

"Sun Tzu has much to say in the matter of hiding a large force," Holts offered. "We encountered or were allowed to see a few of their weapons, but what did they hold back? What lay hidden inside the black field?"

"And what is controlling them this far from any detectable vessel, station or even satellite? If these 'weapons' are run through advanced artificial intelligence," Falco leaned back, "it is far beyond the UN's current capabilities. Or anyone else we know of."

"Yes, Captain and what if it is not AI controlling them? What if the weapons are actually 'crewed' by someone or some*thing*?" Holts emphasized the last word.

"Either way," Commander Shar'ran stated, "these sentient or crewed weapons did not destroy us when they could have. We turned and headed for Station Pluto... and they let us. Still, we know nothing of what remains hidden behind the field. We are blind."

The flashes from outside the bridge portside windows ceased. Captain Fei's next message was translated and sent to Falco.

'I agree with your assessment. However, Admiral Chen has ordered me to the quadrants of your last encounter near the edge of the 'black field.' Based on our current information, our battle group should provide us with a sufficient tactical advantage, if necessary. Director Lipinski of Station Pluto has asked me to pass along your docking information, which is Beta-Four. A crew is standing by to make your needed repairs and the station COM-Sat is up and functional, though it does you little good in your current state. I wish you and your crew peace and prosperity.'

Falco had been sporadically tapping his data-pad while reading Captain Fei's response. "Lieutenant Wallace, translate and send Holts's analysis over as fast as possible."

Falco felt an instant liking of this Captain Fei, but with a Viper class vessel named after the Chinese Goddess of Mercy and Compassion, he was not surprised. Fei had a quiet confidence about him, even through their current archaic means of communication. Based on Fei's personnel file, it was a confidence born from a philosophy of ambassadorship first, the heavy stick last – if there was absolutely no other option.

Lieutenant Wallace passed on the final message from the captain of the *Kwan Yin*. Falco read it in silence, knowing that his colleague's orders were taking his battle group to face a few hidden weapons or something far more dangerous.

The final image from the video feed was all Falco could see. A swarm of fireflies... lightning... In any case, Admiral Chen had seen all of the latest data and his orders remained.

"Fire her up, Lieutenant, best speed to Station Pluto, docking area Beta-Four." Falco pushed off the worn leather of the captain's chair, his thick, calloused hands scraping across the smooth grain. He joined Commander Shar'ran and Ensign Holts as the three officers gazed out the port windows to see five black predators slide through a desolate chunk of space, towards a destination known only as the black field.

Holts was first to state what they were all thinking. "Why would we be able to see this 'lightning storm' of vessels behind the field when previously, every sensor linked to the Battle-Net gave us nothing. Not even a false signal or errant blip until the weapons lying in wait outside it came online or passed through it into open space?"

Falco turned toward his ensign, always looking a bit to intently into her eyes. "A strong force reveals only what it wants its adversary to see, Ensign," answered Falco.

Shar'ran slid to the side of Holts, jaw clenched then softened as his stare met that of his captain's. "What is it, Commander?"

Seeing his warrior-friend locked in a mask of dread literally knocked him off balance. Falco realized Commander Shar'ran was looking through him.

"Commander?" Falco grounded his stance. "Commander Shar'ran, if you have something to add, now would be the time."

Shar'ran's eyes briefly closed as he exhaled.

"When I was a much younger man, the Israelis grew tired of their hopeless aerial assault and met us in the sands of Yemen. We used our blowing and shifting dunes as camouflage. Charging then slashing and tearing at our enemy out of its protective cloak, only to return and wait for the next opportunity, disappearing in a sea of gritty-chaos."

Falco patiently waited as his commander sifted through the many histories of his life, finding the pieces of his past that echoed, fought and reflected the pieces of his present.

Each man was at ease with these quiet spaces, Falco even found comfort in them. He noticed Ensign Holts had turned and was now facing the men. The quiet strength of this woman had unknown reserves and he felt pride that she would not stand in the shadow of anyone.

Shar'ran's eyes flashed to the present and the power of the movement seemed to ripple through each muscle and tendon, flexing and relaxing. Falco noted it seemed like a warrior's reflex, readying for a fight.

"These are their sands," Commander Shar'ran stated. "This

black field is their sandstorm and if needed, I believe 'they' will use it to destroy us."

Falco's newly found sense of calm evaporated. "Then let us hope, Commander, the need does not arise."

"Station Pluto dead ahead, sir." The relief in Lieutenant Wallace's voice spread through the bridge. "Should be docked in an hour."

A heavenly lighted Frisbee, Falco thought. Ah, but Pluto... She is magnificent. Thank the Gods she is still close. He felt her power flowing into the *Anam Cara*, as Pluto was again his focus, his muse and his anchor. Yet a day's burn from this beautiful planet was an invisible force: powerful and potentially deadly.

"Once she's out of our sight, 248 years till her return," Falco whispered to the *Anam Cara* as much as anyone. "Take a good look."

25

Captain Falco
Station Pluto – Beacon of Humanity

"Twenty minutes to docking, sir."

Captain Falco nodded towards Lieutenant Wallace and continued studying the file on Station Pluto. It was more an attempt to take his attention off the current thoughts battering his mind, knowing he needed distance from the encounter that nearly ended the lives of his crew.

Gently fixed on a two-degree tilt, he read, sure it was for no other reason than it looked more impressive that way. But how do you know it's on a two-degree tilt in space? Falco pondered. Regardless of the station's marketing, he had to agree that the near completed Station Pluto was a stunning technological and architectural achievement. It exuded the purity of humanity's absolute arrogance regarding their perceived importance in their known universe.

Falco turned and looked out the starboard window. At this distance he could see the steady, subtle glow of the Infinity Wall.

It produced a beacon that someday soon would welcome incoming visitors, dignitaries and the ultra-wealthy of planet Earth. The station was packed with contractors, military personnel and those few who could afford the small fortune it took to purchase fare for a trip to the new edge of humanity.

Falco continued reading, swiping through pages of data, blueprints and maps he had looked at over the previous five years. Blue-collar, working class mixing with soldiers, marines and silver-spooners, it was the common thread that created community on Earth. Now this same mixture was creating communities in three space stations spanning an ocean of stars.

Falco paused, reread the statistic and spun around to face Commander Shar'ran and Ensign Holts. "Did you know that when completed, Station Pluto will eventually be home to over ten thousand men and women hailing from over one hundred nations?"

Holts nodded. "That is why they are about to finish this floating city in just under seven and a half years." She looked to Shar'ran. "An incredible feat for such a skeleton crew."

Commander Shar'ran nodded, feigned interest for a few more seconds and returned to the Battle-Net screen.

Holts smiled. "One hundred nations will be the impressive part. Everyone working, eating and playing nice together, achieving as normal an existence as one could expect five years' travel time from Earth."

"And that is why the United Nations is the most popular organization on Earth. We get along so well." Falco left the sarcasm hanging in the air as Station Pluto came into full view.

Falco closed the file, stood and gazed out the window, following its gentle rotation, a bright beacon of humanity floating close to the elliptical path of a scorned and former planet. Shiny, new and filled with life, he thought, filled with hope and soon to be occupied by ten thousand souls who have no idea what or whom is out here with them.

the Darkness
the Chosen One

ARIS'S newfound power was intoxicating. Harnessing the warrior's rage was changing her, a forced evolution towards something beyond Prox. It was exhilarating and terrifying as her control over one gave life to the other. If I can control the warrior's rage, but not where it takes me, then what have I gained?

With a single thought to the clans, Aris could now bring a storm of death and destruction that had not be seen for billions of cycles. I am Aris the Chosen One, leader of the clans, guardian of the territories and of the Darkness herself. Even the Creators depend upon my wrath for their protection.

She felt a stab of anger enter her systems at the thought of the Creators and her Oath to protect them. An Oath she and all that guarded the Territories were forced to take. Aris wondered if the Oath was a means to unite the clans or was simply another mechanism used by the Creators to control them. It was a sign of her evolution... she now questioned the Creators.

A slight burning sensation and her private thought-stream closed. Aris opened a direct thought-stream to the eldest of the Warruqs and as was tradition, commended him on his ascent to the rank of LOR, leader of the Warruqs and second-in-command to Aris herself.

The previous LOR had died in the Void as her mentor had; as a warrior fulfilling his Oath to the Creators. She wondered if he had made the journey to the Realm of Warriors or was that also a means of control implemented by the Creators? If you died within the body of the Darkness, your carapace and systems would slowly fade, until all of what you had been traveled to the Realm of Warriors. Her mentor had taught Aris that dying in the

Void was different. Your carapace would float lost and alone, but your 'essence' would find a way to the Realm of Warriors... eventually.

A Warruq entered from the Void, sent Aris a message then disappeared through the Veil to guard the boundary.

Aris opened a thought-stream to all the clans. *The enemy has returned and is moving toward the Darkness. We must be ready to defend our territories and the Creators.* The thought-stream filled with the roar of the clans. Aris switched back to her private thought-stream.

Warruq clans outnumbered the Prox clans ten to one and their roar of support, or was it their backing of the newest LOR, overwhelmed the thought-stream. I will need to keep LOR close, Aris thought as she switched back to the clans.

We will use the Darkness to hide our numbers and from her mass, we will defend our clans and our worlds if the enemy voices do not return to wherever they were spawned.

The clans roared again and Aris returned to her private thought-stream, going over the plans now being uploaded into her systems by the Creators. Plans to defend not attack. The upload finished.

The steel beast is gone, she thought. These voices are different; the carapace in which they travel is strange and quiet. She sent the plan to the Prox and then to LOR to transfer among his minions'. LOR would lead the Warruqs and Aris the Prox.

If needed, she could call upon the Krell, legendary beasts from the deepest, oldest parts of the Darkness. A clan that in the current cycle was only rumor, as their kind had not been seen since the first defense, billions of cycles ago and long before the Prox came into existence.

Aris pushed through the mass of the Darkness towards the Veil, the tips of her fins breaking through and entering the Void, the four Seekers shifting in their muscle-bound sacks on her back, sensing the change. You will burn bright young ones. You will silence the voices and find your way to the Realm of Warriors.

Moving away from the Veil, Aris floated in the Darkness, her internal systems surging with the power of the clans. Their sheer numbers were potent. Wave after wave of Warruqs floated at each flank. Perfectly still, fueled and ready for full burn. Rows of fodder, Aris thought. Warruqs were good for dying and Prox for leading.

It was time to issue the final order. While Aris completed her upload to the clans, hundreds of Warruqs combined their thought-stream into a single feed for battle and pairs of Prox, mentor and student, joined their systems as one.

Everything fell into shadow within the swirling camouflage of the Darkness as each warrior shut down its heat-core to save energy and fuel for the battle to come.

There they waited behind the Veil, hundreds of warriors of the Darkness, waiting to fulfill their Oath to the Creators. Waiting to silence the encroaching enemy voices and defend their territories. Knowing that the invaders were blind to their numbers and to the worlds that lay behind them. Even the clans would be sightless within the Darkness without her permission, but the Great Mother was on their side, the Darkness would protect them for now.

And that was all that mattered.

26

Captain Falco
Station Pluto – Safe Harbor

"PREPARE FOR DOCKING." Lieutenant Wallace leaned back into the pilot's seat, his harness tightening around his shoulders as he placed both hands behind his head and allowed Station Pluto's docking system to bring them into the moorings.

Falco felt a wave of relief as the *Anam Cara* came to a complete stop in the Beta-Four docking zone. He shut off the main COM, pushed the release on his harness and turned around to find an already standing and hollow-eyed Ensign Holts holding a tiny sealed container in the palm of her hand, yet bracing it with her other hand. Her biceps flexed, straining with the weight of it.

"Find the stations lab and drop off..." what the hell would you call this, he thought, "the remains, Ensign." Falco found himself staring at the floor. "Let's get a second opinion from the best tech-lab around."

"Yes, Captain." Ensign Holts turned and headed toward the

main hatch. The remains of the round or weapon pried from the battle-bucket seats had to be cleaned of human remains and sealed in a hazard container.

"Ensign Holts?"

She stopped mid-stride and looked back at Falco. "Captain?"

Falco pointed at the vessel in her hands. "Did these smaller weapons show a similar make-up to the larger ones that destroyed the Data-Pods?"

"Yes."

He tilted his head. "And yet, you can lift a small haz-container filled with particles of a neutron star?"

"The Battle-Net can only give us its best equivalent, sir and yes, according to its analysis, at this very moment I am able to lift particles of a neutron star. All on my own." Holts's eyes were glossy, soft and tired. "I'll send the station techs to collect the bigger pieces."

"We have much to learn about these weapons. Thank you, Ensign. Carry on."

"Sir."

Falco watched her walk away carrying a minuscule piece of something that had rendered two of his crew into a jelly-like pulp. A container that, based on their best analysis, should weigh as much as the *Anam Cara*.

The spinning sound of the massive steel threads of Station Pluto's new high-tech grav-locks echoed through the bridge and ended with a crunch as they griped onto the *Anam Cara*'s hull.

"Jesus fucking Christ," Falco swore. "Take it easy."

He found Lieutenant Wallace fighting to stand up after he shut down all systems and readied the boat for the disembarking process.

The Scotsman punched his harness release and practically launched out of his pilot's chair, the release mechanism shot open in response to the ensnared beast prying itself free.

"By God she's taken enough from those bastards out there!"

He pushed up the sleeves of his uniform showing muscled arms covered in Celtic tattoos and pointed towards the bay door in the direction of the dark field. "And to have these idiots smash her in a poorly set grav-lock! She stood between us and death!" Wallace crashed through the bridge heading towards the hatch that Station Pluto's umbilical was now connecting to.

Falco shot Commander Shar'ran a look. "You better get to him before they are able to unlock our hatch."

The commander nodded in agreement.

Falco had seen this before. His Scottish brother shared the warrior's spirit and protecting his own was at its core. The *Anam Cara* was as much 'their own' as anyone and though Wallace shared the warrior's creed, he did not have the warrior's patience.

Shar'ran was up and moving. He looked like a foot trying to fit into a shoe three sizes too small as he ducked and weaved his way off the bridge and towards the hatch.

"You're paying the brig fee and any medical bills for the sorry bastard who's at the controls!" Falco yelled after the man and began to work his way toward the hatch.

A bellowing lieutenant echoed throughout the passageway. Falco turned the corner and stopped, a few meters in front of him a commotion played out at the main hatch.

Another clang, followed by the immense suction-cup-stick of the station's umbilical.

"Oh shit!" Commander Shar'ran yelled from the front of the waiting crew, he was losing his grip on Lieutenant Wallace. The main hatch slid open, light from Station Pluto filling the void.

"Who was it?" Lieutenant Wallace yelled toward the maintenance crew as he staggered through the station's umbilical with a large grinning Yemeni commander clinging to his back.

Falco emerged seconds later and Shar'ran seemed to have a spirited Wallace under control or at least enough for Falco to notice the sparks already flying outside the bank of windows that looked over the *Anam Cara*.

Lieutenant Wallace also took notice as he stopped berating the deck officer and like a good horse, brought his rider, Commander Shar'ran over to view the work in progress.

Torches spat and puffs of glowing sparks surrounded the *Anam Cara*. Station Pluto's repair crews were practically fighting over the opportunity to work on the iron vessel. Repair personnel were dragging over totes stamped in large black letters with 'welding equipment (steelwork)'.

Falco learned that poly-panels and epoxy technologies had made the art and use of brute force to melt and grow iron antiquated, and virtually useless. But the United Nations recognized there was a good chance they would be repairing and servicing the old US Fleet, so welding gear was stowed early in Station Pluto's beginnings.

"Absolutely incredible," Falco stated, scrutinizing the crews already buzzing around the *Anam Cara*. "They said she would be good as new in eight hours, judging by the speed in which they started on her, I believe them. Holy shit!" Falco pointed toward a long, steel cylinder comprised of seven barrels. "Well, look at the new toy she gets. Always thought a Gatling gun under the bow was missing." Falco put his hands on his hips. "They even have a 'shaper.'"

A highly skilled crewman ground out the poly-foam sealing the holes through the *Anam Cara*'s hull. A stack of steel mending plates and welding gear sat next to her.

Still hanging on Lieutenant Wallace's back, Shar'ran patted the top of his head. "You good? Can I get off now?"

Wallace growled, but a smile finally appeared. "She's going to be good as new, even better."

Commander Shar'ran extended his legs to the floor and let go.

"See, they're taking great care of our lady." Falco met the

glassy eyes of his lieutenant and then looked to his commander. "I need a few drinks."

27

Captain Fei
Viper Battle Group

"Keep the formation tight, Commanders." Captain Fei observed his screen from the captain's chair while his five Viper class patrol boats made slight adjustments, then moved as one group. His ship, the *Kwan Yin*, moved in the center and was flanked by four vessels two forward of its position a thousand meters and two astern two thousand meters, spread wider like an upside down 'W'. Fei rolled powerful fingers over his datapad. His screen split into six different boxes. The Battle-Net displayed real-time views from all four sides plus top and bottom of the Battle group.

At 20,000 clicks out from the black field, Captain Fei pictured his mighty Viper class vessels as ants staring up from the base of the Great Wall of his homeland. The immensity of this dark barrier was dizzying. The bridge was silent; every breath hushed and protected.

Fei focused on his monitor. Four of the six boxes were filled with brave, silent crews waiting for hell to open its doors or simply to float and wait for orders to return to Station Pluto. The formation was simple. With five patrol boats, similar armament and capabilities, the only formation that made sense was the 'Fighting Wing.'

It gave each vessel the ability to afford protection to the others while providing maximum cover for the command vessel at its center.

Great when you were expecting an attack, Fei thought, but we have no idea if or when it will come. However, we do have solid data on where it will come from, or at least where it came from. The endless wall in front of us.

"Lieutenant, prepare to test full VSV." Captain Fei gripped his armrests while the rest of his personnel on the bridge grabbed something to ground them to their stations. He was getting comfortable with the new technologies and Virtual Surround Vision (VSV) was at the top on his list. He had yet to find a military reason to use the system, he simply loved the view.

Captain Fei was reminded of the first time he and his crew took the *Kwan Yin* on her maiden voyage to Luna Station. While in orbit the technician's on board had asked the captain if they could give a presentation to the crew regarding the new technology behind the VSV. Twenty minutes of tech speak went by and Captain Fei and most of the officers on the bridge were stoically and rigidly fighting off boredom.

Seeing the 'thunder' of their technological brilliance being stolen by the sleep-inducing effect of their own impressive jargon, the lead technician offered a 'live example.' Fei, looking and feeling relieved, practically begged them to stop torturing them and show the crew something they could understand.

"We are ready, Captain Fei, with your permission we will begin the 'live example.'"

Fei, keeping a professional and military posture, looked at the lead. "Begin," he stated.

"Holy shit," flew in all directions in a dozen or so dialects as the deck beneath their feet, dissolved to show the moon's surface. Fei had never seen a Chinese crew completely lose their discipline in an instant. Not bad for a dog and pony technology—

"Captain?" The COMs officer patiently waited and tried again. "Captain?"

Fei returned to the present, finding himself clinging to his armrests using his best death grip and expecting to see the moon beneath his feet.

"Captain, VSV is ready to engage."

Fei nodded. "Keep the deck, Lieutenant, I want to see my boots on a solid surface. Engage VSV." The bulkheads fluttered and then dissolved. All that remained to the human eye was the floor. It never disappointed, Fei thought.

He picked up the ember glow of the two Viper engines ahead. Fei swiveled his command chair to view the vessels at the rear tips of the 'Fighting Wing' through the VSV stern cameras.

Squinting Fei grunted, "Lieutenant, magnify five point five, stern. There they are, perfect formation." He exhaled hard and fast. "VSV off." Seconds passed, a slight visual ripple and the hull was back, providing the false sense of security that humans needed during space travel.

"COMs, open channel."

The COMs officer connected with the other boats. "Channel is live, sir."

Fei gave the young man a short, curt nod. "Commanders, this is Captain Fei. Our orders are to continue our current heading until we reach the coordinates of the first attack near the face of the black field." The words felt ridiculous coming out of his mouth. An attack out here in the middle of nothing, the edge of humanity's solar system did not make sense. Even if someone did manage to beat the UN to this area all they would need to do is file their claim or build their own space station.

There was not a lack of opportunity once you were past the Mars Station.

"ETA, one hour. You have seen the data from the encounter. Test and retest your systems, Defender missiles in the forward launchers with Interceptors in the mid and aft tubes. Keep sharp, someone beat us out here and went to a lot of trouble to keep us away. We will connect our Battle-Nets to the *Kwan Yin* in ten minutes." Captain Fei motioned to his COMs officer to close the channel.

He left the six views of his battle group up and running. The Battle-Net sensors showed him everything they were designed to find. The split screen video feeds gave him little comfort, but they provided a backdrop of the black field, the endless face of a massive fortress with no doors, or windows. Or, was it all a doorway?

He turned to another display and ran the video feed uploaded from Captain Falco. The 'lightning storm' could be anything or nothing, but the glow of combustion-based engines close to the face made a lot of sense. Falco's last message had stated that very theory. The glow the result of moving vessels or weapons systems close to the face of the black field.

Admiral Chen had questioned the accuracy and validity of the data along with Captain Falco's theories. Something so vast, he could not see the top, nor find the bottom. It seemed to be infinite, though the scanners and computer modeling provided an estimate. It was as much dark matter as anything else scientists could label. The reality of knowing so little about their environment was unsettling at best.

Fei rolled over his controls and replaced the image of a 'lightning storm' with a hologram of the dark wall that lay before them. He adjusted it, wanting to look around or through the image, trying to see what it was hiding. He read Ensign Holts's report and ended with the notes added by Captain Falco. All this time, he thought, we looked at this dark field and assumed it was remnants of the violent birth of the universe. Now we find someone or something hiding in it. How in Lord Buddha's name could it be used to hide weapons? If we do not possess the technology to see into it… who on earth figured out a means to see out of it?

What if we are wrong? From meetings with Admiral Chen, Fei knew the Russian Federation and the Euro-Arab League had denied placing weaponry beyond Pluto. The United Nations did not believe them and assumed one of the two dominant powers outside of themselves were responsible. Certain words that Captain Falco used during their conversation kept coming back to Fei.

'Them, they…' For centuries we have dismissed every satellite launched from Earth that disappeared or changed course as it approached this section of our solar system, ignored our probes that kept skirting around the borders of this dark field. It must be some type of interference coming from the field was the common theory. But, maybe it was sending us a message to stay away, to keep our distance and yet, here we are. A battle group crawling towards something that does not want to be found, or bothered, five Viper class patrol boats, a pin to prick a lion. He expanded the hologram and stared at the five pricks of light representing his Battle group sitting in front of a vast nothingness. A full day's burn from Station Pluto.

Captain Fei considered the countless governments that comprised the United Nations and unanimously voted to fund and resurrect Project ORT-133. The cost of Station Pluto would be a fraction of what the UN estimated they could make in ore revenue. They wanted something out here and would use Station Pluto and all its resources to get it. We are but pawns, he thought, but are we guardians of this immense black or fodder for what lurks behind it?

Fei tapped a key and the hologram disappeared. He turned back to the split screen. Their formation remained tight. The dark field overwhelmed the center video feeds. It seemed to be expanding, eating away whatever open space was left between it and the vessels that pushed closer. Fei observed the forward and roof top video feeds fill with the shifting black mass until the entire view from the split screens formed a dull, oily cloud. The two lead Vipers' engines became eyes staring back at Fei from an endless shadow.

---

the Darkness border
LOR and Aris

Now is our time! We must crush the voices and destroy the weak vessels they bring to our frontier!

The newest LOR was already giving in to the warrior's rage. Aris the Chosen One listened to the leader of the Warruq over a private thought-stream. She towered over LOR who showed his respect for her position by hovering well below her optical sensors.

Aris brushed a massive fin across the crown of his unbreakable skull. Remarkable, she thought, making sure to separate her personal observations and keep them safe on her private stream.

Your time will come, mighty LOR. You and your clans will fulfill your Oath and take the journey through battle and sacrifice to the Warrior's Realm. The Creators will be pleased. I have a message to send. Break the Veil and connect me to the clans in the Void.

Aris felt the fury pulsating from her second, through waves of energy rippling one after the other from within his carapace. LOR remained silent and was close to losing control of his systems to the warrior's rage. Aris was intrigued by the possible outcome as most Warruq lacked the discipline and power to suppress the rage once it began.

To her surprise, LOR continued to radiate heat, but the waves cooled, slowed and subsided. LOR turned towards the void and pushed his carapace through so half of him was in the Darkness and half in the Void. Aris used LOR as a conduit to connect her ocular systems to the waiting clans.

Aris watched the five invading vessels closing in on their territory. The clans of Warruq remained stationary, using only a miniscule amount of power to run their tracking systems. She switched to a private thought-stream. These invaders are spawned from a different beast, she contemplated. The voices were also using another form of communication. The vessels were silent; they made no attempt to reach out to her. Predators, she was sure.

They move as one. Aris continued to track their movement. There, she picked up the slightest discrepancy between the two on the outside of the group. She began sifting through the data being streamed to her from the Warruq positioned in the void.

These warriors would serve their purpose, but only if Aris had the opportunity to release them. The five crafts continued their advance. Soon, she thought, we will offer the gift of oblivion to all those who would attack the Darkness.

Aris opened a thought-stream to the Creators and uploaded her findings. She added an extra data packet at the end, one that contained her new battle plan based on her latest observations. There was a long pause in the thought-stream, one that she had expected. Prox, even Aris, the leader of the clans, did not make plans and even if they did, they did not send them to the Creators.

Orders erupted, filling the stream and jolting her systems. Bright pain overwhelmed her and a powerful current ravaged through her carapace. The Creators closed the thought-stream and left her reeling in the Darkness, curled into a defensive ball. The shifting, swirling shades of gray and black were gone, the thick warmth of the Darkness was no more, sound waves that filled her thought-streams vanished, there was nothing, the Creators had shut her down…

Another jolt and Aris uncoiled her clenched form, each plate of her carapace unlocking, releasing itself from its instinctual position of defense. The warrior's rage flooded through her and she fought to control it. Slowly, Aris regained control and her systems started coming back online. She detected a new data packet uploaded into her system and opened it.

Plan accepted. You may begin.

2 8

Captain Fei
Viper Battle Group

"Harnesses on. Slow to a full stop," Captain Fei ordered. He sat rigid in the *Kwan Yin*'s captain's seat, clicking into his harness with only the slightest of movements. The bridge wasted space with modern designed workstations and molded poly-panels swooped into the deck. Yes, it looks stunning, he thought, but the facade did something else, it took a lethal vessel and softened the edges, making it feel like home.

Fei's smooth skin took years off his true age, but his eyes replaced them. They had seen the horrors of war, the massive losses inflicted by the Korean Terror Militia. And they watched his wife desperately trying to tear the LINK from her neck as Fei raced across their small backyard, screaming for her to release the ultimate global connection.

The memory always begins when the order came buzzing through Fei's head. Fei instinctively pulled his LINK out while yelling to his wife as she planted vegetables. His empty teacup hanging loosely from his fingers as the LINK sent a massive electric pulse through her body, stopping her heart instantly. She lay crumpled like an old pair of pants on the grass. Did I wait an extra second as I pulled mine out before I warned her? Did that second cost her her life? He pressed his eyes tightly shut until the tears that threatened to come, fled back into the hellish part of his memory that he desperately tried to bury.

Thrusters lit up the bow of each vessel as they burned and fought to eliminate any forward momentum that each had worked hard to earn. And there they sat, five matte black Viper class patrol boats, waiting.

"Captain." His lieutenant held a finger to his screen, working down the report. "Battle group is armed and ready. I have forwarded the report to your display."

Fei gave the man a quick nod and glanced at the split-screen one last time. He spun to his other monitor and pulled up the report.

Confidence grew while he skimmed the munitions stock. We could conquer a small fleet. The Viper class boats were missile heavy. The Chinese knew that if the peace treaty between the Euro-Arab League and Russian Federation ended and there were battles in space, they would be fought far from Earth's warring regions.

Starships could rain down ordnance from above making bullets or even the cumbersome rail guns of little value, though Captain Falco's crewman had made one hell of a shot with the old cannon they had on board. Pride swelled and Fei permitted the feeling to almost turn to admiration.

"COMs."

The young ensign looked up. "Yes, Captain," he asked, not making eye contact.

"Ensign? Don't you want to know with whom I want to speak? Or is this open-COM link to Lord Buddha himself?"

The youthful communications officer sheepishly looked at the glowing red link. "Sorry, Captain." Fei held back a grin and noticed that his other officers were respectfully doing the same.

"Admiral Chen. An open-COM is fine." Fei waited for the light to turn green, knowing that his officers would follow the conversation.

"Admiral Chen."

Captain Fei looked hard to his right and let out a sharp exhale. "Admiral, we are in position and holding. What are my orders, sir?" There was a long and drawn out silence that was the admiral's usual manner of letting Captain Fei know that he was 'just a captain.'

Chen broke the silence. "Continue holding present position and continue full data feed to Station Pluto. According to your Battle group's sensors there are no signs of the enemy."

Fei looked at his lieutenant, his eyes stating the obvious. Did the admiral think they would be out here mulling about, waiting for us?

"Admiral, the black field shows no signatures of any kind. Nothing like the 'lightning storm' image sent from the *Anam Cara*. If they are out here, they are probably hiding within it."

Another long pause. "Captain Yue Fei, remain in your current position and continue your surveillance feed." The COM turned red.

"Yes, Admiral Chen, I know, I am a captain in the People's Navy," Fei whispered to the dead COM-link.

---

the Veil
LOR and Aris

WHY DO THEY WAIT, *Aris the Chosen One? They are afraid of the Darkness and the warriors that protect it*, LOR pushed through their thought-stream. *I want them closer. They must breach our border so you can release the Warruq upon them!*

If only she had left LOR in the open where he belongs, Aris thought to herself, out in the void, unprotected and at the mercy of the invaders cutting weapons. The Darkness is for the Prox. Warruqs are mindless warriors that fight carapace to carapace without thought or care.

Aris the Chosen One rolled her head downward to look at her second-in-command. Enormous sinewy muscles covered with thick layers of cartilage and bony plates, flexed and adjusted as her optical sensors neared those of the much smaller LOR.

She looked deep into the Warruq. Twisted and formed by the Creators for one purpose, to die in defense of the Territories. *Like us, they possibly wait for their directives. They wait for their own Creators to send them a plan to attack the Darkness or turn and flee, a coward's fate that would last an eternity.* Aris added that thought for LOR.

LOR filled their shared thought-stream with a warrior's pride.

Yes, LOR, if they run, we remain in the Darkness, but if they enter our territorial boundary that lays just outside of her protection... where she meets and fades into the Void, one becoming the other—

It begins, LOR pushed.

Aris gave LOR his orders and with great satisfaction the warrior swiftly moved towards his position, using his eight appendages for propulsion.

So that is what death looks like, Aris thought. She opened her direct stream to the Creators and sent her request. All the invaders need now is courage to continue their forward progress, enter the territories and see what lurks behind the cloak they have come to fear.

But there was no need for courage, the invaders were close enough and soon she would have vengeance for her mentor.

Soon they would know of Aris the Chosen One, whether they entered the territories or not, Aris would make sure they would be punished.

Admiral Chen of the People's 10th Fleet
Station Pluto – Command Center

THE DISTANCE from the patrol group limited station Pluto's connection to the vessels. The ability to share the distance between them through networking their sensory instruments, gave them a simple window into what was happening on each end.

The five Viper class vessels were denoted by five embers floating in front of a horizontal sea of black at Station Pluto. Their formation was meaningless in the vastness of their position. Admiral Chen knew the Fighting Wing formation was sound. It gave the commanding vessel excellent protection and offered the other boats clear lines of fire, but still kept them close enough to protect one other.

But what good are five vessels in a sea of potential chaos? he thought as he continued to scour the data with his officers, using every piece of Station Pluto's scanning and sensory equipment. At the end of the day, the *Anam Cara* data banks and video feeds were the only evidence he had of the encounter, except for the remains scraped off and out of Captain Falco's ancient boat.

A newer vessel could have linked their sensors, given us something more than data feeds he pondered, but the *Anam Cara* was old and outdated. "Iron, windows, and rail-guns," he spat.

"Admiral?" the senior officer enquired.

"Nothing." Admiral Chen felt tired, old and impatient.

He looked to his officers sitting around a large table in Station Pluto's Command Center known as the Pluto Room. It was little more than a lecture hall with all the latest gadgets and equipment. "Get me a feed to Director Lipinski," he ordered.

"Feed is live, Admiral." The young lieutenant watched the hologram centered in the table quickly turn from a blurred, sparkling mass to a clear image of an oblivious Director Lipinski siting behind his desk.

Admiral Chen glanced at his young tech officer, and cleared his throat.

"Sorry, Admiral, there is a slight delay with the system."

Two beeps sounded and a flustered Lipinski sat upright, perfect posture, his hands continuing their delicate play over his data-pad. The director visibly gathered himself, slowly turned and looked at the officers, the large pores of his face clearly visible in their hologram feed. Chen moved back from the aberration and waved a hand.

His tech officer quickly reduced the magnification of the hologram feed.

Now comfortable, Admiral Chen moved toward the floating image. "Director Lipinski, when is that report on the remains going to be complete?"

"Give me a moment, Admiral, while I contact the lab."

Chen and his officers exchanged uncomfortable glances. The director tapped a key and another to mute his audio feed. Moments later after a few dramatic nods and chin strokes, Lipinski turned the audio on, exhaled sharply.

"Within the hour, Admiral Chen, we will have a full report on the 'materials' gathered from the *Anam Cara*."

Chen nodded. "You have one hour, Director."

The command center had all the latest technologies in visual, audio and data equipment, not to mention the ability to feed or upload anything from Station Pluto or even surrounding vessels to its centralized mainframe.

"I want a hologram display of all data feeds from Captain Fei's Battle group and remove this monitor." Chen felt uneasy. The five embers faded on the small screen and it descended into the table and disappeared.

The tech officer continued to work the data-pad that slid out from under the side table in the center of the room. A bright light flashed from the center of the top, casting its glare on the vaulted ceiling above. A few moments later, the officer smiled and hit a key with the look of a job well done. The area between Station Pluto and the black field hung over the entire table.

Admiral Chen rose from his executive chair and walked around the floating image, pausing and moving his head from side to side as if trying to find something. Finally, he stopped. "Where is my battle group? This is nothing but a hologram of open space and the black field? Where are my Vipers?"

The lieutenant's look of confidence eroded with the harsh tone exuded from his superior. He slid the data-pad out again from under the table and adjusted the hologram. The light streaming from the center of the table flickered and the holographic image filled the room. Half the room was open space and the other was filled by pitch black.

It looked like someone had pulled a black curtain down the middle of the command center. Chen and his officers moved to open space where they could see.

"Sir, I have maxed out the hologram display while still keeping the image to scale." The lieutenant continued working the data-pad, from the visible side of the room.

Chen walked from one end of the room to the other, dragging his hand across the smoky display. His officers watched in eerie silence as parts of the admiral's body evaporated behind the dark field.

"Where is my battle group? This hologram is showing us nothing!" Chen barked at his officer who was still frantically working the data-pad on a system he had little experience running.

"Sir, I am almost finished." Seconds later, he popped up out of his chair as the admiral was preparing to launch a new verbal assault. His quick movement immediately silenced Chen who was now curiously watching the man moving away from the other officers and followed the dark curtain cutting through the middle of the room.

"Here." The tech officer stopped and pointed at a spot of nothingness a few centimeters in front of the black field.

Chen's patience was at an end. He stormed towards his pointing officer and was a few paces away when the man held up his hand.

"Please, Admiral, just a moment. Lights OFF," he stated. A field of stars appeared over half the table while the Pluto Room lights faded. In front of where the lieutenant's finger was pointing were five pin pricks of red light, barely visible, seeming to come and go.

"Here, Admiral. The People's Navy, your Viper class battle group in the Fighting Wing formation."

The sheer vastness of the dark field was mind bending. Admiral Chen focused on his vessels' formation, still unsure if the five pinpricks of light were even real. The second he took his eyes off them, they were almost impossible to find again. "The feed from the battle group does not seem correct. The field's scale is different. I want Captain Falco and his officers here, now. Lights ON." Chen felt an ocean of panic sloshing in his bowels.

Something stirred deep in the admiral's core. He felt hunted.

A predator just knocked off the top of the food chain by something more fierce, cunning and ruthless. "Lieutenant. Upload the hologram from the *Anam Cara* during the attack. Captain Falco created a scale hologram of this field from approximately the same coordinates." Chen's voice was layered with intensity and dread.

"Overlay Falco's hologram against our current image, same scale and orientation." Admiral Chen's breath came fast and sharp.

"Admiral, I have the *Anam Cara* data uploaded. Image should project," the officer paused and tapped a final key, "now."

A second light burned from the center of the table and a new hologram spread across the Pluto Room, its shape blanketing the battle groups current hologram as it unrolled towards the ends of the room. Then it stopped, half a meter short of the current image.

The officers began to understand the implications and Admiral Chen snapped into action.

"The field is growing. Get Captain Fei on an open link. Where the hell is Captain Falco?" Control fought its way back into Chen's voice not a second too soon.

3 0

Viper Battle Group
Captain Fei

"Yes, Admiral. One moment, the commanders are checking in as we speak." Captain Fei looked towards his COMs officer who was already opening a channel to the other vessels. Fei waited for the other four commanders of his battle group to chime in on the open-COM.

After hearing the fourth 'all clear,' Captain Fei in the rear, center position stated, "All clear. Keep your sensors on full spread and report anything immediately. I will keep the Battle-Net linked. Fei out." Fei closed the line.

"All is clear, Admiral Chen. We have no signs of hostiles. However, we can confirm that the black field has moved towards our position."

Fei scanned the data and changed a single word.

"More accurately, Admiral, the mass has 'jumped' in our direction, narrowing the gap of open space to a few thousand meters." The captain added, "Admiral, our sensors gave no warning of the field's movement, but now show it is indeed closer to our formation."

Another pause from Chen.

"What are your orders, Admiral?" Fei stated, doing his best to temper his growing unease with his battle group's position.

"Hold your position and continue to scan for threats and monitor your distance from the field, Captain. Captain Falco and his officers are on their way to our command center." Admiral Chen swore under his breath, "What is the time lag between your visual feed in real time and the feed we are receiving here at Station Pluto?"

"Seconds, barely discernible, Admiral. We are currently twenty-three point five hours from Station Pluto at maximum burn, which leaves us on fumes into the hangar," Fei stated. This time Captain Fei did not wait for the pause, "I request the battle group falls back ten kilometers, Admiral."

"Denied. Hold your position and continue to monitor the situation." Admiral Chen was gone.

Fei sat stoically, thinking through his battle group's position, weighing the order he had just received, an order that for the first time in his distinguished career, he could not follow. He had been in worse situations during the Korean Empire conflict, surrounded in the Sea of Japan with missile damage that would have sunk most boats... and yet, he felt this was a thousand times worse.

He hammered a fist into his armrest. Every officer on the bridge of the *Kwan Yin* was now locked onto Captain Fei. He straitened his uniform, took a chest expanding breath and released it with slow precision.

"Commander, bow thrusters, low burn. Move the formation back ten klicks. Get us beyond the field's next potential advance."

His order was patched through the Battle-Link and the fighting wing formation began to push away from the dark field at a barely detectable pace.

"Battle group, open-COM." Fei felt the beginnings of adrenaline being pushed through his body.

"COM is open, sir," stated his lieutenant with added volume.

So the officers feel it too, he thought.

"Commanders, this is Captain Fei. We will continue our push away from the field and remain in the Fighting Wing formation." Fei scanned his armament inventory again.

"Our linked Battle-Net will adjust sensory settings on missile launchers according to the size and speed of any incoming hostiles." Fei could hear his commanders' breathing patterns change. "Precautionary measures. Prepare yourselves and your crews for potential, hostile contact. For the People's Republic." Fei closed the open-COM.

You're coming, Fei thought. Admiral Chen had been the first to see the advance or leap of the dark field. Its movement was precise, with purpose. The joined sensors of the battle group gave no warning of the advance, yet they showed the field closer after being alerted by the admiral. Latest generation sensors or not, we are blind to all that moves behind its wall.

"Captain!" The officer waited as the Battle-Net churned through incoming data, his screen filled with rolling text and numbers.

Fei sensed the heightened awareness as every crewman on five Viper class patrol boats waited for the massive wall that loomed in front of them, to erupt, spewing potential chaos at their vessels.

"Report." Fei heard his voice, yet it sounded foreign to his ears.

"Captain, the wall is folding! The area in front of us remains, but the rest is rushing forward." The officer continued to read his monitor.

"Hologram!" Fei wanted a visual, everything still looked unchanged on every camera view. "I need a scaled image now."

"Hologram up." The young officer's voice cracked. "Scale at .000015 percent."

The image floated over Captain Fei's station on the bridge. Fei spun and rose from his chair and faced the hologram. *And we sit at the gate*, he thought. The field was far greater than the sensors' range.

"It's gaining speed, Captain. The center of the dark field in front of us remains. The rest of the wall's movement is escalating."

"Battle stations..." the sailors' calm had taken over. *The beginning is drenched with fear and then it passes and the storm begins.* Fei knew this from experience. There was no reason to run, nowhere to go. The speed of the dark field's movement meant only one thing.

"Pilot, bow thruster burst, ten second intervals." They could not outrun from the speeding blackness, but at least they could try and place a bit of distance between them. *It left an exit; maybe it would like us to leave.*

"Fighting Wing formation is moving away from the mass, sir." The pilot fought to keep his words intact and the fear from his tone.

"Commander, lock Battle-Net control to the *Kwan Yin*. Pilot, five second bow bursts." Fei waited.

Not one turn of head or even a sideways glance. He waited to see if the COM would light up with panicked commanders from the other Vipers but the panel remained dark, they were ready. Fighters, each and every one of them; locking the Battle-Net link could only be done by a captain or admiral in charge of a fleet or battle group.

Once locked, all vessels were under the control of the command ship. The People's Navy had learned that battles were won and lost based on the courage to stay in position, when fear took hold and death was a certainty. It was also why the United

Nations Navy and the Peoples Navy were almost one and the same. Almost.

The hologram hung in the middle of the bridge, a thick, long rectangle of universal mass with a perfectly round, infinitesimal bite taken out of the edge. Sitting in the center of the crescent sat their Viper class battle group.

Five predatory, missile-laden boats alone and a day's burn from Station Pluto.

Darkness - expansion
Aris the Chosen One

ROTATING SLOWLY IN THE DARKNESS, Aris the Chosen One fully extended her fins in all directions. The Darkness was intoxicating as it flooded over her carapace, stirring arousal within her most protected organs that leached the fluid throughout her systems and brought the fire of the warrior's rage.

A voice pushed into her personal thought-stream. Coming and going, fading in and out. First it felt like the Creators... no Aris thought, knowing it was something else. 'It' was uploading data into her systems and probing her carapace with infinite appendages of energy searching for... and then the voice fell silent, the energy gone.

Aris was different, her sensory organs heightened and more powerful. Though still blind in the mass of the Darkness, shades of black, swirls and shadows appeared. The new upload contained information regarding the warrior's rage. It had a purpose. Fashioned to govern the weaker masses of the clans. Those who could not control or at least channel the rage became slaves to its fury-induced euphoria. The Warruq longed for the warrior's rage to return the moment the drip ceased and they returned to waiting to defend the Creators worlds. Lingering in a single spot in the void for millions to billions of cycles.

The Darkness was more than camouflage or 'a cowardice mist to hide in,' as the Warruq clans called it. The Darkness was a destroyer and a healer. It provided methane for their propulsion and respiration, and was the reason the clans needed to be near it or near one of its massive travelers that lurked deep within its mass. Aris knew she was a vast living organism, the Darkness forever evolving to protect and control those who swam within her form.

It was the Darkness who pushed into her systems and uploaded the meaning of the warrior's rage and its use by the Creators. Created to control all the Warruq clans and enhance the intellect of the Prox. But those few who could harness the rage were given title and power. They became Aris the Chosen One and LOR, until they too succumbed to its poison.

For the Prox the warrior's rage heightened their intellect, for the Warruq it brought bravery that bordered on insanity. For the mighty Krell... Aris was not sure as they hid near the Creators' planets, elusive to all but the Creators themselves. But the legend of the Krell were built on the nightmares of stories past when the worlds were few and many of the clans had not come into existence.

Aris the Chosen one, they are moving away from the Darkness. LOR had opened a thought-stream.

The invaders have joined as one. They choose to retreat and may even sense that we are here. She paused. *Their weakness is their lack of numbers, but our Creators have left them a path to peace and they have taken it.*

LOR's voice thundered over the thought-stream. *We cannot let them run! Revenge for our fallen is all that is left! They have become one, let my clans destroy the intruders so we may travel to the Realm of Warriors!* The warrior's rage was taking control of LOR.

Aris would soon lose control over her second-in-command.

LOR was giving in to the bloodlust coursing through his systems. A skirmish would keep LOR and the Warruq under control and was a small price to keep order. But to go against the Creators could mean Aris's end. She kept her thoughts safeguarded in her private thought-stream. An opportunity.

Let it begin, LOR. They are pushing flame and heat from their vessels. A weak attempt to attack the Darkness. The Territories must be protected. She pushed his orders and LOR swam through the shadows, heading towards the hidden clans floating near the Veil.

Aris offered a second proposal to the Creators. Expecting they would approve, the fear of being attacked... No, she realized, it is the fear of being replaced by the invaders that gave her all the influence she needed.

The upload was swift and direct. No pulsing current attacked her organs or sent pain shooting through her systems.

The Creators quickly responded, *Go forth and conquer.*

31

Station Pluto Command Center
Admiral Chen

"ADMIRAL, the black field has overtaken the battle group and surrounds them on three sides." The officer remained still with a permanent flinch hammered into his stance.

Chen looked to the man and remained silent, his eyes searching for an answer or a solution. Captain Falco and his officers had just arrived and were now seated around the command table. "Cut the hologram. Welcome, Captain Falco, your insight would be of value."

The Pluto Room returned to a soft glow, the hologram faded into nothingness and the lights in the center of the massive table went dark.

Falco stood. "Thank you, Admiral. Lieutenant, please bring up the *Anam Cara*'s original image, scaled to the table." He moved towards the center of the room.

Chen and his officers trailed behind Falco toward the newly

sized hologram showing the *Anam Cara*'s encounter. Falco's own officers sat against the wall.

Falco stopped, staring at the blackness floating above the large poly-slab that was crafted into a tabletop.

"Camouflage," Falco stated.

Chen's notorious impatience quickly rose to the surface. "Captain. My battle group is practically surrounded. I need your insight based on your encounter. I need it now!"

Commander Shar'ran looked to Lieutenant Wallace who was making eye contact with Falco while gently shaking his head from side to side. "Let it go, now is not the time," he whispered to his comrades more than his captain.

"Admiral," Falco stated curtly. "Our sensors, like yours, could not penetrate the black field. In fact, the only shred of movement or life that we managed to glean was the lightning storm across its face as we were leaving." Falco again locked onto the floating hologram.

"We know at least some of these 'weapons' came from the field. Our sensors only picked them up as they left the field. If it is camouflage, which it seems to be as it renders our sensors useless..." Falco's eyes fell from the hologram and found Admiral Chen's intense gaze.

Falco continued, "What would such a vast, almost infinite field be used to conceal?"

Chen swallowed hard. "We still do not have any evidence this field could have been designed or engineered by the Russian Federation or any other hostile nation. The sample you have from your damaged boat estimates material from a neutron star."

"How else could something of that mass exist if not from the power and wealth of an advanced civilization? We can't explain..." Falco trailed off. "As you stated, Admiral, there is no history or proof that humanity could produce this type of technology... and hide it from us out here." Falco's hands gestured toward the hologram.

Chen nodded at the captain. "The United Nations agrees, and every government on Earth now knows we have come in contact with something that seems to be of another's making." Admiral Chen felt a storm was coming and Captain Yue Fei was now in its path.

"Captain Falco, is there anything you can offer outside of what we have read or seen from your reports and feeds from the *Anam Cara?*"

"Only that they hit us hard, where it would hurt and then let us go." Falco turned from the holo-display toward Admiral Chen. "We need the full report from Station Pluto's lab on the remains. Until then—"

"Enough." Chen's hardened gaze fell on his commander. "Ready the remainder of 10th Fleet, we depart in two hours. Get Captain Fei on feed, now."

"Admiral," Falco's voice boomed, "there is nothing you can do for them now, they're twenty-four hours out, even at a dreadnought's speed. We have thousands of civilians on Station Pluto! We should prepare for the worst. Ready the civilians for a possible evacuation scenario and ready the station and the remainder of 10th Fleet for a possible hostile situation."

"Captain! Learn your place or you will see yourself a private in the brig before this day is finished. I never took you for a coward, Captain Falco." Chen kept a steady eye on the officer.

Falco moved towards the admiral and was quickly redirected by his officers. Falco muttered something to his commander who released his arms.

"You will soon be the ranking officer of Station Pluto, Captain." Chen stepped toward Falco. "Act like it and do your job."

"Yes, Admiral." Falco faced his officers. "Come with me and find Chief Tenzin. We are going to need him."

the Black Field
Captain Fei

AN EERIE QUIET hung over the open-COM connecting the battle-group as they continued a deliberate crawl towards open space left by the black field. Red lights lit up the screen, the Battle-Net was flooded with potential threats.

Captain Fei turned towards the Battle-Net post while Commander Zhu calmly stated the incoming warnings. A gray streak blazed through the center of his cropped black hair, and gave an added intensity to an already hardened face. "Battle group has lock on 144 targets, Captain. Marks breached the field and stopped." The steely commander raised an eyebrow.

He likes the odds, Fei thought, twenty-nine to one. "Hologram." Fei waited for the image to update to their current position. If ever there was a reason to leave this rat trap, this would be it, Fei thought.

"Captain, the objects are positioned precisely level with our vessels. Holding their positions." Commander Zhu squinted and read the data flowing from the Battle-Net.

"Either they are guarding the gate, have limited military experience, or..." Captain Fei paused as the third possibility rose to the surface, "or they have a commanding technological advantage and do not need to be above or below our position, as neither matters." Fei always spoke his thoughts aloud to the bridge and all that were on it. He had done so since his youthful beginnings, years ago, when boats mainly sailed the seas and oceans of Earth.

"Or," Commander Zhu added, "they have us vastly outnumbered and feel little threat from our five Viper class boats."

"Captain Fei." Admiral Chen's voice sounded over the open-COM.

"Sir." Fei waited.

"Fall back. Full burn. We will rendezvous at the sent coordinates." Chen was gone.

"Coordinates received, Captain."

"Plot them Lieutenant and increase burn. Let's take the exit in the least threatening way possible." Fei wanted to leave whoever or whatever had emerged from the field with a farewell wave instead of a missile barrage.

"Captain, sensor field is clear. Wait. Thirty-four marks." The unflappable Commander Zhu sounded flustered.

"Sir, field is clear again. Captain, Battle-Net tracking eighty-nine potential threats."

"Commander." Fei looked at the man, his gaze demanding calm.

"Sir, the marks are passing in and out of the field, changing their numbers with each pass." Zhu's breathing was softening with each word. "Field is clear again, sir."

"Lieutenant. Full stop. Swing the formation around. Full burn as soon as we are in position." Fei could feel it coming and hoped his battle group could make a dash for the door, if it was still open.

'Door' was nothing short of an analogy. The door represented the only physical area the sensors could get a read. The dark field was covering everything else but the ceiling and floor, both of which were bottomless, their height and depth far greater than the technological range of the battle-group.

"COMs," Fei looked towards his young officer. He mouthed 'open-COM' and then drew his hand in a slicing motion across his neck. The light on the panel turned orange and Admiral Chen could no longer listen to the crew, but Fei could hear incoming orders.

"Almost in position, Captain." Turning five boats locked into the Fighting Wing formation took time. If anything, Fei hoped, it shows that we are leaving. He exhaled sharply, assuming they know our bow from our stern. Not good, not good at all, he thought.

"610 targets locked!" Commander Zhu boomed across the bridge.

"Hold on. Engage main engines, Lieutenant." Fei's voice remained calm.

"Initiating full burn."

Five rocket engines engaged at one hundred and nine percent, generating a combined three hundred million horsepower.

"Incoming!" The commander shouted over the engines' rumble, trying to fight off the Gs while the grav-system caught up.

"Twenty-eight smaller targets have entered open space. In pursuit! Battle-Net signatures match those that hit the *Anam Cara*. 610 marks remain in holding position."

"Commander." Fei remained locked on the hologram feed in the center of the bridge, "Time to impact."

"Our current burn, incoming burn plus acceleration factor… two minutes, Captain, maybe less."

"Lieutenant," the pilot struggled to twist his head to the side. "Exit time?"

"Ninety seconds." The pilot was pushing forward in his harness, as if trying to pull the battle group out of harm's way while they burned towards the small opening in the field.

Fei looked around the bridge. His crew no longer fought the Gs, the *Kwan Yin*'s grav-system had neutralized the sudden force of the engines; all eyes remained on their stations. "Battle-group will be free of the field before the projectiles reach us." Fei paused to look at his captain's screen. One minute twenty-eight.

"Battle-Net has a hard lock on all twenty-eight marks in pursuit." Commander Zhu gripped both sides of his station's smooth surface. "Ready to fire, Captain."

Admiral Chen's voice sounded over the COM. "Captain Fei you are cleared to fire. Repeat, you are cleared to fire."

Fei nodded to his COMs officer. A second later and the orange COM light turned green.

"Yes, Admiral. We have weapons lock on incoming targets. Battle group will clear the field in sixty seconds and fire if necessary."

"The final decision is yours, Captain Fei. Do what is required. 10th Fleet is on its way." Admiral Chen was gone.

Fei exhaled slowly, his posture arrow straight. We better be sure they want us dead before we start something our grandchildren may have to finish, he thought. The consequences of his actions today could echo an eternity; he closed his eyes and prepared to give an order that could change humanity forever. If these targets are not of Earth's making, I am about to start the first interstellar battle with an unknown force. Once started, this action cannot be undone. For the love of Lord Buddha, please let us leave this place in peace.

the Void
LOR

LOR FLOATED in front of the Darkness, watching the tiny Seekers give chase to the fleeing vessels. Strange creatures living and feeding off the Prox, but fearless and deadly. He kept his thoughts his own, the warrior's rage contained for the moment. Aris the Chosen One promised vengeance for the slain Warruq warriors and the thought looped over and over in his systems.

LOR connected to the clans open thought-stream, feeling the hundreds that waited just beyond the Veil, the newest border with the Void. The Darkness had raced forward, expanding the territories again while surrounded the fleeing enemy on three of the six planes. If the Darkness ventured further into the Void, the Creators' Law said it was now part of the territories and must be defended. If only the Darkness would put an end to this game and wash over the enemy. LOR spoke to the Warruq clans. *My brothers, our time is near. The Seekers are pushing the intruders out of our newest territory, but they have not cleared the opening yet.*

Six hundred nine warriors, each representing a different clan, responded with a carapace-rattling roar. LOR made six hundred ten.

He closed the open thought-stream and a massive armored form emerged from the Darkness behind him.

Are the Warruqs prepared, LOR?

Heat radiated from the leader of the Clans. Aris the Chosen One no longer feared the Void. He knew the weak young Prox whose mentor was blown into a thousand pieces was gone as soon as she was able to control the warrior's rage and why she was named to lead them all. *We await your command, Aris the Chosen One.*

The cycle is close, LOR. Let the Seekers enjoy their hunt. They have instructions to chase, not engage, not yet.

Aris shared her optical connection to the Seekers with LOR. They were keeping their distance behind the five beasts that moved as one.

LOR sensed the warrior's rage building in each of the twenty-eight Seekers that were spawned by seven Prox. They were mothers to these young ones, LOR thought. If they survived, the Seekers would be sent to the Creators' planet. Many cycles would pass and some would return to the Darkness as Prox and others would never be seen or felt again among the clans.

LOR caught the flash of an Aris private thought while they still shared the connection with the Seekers... *'Incubators of foreign dregs that grow inside us; a forced attachment that becomes a symbiotic necessity, and now they burn towards their death, hoping to find a realm of peace we do not know truly exists. That I do not know truly exists...'* Aris's private thought-stream closed and LOR was left to wonder what she had meant. He watched her send the Seekers' final order and assumed she was finished when the twenty-eight children of the Prox burned bright and full and increased their speed toward the intruders. Oath fulfilled? LOR questioned and continued to process what Aris had said, private or not, she had allowed him access.

A thought-stream opened and Aris gave the order LOR had been waiting for, no, lusting for. *Unleash your heat bloom.*

And now it begins, LOR thought as Aris disappeared back into the Darkness. He replaced the looping thought of vengeance for the fallen warriors with a new task. Finding the Realm of Warriors, if it existed at all.

Blue flames lit the face of the Darkness. LOR and the rest of the Warruq warriors joined the Seekers' hunt.

33

Viper Battle Group
Captain Fei

"TWENTY-EIGHT HOSTILES INCREASING SPEED. Contact in twenty-two seconds! A second wave has launched from beyond the field, 610 marks incoming." Commander Zhu's voice was amplified, but fear and panic were absent.

"Engage Battle-Net. Damn it," Captain Fei barked. The battle group was only seconds from pushing through to open space.

Missiles flew from cradles buried deep in the protective hulls. The Battle-Net welcomed the attackers with deadly accuracy. Half of the incoming projectiles were shredded into scrap and organic pulp.

"Remaining fourteen marks are locked. Missiles away." The commander waited with the rest of the crew while the twenty-eight missiles honed in on the threat. Two missiles for each attacker, the Battle-Net was compensating for the unusual flight paths the objects were capable of.

"Captain Fei, we are nearing the opening."

Fei gritted his teeth, held his breath and watched the holo-feed. The hologram in the center of the bridge displayed the almost perfect fit of the Fighting Wing formation's fixed span compared to the exit they were pushing towards.

Black, smoky cliffs with no top or bottom hugged the formation's flanks. The portside and starboard vessels skimmed the black walls.

Missiles fired en masse the moment the Battle-Net's piercing proximity sensors flooded every Viper class vessel of the fleeing battle-group. Captain Fei's boat, the *Kwan Yin* was in the center of two meteor showers that erupted out of the black field and hurtled death and destruction from both sides. The hologram faded in and out due to the sheer volume of incoming projectiles. Dispersing exhaust trails from launching missiles created a hanging mist dotted with glowing engines burning to defend the boats. It looked like a massive firework with the battle-group at its center.

"Report!" Fei was fighting to keep his mind sharp and in control. The open-COM sounded like a deep-space version of a hailstorm. Clanks and thuds pounded all of the battle-group except for Captain Fei's vessel.

"Thrusters destroyed, main engines at ten percent, missile bays one through five destroyed. Two hundred twenty-two enemies destroyed, one hundred fifteen unaccounted for. Battle-Net had a hard lock, then they were gone."

"Which vessel is the damage report for and how the hell can one hundred fifteen hostiles be unaccounted for?" Fei knew the answer was coming.

"All of them, sir. All but ours, the *Kwan Yin* has lost her COM-Sat and nothing else." The commander paused as the only reliable communication left to the Fighting Wing formation, the Battle-Net ship-to-ship direct COM, buzzed to life. The defensive system locked the open-COM between the battle group, ensuring voice-to-voice communication. "COM with Station Pluto, 10th Fleet gone. Line of sight only, Captain."

Muffled, static-ridden shouting spat over the ship-to-ship in bursts. "Get a filter on that feed! Who is firing weapons?" Fei imagined each round punching through the interior layer of the hulls, hopefully stopping short of puncturing the hardened, outer poly-epoxy layers and setting off the repair system.

Before the officer could announce the filter was in place, the clarity of the scenario rippled through every crewman on the *Kwan Yin*. The direct COMs became a landslide of clear, panicked voices. Voices from four vessels, desperate, laced with fear, sounds of crewmen fighting for their lives in a guttural and primal death match.

Fei's crew sat in stunned silence. They had found the one hundred and fifteen hostiles that disappeared from their sensors. The enemy had pierced the hulls and were inside the vessels. The ships' repair systems had sealed them in.

"It sounds like a child's rattle," whispered the commander seconds before a scream filled the open-COM then fell silent with a sickening, wet thud. Compression rounds continued to boom and small arms fire popped in rapid bursts.

"Sidearms!" Captain Fei stood, reached under his command chair and punched the release. A compartment door fell open. Fei pulled out a short, thick-barreled pistol and attached it to his waist. The crew of the *Kwan Yin* followed his order, each opening their stations compartment, frantically strapping on sidearms.

"Captain Fei, two of our battle group are falling out of formation, main engines off line, repair systems destroyed, hull integrity below fifty percent, and falling." The commander read the damage report in a robotic tone while the Battle-Net screen flashed red, tracking each new incoming danger exiting the dark field while countering with missiles. The emerging enemy's numbers from their flanks were slowing, but the second wave slowly encroached, keeping its distance, waiting. The rattling sound of the COM grew faint. The screams of the battle group's dying crewmen faded and the small arms fire turned sporadic. The ship-to-ship filled with the panting breaths of those still alive at the helm or slowly dying behind it.

"Battle group this is Captain Fei. Full stop."

"But, sir!" Commander Zhu shouted. "We have not cleared the field! The second wave? We have a chance to get out!"

"Calm yourself, Commander, these are our brothers and sisters who fall behind, dying as warriors and heroes of the People." Fei found his entire bridge locked on his movement. The commander sucked in a deep breath and looked to the deck.

"You are the bravest officer I have ever known, Commander Zhu." Fei waited as his friend raised his head and met his eyes, the look of fear replaced with a warrior's pride.

Fei spoke to the open-COM. "Crewmen of the People's Navy." He knew commanders had perished. Lieutenants, ensigns or even a seaman could be at the helm of the four battered Vipers. "We live together, we fight together and if needed, we die together. No vessel will be left behind. The *Kwan Yin* remains intact and will move into a cover and point position over the battle group.

"Captain, the field is moving!" The commander fell silent, the dark field rushed to fill the exit and pulled closer in all directions. "Second enemy wave is gone, our Battle-Net sensor range is only a few klicks in all directions—"

The hologram in the center of the bridge displayed an endless, impenetrable black-fog circling the battered vessels. The Battle-Net warning sounded again, 610 red dots emerged from the field, encircling the battle-group and stopped, floating in front, waiting.

"We are completely surrounded." The commander squared his shoulders. "Your orders, sir?"

Fei eyed the crew on the bridge then stared at the green

light of the open ship-to-ship COM. It represented the remaining living crewmen of his battle group and the light looked dull and faded. Rasping breaths muted by distance and injury pulsed over the COM. Battered crewman of the battle-group, huddled next to a functioning COM waiting for an order.

Captain Fei leaned in toward the COMs at his captain's chair. "We fight to the end and the People's Republic will tell of our valor and fearless action in the face of insurmountable odds, a story that will be told for thousands of years. A story that will inspire and rekindle the passions of the greatest nation earth has ever known." A predatory grin ended Fei's speech. "Lock on all targets."

"Battle-Net has a hard-lock on six hundred ten stationary marks. Battle-group ordnance inventory post launch will be two percent, sir." The commander nodded toward Fei.

Captain Yue Fei came to his feet. "All vessels, load functional Data-Pods with full situational upload." He glanced at the continuous feed of the latest data on his personal screen. Twenty-one functional Pods will do, he thought.

"Random flight paths to the following targets: five to 10th Fleet rendezvous coordinates, five to Station Pluto and the eleven long-range Pods with solar sails, to Earth." It worked for Captain Falco, Fei considered. If just one Data-Pod got through, there may be something for Admiral Chen to use in the coming battles. The question was whether the Data-Pods would blast blindly through the dark field that now surrounded them and out the other side. Or, he thought, they would simply lose themselves in the field. Fei bet most or all would be destroyed by the enemy upon entry.

The Battle-Net warnings sounded again and Commander Zhu spun towards Captain Fei. "Six hundred ten marks increasing heat signatures, sir. Enemy is stationary, but power sources are growing."

"Launch the Data-Pods," Fei ordered over the ship-to-ship COM.

Twenty-one round spheres streaked out of the battle-group in two waves, adjusted their course and plowed into the dark field.

"All Data-Pods have entered the field and are off our sensors. Missiles ready for launch." Commander Zhu's hand hovered over the launch pad.

"Patience, Commander. If we fire too soon they will retreat into their black camouflage and we waste our only hope of collateral damage. Let them come."

In front of the broken ships of the battle-group still holding a ragged formation, the black field flashed. Data-Pods were dying, Fei thought, exploding within its depths. Destroyed by unseen predators that slashed and hammered the Pods into scrap.

The Battle-Net lit the bridge. Commander Zhu boomed, "Incoming!" Half of the circling enemy streamed toward them.

"Two thousand meter launch cycle!" We will bring you close and slaughter you like sheep. Fei relished the image.

Damaged but functioning stabilizing thrusters fired on all sides of the formation, the sheer number of missiles streaming from the hulls of the five boats pushed the vessels. Within seconds the battle group destroyed all attackers within the two thousand meter killing field.

"Three hundred seventy-two hostiles heading straight for us, Captain."

The final assault, Fei exhaled, "Are they slowing down, Commander?"

"No, sir, they have increased speed by ten percent."

"Good. They feel the pain of losing their own. Fire remaining missiles on my command."

Captain Fei rested a steady hand on the butt of his side arm. "May the winds of hell carry our vengeance to your doorstep in this life and the next," he whispered. "Fire!"

the Void
LOR – Realm of Warriors

MAY *your path be bathed in the blood of your enemies, your end a new beginning.* LOR added his farewell to the Warruq thought-stream; his optical sensors filled with disintegrating carapaces and frozen entrails of his Warruq fighters. He had long given in to the warrior's rage and the exhilarating passion it induced for his self-destruction.

A rope of frozen organs clanked off his skull plate as he neared the worthy adversary. His orders were to leave the center vessel alone. Aris had spoken of its power, the only true voice among these new soft skinned beasts. He was sure the Creators wanted it for themselves, a trophy of a conquered force.

A piece of Warruq armor-plated carapace hammered into his midsection and spun into the Void. Pain pulsated through LOR's systems. *I am close to fulfilling my Oath and in the Realm of Warriors we will meet!* He pushed through the thought-stream without a single response. The Void was a lonely place without a connection to the Darkness and too far away to connect with the clans protecting the Veil. LOR was alone, last of his warriors.

Their numbers were now few but this new enemy had far greater power than Aris the Chosen One or the Creators had known. The vessels carried more warriors than LOR and his Warruqs totaled, but some of his clan had torn into the soft enemy's carapace and he could see the frothing wounds bubbling and oozing on their surface.

LOR streaked towards his target alone. He heard the approaching adversary before his sensors created an image. It seemed to be using one of the ancient tongues to somehow track LOR. Its pulsating voice continued to redirect its course to ensure it would hammer LOR into pieces. None of the words spattering from it brought hatred. The chasing form simply chattered then adjusted its course, directly toward LOR's path.

LOR's systems made the necessary adjustments based on the history of the current battle that no longer uploaded into his core, but enough was learned to elude the pursuing enemy for the split cycle he needed. LOR hardened his carapace by locking his functioning plating, each painfully slipping into place with a sucking click.

For the clans, was LOR's final thought to an empty thought-stream and he ignited the remaining contents of his methane sac. The increased pressure created a breach in his weakened midsection; his organs spilled out of the gash and froze. LOR's lifeless form shot forward, its speed far exceeding its physical parameters.

LOR tore a gaping hole through the enemy; the last Warruq in the Void disappeared, Oath fulfilled.

3 4

Station Pluto
Captain Jack Falco

"Nice view," Captain Falco stated as he strolled up behind Commander Azim Shar'ran, a fully kilted Lieutenant Ian Wallace and Ensign Sierra Holts. Before the barrage of 'what are we here for' questions came his way, Falco asked them to wait. He needed a moment alone with Pema Tenzin, who was on his way. After receiving three nods, Falco moved a few meters down the clear wall that looked out into the beautiful black.

Falco faced station Pluto's Infinity Wall, gravely looking out at the dock. The *Anam Cara* sat proudly in her grav-locks; she was ready, good as new and fully reloaded. But he felt 'it' coming. The same feeling that overcame him the moment over half the world's population dropped where they stood. The moment he lost his wife and daughter.

Admiral Chen had released the latest information on the battle group. 'They had made contact and were making progress,' was all Chen would say. Admiral Chen continued to conceal and filter the incoming data from him. A calming presence appeared behind him. Falco turned to see Pema Tenzin.

"Captain Falco, I was told you wanted to see me."

The two men continued to evaluate the recent damage they had inflicted on each other during their long overdue grav-fighting match.

"Brothers again, old friend, but we could not be together under worse circumstances." Falco smiled at the man who had begun as his greatest foe in the ring so long ago and quickly became one of his closest friends. Falco had chosen the military and Pema the university. Only recently reunited due to the largest terrorist attack in humanity's history that created a road to global peace. And here we stand, Falco thought, five years from Earth.

"Yes, Captain, that is true, but who else would you want at your side when you enter the storm?" Pema Tenzin gently nodded.

Falco folded his arms. "Admiral Chen has taken the rest of 10th Fleet to aid Captain Fei, but—"

Pema finished his sentence, "You fear it is too late. This new adversary will gather its forces and search for the home from which the battle-group was launched. Which also means, you do not believe this enemy is of Earth."

"That is my very concern. The UN has spent mountains of money searching for life beyond earth, even found remnants near Mars of ancient starships. But this is different; this is out our front door." Falco paused, each man turned, looking out the Infinity Wall into open space, the Tibetan lotus engraved in the clear panel before them. "If the 10th cannot stop this force, a force I feel is far greater than we imagine, Station Pluto could be nothing more than a bread crumb on the trail to the Mars Station." Falco turned toward Pema, "And if they find the Mars Station?"

"Luna Station… Earth," Pema said with a sigh. "Station Pluto must be prepared for the storm that rages towards its shore."

Falco cracked an inappropriate grin. "Why is it that you are always using the 'hurricane analogy?' When your country's closest sea access is over a thousand klicks away?"

"Storms come in many shapes, my friend. The Chinese wave broke across my country centuries ago and only recently, has it subsided. The Korean Terror Militia shook the entire planet and now a new tempest moves toward us." Pema turned toward the red wall behind them. "It will try and wash over this station. I believe we have awakened a battering mass of ancient power. I too, can feel it coming, Captain. What are your orders, sir?"

Falco raised a scarred eyebrow. "I guess you knew where this was going." He reached into a pocket, "Take this and we can get on with it." Falco extended a sore limb and dropped a single silver bar into Pema's open palm. "It comes with a UN pay grade raise to Chief Engineer of the *Anam Cara*. At least, as soon as we get back to earth." Falco did his best to hide the sarcasm he felt.

"Can you do that?" Pema looked less than convinced.

"It will take paperwork… a bit of bureaucratic wrangling," Falco stated, "but that can wait. Now pin that bar to your chest." Falco stepped back then snapped his lean form ramrod straight. "Chief Engineering Officer Tenzin report for duty," he bellowed in his best captain's voice and looked to where his other officers were waiting. Falco waved them over.

"Meet our new Chief Engineer," Falco announced to his approaching officers.

"Honored to serve with you, Chief Tenzin," Commander Shar'ran said with a grin.

"About time you got back into the action, Chief. Pulling the grav-sleds around has kept you in shape at least," Lieutenant Wallace noted.

"Ensign Holts." Holts reach out a hand. "Pleasure to officially meet you, Chief Tenzin."

"Pleasure is mine, Ensign Holts. Captain Falco speaks very highly of you."

Falco cleared his throat and looked to each of his officers. "We have a problem. Few things are more difficult than trying to defend a fixed piece of real estate in space that is also a shining beacon of humanity. We have a lot of work to do.

"Lieutenant Wallace, change that skirt and run a full systems' check on our girl, the *Anam Cara* needs to be fully capable. Commander, get our new chief his uniform and both of you start tallying up every usable weapon on Station Pluto and check the mining gear. Ensign Holts get every shred of data you can on who or what we are dealing with."

Falco looked toward his antiquated watch. "We meet aboard the *Anam Cara* in two hours, have your reports ready. Get busy."

While his crew moved in various directions, the mapping system chimed away in the background with each officer punching in differing coordinates into the wall monitors. Falco felt the uneasiness of what was coming. Admiral Chen, he thought, I need to contact 10th Fleet and our lives may depend on the arrogant ass.

First things first, I need to find Director Lipinski and begin evacuating the thousands of non-essential personnel, in other words, anyone who cannot pull a trigger. Falco knew time was short and priorities would decide their future, their lives and in the worst-case scenario, every life between Station Pluto and Earth.

Falco picked up his pace, feeling like Atlas with the world on his shoulders.

35

Full burn – the Black Field
Admiral Chen, 10th Fleet

"WE HAVE LOST COMs with the battle-group." Commander Zhu again tried to hail Captain Fei, without success.

Admiral Chen slammed a thick fist into his armrest. "Keep trying, Commander." He leaned forward in his admiral's chair, tapped the controls on the side of his armrest and set his COMs to Fleet-wide and sucked in a deep breath. "Captains and commanders of 10th Fleet, maximum burn, any ship that falls behind will be dealt with harshly!" Admiral Chen bellowed then felt another quake while the grav-system adjusted to the increased speed of his dreadnought.

Chen would drive each vessel beyond its safety limits to reach his battle group now fully under siege. He scanned the signatures of his vessels on a floating hologram above his left armrest.

Three dreadnoughts, nine cruisers and eighteen patrol boats, the greatest space fleet Earth had ever assembled. He punched at the data-pad on his right armrest reducing the hologram scale; the vessels became small dots on a vast, growing plain leading to a massive black field. Chen touched his data-pad again and his personal hologram disappeared.

He slowly rotated his chair, seeing every station and officer on the bridge until he had returned from where he had started. His flagship the *Qing Long* was the state-of-the-art Dreadnought class vessel when it left Earth. Over one hundred meters long with a fighting crew of close to 3,000 and armament that could lay waste to a small moon. But what good would it do now? What can these vessels do here, in this endless space? he thought.

Commander Zhu turned from his Battle-Net station. "Admiral, battle group vessel signatures should be in range of our long-range scanners... nothing. Admiral, they are gone. The field has moved towards us, sir, and now covers the area of the last coordinates of the battle group. They could have been overrun."

"Or they have been destroyed." Chen looked around his vast bridge and command center, all eyes waiting for their admiral to give out his orders.

"One hundred twenty five percent burn, Commander, Stealth formation," Chen stated.

Chinese officers were long versed in the ancient strategists. Jiang Ziya, General Sima Rangju, Wu Qi, and the great, Sun Tzu provided the foundation of strategy for the People's military machine; the challenge was applying it when surrounded by the vastness of space.

"Admiral."

"Lieutenant?" Chen stated with the usual level of impatience.

"Sir, Captain Falco has asked for an open feed between 10th Fleet and Station Pluto along with all pertinent data regarding the battle-group and our current situation."

Chen's face tightened. With the battle-group destroyed or

incapacitated, he might need the ragtag vessels left at Station Pluto to fight off anything that got through 10th Fleet.

"Grant his request, Lieutenant."

The ashen-faced officer locked an independent COM line to Station Pluto that would immediately begin pushing data packets.

Battles fought in this new arena would come down to numbers, technology and finally, strategy. Technology would become the landscape that created advantages or disadvantages. The number of vessels could buffer a force that had a distinct disadvantage in technology, but no longer could a small force of 'peasants' rise to topple a king. There was no forest to run to, no caves to escape bombardment, nowhere to hide.

The image of an ancient and outnumbered force sifted through Admiral Chen's thoughts. Many centuries ago, lowly colonials had beaten the formidable British Empire by using native tactics, attacking in small numbers and then fleeing into their natural camouflage, the forest, the mountains and the grasslands, thinning Empire numbers until their advantage was gone and then the colonials struck in force. Of course, this force was bolstered by an ally.

"Continue to hold stealth formation."

"Yes, Admiral." The commander passed down the orders and moments later the greatest off-planet gathering of firepower in the history of humanity, floated in a sea of blackness. The stealth formation was simple and based on the latest sensory technology.

Clustering the vessels in hull-scraping tight formations forced enemy sensors to read them as a few large objects or even a single one, hiding their numbers.

"Commander, bring up the tactical hologram." Admiral Chen stood and moved toward the circular table in the center of the bridge. A hologram shimmered into existence and hung over the table. Even the Battle-Net showed only three large signatures.

In the China Sea on Earth, this would be a small but powerful fleet, Chen considered. *Here at the edge of our solar system it is all we have.*

"Link the Battle-Net, begin combat drills and operational testing." Admiral Chen returned to his chair, "I want every system and crewman ready for what lies ahead." He looked toward the center of the bridge, at the hologram floating tabletop to ceiling. Three dots crawling across open space and still, Chen pondered, *we have no idea who or what we face or how it got out here... or who put them here.*

So small and trivial we look. We wait and see if this new enemy has the patience of a master or the fervor of a fighter. Let you be the latter and let my name be made on your destruction.

the Darkness
the Krell

ARIS THE CHOSEN One floated just behind the Veil of the darkness. Her sensors were hindered at the edge, but were able to watch the battle and passively connect with the Warruq thought-stream each time she passed into the Void.

The Voices are strong, she considered and again made sure her thoughts were protected. All five vessels remained, though four were battered and her sensors could find few voices or systems that were still intact and functioning within their soft-layered carapaces that continued to froth and foam from every wound.

As ordered, she had left the strong voiced beast untouched. She felt the rage within her growing and adjusted her systems to control it. It felt strange that the vessel remained with the damaged ones. Aris had been sure it would flee. It did not, and now hovered over the others like a mentor protecting her apprentices.

Maybe they are like the Warruq and refuse to leave their clan. Or maybe they know what lurks in the Darkness. Yes, she thought, that is the truth as it follows the logic of fear that enshrouds the enemy Voices themselves. Another time, she thought, another battle. The Creators want to study these creatures, spread them open and dissect the beasts and the invaders that travel within them.

The Darkness swirled around her fins, each appendage tensed and the slippery mass pushed beyond Aris and grew towards the enemy vessels. Our Creators are increasing the territories, she thought, the Darkness grows more turbulent.

Aris shuddered, fear flashing through her systems. They are here and she wanted to flee, but controlled her trembling carapace and held her position.

A torrent of pain and terror was closing in. The Creators had sent the massive Krell to finish the battle. Aris sensed the cold current while the Darkness thinned its mass to ease the path of the coming demons. Without thought, Aris the Chosen One gave in to her fear and pushed hard, swimming up and away from the approaching Krell's path.

Her thought-stream filled with the guttural shrieks of legend. The Krell had not been seen for millions of cycles. It was said they were caged far from the outer edge of the Darkness, somewhere near the two fiery stars that shone bright on the Creators' twelve circling planets. A place Arial and the rest of the clans could not travel, another place of legend.

There were tales where thousands of Krell fought in the first Frontier Wars. Their shrieking cries filling the thought-streams long before Prox had passed through the Veil and came into existence. Aris's mentor had given her glimpses of the massive beings, passed down from clan to clan. Aris only knew the Krell were not of the clans, nor did they care who lived or died, by their will or any other. She pushed harder to move higher. Again, Aris was overcome by the primal urge to ignite her energy bloom and flee the coming Krell.

That would be her end. The Darkness protected Aris from all that called her thick mass home as much as she did from the enemy vessels in the Void. Suction from below worked at her carapace, the massive Krell moved past her position, just beneath her. The flow of the Darkness swirling into eddies and undertows that pulled and pushed Aris while the Krell's bulk plowed through it. Suddenly, the Darkness fell slack and calm returned. The Krell stopped at the Veil that protected the clans from the cold Void beyond.

Aris heard them pleading with the Creators, filling the open thought-stream without want or care for those who listened. Why do they fear the Oath, she thought? The Realm of Warriors awaits us all. Aris moved towards the Veil of the Darkness. She had to see the Krell for herself, allow her optical sensors to take in the beasts of myth. The fear of being detected by the dying enemy vessels was gone.

Legends no more, the massive Krell were here.

36

Viper Battle Group
Captain Fei

CAPTAIN FEI WATCHED IN HORROR. The missile could not dispatch its target in time. A bright flash lit the bridge of his vessel, the *Kwan Yin*. The final attacker ripped through the hull of their sister vessel, the *Kuan Ti*, a lethal wound that had broken her back for good.

He allowed the guilt of the moment to sink in. We remain unscathed, he thought; *Kwan Yin* is without a scratch. The sizzle of burning plastics and desperate, hurried movements filled the open-COM and soon turned to the sounds of the *Kuan Ti*'s remaining crew fighting to put out fires that ravaged her shredded hull. Muffled screams added to the glowing carnage that lit the black field. The commander of the dying vessel used the last functioning thruster to move the vessel down and away from the group and then the open-COM fell silent.

"Battle group is drifting, Captain." The commander looked toward Fei.

"Weapons inventory?" Fei swallowed the rising bile.

His Commander made a few swiping motions across a glowing screen, "Three missiles. The *Feng Huang* has two," the commander exhaled, "the *Kwan Yin* has one, sir."

"Battle group, damage report." Fei braced himself, but if there was anyone left alive on his boats, he would get them out.

Seconds past as the commander waited for the Battle-Net to compile the data. Eleven seconds later, Commander Zhu read off the list.

Captain Fei remained still, silent as Zhu finished reading the devastating report. He had only one option remaining.

Captain Yue Fei quietly stood on the bridge of the *Kwan Yin*. His words fell heavy, the green light shown bright on the open-COM link, "Battle group of the People's Navy, initiate Zéi Dé, Wú Ái, three... nine... zero... Yí."

Fei was following protocol. 'Z-Y-390-E' was the code for abandon vessel. Any surviving soul would hear the code, suit up and jettison into open space for pickup. Fei could not risk the lives of a rescue party for the three crewmen the Battle-Net listed as 'unaccounted for.' Crewman that were most likely dead, were most likely in pieces or worse.

Protocol also required that he fire a missile at a specified area on each boat to ensure total destruction. With only one missile left, that would have to wait for Admiral Chen to arrive.

"Lieutenant, get us above them, minimum safe distance. Keep us in the center of the open space."

"Yes, sir." The pilot lit the thrusters and the *Kwan Yin* began her lift to avoid any potential collisions between the four Viper class patrol boats aimlessly drifting, 'dead in space.'

"Black field is moving!" Zhu was locked on the Battle-Net screen. "Directly behind us."

"What now?" Fei growled. The Battle-Net alert flashed into life again. "Hologram up, Commander."

"Yes, Captain."

A thick, oily smoke hung in the air above the bridge's command table, the increased in clarity. The holo-feed represented what the Battle-Net was detecting hundreds of klicks dead ahead of their gutted battle-group.

"Commander, what are we looking at?"

Fei wondered if the Battle-Net was damaged. It was possible, he thought. Each vessel's Battle-Net was a supercomputer housed in the core of each boat. It was the guardian of the vessel and could run as a standalone unit or could join with other Battle-Net systems to create a deadly defensive shield. "But it's not possible," he muttered to himself. The *Kwan Yin* was untouched during the fighting.

The Battle-Net was buried in the center of the hull, away from weapon ports, engines or any system that could be detected by sensors and seen as important. The only known way to damage the Battle-Net was to destroy the vessel itself.

"Captain," the Commander kept his head locked on his display while his monitor continued to flash a warning, "Our sensors are picking up... they are picking up a zone of intense turbulence on the surface of the black field directly behind our position."

"What does 'intense turbulence' look like in space, Commander?" Fei fought to keep the sarcasm from entering his voice.

"Sir, the data suggests this 'zone of turbulence' is similar to ocean currents."

"Commander, you mean the field has characteristics of Earth's oceans?" Fei was already reeling from the hopeless scenario he and his crew faced; his connection to the present was losing its grip.

"According to the Battle-Net's database, the specific 'area of turbulence' is comparable to the surface forces created by a massive pod of bubble feeding humpback whales in the waters off the Southeast Alaskan Union." The crew understood when

Zhu stated the 'database,' every soul in range of his voice knew it contained every document and shred of information collected by humanity.

"Bubble feeding whales in the outer solar system?" Fei knew the database used the best equivalent from the known experiences and history of Earth and humanity's limited space travel. "The surface?" Fei looked to his commander. "Captain Falco and the *Anam Cara* detected light changes on the surface."

"Yes, Captain, they called it a lightning storm."

"Hmm." Fei nodded toward his commander. "Its surface may give away an exit point or staging area."

"Possibly, Captain."

"Why did we not detect motion on the field's surface prior to the other attacks?" Fei folded his arms.

Commander Zhu turned toward Captain Fei, "Size. The first two waves were the size of cannonballs and soldiers. Something large is near the surface, large enough to create a disturbance."

Whatever was coming had probably not been seen by his battle-group – what was left of it – or the *Anam Cara*. It was not documented in the database or it would have recognized it. Captain Fei slowly rotated his chair, feeling the black field closing in. Whatever was going to surface from that hellish field was not going to be pleasant and it was not going to be a bubble-feeding pod of humpback whales.

---

the Darkness
the Krell
Aris the Chosen One

LEGEND TELLS of mammoth aberrations spawned by the Creators. Entombed in a far away piece of the Darkness and cut off from the clans. They were beasts twisted from the pain and torture of millions of cycles of design. They were forged in fire and said to be devastation in its purest form. They were known as the Krell.

———————

ARIS THE CHOSEN One drifted in the Darkness just above the four Krell. They felt foreign and alien to her and though Aris could feel heat rising from their mass, she could not see them through the thick, dark mass of the Darkness. She listened to their pleas over their thought-stream.

The Krell of legend could not be cowards, Aris pondered, while their vast quaking forms vibrated through the Darkness and their shrieking consumed the open thought-stream. But their fear was not of death in battle and the journey to the Realm of Warriors, it was of something else. Fear of endless pain? What did it mean?

The Krell's form was immense. Aris constantly moved her fins to hold her position above them, pushing against the suction created by their rotating girth. Aris needed to know all that was available about them. She accessed the Thought-Stream of Clans that was always open, always updating the history and knowledge of the territories that spanned all cycles from the Rising to now. Updated by each clan and each form surviving within the Darkness.

It was said that even those living on the Creators twelve worlds circling the burning twin stars fed the Thought-Stream of Clans. More myth and legend, Aris thought, if those who lived on the planets shared their histories, then why do we not see and learn of these worlds? But she knew the answer before the thought, because it is kept from us, just like the twelve worlds and the warmth of the twin stars.

Aris filtered through the data, allowing new information to enter her systems, but little data told of the Krell. She studied a diagram of the clans. An image of the small and deadly Seeker was displayed with a list of warrior attributes and all of its varying dimensions, but its overall size was exact and never varied. This was true of all the different clans of the Darkness. Dimensions varied but the size was exact, as if each Prox or Warruq was made to fill an exact area and nothing more or it would perish without a trace.

Aris moved through the physical hierarchy. A Seeker was smaller than a Rover that in turn was half the mass of a Warruq. The fierce Warruq were smaller than the skillful Builders who were smaller than Aris, a Prox, one of the largest of the clans. Or are we? she wondered. Whatever the size and dimension of the clans, they must be determined by the laws used by the Creators. But the Darkness... the Darkness seemed to grow and expand on her own. No, maybe it was simply that Aris the Chosen One wanted the Darkness to be free from the Creators' laws and rules.

Aris searched more data. Finally the increasing movement from below reawakened the fear of these beings with no loyalty or allegiance and she exited the Thought-Stream of Clans finding no new data on the Krell that lurked below her. They were real and soon they might be released into the Void.

Regardless of her presence, the Krell showed no interest in Aris hovering above them. The Creators' thoughts cut through the constant shrieking flooding out of the four creatures and they fell silent. Their quaking forms rippling the Veil of the Darkness in front of them.

Aris adjusted her position in the torrent created by the beasts. The Darkness concealed them so Aris gently moved her fins and pushed herself slowly through the raging flow until she hovered directly above them and for the first time in millions of cycles, a Prox looked upon the Krell.

Creators, what have you done? Aris thought. She was consumed by the guttural fear of those who were born to it. The sight repelled her sense of curiosity and the Krell's tortured thoughts again poured over the thought-stream and burned into her memory.

Aris was overcome by something new. Not only did she fear for her own existence, but she felt terror for the invaders that would soon meet the Krell in combat.

Captain Fei
Viper Class Battle Group

FEI KEPT his eyes on the hologram and pushed to find the answer. Why leave us in the open when they could have covered us in the black field and destroyed us without even revealing themselves? Fei shook himself from the image of the suffocating black field and looked around the bridge.

"Why not kill us in the dark where we are defenseless? Why risk the losses?" Fei stood as he moved around the bridge. "And why did they not attack our vessel?

"Think. Our lives depend on it." He continued to prowl around the bridge. "We are surrounded by black field controlled by something, yet we sit in the open? Blind to all but this small patch of open space." An area now shaped like an endless tube and for all he knew, the *Kwan Yin* was in its center. No ceiling or floor as far as the sensors could tell.

Fei was missing something and it was infuriating. It literally is right in front of us, he thought, as the madness of knowing their survival depended on one of them making the connection.

"Captain," the young lieutenant was working hard to keep emotion from his voice, "we know the black field is thinnest directly in front of us... or was. We have full burn capabilities and Admiral Chen and the rest of 10th Fleet is underway..." the lieutenant stammered and lost control, "We could make it, sir! A full burn towards 10th Fleet! We must get out of here!"

Fei shot a steely glance toward his lieutenant and the man quickly regained his composure. Fei nodded and turned toward his commander.

"Yes, we could run toward open space, but this must be the end move our enemy has orchestrated. That's it." Fei raised an open hand and clenched it into a hammer-like fist. "Go!" he exclaimed to a bridge filled with confused officers.

"Captain?" Fei's commander looked unsure of whether he had received an order or an idea.

"The strategy game of Go." Captain Fei, like every other officer candidate, Fei had studied the ancient game at the military academy. "Simplistic in rules, but it is the most complex strategic game on Earth. Surround and capture your foe."

He moved toward his captain's chair and sat down. "Go has no equal. The most advanced computers can only reach the proficiency of an average human player," Fei said.

"There are almost limitless possible moves," added the lieutenant.

"Once we became masters at Go, we had up to five hours to place a single stone. Day one of a match could end with only a few stones being placed," Fei stated as his mind was close to the answer that had plagued them and left four ships and one hundred and twenty crew dead.

"Captain?" His commander was abrupt. "What does the game of Go have to do with our present situation?"

Fei let the anger and fear in his commander's words wash

over him and calmly stated, "The enemy has played his first ten stones and has us surrounded for capture. They have played us into an action that we must take to survive, or they think we must take to survive." Captain Fei looked to his officers. "What this enemy has not taken into consideration is that we have limitless moves."

The Battle-Net warning sounded. A burning glow appeared on the holo-feed, floating over the command table and grew into a radiant mass.

"Captain, the area of turbulence is increasing, heat signature detected."

"Yes, Commander, they are coming." Fei remained motionless in his chair; the bridge of the *Kwan Yin* was silent. Crewmen and officers watched the roiling area of the black field now magnified on the hologram. Yes, soon they will come, Fei thought, and soon I will decide our fate.

"They want us whole, they want us captured," whispered Captain Fei with chilling effect, "another stone is placed."

---

the Darkness
Aris the Chosen One
the Krell

ARIS THE CHOSEN One hung above the beasts. They calmly bobbed in the Darkness while the Creators uploaded their orders through a thought-stream. The Darkness thinned its mass around the four and for the first time, Aris could see the details of the Krell. Each was a massive orb covered in a thick, transparent layer that rippled as the creature moved its only fin. The fin itself was an abomination and hung like a long, clear, circular sheath that was hollow and surrounded a vast orifice at the base where it connected to the body. Controlled energy bloom was the only use for such a horror, she thought.

Slowly, Aris moved around the Krell, studying each piece, memorizing each detail. This could be the only opportunity to gain insight into the creatures. Not a single optical sensor, she added this detail to a special area of her memory and continued her search. Thousands of sacs lay deflated under the thick, outer viscous layer. Not an organ to be seen... she again positioned herself above the foursome.

Aris froze, the open thought-stream filled with a shrieking terror that flashed throughout the Darkness and across the territories, silencing anyone connected to it. Instinctively, she curled up into an armor-plated sphere. This time she left room for her optical sensors and focused them on the Krell, unable to look away from the scene beneath her.

They formed a tight line. Four colossal gelatinous orbs, each close to three times the size of Aris, pressing into each other while their bodies quivered and shook. Terror, Aris thought. What could such beasts fear?

Thousands of sacs expanded under the Krell's outer skin, the soft, clear layers of each beast flexed and stretched. Aris tried to move out of the expanding mass, but her own terror had shut down her systems. Soft mush surrounded her hardened carapace. The Krell's skin pushed Aris away only to suck her back into its warm expanding mass, then grew hard as the sacs continued to fill.

A gentle pressure and then a powerful force flung Aris up and away as the Krell were now twice their original mass. They continued their shrieking wail, pushing and flinging themselves at each other's sides, keeping just inside the camouflage of the thinning Darkness.

And then it happened and Aris the Chosen One now understood their fear, their panic and their pain.

A dim glow grew from deep inside each massive orb. The light increased and the shrieking grew louder until Aris was sure the thought-stream could handle no more. The clear skins of the Krell grew brighter still and Aris adjusted her ocular filters to stem the searing light and protect her sensors. The mass of the Darkness surrounding them was little more than thin, gray mist now.

The Darkness exploded around Aris, the Krell ignited into four flesh powered infernos and blasted into the Void, leaving burning chunks of their bulk along the way. The thought-stream fell silent, the Krell were beyond the Darkness. Aris slipped outside into the Void. The thought-stream blasted her sensory systems with the wailing of four fiery forms using their flesh as fuel to propel them towards their targets.

The Krell's screams turned to whimpers and the thought-stream fell silent. Aris reached out to them, her carapace singed, fins damaged from the heat. This is your path to the Realm of Warriors great Krell, your Oath fulfilled, the invaders destroyed. A surge of pain flooded her. Something pulled Aris back into the Darkness and her damaged systems began to shut down.

She floated in and out of existence while the Darkness seeped into her wounds. The warrior's rage fused with the Darkness' life preserving mass. Within fractions of cycles, her carapace healed and data flowed through previously destroyed feeds. I must silence my wail, Aris considered. I am Aris the Chosen One, fear and young-one cries are for the weak, for the Krell. Strength continued to flow into her; the Darkness would heal her again and again as long as Aris returned to its mass.

She's expanding. The Darkness moved in all directions, swirling and flowing around her. A growing pain and fear pushed closer, again the thought-stream filled with shrieking. But it is not me, Aris thought. The Creators have released a fifth Krell.

Still too weak to move, Aris stretched her mending carapace to its capacity and allowed the healing liquid of the Darkness to enter between each armored-plate, pushing into her organs at will. Fear was conquered; Aris fully gave herself to the Darkness and lay helpless in the path of the Creators' ultimate destroyer, the Krell. She found herself wondering if that were still true.

Other clans must exist. Hidden from the warriors of the Darkness, waiting to be unleashed. Aris the Chosen One rose and fell. The fifth tortured abomination was close and moving closer towards the Veil of the Darkness. She lay in its path and would let the Darkness choose life or death for the leader of the clans.

Aris would never let fear control her again.

38

Captain Falco
Station Pluto

"She is ready to go, sir," Chief Engineer Pema Tenzin stated with confidence. He walked over to the long table that ran the length of the galley of the refitted *Anam Cara* and set a fist-sized black box in the center.

"That's it?" Falco said.

"Captain?" Tenzin was at a loss.

"Chief, that little black case is going to broadcast this meeting to every COM box on Station Pluto and 10th Fleet?" Falco was sure his newly appointed officer was back in the Chang business.

Pema closed his eyes and drew a deep breath. "Sir, not only will that little black case securely broadcast the meeting, but it will also push data packets to every hologram station onboard." The chief glowed with the power of his brilliance.

"Well then, good work, Chief." Falco could see the cocky bastard he loved behind those steady eyes. He walked towards the hatch to gather the others that were scouring over the exterior hull of their newly repaired boat.

Falco punched the release and the hatch slid open. He caught himself midstride and turned back to where Chief Tenzin made a few last second checks.

"Remember, oh Great Lion of Tibet, I kicked your ass," he lovingly whispered just loud enough for the stoic Tibetan to hear. Falco strode out of the mess hall to meet his crew, muffled Tibetan slang filling the galley behind him.

"I've got it! I know what you did!" Lieutenant Ian Wallace was in rare form. Falco waited for his pilot to finish running a loving hand over one of the new compartments added during her repair work.

"She looks bloody fantastic, sir! A right good beauty she is!" His Scottish accent was in full bloom as was always the case when he spoke of his love.

"It will have to wait, Lieutenant. Meeting first, secrets later." Falco was relieved to see his lieutenant's glowing approval. If any of his crew were to break regs and beat the hell out of a higher ranked officer, friend or not, it would be Ian Wallace over the wronging of the *Anam Cara*.

"Aye, our boat looks ready and your ribs should be healing by now."

Falco grinned at the sound of his commander's voice. He looked up to see the big Yemeni bastard keeping the same deadpan expression he always wore when placing a friendly dig.

"Not well enough, Commander Shar'ran, but I'm better off than the one who lost." Perfectly timed Falco thought as Chief Tenzin exited the galley with a scowl plastered across his seamless face. However, his true nature was too strong for his weak-willed attempt at anger and the scowl naturally turned into a lighthearted smile.

Falco took in the scene. His crew was crammed into the galley and finding a place to sit, stand or, in Commander

Shar'ran's case, both. He was without a doubt the biggest of the *Anam Cara*'s crew and outside of Falco himself, the most respected and even feared.

Falco enjoyed the movement of those around Commander Shar'ran. The rookies pushed hard against other crewmen standing near the commander to ensure they would not make contact with the man, their eyes never rising much higher than his special issue size sixteen boots. It was like watching a school of mackerel avoid the shadow of a shark near his childhood home in New Sicily.

But in a shit-storm, Falco knew that there were three people he wanted at his side and that big bastard taunting the newbies without a sound was front and center. Four, he corrected himself.

"Captain?"

Falco turned to see his science officer carrying a stack of data screens that held every known report and findings on a potential new life form that seemed to be growing hostile... or are we the aggressors? he pondered. He once again thought of Captain Fei and the battle group being swallowed by the dark field.

"I am ready to proceed when you are, sir," Ensign Sierra Holts stated with the focus and tone of someone carrying a heavy burden.

Falco found Lieutenant Wallace, raised his head and motioned his hand across his neck. The lieutenant answered the gesture with a nod and released a high pitched, eardrum-splitting whistle that silenced the crew out of pain if not volume.

"Captain on deck!" Wallace relaxed his shoulders and all eyes were now on Falco.

"Ensign Holts, you're up in five minutes. Chief Tenzin, do we have clean audio and hologram feeds to all centers of Station Pluto and Admiral Chen's flagship vessel, the *Qing Long*?"

"All feeds are clean and ready to go." Pema held a finger over the small black case and waited for the captain's go ahead.

Ensign Holts sat in the middle of the long table near the hologram feed and organized her data. Falco watched her movements, noting there was not an ounce of fear emanating from any part of her graceful, yet powerful form. Soon Holts would offer her insights and any factual clues to humanity's greatest and potentially, most deadly discovery in its history. She locked eyes with Falco and after a few moments, gave a confident nod.

"Light up the feeds, Chief." Falco gave his full attention to his ensign.

Holts moved her hand across her first data-screen and the hologram came to life.

"We are looking at the current mass and scope of the dark field utilizing the best models programed for the Battle-Net. Based on all data we have sent to the United Nations top scientists and military advisors, the defensive forces within and around the field are not manufactured with Earth-based technology."

Falco heard the words and knew Holts and the UN were right. The crewmen and officers remained silent, but many nodded gently and like Falco, he assumed they believed something unexplainable through the human experience had been found just beyond humanity's solar system.

"The UN Space Agency has assigned a name for those who have created the weaponry we have faced and continue to have contact with." Holts took a deep breath. "We call it the Oortian Civilization."

The word Oortian was whispered throughout the galley. Falco scanned the room, every face taut and locked onto Ensign Holts's every word. The act of naming something made it real. No longer could humanity look at a universe filled with a patchwork of dark fields without considering something deadly cloaked within them. Hidden from its best technology.

Holts continued, "We believe the Oortian's territory may be

larger than our own." She tapped another data-pad. A new hologram appeared showing two black disks floating alongside one another.

"This is the dark field the *Anam Cara* came upon seven days ago. As discovered by Admiral Chen of the People's 10th Fleet, the field is growing. The battle-group led by Captain Yue Fei was quickly overtaken and all communications cut," she paused and then added, "or jammed. This is the dark field now." The larger disc grew bright and the room filled with muttering crewmen.

"Keep it down! We have a long way to go." Captain Falco added a little extra grit to the last word and the room fell silent.

"The smaller field is roughly the size of our solar system in circumference." Ensign Holts waited to let that sink in. "Defining the size of our solar system is debatable as there is no clear boundary. The United Nations uses the unusual orbit of Pluto as the boundary of our solar system. Due to its unique path we use the average distance between Pluto and the sun then add fifteen percent, which gives our solar system a diameter of approximately eighty-nine astronomical units. Currently that equates to ten years and two months' travel time by the latest solar assisted sails, but the newest models may cut that time by thirty-percent," she added to a smattering of cheers.

The hologram changed and the science officer continued her report. Murmurs ran through the crew as implications of the hovering image before them sunk in.

"The black field is currently sixty-two percent larger than our solar system based on my calculations."

Commander Shar'ran broke the silence. "Ensign Holts, how can something this size grow at will? The Oortian field moved with purpose and speed to surround and finally overrun the battle-group."

Holts's eyes lifted from the data pads she was studying. "Based on its sheer size, we can assume that somewhere in the dark field, there may be a solar system. A sun with at least one planet, possibly more. The real question, commander, is how do the Oortians move a field of this size against the gravitational force that captures planets and creates orbits?"

"In other words," Falco added, "there is not enough information to have a working theory beyond your current assumptions?"

"That is correct, sir." Holts shook her head. "There must be something within the field that dictates its size or why would it exist? Everything is purpose driven to ensure efficiency of resources."

"Right," Falco moved away from the holo-feed and leaned against the bulkhead, "but again that assumption is based on our own realities, technologies and experience this far from Earth."

Lieutenant Wallace was shaking his head.

"Lieutenant. Do you have something to add?" Falco wanted his officers engaged in this discussion and his pilot knew more about moving through open space than the rest of them combined.

Wallace looked at his captain then eyed the commander and finally his gaze fell to Ensign Holts. "A hidden solar system makes sense. The Oortians' weapons came from somewhere and the simple fact that our scanners cannot penetrate a meter into the field, reveals its purpose." He moved towards the holo-feed and sat next to the ensign.

"Do you mind?" Lieutenant Wallace pointed towards the visible data-screen resting on top of the others, its screen lit, data rolling across the bottom of the display.

Holts nodded. Wallace tapped on the input pad and the hologram changed again. This time the dark field enlarged and hung a few feet above the galley's table. It resembled an oval platter with one square end. A few meters in front of the square end sat a tiny glowing orb, Station Pluto.

Wallace looked to Holts for help and without a word she entered the missing data.

A deep red glow started at the curving end of the floating oval and slowly grew outward, towards the square end and then stopped.

"It's growing toward Station Pluto," Holts stated. "More accurately," she corrected herself, "it is leaping in our direction. For now, the field is stagnant, but if it follows the same pattern of movement, at some point we can expect it to leap an additional sixty-two percent toward Station Pluto."

Falco didn't like the scenario that was running through his head. "Based on the current findings, how long until this field is at our front door?"

Holts reached under the stack of data-screens and pulled out the bottom display. Her hand worked the screen and stopped.

"Six days, twenty-two hours, sir. But that's an estimate."

"Admiral Chen. Are you getting this?" Falco was not surprised the admiral had not said a single word to this point. The leader of 10th Fleet was the only officer patched in on the COM link.

"Captain Falco?" An unknown voice sounded from 10th Fleet. "This is Commander Lee of the Admiral's Flagship, the *Qing Long.*"

Falco found his officers now standing in front of the holo-feed, each wearing a variation of concern on their faces.

Commander Lee continued, "We are recording the findings and will present all pertinent data to Admiral Chen."

Falco quickly answered, "Commander Lee, 10th Fleet is in the direct path—"

"Based on the assumption, Captain, that the field is 'leapfrogging' by sixty-two percent of its area each time it grows, you would be correct," responded the commander in a flat tone. "Thank you, Captain. Lee out."

Station Pluto is alone, Falco thought; a potential bump in the road towards Earth and the only person in 10th Fleet he hoped he could trust, disappeared in a leaping dark field twenty-four hours ago. Falco knew the odds of Captain Fei surviving in that predatory soup were slim at best.

But Captain Fei gave off a quiet strength; Captain Falco had faith in that and belief in his crew.

A figure in white burst into the room and scrambled toward Falco.

Short of breath with his lab coat marked with sweat, Lab Specialist Campos held up the data-pad. "Captain, you need to read this."

"Autopsy Report?" Falco was already grabbing the data-pad as Ensign Holts, Lieutenant Wallace and Commander Shar'ran joined the circle.

Captain Falco's eyes locked on the scrolling data and exhaled sharply. "Son of a bitch. Back to work people. Meeting adjourned. "Ensign Holts, send a summary to all officer stations and Admiral Chen."

The room cleared and Falco handed the data-pad to Holts who scanned the first few pages, her hand dropping to her side, the data-pad loosely swinging. Holts looked at her captain, mouth open and eyes wide.

"Station Pluto lab, ten minutes." Falco looked to his officers. "All of you. Holts get your head right, you're going to tell us," Falco pointed to the data pad, "what the hell that means."

39

Captain Fei
Battle Group

THE BATTLE-NET roared to life when four, patrol boat sized flaming spheres, erupted from the black field and into open space, each heading a different direction. Two of the blazing masses arched back into the sides of the dark field, disappearing into its camouflaging depths only to burst out seconds later. The two other orbs avoided a collision when they broke through the field, erratically changing course at the last second.

They stabilized their paths and homed in on the beleaguered battle group. Commander Fei and his crew followed the flaming spheres burning toward the broken; drifting remains of their comrades and their once sleek, predatory vessels that were now tombs. Long fiery tails trailed behind them. The *Kwan Yin* floated a few kilometers above the four lifeless boats.

"Silence!" Captain Fei ordered the bridge. "Basic life support and Battle-Net only. Shut everything else down. I want the smallest signature possible."

The Battle-Net tracked the four new enemy marks locked onto the battle group's dying vessels below. Fei kept an eye on Commander Zhu's station, the Battle-Net continued searching for additional threats while charting the course of the incoming enemy.

Commander Zhu turned toward Fei. "Twenty seconds to impact."

"Hold current position, prepare for full burn," Fei locked onto Commander Zhu, "ready the final missile. Fire on my command."

Fei thought of the *Anam Cara*, her windows on the bridge and the need for the Americans to have visual access to the black of deep space. Thank the Lord Buddha for new windowless Chinese designs, as seeing the obliteration of four Viper class vessels would take the fight out of any crew and we are not finished yet, Fei thought. There is still hope.

"Impact." Commander Zhu practically spat the word out. The battle screen glowed bright red a moment after the four fireballs engulfed the four dead vessels. Pulses of depleting energy washed over the bridge, vibrations coming in gentle waves. The grav-system softened each rolling swell until there was nothing.

The Battle-Net lit up. Another burning sphere ejected from the dark field.

"Incoming! New target locked." Commander Zhu followed the Battle-Net data flashing across his screen. The sensors tracking the distant orbs movements and then it stopped, reversed course and stopped again.

Seconds past, Commander Zhu tracking the movements through Battle-Net feed.

"Target is dead ahead, Captain." Zhu swore under his breath. "It's partially hidden in the field, sitting on the surface."

Captain Fei nodded to his commander. He assumed the enemy had locked onto their position. Locked onto the *Kwan Yin*'s faint signature from two thousand klicks away? Who knew? Fei again saw the beginnings of the connection that could save their lives.

Open space, he thought. Why leave us surrounded by your camouflage, but in the open? You burst into the open erratically to... avoid our weapons lock? No, Fei thought. Based on the initial battle, they would know how quickly his battle-group locked onto their vessels beyond the dark field.

"Energy signature growing, Captain," Commander Zhu stated. "Looks like capture is off the board, sir. Signature gone, enemy has moved back into the field."

"Low burn, keep us in the center, Lieutenant." Fei had a good idea where the enemy would attack from and, if he were wrong, he would kill his entire crew. It wants us to flee through the area we came, Fei thought, where our experience tells us the black field is thinnest.

Commander Zhu was probably correct. Capturing the *Kwan Yin* may have been the goal in the beginning as nothing else explained why she was left without a scratch. But regardless of his battle group's losses, they turned the trap of open space into a killing ground until there was nothing left to die. Well, almost nothing.

"Commander, switch the Battle-Net to manual fire. Make sure the enemy is close. You have one chance." Fei looked toward his pilot. "Lieutenant Ko—"

The pilot spun to face him. "Yes, Captain?"

"Turn the *Kwan Yin* towards the area where the enemy first emerged. I want our bow pointing like an arrow at that spot." Fei could see the confusion in the young officer. "When I give the command, I want a hard bow thruster burn, on my second command, kill the thrusters and initiate a full burn, thirty percent downward plane."

"Captain, we will be heading away from Station Pluto."

"Yes, Lieutenant, we will be heading away from home and away from the ambush that would shred us to oblivion." Fei was betting the Data-Pods had met a similar fate. The captain observed his officers. There it was, the healthy look of fear that he needed to keep them sharp.

Leaving the battle group in open space had Fei puzzled as soon as they realized the enemy could move the dark field. Why leave us in the open where we can use our weapons and sensors? He had pondered long and hard. Now Captain Fei had a theory, one that would save his crew or destroy them.

The enemy cannot see in the dark field either.

4 ○

Captain Falco
Station Pluto, Lab

CAPTAIN FALCO, his officers and the lab personnel sat tensely. Ensign Holts with data-pad in hand, stood before them with a short man, balding with loose skin drooping around his mouth like a bulldog.

"Dr Torbose, I've heard great things. Nice to finally meet you in person." Falco hated labs and they were always was too bright, too white, or maybe I miss the rust and welded seams of the *Anam Cara*, he thought. Either way a lab was uncomfortable in every sense of the word.

"Thank you, Captain. I have also heard things about you and your crew." Torbose moved toward another room adjacent to the main area of the lab.

Falco shot a questioning glance to Ensign Holts who simply shrugged and followed.

Dr Torbose stopped in front of a hatch, turned toward the

group and calmly held up his hand. "We felt a display would be easier to explain," he said, releasing the hatch.

When Falco and his officers were all inside the room, a pair of straining lab techs wheeled in two black objects the size of hubcaps resting on a thick steel powered-lift, the wheels squeaking loudly.

Dr Torbose pointed at the lift. "We believe these – hull-pounders you call them – to be similar to 'skulls.' They are intact, cleaned and free of any known contaminant." Dr Torbose took a step back as the techs parked the powered-lift in the middle of the gathering.

"Wait a second, Doc." Falco took a deep breath. "Are you telling us that these are not the weapons, but the Oortians themselves? These hull-pounders that punched through our boat, killed crew members, these are fucking soldiers of some sort?"

Ensign Holts knelt down next to the dark shinning discs while Falco and rest of the group walked up and silently surrounded them. Dr Torbose launched into a scientific description of the autopsy findings.

Falco cut him off. "Doc, no disrespect, but I didn't understand a word you just said. I need layman's terms. Time is short and we need to understand what we are dealing with."

Dr Torbose turned a reddened face to Ensign Holts. "Science Officer Holts, please." He stepped back and Holts stood.

"Most of the human body is comprised of mainly six elements. Carbon is the glue that bonds them, allows for the formation of DNA and enables dynamic organic chemistry to occur in our cells."

Lieutenant Wallace look relieved. "And why, we humans are termed a carbon-based species."

"Exactly." Holts pointed toward the skulls. "These have many of the same elements as the human body or at least we have a record of the elements that comprise them, except," she again knelt over the dark skulls, "they are not carbon-based."

Dr Torbose stepped forward. "Carbon is roughly eighteen percent of human body weight and is synonymous with life on Earth."

Falco just stared at the skulls. "If they are not carbon-based," he looked up at Dr Torbose and down to Ensign Holts, "then what the hell are they?"

Ensign Holts tilted her head, "Our scanners found a material in these plates that had the closest match to material from a neutron star. But what the material is, we have absolutely no idea." She continued to scan the data-pad. "According to the autopsy, there is no trace of carbon in the remains, but there is an element, or material that we do not have a record for."

Torbose added, "And like the systems on the *Anam Cara*, the closest material that any of our scanners can match it to—"

"Is a neutron star." Falco shook his head.

"We also found what looks to be the remains of 'organ-type' parts that were badly damaged and methane residue in a 'sac-like' pouch that ended in a type of orifice." Dr Torbose shrugged his shoulders.

Commander Shar'ran nodded and for the first time spoke, "Organ-type?"

"Sorry, Commander, but we have no clear-cut data leading to theories that support any specific functions of the remains, but with time…" Dr Torbose shrugged. "Except for those." He pointed at the black skulls. "The element that is foreign to us is what the skulls are comprised of and it also runs like veins or arteries through the softer, 'body' of the Oortians."

"Is it possible to surmise that these Oortians have a bone structure made of something similar to a neutron star?" Falco folded his arms.

"If you're going to fly through space without a suite, a

neutron star skeletal frame… would come in handy." Lieutenant Wallace swallowed hard, smiled and started shaking.

"Funny, Lieutenant," Falco said, ignoring the high-five between Commander Shar'ran and Lieutenant Wallace.

Ensign Holts put down the data-pad and ran her hands over the dark discs. "Not a scratch on them, or a single detectable imperfection." She looked up to Captain Falco. "These went through our layered, steel plated hull—"

"Without a mark on them," Falco cut in.

Ensign Holts stood and faced Dr Torbose. "You stated that you refer to these," she pointed to the black discs, "as skulls?"

"Yes, our only theory so far is based on a web-like ball made of the unknown material found on the underside of the skull. Its placement in the most protected area would suggest its importance, a brain or processor for the rest of it."

"Was it damaged in any way?" Falco asked Torbose.

"Possibly compressed into the plate on impact, but we have no idea what it looked like before, Captain," he turned towards Falco, "what we do know of this unrecorded element is that it cannot be measured on the hardness scale."

"You have diamonds on board?"

"Station Pluto has a significant mining operation, Captain. Of course, we have diamond bits for drilling. But diamonds are not the hardest mining bits we have."

"Pressurized Lonsdaleite." Ensign Holts nodded. "Makes sense out here, just in case."

"Fifty-eight percent harder than diamond, but we also have other materials made of carbon atoms that are even harder." Torbose pointed to dark skull plates. "Our best drilling bits did not even scuff them."

Falco turned to his officers. "Ensign Holts get a report to 10th Fleet ASAP."

"Already on its way," Dr Torbose stated. "Admiral Chen had an open feed to the earlier meeting, report was flashed his way as soon as it was finished." Torbose looked sheepish, cleared his throat, "He is the admiral, Captain."

"Of course," Falco growled in the doctor's general direction. "Let's go people, we have work to do."

"Captain."

Falco spun towards Dr Torbose. "Yes, Doc?"

"Pick it up." He pointed toward the two skulls on the power-lift.

"Excuse me?" Falco stated.

"Try and lift one."

Commander Shar'ran smiled, squatted down, wrapped two massive hands around the smooth edges and lifted with all he had. The hubcap-sized disc did not move.

"Each one of those half meter skulls weighs over six tons." Dr Torbose looked hard at the officers. "These things are battering-rams. They may be weapons or a type of Oortian soldier, or both. They are also the smallest 'objects' we have seen of the Oortians and possibly the most basic. We should proceed with great caution."

"Point taken and make sure you add that to the admiral's report." Falco scowled. "Doc, any more information comes to light—"

"You'll be the second to know, Captain."

Admiral Chen
10th Fleet

THE BRIDGE of the *Qing Long* was energized. Admiral Chen scanned the autopsy report from Station Pluto. Commander Lee sat at his station reading the data file sent by Ensign Holts.

Commander Lee had listened intently to Ensign Sierra Holts's thorough report. Her ability to scrutinize zona-bytes of data and create an in-depth report in layman's terms proved that the officer was of the highest intellectual caliber.

"These 'Oortians' may be hiding an entire solar system?" Admiral Chen asked no one in particular and continued to read out loud at a mumbling pace. "Non carbon-based life," he said and dropped the data-screen into its slot on the side of his chair.

"Oortians are a civilization that may be far older than humanity, but according to Ensign Holts's report their technological capabilities are limited and seem to be based on an organic foundation." The admiral rapped his fingers on the arm of his chair. "The autopsy findings back up Holts's theories. So far."

"Thoughts?"

Commander Lee spoke. "With great respect, Admiral, Ensign Holts's most educated guess was that the Oortians were not technologically inferior, rather we have encountered their defensive perimeter. Similar to a space defense missile system and the simple existence of a controllable field of that size lends weight to an advanced civilization."

"So Commander, are we currently clashing with something that has been on the edge of our solar system before humans even knew... we had a solar system? We've encountered some type of guarded boundary?"

"Yes," Commander Lee stated, "a boundary protected by weaponry made of materials that can shred our hulls and possibly, adjust to our tactics independently as we have found no sign of a base or vessel beyond the small Oortians we have destroyed."

Chen leaned back, folding his arms. "If this path is irreversible, have we awakened a massive war machine that has sat silently in the far depths of our solar system?"

"There are many possibilities Admiral," Commander Lee said as the Battle-Net screen registered friendly craft on its scanners.

"Admiral, we have twenty-five confirmed Data-Pod signatures on the long-range scanners," Lee continued to scan the screen. "Three groupings, Battle-Net calculates five are heading towards 10th Fleet, five towards Station Pluto and fifteen towards Earth."

As Commander Lee finished, the entire bridge fell silent. Every officer within earshot knew the sound of a final act when they heard it. The battle-group must have been destroyed and Captain Fei was trying to warn them.

"Should I prep the grappling-bot, sir?"

Admiral Chen grimaced, he could not remember the last time

he had seen anyone use the robots for anything other than dust collectors. "Have them prep the bot, and Commander make sure they do not use a mag-lock to drag them in. Nets only."

"Yes, sir." Lee turned to his data-pad and sent the order.

"Commander," Chen paused to allow his officer time to finish, "alert Captain Falco that Station Pluto will be picking up twenty Data-Pod signatures in the next eighteen hours and five will head their way."

An entire battle-group gone. Chen had already lost five state of the art, Viper class vessels and knew little of what had destroyed them, no he thought, consumed them. What the admiral did know, 10th Fleet would respond in a manner the Oortians would understand.

Captain Falco
Anam Cara – Station Pluto

EVEN IN HIS personal quarters in the stern of the *Anam Cara*, Falco couldn't get a moment's rest.

"Thank you for the heads-up, Commander Lee. Twenty Data-Pods en route. We will expect sensor contact in eighteen hours."

"Your update for Admiral Chen?"

Falco thought hard on the orders he gave his officers an hour prior. "Preparations continue on Station Pluto and we are doing everything we can to turn her into Battle Station Pluto..." he exhaled, "with what we have, and Commander Lee, I am deeply sorry for the loss of the battle group's crew."

"Thank you, Captain. I will let the Admiral know you have things well in hand. Lee out."

Falco swiped a tired hand across the COM box next to his bunk, barely missing the near empty glass of scotch next to it. The COMs green light faded. Falco closed his eyes, trying to embrace a brief moment of peace in what felt like years. His eyes fell to the bottle of scotch. A necessary drink was never a bad thing, but a bottle? That could change the situation.

Ensign Holts's report was a wake-up call and then there was the autopsy findings. Falco swore under his breath. Holts did an exceptional job; the detail in her summary alone gave him confidence in his newfound knowledge of chemistry and biology. From the moment the United Nations named the civilization, the Oortians became a sobering realization. Humanity was sparring with something that lay hidden from their most advanced technologies. "Right on our fucking doorstep," Falco whispered.

He had always held out hope that the Russian Federation had finally got their shit together and headed back into space or at least the Euro-Arab League had beaten them to Pluto.

"But Oortians lurking behind a black field at the edge of our solar system, hammering our ships to scrap... or letting them go." Falco sat up, listing the casualties. "Captain Fei, the crews of the battle-group, my crewmen, this shit is real, this is happening." The words sounded from another part of him, a darker side that had been held in check since – Falco swallowed hard – since he met his wife, Luciana.

His quarters loomed darker, shadows growing and he took another slow sip of scotch that reached the disappointing bottom. Falco looked away from the empty glass, his hand resting on the release of a drawer embedded in the hull near the head of his bunk. The drawer slid out and Falco stared at the photo of his murdered wife and daughter. The picture lay alone, entombed in the steel compartment. He refilled his glass, took another deep draw, ashamed of his need for liquid therapy.

Commander Lee's call from 10th Fleet confirmed the worst. Captain Yue Fei and his battle-group were completely destroyed or in a serious shit storm. A brave captain always sends every shred of information on an enemy he can, before he can't. Fei fit the description of a brave captain.

Falco reached for the glass and thought better of it. Again, his booze-clouded mind began tracing over his science officer's report and back to the images of the black skulls or plates or whatever the hell they were.

"Closest match was the material from a neutron star? What does that even mean? No carbon, sacs laced with methane, things that look like organs, and then add a healthy amount of some unknown *element* harder than anything known to mankind and weighing as much as a shuttle." Falco's whisper grew to a snarl and he threw back another healthy gulp. "Pulverize a few of my crew into hamburger, destroy a battle group, have a fancy fucking skull and BAM!" He smashed the glass against the bulkhead. "You have a fucking Oortian!"

Fragments of glass and a mist of scotch covered the photo of his wife and daughter; Falco gently pulled the silver frame out of the compartment. His hands shaking, he carefully cleaned it off.

"I'm sorry." Tears streamed down his cheeks. "I failed you both. Seventeen seconds. If I could have fired seventeen seconds earlier… twenty billion people would still be alive. You'd still be alive and I'd be back on Earth." Tenderly he placed the photo into the drawer and pushed it back into the bulkhead. "Get your shit together, Captain," Falco told himself as he put the scotch away.

"How long can it take to turn this neon Frisbee into a defensible fortress anyway?" he grunted while he stood and walked out of his quarters. Falco had gotten word from Commander Shar'ran that the evacuation had gone smoothly. Of the initial inhabitants of Station Pluto, five hundred were left. The rest were packed onto the shuttles, mining boats and anything that had the capabilities for the five-year voyage to Earth. The last vessel to leave included one stowaway, Director Lipinski who had hidden in a storage crate on the supply bay.

Falco grinned at the thought of Commander Shar'ran having the deck crew stack a dozen crates filled with legumes on top of him. Director should have turned off his locator, his grin turned to a smile, but glad you didn't. Crew will let him out after a good cry, he thought as the smile faded.

He paused in front of the newly repaired rail gun compartment. Falco looked at the plate welded to the hatch as he always did since the loss of his crewmen and whispered the same sentence in his native tongue. The words rode a heavy Sicilian accent born of rage and sorrow, "l'eredità degli eroi è il ricordo di un grande nome e l'eredità di un grande esempio (the legacy of heroes is the memory of a great name and the inheritance of a great example)."

Falco ran his fingers over the plate that simply read, *Martinez & Conlin*, wiped at his eyes and headed for Station Pluto's ops-center. One stop, he thought as he exited the *Anam Cara*. He found the hangar COM-box and stood in front of it. Immediately identifying him, a yellow light appeared. Falco cleared his throat, leaned in uncomfortably toward the box. "*Anam Cara* officers to the Infinity Wall, lotus section."

Ensign Holts was last to arrive. She silently joined the awestruck group, adding her subtle reflection to the clear wall looking out onto the universe. Her smooth ebony head and striking features adding comic contrast to the scarred, scruffy and 'lived in' features of the four others.

Falco found their slight reflection off the Infinity Wall comforting. Commander Shar'ran stood a good ten centimeters above himself and Lieutenant Wallace, Ensign Holts was just shy of Falco's height and then there was the brick of Chief Tenzin. While he stood eighteen centimeters below Falco, he was twice as broad.

"Four hundred and five vessels beginning 'the Crawl'," Commander Shar'ran growled the last two words as he shook his head back and forth.

"There is always the pungent red-light section on Mars Station to break up the monotony." Lieutenant Wallace loved to jab his friend and as he and Falco knew, Commander Shar'ran was not fond of confined spaces, let alone five years' worth.

"They have a glow. I never knew what they looked like en masse." The elegant beauty of the solar sails surprised Ensign Holts. "They remind me of a school of jellyfish."

"Version fives are the brightest, collect the full spectrum of radiation," Chief Tenzin stated with pride while the four hundred and five glowing sails pulled their vessels away from Station Pluto.

"It will take weeks before they reach MACH 2," Falco stated. The officers stood in silence. The blackness of deep space returned, only the faint silver glow of Pluto adding any kind of warmth. "As we have seen first-hand, the Oortians can easily match our fleets best speeds."

His officers remained quiet.

"Thousands of lives may depend on us." Falco continued to stare out the Infinity Wall. "If the Oortians attack and we fail to defend Station Pluto," he turned, to face his officers who continued to look the direction of the fleeing ships, "they all die and that may just be the beginning. You have your orders, let's get to it."

Falco observed the last sail's glow disappear, its faint warm light replaced by a desperate and hungry cold.

43

Chief Engineer Tenzin
Station Pluto

PLUTO LOOKED distant through the Infinity Wall. She is leaving us alone, Chief Pema Tenzin thought. He walked past a team fitting a final panel on another newly created 'Battle-Cube', paused and scrutinized the sizzling epoxy that fused the piece with the others.

"Make sure you add an airtight hatch on each wall." The chief continued to examine their work. "Any one of us may be using this bunker. Act as if your own lives depend on the work you do now, as it may in the days to come. Damage control is the key to the Infinity Hall. Each bunker must work as an independent unit."

The 'Infinity Hall' that clung to the edge of Station Pluto was quickly becoming the equivalent of one hundred and fifty foxholes.

Pema was proud to see a Tibetan engineer leading each team. All of his countrymen had chosen to stay when Chief Tenzin explained in great detail the situation at hand over a mug of Chang. The old Tibet lives on he thought, she embraces her warrior heritage yet struggles to fuse it with her Buddhist longings. Warrior Monks defend, never attack. His thoughts spoke to his ancestors, ancestors he knew were at his side.

"Chief. How goes the progress?" Commander Shar'ran asked as he pulled himself through the small hatchway of a newly constructed bunker.

Pema smiled at the giant of a man and felt sympathy for the man's mother. Childbirth is a warrior's pursuit of which women are the only ones strong enough to endure, he thought.

"As you ordered, Commander Shar'ran, we are creating the bulk of the bunkers facing the direction of the Oortian field." Pema pulled out his data-screen and scanned the completed bunkers. "One hundred completed, thirty-five meters long by ten meters. The remaining fifty will protect our stern and be seventy meters long by ten meters. You realize if we cannot keep the station facing its current direction, the positioning of the bunkers won't make a difference?"

"Yes, Chief, duly noted, but we have a plan for that. Did you say one hundred completed? Finished." Commander Shar'ran looked surprised.

Tenzin nodded with pride. "Yes, Commander, my crews are incredibly efficient, highly skilled."

Shar'ran grunted. "I can see that. What about hatch doors, oxygen feeds, and missile cradles?"

"All in place, Commander. Oxygen lines feed to separate tanks that are stored outside of the Infinity Bunkers for safety. Extra munitions are stored in old steel mining footlockers bolted to the interior red wall. They should keep a direct hit from taking out more than one or two bunkers."

"Rail guns are up and online!" Lieutenant Wallace shouted as he came swimming through the hatch that Commander Shar'ran had literally popped out of. "What is taking you so long, Chief?"

"Great work, Lieutenant," Shar'ran said mockingly. "Chief Tenzin only has one hundred chambers completed and fifty in the works. But it is good to hear that the two rail guns are in place."

"They're big, ya bastards! Much bigger than these wee little rooms with a view!" Wallace stormed off grinning, but turned as he opened the hatch to exit the newly created Infinity Bunkers. "Well done, Chief. Thank the Gods you were stationed on this plastic disc."

Chief Tenzin and Commander Shar'ran continued going over the checklist when Lieutenant Wallace appeared again from a hatch.

"Forgot to mention, the captain wants to see us in the Pluto Room in thirty. Update of sorts." And he was gone.

Chief Tenzin looked to the commander. "Where did the rail guns come from and where did the lieutenant place them?"

"They were stored with the old welding equipment, steel plating and rifles."

"Rifles?" Tenzin wondered why Station Pluto would have rifles in storage.

"Not just rifles." Commander Shar'ran lowered his voice. "Found fifty M40 combat shotguns." He leaned closer to Chief Tenzin. "If you were going to control riots or other potential hazards, a gas operated semi-automatic 12-gauge made a lot of sense when holes through the hull were not on the list of desired outcomes."

Chief Tenzin raised an eyebrow. "And the rail guns?"

"Lieutenant Wallace placed one on the upper deck and the other in the lower storage compartment. Both have a 360-degree view and the same poly-glass that the Infinity Wall has, the areas are sealed and the infinity glass is cut and ready for removal. Best placement if you only have two rail guns to cover a massive range."

The chief was concerned. "Commander, are both guns locked in a fixed position?"

Tenzin knew the answer before he asked the question based on the time they had and the materials they did not.

"Yes, Chief, the rail guns are facing the same direction as your one hundred foxholes, towards the Oortian field. They are bolted to the decks. Their range is limited to rails minimal rotation, but still covers a big chunk of space. Rooms are sealed off with oxygen lines and ammo storage just like the bunkers. Two crewmen will suit up, tie into the safety line, punch out the glass and strap in for the show."

"No rear guard." Chief Tenzin exhaled hard. "We can do better, Commander."

Shar'ran looked to cut in, but stopped and allowed Chief Tenzin to continue.

"I can take one of my teams and use the steel plating, strip the wheels off the heavy loaders and use the welding gear stored on deck three to create a revolving base." Pema's intensity grew. "We will need the rail guns functional in all directions."

"Do it, Chief."

"Yes, Commander."

"And Chief, I'll notify the captain of your whereabouts. We can tie you in to the nearest COM-Box if we need to. Tenzin spoke to his crew of engineers, grabbed two of them and headed on his way.

COMMANDER SHAR'RAN INSPECTED the hatch leading to the corridor supporting the newly created bunkers. He already missed the view and open space of the Infinity Hall. The nearest COM-Box came to life with Captain Falco's muffled bark. Shar'ran crawled through the hatch and tapped the side of the COM-Box embedded in the far bulkhead.

"This is Commander Shar'ran."

"Need you in Bay-3. Single incoming Data-Pod, looks to be damaged and I need someone who can still capture it the old fashion way. You'll need to net it with a bot so Ensign Holts can download the data from it."

"On my way, sir." Shar'ran tried and failed to keep the lightness from entering his tone. "No meeting, I assume."

"We'll send updates through the COMs. On the move, Commander. Falco out." The COM-Box fell silent.

CAPTAIN FALCO RESTED his hands on the slab top of the long table in Station Pluto's ops-center. He glanced at Ensign Holts while she followed the visual feed of the Data-Pod's course and inevitable capture. She was already prepared to download the files from its banks as soon as Commander Shar'ran could wrangle the pod into Bay-3 and attach one of the station's hardwires to its battered storage banks.

Falco was impressed with the ensign's quick, efficient work. He was looking forward to a time when he could get to know her on a more personal level. She had a depth that fascinated him. One day—

"The signature on the Data-Pod," Ensign Holts looked up from her screen, "is consistent with the vessel *Kuan Ti* of Captain Fei's battle-group."

Falco felt a real sense of loss for a captain he barely knew.

"Ensign Holts."

"Captain?"

"Let Admiral Chen know we have a lone Data-Pod. Signature is a match for the *Kuan Ti* and it has taken a beating. Also the course it took is outside of the battle group's last known position and far outside the path of the incoming Pods."

"Sir," the ensign was again scanning the data being uploaded to her screen from Station Pluto's Battle-Net. Falco patiently waited for the officer to finish her statement.

"Sir, according to these images, the Data-Pod..." she again paused, her eyes squinting, her head slowly moving from side to side. "Captain the Data-Pod has been damaged. There are multiple impacts," Holts tapped her screen and zoomed in on the image, "and what looks to be slashes across its plating."

The plating that protected the Data-Pods was a blessing and a curse. Heavy steel and lead layers alternated with poly-resins to create a virtually impenetrable shell that protected the data from all known methods of attack from cyberterrorism to a nuclear blast.

The disadvantage was the downloading of the protected data. The data had to be manually received after the plating-shell was unlocked by entering a twenty-one-digit key. If the correct key was not entered within three attempts or if the shell was breached, the Data-Pod would destroy the files.

Falco studied the images. "Not a surprise based on the battle that must have ensued, but how would a damaged Data-Pod arrive so many hours ahead of the rest of the pods 10th Fleet had informed us about?"

Holts scanned her screens. "This pod must be separate from the group that passed by 10th Fleet."

Falco stood. "That makes twenty-six." He tapped his fingers on the tabletop, "Viper class carry five each?"

Holts slid a data-pad over and accessed another screen under it. She looked up and Falco froze. The look on her face was enough.

"Captain," Ensign Holts pointed to the screen to her left, the image of a grappling-bot towing the netted pod toward Bay-3, "this pod makes twenty-six. The battle group had twenty-five confirmed Data-Pods."

"Oh God." Falco flew towards the COM-Box, placed his mouth inches from the sensor. "Captain Jack Falco, CODE RED."

A red light pulsed on the surface. He punched in his emergency code followed by the three-digit pin for Admiral Chen's flagship, the *Qing Long.*

"God damn it!" Falco shouted at the COM-Box. "CODE RED! Pick it up, Chen!"

Falco helplessly watched the red light continue to flash.

44

Captain Fei
Kwan Yin

CAPTAIN FEI WIPED the sweat off his brow. What began as a sporadic push and pull of air had become a rhythmic inhale and exhale as his officers now fed their lungs in unison. Basic life support was uncomfortable at best. The cold of space could not overcome the intense heat produced by the spinning grav-fluid that traveled between the third and fourth layers of the hull.

Brilliant engineering, but with the cooling system on low, the entire ship was sitting at a not so pleasant 30.5 Celsius. Thank Lord Buddha for the humidity filters or he and his crewmen would be swimming in their uniforms, he thought. Nothing wasted on a Chinese boat.

When your country has five billion citizens you learn to reuse everything no matter what it smells or looks like. That was Fei's father's favorite statement when he was a boy. He tamped the wet cloth on his forehead and waited. The enemy had not shown itself again and sitting in the center of the open space with the *Kwan Yin* pointed away from a previously safe harbor seemed dangerous. Trust your instincts, captain, they have never led you astray. He reassured himself.

The calm before the storm, Fei was sure. For a brief moment, it seemed the enemy could not find the *Kwan Yin* in the open, or was simply letting them know it was there. Sensors are based on the evolution of a species. You design technology for the signatures you know exist in yourself, your environment and your world.

There must be at least a few shared characteristics between humans and this new... Fei still had no idea what they had encountered. Heat was the most obvious. Each used combustion to power their vessels and each had means to destroy.

Do they hone in on the sound of human voices, the sound of pumps and moving liquid? Contrary to what people believe, sound travels sporadically through space on particles of dust and debris. The five-layer hulls deadened ninety-nine percent of sound outside of the boats. Or could it be as simple as line of sight? He thought of the new telescopes that could pry into distant solar systems. Line of sight depending on the technology or evolution could be far superior to computer-based sensors.

Red flashes caught Captain Fei's attention. Commander Zhu scanned the Battle-Net screen, stood up and walked to the hologram that floated in the center of the bridge. He touched the data-pad and a red glow appeared on the edge where the dark field ended and the oval piece of open space they found themselves began.

The enemy was skimming the camouflage just enough for the Battle-Net sensors to pick it up. It has almost gone full-circle. Any moment now, Fei thought, and readied himself.

"Ready yourself, Lieutenant," he whispered to his pilot.

The pilot turned. "Ready, Captain."

Fei saw resolve in the man's face or maybe just fear. Either way, he was ready.

"INCOMING!" Commander Zhu roared as the giant orb flew from the dark field. The commander's hand slid towards the right side of his data-pad and hovered over the launch controls.

"Hold your fire, Commander." Fei could see panic rushing over the man. "We have one shot, let it come closer."

Commander Zhu took a deep breath and held steady. "There is no heat lock from the Battle-Net."

The sphere the size of the *Kwan Yin* had an amber tint, no flames, no glow, just a vast glob of mottled-jelly moving towards the center of the cleared area. Pushing towards the *Kwan Yin* at a steady, but measured pace.

The Battle-Net had a visual lock based on the movement, but that was all, and that was not good enough. Captain Fei knew the stakes were too high for anything other than a heat-lock. A heat-lock was a guaranteed hit or as close to one as the Battle-Net could get.

"Ready Lieutenant." Fei waited for the rush, waited for the predator to make a kill-run at them.

"Heat source, Captain! Battle-Net has a heat-lock!" Commander Zhu moved to fire.

A massive burst from the orb and it shot away from the *Kwan Yin*. The enemy cut its burn and with it the heat-lock. In seconds, it was hidden once again in the camouflage of the dark field directly in front of the *Kwan Yin*.

Zhu thumped a hand near his data-pad. "I should have fired. We had heat-lock." He looked to the decking under his feet. "I have failed you, Captain, I have failed this crew."

"Focus, Commander. If you had fired we would be defenseless and our last missile would be harmlessly chasing ghosts in the field."

"Lieutenant prepare—"

The bridge lit up, the hologram in the center erupted with light. The sphere tore into open space, covered in blue flames with fiery debris trailing behind it. A bulk of flames raged towards the *Kwan Yin*.

"Hold, Commander!"

"Full bow burn, Lieutenant."

The crew on the bridge slammed toward the bow, each harness straining until the grav-system caught up to the sudden thrust. Fei saw that the angle was off, but it should buy them the seconds they needed by increasing the distance.

"Fire!"

Commander Zhu hammered the control and the Battle-Net unleashed a single missile from a lone, now empty cradle.

"Full Burn! Twenty-degree up-angle." Fei's body smashed into his captain's chair, the *Kwan Yin* unleashed its main engine and powered up and away from the flaming orb.

"Direct hit!" Commander Zhu rattled.

Blue flames engulfed the hologram, the *Kwan Yin* shuttered, the force of the explosion pushed her close to vertical. The lieutenant adjusted his flight path while a shower of burning debris thumped against the bottom of the hull.

Commander Zhu's screens flashed, data streaming across in a solid line. "Fire suppression system is overwhelmed, Captain!"

"Do what you can, Commander." Fei felt the strain ease on his chest, the grav-systems balancing out the force of acceleration. The *Kwan Yin*'s outer layer foamed and frothed while its fire suppression system fought to extinguish the chunks of burning mass and fill the voids they left behind. The repair system pushed its sticky epoxy through charred holes, sealing them shut until the hull warning lights ceased flashing.

"Captain! Twenty seconds until we enter the field!" Fear had taken the young pilot as they approached the harbinger of death that surrounded them.

Captain Fei hit the open-COM key. "Brace for possible impact in fifteen seconds. Once we enter I want full silence, not a sound from anyone on this boat." His calm was more unnerving than the scenario from which it sprang.

... TEN... NINE... EIGHT...

Fei clamped down hard on his arm rests, watching the numbers light up the bridge of the *Kwan Yin*.

"Lieutenant, cut the main engines and ready the bow thrusters." Fei looked to the Battle-Net station. "Commander, shutdown the hologram, emergency power only and that includes the Battle-Net, remain on basic life support." Let's hope there is nothing in our path, he thought as he prepared to slow their forward progress.

Silence consumed the *Kwan Yin* while the Battle-Net counted down the seconds to contact on every screen, at every station on the *Kwan Yin*. Each numeric change lighting the tense faces on the bridge with an eerie glow.

The Battle Net flashed ... FOUR... THREE...

"Fire the bow thrusters, Lieutenant."

... TWO...

"Shut it down, Lieutenant." Captain Fei calmly stated, his heart pounding in his ears.

... ONE...

Aris the Chosen One
the Darkness

A PRIVATE THOUGHT-STREAM opened and the upload began. Aris
the Chosen One hung in the darkness tired and aching from its
restorative infusion, but alive and close to fully healed. The
Creators continued to push data into her systems. Her carapace
ebbed and flowed with the warrior's rage coursing through her
mended organs and systems.

The Creators had a new plan. Aris continued to scan the
incoming data. She was not allowed direct communication with
the Creators yet. But of course, they knew this as they knew all
things that went on within the clans. They knew of all things
except the Darkness, Aris thought on her private thought-
stream. The Darkness has her own plan, but how Aris knew this,
was not known to her, it was simply part of her memory.

Aris was pleased that the Creators had championed the eldest
Warruq as the new LOR. Warruqs followed the title and each
time the leader of their clans completed his journey to the Realm

of Warriors, chaos ensued until another leader was named. They were a warrior class that needed an iron fist. Aris the Chosen One commanded the Warruq, but only through a LOR.

Aris uploaded the latest records on the invader's five vessels. Pleasure pushed through her systems. The leader had escaped capture and was hurtling towards the Darkness itself. It had not run towards the direction it came, and fled towards its home as the Creators had planned, the location where fifty-five Warruq waited for glory. Instead the lone craft felled a Krell with a single ember that turned the beast into flaming shards and bravely pushed into the Darkness and vanished in her mass.

Fearless, Aris thought, a warrior among them. This vessel would be worthy of battle, worthy of death by Aris the Chosen One. She hesitated after the upload terminated. The last of the feed was unusual for the Creators. Aris was to choose four Prox and hunt down the remaining enemy and LOR would lead the clans against another invading force moving toward the Darkness.

A battle without a Prox? Aris had never heard of such a strategy, but the Creators had their reasons and she, her orders. Aris opened a thought-stream to the clans, searching its traffic for four specific beings.

Aris would gather the four Prox that her mentor had spoken of before she passed to the Realm of Warriors. She would bring the ancient ones that existed when the Darkness protected but a single planet. The four that could be forged into a hunting pack and find the invader that boldly charged into the Darkness.

The territories must be protected.

4 6

Admiral Chen
10th Fleet

ADMIRAL CHEN BEGAN THUMPING A LOOSELY closed fist on his armrest. "Twenty-five Data-Pods would account for their entire inventory?" Chen looked around the bridge, his eyes finally falling on his commander.

"Why would Captain Fei send fifteen towards Earth? His COMs are out, but 10th Fleet is less than twenty-four hours from his last location and Station Pluto is only a few hours further? We could flash a message to Earth in four point five hours?" The Admiral had been doing so daily with his United Nations superiors updating the situation and receiving his orders. Quietly the admiral also used encrypted back channels with the sovereign Chinese government to keep them up to date.

Chen was getting uncomfortable. The orders received from the UN and the opinions of the Chinese government were no longer congruent. Though the United Nations accord stated that the combined military was under their leadership, China is the country with the majority of lives at risk at Station Pluto and the 10th Fleet are their vessels, filled with Chinese crewman.

Commander Lee broke the silence. "Captain Fei's battle-group may have assumed that the mass of the Data-Pods should be sent to the target with the greatest..." Lee paused and gathered himself. "A target with the greatest chance of successful contact."

Chen felt adrenaline enter his veins. "And 10th Fleet was not believed to fit that assumption?" If Captain Fei's battle-group encountered a force he believed was superior to Chen's armada he would look to Station Pluto then Earth.

"Admiral?" Commander Lee scanned the Battle-Net screens.

"Yes, Commander."

"There is something that does not fit, sir." Lee was examining the data as he spoke. "What is the probability that after the battle-group was surrounded by the black field and engaged by enemy forces—"

"Could they have launched their entire inventory of Data-Pods and not lost one to the enemy?" Admiral Chen asked aggressively.

Chen rose and marched to Commander Lee's station. The Battle-Net screen continued to track the Data-Pods. Five were slowing down as they neared 10th Fleet. Their trajectory would place them just within the range of the Grappling-Bot.

Five other signatures where moving wide starboard of the Fleet's flank and another fifteen were further starboard of those. All would pass the Fleet in minutes while they traveled towards Station Pluto and Earth.

"Commander, Battle Stations level ONE." Chen was following protocol, but he felt the need to raise the alert to a level THREE. Calm, he thought, Level ONE is a defensive position.

The grappling-bot released from its cradle on the underside of his command ship, the *Qing Long* and moved towards the waiting Data-Pods. The Battle-Net continued to track the twenty other signatures passing wide off the Fleet's starboard flank.

"Two minutes to contact, Admiral." The lieutenant's fingers continued to skate over the small navigation screen while she skillfully maneuvered the bot through the Fleet's hull scrapping Stealth Formation. Once in open space the grappling-bot would net the Data-Pods, one at a time.

"Emergency Flash coming in, Admiral," the COMs officer stated in response to a pulsating red light on his screen, "CODE RED from Station Pluto, Captain Falco's authorization cypher." He opened the protected channel, as was protocol for the seldom-used line and fed it to the admiral's station.

Captain Falco's desperate voice sounded. "Admiral, badly damaged Data-Pod was brought into Station Pluto. Signature is a match for the *Kuan Ti* of Captain Fei's battle-group.

"All of the incoming Data-Pod signatures match the battle group pod signatures." Chen scanned his personal Battle-Net feed, "Five Pods from each vessel."

"Yes, Admiral, with the damaged pod, count makes twenty-six, one more than battle-group's inventory. I repeat, count makes twenty-six!"

"Battle Stations level THREE! Battle-Net to protect 10th Fleet vessel signatures only!" Chen's voice boomed through the command center. "Data-Pod signatures may be compromised. Commander Lee, optical scan, as close as we can get on the nearest of the five Pods. Keep tracking the twenty off our flank."

"On your screen, Admiral."

Chen flinched at the image of what was reading as a Data-Pod. The newest model was a layered-plastic sphere covered in sensors and solar skins with an unhackable, coded Fleet Signature, specific to pod vessels. What the Admiral was looking at on the optical-zoom was something else. A rough, shiny skin stretched over a hard sphere with a loose fleshy appendage on the rear that appeared to be venting steam or—

"Optical match to the 'Hull Pounders' that hit the *Anam Cara!*" Commander Lee frantically moved his hands across his data pads. "Signatures are good, but these are not our pods!"

"Lock onto all pods, Commander…"

Commander Lee input the order the second it left the admiral's lips and the Battle-Net's warning systems screamed inbound alerts from bow to stern of 10th Fleet's formation. Twenty Hull Pounders ignited into a full burn. Five toward the bow and twenty from the starboard side.

"INCOMING!" shouted Commander Lee.

"FIRE!" responded Chen.

47

Captain Fei
the Black Field

COMMANDER ZHU of the *Kwan Yin* turned toward Captain Fei. "Sensors are useless. We are blind beyond our hull," he whispered.

Fei felt the words more than heard them. There was a familiarity upon entering the camouflage. A feeling from the past that skirted just outside of his memories. The soft resistance to the *Kwan Yin*'s forceful plunge had been unexpected, soft and pliable.

The crew braced for impact anticipating the dark field to feel like a solid wall. Instead the dark mass gently pushed against the boats hull, gripped her tight yet permitted her to enter without damage. The *Kwan Yin* slowed against the soft resistance, crawled forward and finally came to a full stop. How far they had traveled into the dark field was anyone's guess. A hundred meters or a hundred klicks.

Captain Fei surveyed the bridge. Stations dark, each screen

black, holograms off, a faint glow from the Battle-Nets reduced function gave Commander Zhu a fierce lighting from beneath his angular face.

Here we sit in a sea of black with no means to protect ourselves, no method to detect the enemy that lurks within it and no way of knowing which way to go. But we are still alive, Fei thought.

He risked their lives by entering the field, but believed it was their only hope. Fei put the final pieces together as the lone, massive orb circled them. It was using the field as cover, yet it would appear and then vanish beneath its camouflage.

Fei deduced then that it could not see his vessel unless it was in the open space that had been left for them; a trap for the *Kwan Yin* and at the same time, a killing field for her weapons. Even then, he thought, it had to search for them. Keying in on a sight or a sound within the vessel itself? Human voices or the *Kwan Yin*'s systems? The ping from her searching sensors, radio waves maybe or even the scanning Battle-Net? If the field can hide the enemy from us, it can hide us from them, was his theory and, so far, it seemed correct.

Fei reached for his harness release, the click echoed through the bridge. Slowly he stood and moved toward the Battle-Net station and Commander Zhu. Leaning down, Fei and Zhu began whispering back and forth, afraid a sound may give away their position.

"This field hides their form, but we must assume that they have a way to communicate their location with the others and some means of moving within it."

Fei nodded at each barely audible word. "Yes, we must assume, but how would they communicate in this field? See or travel?"

A shrug was all that followed and Fei moved back to his captain's chair.

Fei's crew continued to go over the *Kwan Yin* with a fine-tooth comb, outside of the epoxy-filled burn marks on her belly, they could not find a dent or scratch. The commander wanted to send out a probe to get a sample of the dark field that covered them. Fei agreed, but not until he knew they could do it safely without giving away their position.

We need to warn Station Pluto. The only means to communicate would require being close enough to use Morse code or dock at one of the station's bays. The *Kwan Yin*'s COMs satellite was smashed into scrap.

Fei caught himself assuming 10th Fleet would be overrun and destroyed, leaving Station Pluto as his only refuge. No, he thought, they have a chance. 10th Fleet has immense firepower and an admiral that knows only stubborn victory.

A rising humidity glossed over the bridge. Crewmen glistened and Fei felt a lone drip of sweat run down his back. Even at the lowest setting, the life support systems kept humidity low. A problem for another time, Fei thought. Let's see this dark field. He pushed off his captain's chair and soundlessly moved toward his Commanders station again. "Engage the Virtual Surround Vision," he murmured.

Commander Zhu nodded, grabbed one of his data-pads, powered it up and quickly tapped the keyboard and held it up to Captain Fei.

FULL VSV – PREPARE YOURSELF – ENTIRE HULL – 10:00'

Fei nodded in approval. Commander Zhu tapped the screen, started the countdown and made his way through the bridge. Each time he stopped at a new station, the officer read the note. After finishing with the bridge, Zhu handed the data-pad to the COMs officer who crept off the bridge to alert the remaining crew-members.

It was the look of fear overcome by curiosity, Fei thought or possibly curiosity overcome by fear. Either way, his crew was about to see something new. What if the VSV shows nothing but true blackness? Deep space was dark with lighter stretches of gray mixed with pinholes of distant light, but what if the camouflaging field consumed all spectrums of light? With no stellar map to guide them, no sensors to lead them, the *Kwan Yin* could be lost for good. A drop in an ocean. I will find a way out of this, Captain Fei promised, there is always a path if one can find a way to see it.

The COMs officer crept back onto the bridge, held the Data-Pad up for everyone to see.

'FULL VSV – PREPARE YOURSELF – ENTIRE HULL – 1:37'

4 8

Aris the Chosen One
the Darkness

ARIS THE CHOSEN One drifted in the Darkness with a new sense of purpose. Three of the ancient Prox had arrived and as was customary for Prox of a lower rank, they remained just below her and waited for the last member of their pack.

When the forth arrived the hunting pack would be whole. Aris would be the fifth and final Prox, completing the ancient tradition of 'forming the five' and the uploads from the Creators would commence.

Aris studied the three ancient ones. Each gently brushed against one another. But do I? she thought, do I see them or is the Darkness feeding the images to my sensors? And are the Creators uploading to the Darkness? No, she concluded, the Darkness feeds itself. Fins continued moving below her, just enough for the Proxs to keep their positions in the Darkness that swirled, pushed and pulled against their carapaces. All Prox shared the same carapace overall size but she marveled at the various shapes of the three below her. This was the truth of the Creators' offspring, each clan had its own bulk, its warrior's symbol that represented the space they consumed with their form and all were created within its rubrics. But how each of them filled that space was fascinating to Aris.

A current pushed past her sensors, the last of the four approached. The eldest of all the Prox was moments away and it was her right, even her duty to arrive last. Aris felt the warrior's rage begin to drip into her systems. Soon it would seep into her organs once the hunting pack was whole.

Where are the Creators' plans? Aris thought on a private thought-stream. The hunting pack continued to jostle against one another, the warrior's rage growing within each Prox and with it, fearless aggression would soon overtake the pack. The Creators must upload the plans before the four lost control of their systems to the building fury.

Serenity washed over Aris. She closed her private thought-stream and opened one to the pack. The ancient Prox swam into their midst. The pack was whole and their prey was close. A surge pushed into the pack, each of the five carapaces arched and stretched. The Creators began to upload their plan.

Aris heard the singular voice echo throughout all of her systems and vibrate through each plate in her carapace. Even her fins twitched and flexed with the sound of the Creators.

The enemy has entered the Darkness, invaded the territories. A warrior's action and an opportunity for a Prox hunt that has not taken place in the territories since the ancient conflicts, billions of cycles ago, before the Darkness herself came into existence. The upload continued until all known data of the invading vessel was stored in the Prox core organ.

Aris the Chosen One, new leader of the Prox and the clans with the aid of the four ancient beings that had existed for billions of years, would finally fulfill their Oath and protect the

Creators and defend the territories. The data push slowed and then stopped.

Aris gently moved her fins and slipped through the oily-black current towards the last known location of the enemy voices and the foreign beast they traveled in. Four ancient shadows followed her while the warrior's rage coursed through their carapaces, turning them into a predatory force with a single purpose.

The voices must be silenced.

49

Admiral Chen
10th Fleet

ADMIRAL CHEN OBSERVED from his flagship the *Qing Long*. The chasing missile locked on to one of the few remaining enemy targets so skillfully cloaked as one of their own Data-Pods down to the electronic signature. Moments later, the missile made contact, turning the Hull Pounder into flame for a split second before the vacuum of deep space erased it from existence. Shrapnel thudded against the outer hull, close to the bridge. Chen thought about the creation of 10th Fleet, its purpose and its reality.

Far cheaper than iron, poly-epoxy plastics gave vessels the ability to carry vast amounts of fuel and supplies for short-range missions. Layered across lightweight carbon-fiber frames, they created a superior hull and allowed grav-fluid to flow and spin at incredible speeds between layers creating ninety-eight percent Earth gravity.

Other spaces between the five layers were filled with patching epoxy to ensure any punctures or even a heavy impact crater could be filled and sealed within seconds. The downside of the lightweight materials, Chen thought, they may have no place in combat. 10th Fleet represented the pinnacle of technology and power. In reality, it was a horse and pony show meant to awe their competitors, the Russian Federation and Euro-Arab League and inspire the Chinese people now under the umbrella of the United Nations. But most importantly, 10th Fleet gave China immense influence within the UN. Another warning siren pulsed over the COM.

"Damage report, Commander." Chen kept his eyes level and back straight. The Oortians used 10th Fleet's stealth formation against it, but they had not caught them with their Battle-Net down. The close proximity of the vessels allowed many of the Hull Pounders to inflict damage, but it was minor.

"COM-Sats off line on..." Commander Lee read off each code name for the eighteen damaged boats. As he finished a flash lit the Battle-Net screen and the final attacker exploded along the Fleet's port flank.

"All enemies destroyed, Admiral," Lee added, and the alarm fell silent.

Chen gave his usual nod and tapped the control panel on the right arm of his admiral's chair. A smooth, clear screen emerged from its sleeve on the side and silently followed its track until it rested over his lap.

The flagship *Qing Long* was bustling with hushed activity. Each crew-member went about their duties, but from here on out, anything could be an attack or enemy. After studying the information that passed over the screen, Chen looked to his commander.

"Eighteen COM-Sats destroyed..." The admiral let his statement hang in the air. "Five of these... 'things' imitating our Data-Pods came at us from the bow and twenty more skirted our starboard flank, then attacked our stern after creating the illusion they were heading to Station Pluto and Earth."

Commander Lee listened, his eyes never leaving the admiral's face.

Chen continued, "Yet, they destroyed eighteen of our fleets COM-Sats." Chen tapped his screen, slid it over the arm it sprang from and pushed himself to a standing position. "They attacked what they knew. They hit only our Viper class patrol boats, just as they destroyed Captain Fei's battle-group. They took out their ability to communicate with the Fleet." Chen wiped the sweat off his brow with a thick, solid forearm. "The Oortians attacked the same vessels they destroyed. This time, they mimicked our own electronic signatures without us knowing it." Admiral Chen paced the small area around his chair. "Without Captain Falco's warning..." He cleared his throat, shook his head and sat back in his chair.

Commander Lee turned from his screens. "They are learning from each encounter," he paused, "and so are we. However the Oortian technology may be far better than we estimated."

Chen looked across the bridge as if he could see through the hull itself. "Yes, Commander Lee, the Oortians mimicked the size of our Data-Pods or already had something similar to their signature." He closed his heavy eyes. "The strategy was sound and based on the destruction of eighteen of our COM-Sats... effective."

"Admiral, our long-range sensors have detected irregularities." The lieutenant continued to monitor the incoming data feed. "Sir, we have detected irregularities in the astro-field 2.012.031.9."

"Commander." Chen gave his second-in-command a nod.

Lee moved quickly to the young officer's station where the lieutenant was already standing to the side of her chair. The commander sat hard and keyed in the field reference code. The vast Kuiper Belt surrounded them. It extended from the orbit of

Neptune and went well beyond Pluto. Within its influence were millions of objects from small asteroids to dwarf planets and everything in between.

"Admiral, we have three small objects giving off faint heat signatures."

Admiral Chen knew it could be explained by one of a thousand different scenarios, but he could feel the intensity rise from those around him. What are the chances, he pondered that after a wave of enemy attacks, our sensors pick up irregular heat signatures a thousand klicks out?

All eyes fell to Admiral Chen.

"Scan the field for any objects similar to what data we have on the Oortians so far." Chen hesitated as he thought of the name Captain Falco had given the round projectiles. "Scan the field for the Hull Pounders. Use the data from our skirmish and the *Anam Cara*'s encounter.

"Admiral Chen?" The young lieutenant kept her tone low, eyes down.

Chen did not know her name, but recognized her mannerisms as old-world displays of respect. From a lower cast, he thought, possibly farmers. "Speak, Lieutenant?" He inflected the last syllable and motioned with his hand.

"Lieutenant Bai, sir." She spoke it like someone used to stating her name again and again. Bai was one of twenty officers of which five were low ranking lieutenants like herself. "If we search for these Hull Pounders specifically, by size, what of the other types that the *Anam Cara* encountered?" She felt a growing confidence and continued. "What of the bigger Oortians we know to exist, but have yet to encounter?"

Commander Lee glanced up from his task and shot the admiral a look of concern. Chen met the glance with agreement. "How do we scan for other potential enemies, Lieutenant?"

"Exhaust, sir. Every self-propelled entity excretes a byproduct or waste by simply burning or using some type of fuel."

Admiral Chen came close to releasing a smile, but kept it at bay. "Lieutenant Bai, you have access to all data on the Oortians. Form a team and find a method to scan for enemy threats. Report back to me within the hour." Chen followed the young officer while she did her best to mask the magnitude of his order, saluted and rushed off.

"Commander," Without a single vessel left from Captain Fei's battle-group, Admiral Chen had no reason to move, nowhere to hide. "Fleet formation, Tzu!"

"Yes, Admiral."

The Battle-Net would sound if anything moved in a way that did not conform to the known physics of space. What bothered Chen were these rules and principles were based on human experience, an experience that had no knowledge of a vast camouflaging field big enough to hide a solar system. And for how long? he thought. Before humans walked the Earth? The Oortians had caught him off-guard and it would not happen again.

Moments later Admiral Chen of the People's 10th Fleet watched his screen as twenty-nine heavily armed vessels positioned around his flagship, the *Qing Long*. The image of the vast black wall looking down upon his 10th Fleet seemed like a damn that could crumble at any moment, releasing a rushing river of Oortians.

So be it, Chen pondered, there is nowhere to run and nothing to hide behind out here but our multiple layers of plastic.

50

Captain Falco
Station Pluto

COMMANDER SHAR'RAN and Lieutenant Wallace sat quietly reading the encounter report from 10th Fleet while Captain Falco scanned the latest update on Station Pluto. The Pluto Room and now command center of the space station sat in shadows, the glow from the paper-thin screen lighting Falco's hardened features.

Satisfied with the station's progress, Falco looked up from his data-pad. "Just as we feared, battle group's Data-Pods were compromised."

"Worse," stated Wallace, "the Oortians somehow hacked into the unhackable, stole the encrypted Fleet signatures and stuck them on Hull Pounders."

"And our sensors let them walk on in," Commander Shar'ran added.

"We hope to fix that soon. Holts and Lieutenant Bai are on it."

Falco looked to Wallace. "Bring up the hologram of Station Pluto, Lieutenant."

Wallace shot Commander Shar'ran a sheepish look. Shar'ran stood, moved to the large tables control panel and sat down. Moments later the center of the table glowed bright and Station Pluto appeared, floating a meter above the cool surface.

Shar'ran raised an eyebrow toward Wallace who simply shrugged and proclaimed, "I fly spaceships."

Falco shook his head. "When this is over, Commander Shar'ran, could you please teach Lieutenant Wallace how to use the holo-feed."

"Not sure much more will fit in that thick skull of his, but I'll do my best, sir."

"Good." Falco stood and moved toward the hologram. "Magnify one point five times, Commander." Station Pluto grew so its edges hung over the table. Falco walked around the station with his hand brushing through the image of the newly created bunkers of the Infinity Hall.

"Chief Tenzin sent me his update while he's upgrading the mounts on the rail guns. All one hundred and fifty bunkers are in place and ready. Those crewing the bunkers need to suit up, tie in and hit the marked glass with the butt of their weapon, it's been cut almost through." Captain Falco grimaced, "And hold on until the bunker has equalized."

Lieutenant Wallace raised his hand.

"Speak freely, Lieutenant, there's only the three of us. Ensign Holts will make it for the end of the meeting."

"Why use the Infinity Hall when the level above is already compartmentalized into crew quarters?" Wallace paused. "And not to mention, the hull is thicker and stronger."

"Yes, Lieutenant, it is. But the hull would also fight against us as soon as we cut into it."

"Repair epoxy." Wallace swore under his breath.

"Infinity Wall itself gives up better line of sight for the small weapon systems, hell of a lot easier to cut through the poly-glass." Commander Shar'ran followed Captain Falco as he continued his circle around the hologram.

"Captain, may I ask what Ensign Holts is working on?" Shar'ran asked.

"Admiral Chen has an officer who thinks she may have a way of detecting the Oortians in open space. For all we know, the Oortian force that attacked the *Anam Cara* is one of many, sitting out here all around us, just waiting. Holts had a few theories so Admiral Chen asked for her help." Falco felt a hopeless silence consume the Pluto Room and found his chair.

Commander Shar'ran sat up straight. "As long as the dark field does not swallow us, being able to find an enemy that can completely shut down its systems to the point of leaving no signature, that would be helpful."

The hatch slid open and Ensign Holts burst into the Pluto Room holding a data-pad.

"I think we have a way!" Without waiting for a response, she moved toward Commander Shar'ran, pointing to his seat in front of the controls, "Commander?"

Shar'ran was up and sitting in the next chair over while Holts linked her data-pad to the holo-feed.

Captain Falco waited until he could see Ensign Holts was prepared. "Any time you're ready, Ensign."

"Lieutenant Bai is going over the report now with Admiral Chen."

Falco nodded and waited.

"At first Lieutenant Bai thought we could program the Fleet's sensors to detect the exhaust or waste created by the Oortians." Holts moved her hand and the *Anam Cara* replaced the Station Pluto hologram, the vessel floating in a sea of stars with four faint red dots off her port side.

"The Battle-Net optically detected exhaust trails when the *Anam Cara* made first contact. Though the autopsy created more questions than answers, one thing we feel strongly about is that Oortians use methane as fuel."

Captain Falco cut in, "Based on the methane trace left on sack of the Hull Pounder?"

"Correct, sir. The challenge is that if the Oortians have fully shut down their 'systems' they simply read as debris with no perceivable exhaust or energy signature." Ensign Holts gestured at the hologram of the *Anam Cara* with four faint red dots off her bow. "These," she stood up and placed her finger directly in front of the glowing dots, "are four Oortians powering up."

Commander Shar'ran leaned forward, squinting at the hologram. "But how does any of this help us detect the Oortians in open space when they are fully powered down?"

"Agreed," Falco said. "Where are you going with this, Ensign."

"Yes, Captain." Holts sat down, tapped on her data-pad. "Then we looked for shapes through the optical scanner." The hologram became a field of various sized objects. "Once again this could be any debris without a heat signature and even then..." Holts pointed to the four glowing red dots. "The size and shape of the Oortians could be an infinite number of things if they were fully shut down."

Holts tapped her controls.

"But this," stated Ensign Holts as the hologram turned into thousands of strings of numbers floating above the table.

"Beautiful!" exclaimed an excited Lieutenant Wallace. "How I miss those days."

"Yes, Lieutenant, this is one of the old navigation systems. And this is how we believe we can detect them." She motioned with her hand across her data-pad; the numbers zoomed in so only fifty number strings floated above the table.

Holts looked around the table at the three men locked onto the floating hologram. "As you all know, the old NAV systems were simple. Their only goal was to ensure the vessel didn't strike an object large enough to damage the hull." She stood up and moved to Captain Falco's side of the table.

"Each number represents the surface area of an object using meters squared. The NAV system automatically adjusted the course away from anything larger than a pebble or .000096774." She pointed at one number, 11,640.750912 that had four smaller numbers off to the left.

"That's the *Anam Cara*," Wallace stated with great pride. "Know that number anywhere!"

"They're the same." Falco slowly rose to his feet. "Could it be that simple? They are exactly the same. That's impossible." He stuck his finger into the hologram where the four numbers representing the Oortians hung next to the *Anam Cara*. "You're telling us that each," Falco searched for the right word, "variety of Oortian has the *exact...*" Falco let the word hang, "same surface area?"

Commander Shar'ran and Lieutenant Wallace moved to join him. Hanging next to the 11,640.750912 were four other number strings. Falco looked to Holts.

"Yes, Captain, they are exactly the same. 00.387096," she slowly read the number out loud. "Even the size of our own missiles fluctuates within a small measurable parameter. These four Oortians have precisely the same surface area even when we extend twenty places beyond the decimal. Their shapes vary slightly, but the surface area is exactly identical!"

"What about the Hull Pounders that hit the rail gun compartment," Falco swallowed hard, "the ones that killed my crewmembers?"

Ensign Holts looked to her data-pad. ".18580608. The Hull Pounders that hit the *Anam Cara* and 10th Fleet had an exact surface area of .18580608."

Commander Shar'ran shifted his gaze from Holts to the numbers of the hologram. "How is this possible? Even with our Nano-tech and the newest robotic production facilities, nothing produced is 'perfectly' the same. It is simply impossible for *anything* to be absolutely identical in any way."

"Yes, Commander. For humans, at this moment, it is impossible to reach perfection in production," Holts placed her hands in her lap, "but the Oortians can and in a very specific way, they have."

Falco leaned down towards the table, grabbing its thick top. "Can you create an upload for the Battle-Net that can scan specifically for these exact numbers?" Falco spoke in hushed tones.

"No," Ensign Holts leaned toward Falco, "but Lieutenant Bai can."

"Do it," Falco growled. "Admiral Chen and 10th Fleet are going to need it," he turned to face his officers, "and so will we."

Ensign Holts was up and on the move.

"Holts." Falco released a predatory grin as the ensign turned around. "Great work. You and Bai just moved the advantage back to our side."

Captain Fei
the Black Field

TWO MINUTES, fifty-eight seconds had passed without a sideways glance. Not even a heavy breath was audibly exhaled. The *Kwan Yin's* hull ceased to exist. Workstations attached to bulkheads floated in a sea of churning blackness. Crewman of the Viper class patrol boat sat strapped into chairs that hovered over a dark infinity.

Captain Yue Fei fought to keep his eyes open while his body desperately tried to moderate the avalanche of stimuli coming at him from all sides. His mind needed a reprieve from the vertigo. I must show strength.

Hands flew to mouths in unison. Two young crewmen reached for vomit-bags in time and soundlessly leaned towards the bags sealed over their mouths. Shame embedded on their faces. Fei recognized the look, a need to apologize but having no means to do so.

A moment later he stood and moved across an invisible deck.

He walked on a slow swirling current of oily-black cloud. He kept his eyes locked on his crew to ensure his feet would naturally find the unseen deck below them.

Glossy eyes met Captain Fei's arrival. The two young officers sat in shame, the stench from the contents of their stomachs slowly filtering out of the command center. The *Kwan Yin's* systems were running at minimal life support levels and the smell lingered far longer than it should have.

For the first time since engaging the Virtual Surround Vision, the crew of the *Kwan Yin* had stopped staring at the foreign matter that enshrouded their boat. With hands clutching anything visible at their stations, they turned towards their captain's motion, watching the god-like movements of a man suspended over a swirling nothingness that shifted between absolute black and charcoal gray, the colors so similar it was hard to tell the difference except for the flow of motion between them.

Fei rested a powerful hand on each of their shoulders and gave them a simple nod. He watched the shame leave their faces. Time, he thought, striding back to the Battle-Net station and Commander Zhu, we only need a few more moments for the mind to adjust to its new environment. The human body is resilient. It was already happening as he noticed subtle differences in the field's oily composition, shading... it was strangely beautiful and menacing at the same time.

"Sir, now may be our only chance to take a sample. Use the grappling-bot." Commander Zhu kept his voice low.

Captain Fei nodded toward his commander who sent the order to the maintenance crew in storage bay. Fei remained locked onto the changing, swirling mass outside the *Kwan Yin*. Soon we may know some of your secrets. Soon we may know the order and scale of your building blocks... or nothing at all. He found his captain's chair and sat down, still following the swirling shadows moving around and beyond his hull. I can hear it, Fei thought, no, he reconsidered, I can feel it moving around us, studying each weld on the thousands of poly-plates or inspecting the damage from the destroyed COM-Sat. It felt like sand on an open wound.

The image of the bot scooping up that primordial soup scared the hell out of Fei. What would they find? He was far from a scientist and barely a student of the sciences, but he knew the pure simplicity of the universe. Currently, there were 136 elements in the periodic table with 101 found or occurring on Earth. He felt the gnawing sense that humanity's best attempts at creating a system of classification for the universe in which their microscopic blue planet called home, was about to be shattered.

And such are the ways of a fledgling species, Fei pondered. But can we adapt fast enough in this situation to find a way to save ourselves? A heaviness hung on his face while he pondered the past for an answer to the future. What Fei found was not hopeful. Visibly shaking his head, he focused on the moment, his boat and the lives of his young crew.

A hatch slid open and a tall, lanky crewman cautiously entered the bridge. He stopped in front of Captain Fei, his eyes never leaving his perfectly polished, black boots that were a stark contrast to the grease and grime smeared on his uniform. The crewman leaned in and began whispering to Captain Fei. Finally, Fei nodded and the crewman left the bridge. Fei looked toward a waiting Commander Zhu sitting tensely in front of the glowing battle screen.

Fei held up a single fist, turned it and extend his thumb straight up. Zhu turned and tapped at his data-pad. Minutes later the dimly lit screen filled with streaming data.

The results of the sample were already being analyzed.

52

Tzara Creator of the Prox
Leader of the Creators
Planet Tzara

TZARA'S LEAN, black form drifted in the open territories, her plated carapace hanging just outside of the Darkness. She looked upon the twelve worlds that circled the mighty twin stars. The warmth of their fire kept at bay by the clear field that surrounded them. The Darkness ebbed and flowed at the edges, providing protection from those that lived and killed in the Void far beyond, but always looking like it would rush in and consume the bright open space that it shielded.

Each planet revolved at its own speed, a speed chosen by the Creator that managed it. Each world designed to provide safe harbor for the unique clan that called it home. Like the fiery twin stars, each world had its own field that provided precisely what it required for optimum production. A spike of remorse pulsed through Tzara's systems. As perfect as these worlds are, many of the clans born to them would never see them again.

Instead, they now sit idle in the Darkness or at its border with the Void. Defenders hunkered in the cold. Alone in the dark they sat, Prox, Warruq and that which was hidden for the times when more was needed to protect the territories. A life of waiting... that drove many of them insane, their warrior's rage almost uncontrollable. But that is exactly what Tzara wanted, what the Creators needed to ensure the defense of the vast frontier along the border between the Darkness and the deadly and infinite Void.

Tzara initiated a quick, energy bloom pulse, propelling her into the mass of the Darkness, but still keeping her optical sensors in the open. She could now swim and pulled back with her fins, effortlessly skimming the interior Veil. The planet of the Warruq passed in front of her. Even with the parameters in place, the massive rock always looked as if it would smash into the smaller, gas world of the Krell. The twelve worlds moved in a frenetic dance. Each turning, whirling in a slightly different orbit that avoided collisions at the last possible cycle. Even the vast, twin stars adjusted every few millions of cycles to avoid consuming one of the planets.

How the Darkness could control such things was even beyond Tzara's reach, beyond her known history and that of all the Creators, or simply kept from their memory. But she knew the clear fields that surround each world and the twin stars were somehow part of the Darkness. Soon the meeting of the Creators would begin and it was time for her to go back to her own world, a world of vapor and iron. The planet of the Prox, where Tzara created all in her image.

Almost, she thought as she locked her plates and hardened her carapace. Tzara would always be the largest of her kind and always the strongest. Creators had the right, it was meant to be. She fired a quick energy bloom and moved further into the Darkness. Quickly Tzara unlocked her plates, softened her carapace, extended her fins again and pushed toward her planet's known location. The only world without rotation, without an orbit and the only light source was the planet itself. A tiny creature had survived on her world. Tzara's optical sensors had never seen the minuscule life form, but it covered the planet's surface like a glowing dust that could be wiped away for a moment only to return in the next.

Nearing her world, again she strengthened her long, sleek carapace, each plate clicking and locking into the next creating an itch that worked its way from top to bottom. A warmth washed over her upon entering the protective field, the cold grip of the Darkness gave way to the warmth of Tzara's atmosphere. Finally, she passed through a dense gaseous cloud and the glow of the world lit her path.

The other twelve Creators would soon arrive at Tzara's ancient planet. The planet cloaked and hidden within the Darkness and the oldest among the worlds of the Creators, each named after its lord and master. A private planet for each to spawn a clan in their own image, A clan to protect its world and the territories they passed through while orbiting the twin stars. Planet Tzara sat entombed in the Darkness, hidden from the other Creators' worlds that spun in light and heat, in the open.

The twelve have left the territories and entered the Darkness... soon they will arrive. Tzara recognized it was not a personal thought, nor a newly opened thought-stream, as the Creators did not need them to communicate. Thought-streams were for the clans, another means to control and monitor their masses.

It was the Darkness, pushing itself into her awareness, gentle yet persistent. We have been together since our beginnings so many cycles ago. Tzara was no longer sure where she began or the Darkness ended. It was why Tzara was the leader of the Creators, the twelve knew she spoke for the Darkness, she had chosen Tzara to lead.

Twelve fiery streaks appeared far above her lair, each protective pod passing through the planets field and entering the upper atmosphere of the gas giant world known as Tzara. The Creators would come together for the second time in the billions of cycles of their existence. Another enemy had invaded their growing territories.

This new threat came from the far side of the Territories where their Warruq defenders were few. A place thought to be safe and of little threat. An area with a single planet pulsed with the basic waves of a beginning civilization of little significance. Waves that billions of cycles ago, the Creators themselves, used to communicate, before they realized the waves carried far into the Void where others could detect them and follow them back to their origin. This was how the first conflict began so long ago.

This fledgling civilization was now stretching its reach far beyond its world. The Creators underestimated this new rival and its stationary structures that hung in the Void. Tzara once warned the Creators the latest glowing sphere was far too close to their territories. But the twelve would not listen, always avoiding conflict until clans were sent to the Realm of Warriors in numbers that filled the Darkness with their shattering remains.

How could this new enemy extinguish entire clans in battle when their invading forces were so few? Tzara let the thought fade, a discussion that can wait for the gathering.

They are here. The Darkness pushed the thought into Tzara's systems.

An image appeared on the face of the protective field that formed the exterior wall of her lair. Twelve smoking pods of various shapes and sizes rose and fell with each passing wave of the hydrogen sea that broke their decent. The pods slowly turned until each Creator, protected deep in their fleshy womb was positioned for the short journey.

A searing flash of anger and malice surged through Tzara. With it, an idea, but whose idea, she was no longer alone, no longer in control of her own thoughts... or was it a need...

destroy them all, they are vulnerable, trapped in their protective pods. The Creators snaked their way closer and Tzara's rage subsided, leaving her to her own thoughts. The Darkness released her.

Hovering inside her lair, Tzara prepared to begin the gathering and with it, the development of a plan to extinguish this new enemy that dared to enter the Darkness. Another idea moved through Tzara, the Darkness flowing into her memory. *I will expand my mass and consume more territory. The Creators will follow.*

Tzara needed a stronger leader among the Clans. Aris the Chosen One was weak, she thought of herself as unique and was beginning to believe it. Aris had become dangerous and reckless. The Darkness would take care of her, when the moment was right.

It was time to awaken the fallen. An ancient Creator who long ago lead the clans and was the hero of the Dakkadian War until her desire for power twisted her into a being that could not be tolerated. Banished and caged by the Darkness herself, it was time to release Kalis. The Darkness could control her while she traveled within her mass, but once she reached the Void, Kalis would be unleashed upon the enemy and neither the Darkness or Creators would be able to completely control her. Kalis was needed to destroy this powerful invader and if all went as planned, she would be destroyed in battle and travel to the Realm of Warriors, her oath fulfilled.

53

Captain Falco
Space Station Pluto

CAPTAIN JACK FALCO sat motionless in the Pluto Room while the rest of the station was abuzz with activity. Every able-bodied person was at task working to turn Station Pluto into a defensible, Battle Station. Which is critical, Falco thought, but the upload for the Battle-Net conceived by Ensign Holts and programmed by Lieutenant Bai of 10th Fleet could ensure that the Oortians could at least be detected outside of their dark field.

Chief Pema Tenzin was hanging on every word that left Ensign Sierra Holts's mouth while she explained the upload. "In open space," she was restating, "it simply tells our sensors to compare the surface area of all objects within its reach. If any are an exact match, which is statistically near impossible, the Battle-Net will lock onto them and sound a warning."

Falco could see Ensign Holts was exhausted but he remained silent and ran his hand along the smooth, dreaded plastic edge of the slab-table that consumed the center of the Pluto Room. Falco reached towards the center and brushed the pads of his fingers across the small black box that linked the Pluto Room with Lieutenant Bai on Admiral Chen's flagship. "Even this is god damn plastic," he grumbled

"Captain?" Ensign Holts looked his way.

"Sorry, Ensign." Falco held up a hand, turned back toward the table, mentally dusted off his Mandarin and leaned in, as close as he could get and bellowed into the black case still under hand, sure the device could not hear him.

"Lieutenant Bai." He needed another voice of assurance the 'upload' would work.

"Yes, Captain Falco?" answered Bai in perfect English.

"Are you willing to bet your life and that of every crewman in 10th Fleet and Station Pluto?" Captain Falco remained focused on the COM-Box. "Are you certain that your upload will detect the Oortians when lives depend on it?"

"Yes, Captain. The 'upload' will detect the Oortians identical surface area and that is all it will do."

"Detecting objects sharing identical surface area is our best data-driven option, Captain." Ensign Sierra Holts chimed in, "And Lieutenant Bai's 'upload' will do this."

"Good." Falco leaned back hard on his chair, lacing his fingers behind his head. "Let's get the 'upload' to Admiral Chen. The Battle-Net on the *Qing Long* can encrypt it and send it to the rest of 10th Fleet's boats. Lieutenant Bai." Falco paused then decided, "Send Station Pluto the 'upload' in a Data-Pod ASAP. I want it protected from prying sensors, even on our side of the Oortian field."

"Yes, Captain Falco, I will send it via Data-Pod, but…" Bai fell silent.

"Lieutenant?" Falco had a good idea what she was thinking.

"Captain, the Oortians were able to access the encrypted signatures of our Data-Pods—"

"Why does it matter how we send the uploads?" Falco finished.

"Correct, Captain," stated Bai.

"Lieutenant, we have no idea how the Oortians accessed our pod signatures, so for now, we do what we can."

———

FALCO MARVELED at Ensign Holts's laser-like focus on the COM-Box centered on the massive poly-slab table of the Pluto Room. The rest of his officers were checking and rechecking every added weld, weapon and oxygen line of the newly christened, Battle Station Pluto. Admiral Chen continued to grill Ensign Holts from his command ship the *Qing Long* that sat in the center of 10th Fleet and stood between Falco's jerry-rigged battle station and the Oortians' black field.

Holts stood confident, hands grabbing the smooth poly-slab as she leaned toward the squawking COM-Box that had finally fell silent. "All I can tell you, Admiral Chen, is that we have uploaded the sensor upgrade. It looks to be working as programmed, the data shows the area around Station Pluto is clear."

Falco looked over to his science officer and the co-creator of the aptly named Oortian Detector. Ensign Holts held his gaze and nodded.

More a sign of support than confidence Falco thought, as I would feel a hell of a lot more confident in the 'upload' if it found enemies in waiting, but what if there were only one? As long as the 'one' had already been found by prior scans, its surface area would be documented and added to the Battle-Net database.

A first contact, a single mass without others to compare it to, would be a problem. Cross that bridge when and if it came. At the same time, he was ecstatic that their piece of deep space was

Oortian free. Admiral Chen barked another question and a poised Ensign Holts continued to answer after each pause.

The principle of the Oortian Detector was brilliant in its simplicity. By sheer luck, no Falco thought, it was not luck. It was Ensign Holts looking through fields of data and having the ability to find something out of place.

The COM-Box rumbled, Chen breaking the silence. "You and Lieutenant Bai both assured me this 'upload' will work." Chen exhaled like a man without choices. "The 'upload' is in progress and we have nothing to lose, everything to gain. You have answered all I need, Ensign. Do you have anything to add?"

For the first time Ensign Holts looked unsure, caught off guard. As well she should, Falco thought, Admiral Chen rarely asks for additional information he did not have the acumen to ask for himself.

Holts quickly gathered herself. "We estimate the range of the sensor upload to be the equivalent of the long-range debris scanners." Holts did her best to keep the uncertain tone out of her speech. "2500 to 3000 klicks line of sight, Admiral."

"How certain are you?" Chen paused. "Of the range?"

Holts turned and shot a questioning look toward Falco, "Seventy percent, Admiral, but the 'upload' should be effective at the same distance as our debris scanners."

"Hmmm." Admiral Chen's breath came rasping over the COM-Box. "The debris fields in the outer solar system are vast, Ensign Holts. The Kuiper Belt alone is constantly pushing and pulling objects in and out of its influence."

The three officers fell into silence, Falco found himself staring at the COM-Box with Ensign Holts.

"Continue your preparation of Station Pluto, Captain Falco," Chen stated. "Captain, we will keep an open-COM to the station and the *Anam Cara* for as long as we are able. There is no help out here, it is left to us, here, now."

The COM-Box light's green glow faded to black.

"Seventy percent?" Falco stood, looking intensely at Ensign Holts. "That it will scan 2,500 to 3,000 klicks and detect Oortians that are completely powered down?" His jaw tightened, "or that it will work at all?"

"Yes, Captain, I am seventy percent certain that the sensor upload will detect Oortians within the range of our long-range scanners."

Falco swallowed hard. "Good enough."

5 4

the Creators
Planet Tzara

THE ELEVENTH SHIELDING pod moved through the field and into the protected chamber of Tzara's lair. Moments later the smoldering shell split and released its contents.

Welcome, Creator of the Warruq. Tzara towered over the being that bowed ever so slightly to the leader of the Creators. His carapace wet, glistening from the dampness, appendages hanging loosely with each sinewy length tipped with an almost indestructible piercing end. The Warruq were the foulest of all the clans and by far the most deadly, but also the easiest to control. Warrior's pride was everything to them.

One left. Tzara knew the Creator of the Krell would be last and make an entrance for the rest to remember. Flames erupted outside the protective field; a massive pod lay just beyond her lair's protective veil. Tzara moved back and made room for the last Creator to arrive. Her grand entrance would consist of crossing from the harsh elements into Tzara's protective lair, and she hoped the pain would make the beast whimper.

The giant smoldering pod cracked then shattered. The Creator of the Krell hovered, her massive orb of sloughing flesh turning her shape oblong without the frame of her pod to support her girth. Storm-pushed crystals plunged deep into her layered mass, creating a thousand wounds and sadly, Tzara thought, without the slightest whimper. Through the protective field she pushed as slowly as she could until her towering form stood far above the rest.

Better than expected, Creator of the Krell, thought Tzara, one day you may rise and lead the Creators. But only if the Darkness allows it. *Welcome great Creator of the Krell.*

The vast glistening orb shook ever so slightly. Tzara moved a fin in a circular motion. The thirteen Creators slowly moved into a circle, floating higher or sinking depending on their importance among the group. Tzara was the highest followed by the Creator of the Krell then the Creator of the Warruq. The remaining ten hung below them, equals with a vote in matters, but having only a single voice, the Speaker of the Ten.

Tzara began the meeting. *The voices, our new enemy stands in the open prepared to attack or invade the territories. The Darkness has expanded her protective reach as far as her resources allow. She cannot overtake and surround the second fleet that closes in on our border.*

But they will not leave, the Creator of the Krell echoed through the chamber. *They look to invade our system. They have destroyed our clans in numbers that will take millions of cycles to replace.*

A hum grew from the ten Creators below. They search for a resolution, Tzara thought, an answer to the invading enemy that carries powerful weapons. Weapons it used without hesitation. A sign of a conquering civilization that must be dealt with. Below her, the hum from the ten Creators changed, pulsated which signaled each was following a separate and private conclusion to an idea or a solution. Tzara waited, the volume from the ten increased, decreased and finally, they succinctly fell silent.

As was the tradition, the three most powerful Creators remained quiet. The Speaker of the Ten would provide the first option. Her clan were builders, her carapace was small, but from this round shell grew huge appendages, thick and powerful for lifting and towing. She was larger than the Warruq but peaceful and kind. She raised the skull plate out of her shell and communicated for the Ten.

We have grown the territories as far as our resources will allow. The Speaker looked to the three Creators. *Prox, Krell, Warruq and even some of the lower clans have fulfilled their Oaths to us and traveled to the Realm of Warriors in our defense and preservation. If too many are lost, we become vulnerable to this new enemy with its formidable weapons and what if the Dakkadians return to the furthest frontier?*

Tzara clicked the thick plates under her head, a sign of respect. *If too many are lost,* she pushed her long carapace forward, floating above the others in the center of their circle, *the clans may begin to question their purpose and then they will begin to question ours.*

The hum of the Ten began anew while they searched for a solution to this new and alien threat. Now Tzara or the other highest-ranking Creators could speak freely.

The Darkness cannot be extended beyond its current borders until our resources are replenished. We need her protection from our enemy's weapons, they are too powerful. We must move the clans within the mass of the Darkness. Tzara waited.

Feed the Darkness! The Creator of the Krell bellowed in deep, wet rasps. Feed her the weaker clans! The lower clans! The worker clans! Use their mass to protect the warrior clans! And grow the Darkness!

The ten Creators shot towards the Creator of the Krell who

met their tentacles, fins and bony spikes in the center of the circle with her fleshy mass glowing and ready to ignite.

Enough! Tzara roared, the Creators stopped their aggressive posturing and slowly reformed the circle. *The Darkness will have its resources soon enough! The clans will meet the enemy in the Void as we did in the days of old, when we were a single clan with a lone world without the protection of the Darkness.* She looked down on the twelve Creators, pushing herself higher above them. *The clans are needed, their moment has arrived and they will earn the right to travel to the Realm of Warriors. They will fight in the Void and we will expand the territories!*

That is not enough. The Speaker of the Ten moved toward the middle of the circle, hovering below Tzara. *A chance to reach the Realm of Warriors will spur the bloodlust and warrior's rage in many, but the clans will need protection in the Void.*

The Darkness is not ready to expand, Speaker of the Ten. Tzara lowered herself and looked directly into the ocular sensors beneath her curved skull plate. The Leader of Ten was Creator of the Chakook clan. Peaceful builders, but they were also willful. Tzara's lower carapace hung below the Speaker's thick appendages that could carry and move immense amounts of material. They were miners and builders, engineers and farmers. Without the Chakook, all the Creators' worlds would be barren, without structure, food or minerals. And they were almost impossible to kill... almost, Tzara thought, floating back to her position above the group.

The Speaker of the Ten began thumping her thick limbs together, faster and faster. Here it comes, Tzara waited, the drumming and pounding speeding to a deep drone. Say it, Speaker of the Ten, let it be your idea, you will close the circle and the Creators will be as one.

The droning stopped. *Yes, mighty Tzara, your Darkness awaits its feeding. But we still have our shields and their endless stalks, and the warrior strongholds they carry!* The Creator of the Chakook clan raised her stout limbs and began to spin in the center of the group. *Release the shields! Release the shields!* she spat, spinning faster and faster, creating a living tool that could dig through rock, ice and ore.

Tzara curiously watched the display below her. The spinning blur of the Speaker of the Ten slowed her rotation. Tzara was impressed with the needed spectacle. *I will release the shields and the clans will use their massive cover and immense resources to reach the enemy in the Void.* Tzara looked to the Creator of the Warruq. *And a LOR will lead them!*

Plates clicked, bony spikes clattered and flesh vibrated; Tzara worked the Creators into a blind warrior's rage. She clicked her chest plates, hardened her carapace, did everything she knew the uncontrollable warrior's rage would cause. Tzara sensed the drip and tight push of the thick substance beginning to course through her systems and she remained completely in control while the Creators below her could barely keep from killing one another. She slowed her movements, relaxed her armored plates, and the Creators followed until all was quiet, the stench of gasses and fluids from them, filling Tzara's lair.

The clans will die – the thought hung in Tzara's mind, plucked and placed there by another. She was here, the Darkness was in control. *You will die by the thousands and your broken, ragged remains will replenish my resources and I will grow.*

55

LOR and the Shields
the Darkness

THE UPLOAD from the Creators slowed, pulsed and stopped. The eldest of the living Warruq was now elevated to LOR, his time had come to lead the clans after endless cycles waiting in the Frontier. The Creators had already released the ancient shields and soon the massive guardians would carry thousands of warriors from many of the clans into the great Void. The shields' protection came at a cost.

LOR had swum under one of the massive shields after his awakening millions of cycles ago and followed its protected umbilical stalk to his own warrior stronghold. There were many of the beasts then but now only a few were left. Shields consumed far more sustenance than the Darkness could provide.

LOR fired a quick energy bloom and left the edge of the Void and entered the Darkness. A current formed and carried LOR at incredible speeds. He hardened his carapace and drew in his appendages. The mass of the current thickened and slowed his pace. LOR crossed a vast black arching plain. His journey continued in front of a shadow the size of a small moon, only the slightest bit darker than the Darkness herself, but there it was, the shield's protective plate.

The current slowed, carrying LOR across the surface of the shield and finally dropped off the edge and flowed to the center of its soft fleshy underside, releasing LOR at the stalk. Warrior strongholds were clustered beginning at the base of the stalk where it connected to the underside of the shield until the stalk ended far below. Each sac would only open for its intended warrior.

The cool mass of the Darkness rejuvenated LOR's systems, coursing through every joint of his armored carapace. He softened his carapace, extended his appendages and allowed them to be taken in the current, freely moving while the current spiraled down the shield's stalk, passing grouping after grouping of various sized pods.

Too many cycles, LOR thought, too long since he last moved through her healing mass. His Warruq clan spent most of their time positioned outside of the Darkness just beyond her Veil, only returning for fuel and the gases for their respiration.

The Darkness diluted the current he rode to a gray mist, enabling the clans following the stalks to their protected strongholds to see. His optical sensors were able to pick up endless faint shadows while his warrior's migration continued. Pride filled his systems, the Warruq clans were well represented.

He toggled between the open thought-stream that allowed him to track the locations and movements of his clans and his own private stream. The ability to use his vision within the Darkness, even poorly, had rarely been allowed, but she gives us a gift on our way to destroy the invaders.

Her secrets were her own, but the Darkness had always aided

the Warruq clans. There were even legends of her bringing back the most heroic of the fighters from the Realm of Warriors. After millions of cycles the Warruqs had learned many things. Each lesson aided the whole and filtered back to the Creators and their clans through the Darkness herself. LOR slowed his sinewy-appendages until their movement ceased and the flowing mist of the Darkness slid over and around his plated carapace. Slowly turning, LOR took in the shield's stalk. Infinite fibrous tendrils woven and braided into an endless, living trunk. Even the warrior strongholds moved, pulsed and expanded with life. Interesting, LOR pondered, the small fibers that created the stalk looked similar to his own, smaller, but the shape was exact.

LOR's muscles contracted and stretched as instinct pushed past curiosity and again he was pushing his fins ahead of the smoky flow. Another gelatinous group of pods clung to the massive stalk. Each orb contained precisely enough room for its designed contents to fit within its protective walls. Each orb constricted and stretched to its contents mass.

LOR slowed as one of the empty spheres was sized for a Warruq, but again this was not his stronghold. The orifice that lay at the strongholds furthest point from the stalk did not open at his arrival, so he pushed on without the aid of the Darkness, as she no longer gave him a current to ride.

Shadows loomed ahead and LOR came upon a cluster of mammoth strongholds. He swam close to the outer layer and the stench of fear filled his sensors. They were Krell and would play a key role in the coming battle. Knowing these tortured creatures were part of the attack was comforting, but realizing there was an entire planet of them was not.

LOR learned much of these abominations from the history of the previous engagement. An engagement that silenced his predecessor's thought-stream. Krell were powerful creatures that must be honored for their strength and pitied for their cowardice. There is something else; LOR came to a gliding stop above another of the large orbs.

He gently settled into its gelatinous skin, allowing his carapace to sink into its wet, spongy armor. The emanating fear was clouding its thoughts, but there are distinct and separate thought-streams within. LOR remained still and quieted his systems, rotating through the millions of thought-streams that flowed through the territories; each connecting various clans and groups for different purposes.

Twelve, there are twelve joined with this Krell. No, he thought, they are inside of it. There are twelve Seekers inside of this Krell. Prox would fight to the death before giving their Seekers to another. How this was possible or why, LOR had no collective knowledge of, another first by the Creators.

As was its duty, the Krell's stronghold released LOR from its life sustaining armor. The Darkness consumed the sticky layer left by the stronghold on the front of his carapace and LOR continued to follow the shield's stalk, searching for his own stronghold.

Pride filled his thoughts and LOR quickly switched to the open thought-stream, he wanted all the clans to know of his position. Directly in front of him stood the last pod on the stalk and the final warrior stronghold. A great honor bestowed on the bravest of warriors, the stronghold was furthest from the vast protective shield built of the Creators ultimate armor. LOR hardened his own carapace, clicking his armored plates to pay homage to the great Shield that carried the clans of the Darkness safely through the Void and smashed through their enemies.

A single stronghold sized for a Warruq, the leader's position. The orifice opened and LOR, leader of all the Warruq clans pushed through the narrow entrance. The opening sealed the moment his last appendage moved inside, then flashed open, belched out the Darkness within and closed. The protective sac adjusted to its contents then hardened into a protective shell.

FAR BELOW LOR's stronghold sac, the shield's stalk continued through the churning mass of the Darkness and ended in the territories where the planets of the Creators orbited their fiery twin stars in open space. The ends of seven other stalks joined it, each swaying a great distance from the other in the confluence where the open space of the Clans Territories ended and the Darkness began.

In the great-open, eight creatures the size of small moons, ignited a full energy bloom and freed themselves from their orbit around their home world. Streams of flame shot from behind them, lighting the dead space while they moved toward the swaying ends. Each of the creations known only as Movoo, slowed their colossal bulk by cutting their burn, rotating and sporadically firing their heat bloom in the opposite direction until each was positioned under a stalk.

They attached to the swaying umbilicals, adjusted their positions and ignited a full energy bloom. Each Movoo shook and vibrated, their thick, layered hide rippling with the force of their heat bloom pushing from underneath. Each stalk tightened its endless web of fibers. Fractions of cycles passed and stalks began to move.

The Darkness welcomed the eight Movoo and the shields they pushed by thinning her mass and creating currents to speed their movement toward the Void. Each shield protected and concealed a stalk with hundreds of stronghold sacs attached.

LOR OPENED his systems to the pleasing pressure of the stronghold. Where his carapace started and stopped was impossible to tell, the fitting of the protective shell was designed for the mass of a Warruq and then adjusted to LOR's individual shape. The drip of the warrior's rage began as it always did before a battle. The gentle movement of the mighty shield pushing through the Darkness only added to his stimulation while the drip of the warrior's rage fueled his need for battle and the opportunity to reach the Realm of Warriors.

56

Captain Fei
the Black Field

CAPTAIN FEI WIPED his dripping brow. The dark field swirled and flowed around the *Kwan Yin*, the lone surviving vessel of 10th Fleet's Viper class battle group. He feared running on anything more than emergency power. Most sensors would only show his boat as a minimal heat signature, similar to those created by a thousand different scenarios on the edge of the solar system. But this scenario was different. Whatever or whoever hunted the *Kwan Yin* had never been seen or dealt with before.

He pushed up and away from his captain's chair and moved across the bridge toward his pilot. The Virtual Surround Vision was almost feeling normal, he thought, except for the motion sickness induced by the ever-moving dark field that rushed around them.

His pilot estimated the *Kwan Yin* was anywhere from ten to five hundred klicks from the entry point into the enemy's camouflaging field. It was little more than a best guess based on systems that could only read a meter off the hull, after that the black field blocked everything. And what if the field had moved again, would they notice or see it?

If they had a chance to make a run at open space Captain Fei needed to know how far they would travel blind in the field. But, he pondered, we have no weapons and if the enemy is blind within the field as well, we are safer to remain hidden.

Fei focused on the far bulkhead. His peripheral vision continued to take in the swirling black and dark grays of the murkiness that surrounded them. He made his way towards his science officer who continued to pour over the streaming data from the processing sample taken from the field. It flowed across his screens in waves of formulas and symbols. Captain Fei stood behind him, seeming to float over a dark storm.

The officer's eyes jumped from screen to screen, while the underpowered Battle-Net processed the sample at a slower, but efficient rate. Every few minutes a number dropped out of the streaming data into a dimly lit square on the bottom of the center screen. A few minutes later and the fallen digit had a decimal number attached to it.

Captain Fei watched as one of humanity's greatest achievement, the Battle-Net, continued to process the sample of the dark field. The Battle-Net was based on the recent TERRA Computer designed and used for the 2217 Global Species Survey (GSS'17). The supercomputer processed twelve months of data compiled from every conceivable means of gathering information from outer space to the ocean floor and everything in between.

In the end, the data from the GSS supported the growing thesis that the Earth, losing half its population in the 2214 terrorist attack was now able to heal itself due to humanity's population base being forced into a sustainable model. Scientists had estimated there were nine million species. The TERRA Computer recorded and identified over thirty-two million species living in, around and with Homo sapiens.

And now we can add a few others to that list, Fei thought, seeing another number drop to the glowing box, plucked from the stream of data that continued to drift across the monitors. Seconds later .00023 was added behind it. The *Kwan Yin's* science officer remained focused on his screens, occasionally writing down a number or sequence that was of interest.

Suddenly he stopped, turned and looked at Fei, paused and quickly shot forward and began writing again. Fei leaned closer to the monitors. The officer motioned him downward.

He spoke in a barely audible whisper. "Normal exterior hull temperature this far from our sun should be thirty-five to forty Kelvin."

Fei raised both hands, palms up, confused.

"Negative 250 degrees Celsius," whispered the officer.

The science officer raised a finger, pointing to one of the numbers he had just written down. 275.15 was underlined twice.

"That's Kelvin, sir." He scratched down another number. "*Kwan Yin's* exterior hull temperature is 2 Celsius."

That is impossible, Fei thought. We are nowhere near a sun or any known heat source. Even our cutting-edge solar skins were straining to filter radiation from any spectrums before we entered the black field.

The oxygen was sucked out of the bridge. The black field surrounding them thinned to a gray mist seconds before a vast shadow pushed past the starboard side of the *Kwan Yin*.

Captain Fei caught the flash of red from the Battle-Net station and hurried toward Commander Zhu.

"Captain, Battle-Net sensors now have a limited ten-klick range, partial scan of eight objects, starboard side, each similar shape, but larger than Station Pluto."

Fei caught a panicked motion and found his science officer waving an arm.

"Keep tracking them, Commander, as long as we can," Fei ordered and moved back across the bridge.

"Analysis is complete, sir. Wait..." The science officer's station started scrolling data again and it streamed across each monitor. "The Battle-Net is updating the analysis based on the new sensor range. We should get a better breakdown of the sample if we obtain additional data on a larger area." The data stopped. "It's complete, Captain. Or at least finished for now."

Fei was tired of focusing on each whispered syllable, it was exhausting and scary as hell. "Let's hear it."

"Black field sample assessment: *UNKNOWN ELEMENT. COMPARABLE DOCUMENTED EQUIVALENT: MARINE ENVIRONMENT, MARIANAS TRENCH, WESTERN PACIFIC OCEAN.*"

Fei pointed at the now gray mist beyond. "You're telling me this," he paused and looked out at the shifting shadows beyond their hull, "field... beyond Pluto... is comparable to the deepest ocean waters of Earth? An 'environment,' not something off the periodic table or a substance?"

The officer turned and looked directly at Captain Fei. "Yes."

"A marine environment?" Fei looked at his science officer. "How does the Battle-Net define it?"

The officer entered the term and the answer scrolled across the main monitor.

SEA OR OCEAN INHABITED BY ONE OR MORE SPECIES

Captain Falco
Battle Station Pluto

FALCO SAT heavy on his bunk staring at the shaking glass in his trembling hand. He grabbed the scotch bottle on the steel fold-down-table next to his bed and left the bottle in the air a bit longer to get the heavy pour he needed. His breath came in quick puffs only stopping when gulping his scotch.

When it starts, this may be the last peaceful moment I have left, he thought. The storm is close and we are as ready as we can be. So, we wait.

A gentle rhythm wrapped on the hatch. An unintended smile pulled at his unshaven jawline and his hands steadied. Only his officers knew he was on the *Anam Cara*, tucked deep inside Station Pluto, hoping to steal an hour of peace in his personal quarters.

"Enter Ensign Holts." He added his usual grit for show, but Falco was happy to see her. A muffled thump sounded and the hatch slid open. Holts stood in the opening, a tall elegant form pushed in all the right directions. Her snug uniform only accentuated her natural gifts. Her collar was unbuttoned; a sure sign Holts was off duty and also intent on finding a moment of peace.

"In or out, Ensign." Falco reached for another glass. "Either way, close the hatch."

Holts took a step forward and pushed the release. The door hissed shut and she stood in silence, eyes scanning her captain's quarters.

Falco started to laugh. "Smaller than you remember?" He poured three fingers for his guest. "I think it was once maintenance storage. You know I couldn't pass up the location."

Holts smiled. "This is not the usual placement for the captain's quarters."

"Ah, but then I am more of a back of the boat type of captain." Falco found her presence more than comforting. Sierra Holts rarely ventured to the stern of the boat and this was only one of a handful of times she stood inside Falco's private room since they left Earth over five years ago. The other times were purely professional, an on-duty officer with a question for her off-duty captain. This time was different.

"How did you know it was me, Jack?"

Falco swallowed hard at hearing her use his first name. "Here, Sierra," Falco made a grand gesture with his free hand, "in these lands, the United Nations and its Navy do not exist."

He held out a glass, pulled out the chair that lay hidden under the steel desktop connected to the bulkhead. Sierra smoothly took the glass and pushed the chair back under the desktop.

"Slide over."

Falco's body moved before his mind deciphered the order. Her natural scent was intoxicating. She simply smelled right, Falco thought as he took another drink and watched Sierra take a sip followed by her tongue sliding across perfect lips.

"You never answered my question. How did you know it was me?"

Falco again found it impossible not to smile. She was a strong soul and one of the few that found peace in conversational pauses. Sierra could remain quiet while maintaining full eye contact far longer than he was comfortable. Most would take her silence as a method of manipulation or a power play similar to that used by Admiral Chen. Falco knew the woman well enough to understand its natural role within her character.

"Your knock." Falco moved the glass under his nose, inhaled deeply. He had smuggled five cases of the finest single malt onto the *Anam Cara* from the Mars Station and it had not disappointed. He glanced towards the corner of the room, taking great pride at the site of the large wooden crate strapped to the bulkhead.

"My knock? You can determine who is at your hatch by the knock?" Sierra looked to the hatch and slowly moved the glass towards her lips.

"Well, there's the walk up to the hatch, the length of the pause prior to the knock, and the knock itself… knuckles, fist or a back of the hand tap."

"Which tells you it's me?"

Falco's eyes fell to his glass, and the now steady hand that held it. He turned, their faces only centimeters apart. "The sound of your uniform on your hips as you walk, a light, yet purposeful footfall of your stride, the bottom pad of your loose fist rhythmically wrapping on the steel, almost as if you hope I won't hear it."

Sierra stared at him, slowly raising the glass to her lips for another sip. Falco followed her progress. "You can leave the polite sipping routine outside." Sierra stopped the glass just short of her lips. Her stare gained focus as she waited for the rest, a devilish grin showing white teeth.

"I saw you chugging Pema's Chang at the fight," he told her.

"If you can toss back that Tibetan's firewater, you can handle the finest Scotch in the outer solar system."

A bright smile greeted the liquid as she took a sip that happily grew into a swig. A hint of rose warmed her high cheekbones and seemed to migrate up and over her smooth scalp and she leaned into Falco. Nestled her head against his shoulder.

The dragon tattoos that covered it, were stunning. Falco had never seen them this close before. The ink was a shade darker than her skin and the detail was staggering. Perfectly scaled limbs with rippling muscles on a sea of clouds.

Sierra pushed away, threw back the contents of her glass and gently set it on the table next to the bunk. "For over five years you and I have danced around one another..."

Falco opened his mouth only to find her finger pushed a crossed his lips.

"I'm not finished, Jack."

Sierra moved so close he could see the striking green flecks circling her pupils, that perfectly smooth ebony skin, the smell of scotch, the warmth of her breath.

Sierra pushed even closer, her lips brushing his as she spoke. "If this is where our journey soon ends, no more dancing."

Soft, wet lips covered his own. Falco dropped his glass to the side and gave into the only person that could heal his battered soul.

5 8

Admiral Chen
10th Fleet
Crawling Toward the Oortian Field

ADMIRAL CHEN and 10th Fleet awaited the upload that could give their scanners the capability to find Oortians in waiting. I miss Station Pluto, Chen thought. The difference in location could not be more dramatic as methane clouds and asteroid fields spun off by the Kuiper Belt hung in the distance off 10th Fleet's portside. It looked like a graveyard, no Chen corrected, it felt like a graveyard. Fields of tombstones...

And then there was the light sucking black field, towering five thousand klicks dead ahead. The field was so vast that distance from it quickly became meaningless. All one saw was a flat, endless wall of nothingness. The path to oblivion.

"Upload seventy-five percent complete, Admiral," stated Lieutenant Mi Bai self-consciously from her current position next to Commander Lee at the Battle-Net station. The first sensor pack upload was not precise enough and found multiple objects sharing the same surface area. Chen had learned the meaning of 'exact' was not... well, exact.

He and Commander Lee felt optimistic as Captain Falco and his crew on Station Pluto uploaded and scanned the area around Station Pluto with not a single match. 10th Fleet sat .0044 Astronomical Units from Station Pluto, as soon as the original sensor upgrade had been initialized the Battle-Net found twenty-four potential 'Oortians' lying in wait.

That had not inspired confidence with his twenty-nine captains and their crewmen were less than impressed, and may still be recovering from the full-fledged alarm it caused. If the Fleet had been at battle stations Level Four instead of Three... missiles would have been wasted.

On the bright side, the original sensor upload worked and found exactly what Bai had programed it to. Like a microscope, Lieutenant Bai had stated, 'we need greater magnification due to the number of objects and size of the asteroid fields.'

Admiral Chen still grappled with the vastness of space. He looked over the current holo-charts showing the asteroid field off the Fleet's portside. He ordered Commander Lee to move two battle-groups comprised of five patrol boats each, off the Fleet's vulnerable portside flank. The eight remaining patrol boats protected the starboard and stern of the Fleet.

That left the starboard flank and the stern light, but if you were going to hide, the asteroid field would provide perfect cover.

Lieutenant Bai let out an audible sigh. "Upload complete, Admiral."

Chen nodded. "Here we go. Back to your station, Lieutenant."

Briskly, the lieutenant stood from the Battle-Net station, glanced down at Commander Lee and crossed the bridge of the *Qing Long*. The admiral observed his promising young lieutenant pass by more senior officers. When Bai reached her station and found her seat, Chen turned from his command station, looked across the bridge to the far corner where Bai was once again examining data.

He cleared his throat. "Lieutenant Mi Bai, excellent work, you make the People proud, carry on." A spark, Chen thought, yes, he could see Bai grow from the remark. The statement and the scene were exactly as he had intended.

Lieutenant Bai did not hide from her oversight with the upload, she took ownership of it and improved it. The initial sensor pack worked perfectly, it simply needed to be honed. She was only getting started, Chen was sure of that. He turned toward Commander Lee. "Maximize spread formation for optimal sighting and firing positions."

The commander quickly entered the order over the Battle-Net that instantly fed the data to the Fleet. The laser beacon flashed the order by Morse code to the eighteen Viper patrol boats who lost their COM-Sats in the skirmish that seemed an old and distant memory.

The hologram above the table in the center of the bridge showed slight movements while nine Cruisers and three Dreadnought class boats adjusted their positions, creating space and maximizing their weapons firing lines in relation to the asteroid field.

"All vessels are in position, Admiral."

"Connect the Battle-Nets to our command ship." If vastly outnumbered, and looking at the approaching black wall Chen was betting they would be, precision would decide their fate.

"Yes, Admiral." Lee sent the order and within seconds eleven lines shown bright on the screen of the Battle-Net. Each thin streak ran from a single vessel to the command ship, Chen's dreadnought, the *Qing Long*.

"Sir, what of the patrol boats? They cannot link without a COM-Sat."

They are our wolves, Chen thought, they protect the den at all cost. "Keep to their battle-groups and guard the main fleet."

"Yes, sir." Lonely flashes spat from the laser beacon. The order was received a letter at a time by eighteen matte black vessels, each one in full control of its own Battle-Net.

"Lieutenant Bai, take over the primary scanner station." Admiral Chen adjusted in his command chair and engaged his harness.

"Battle Stations," he took a deep breath, "Level Three." Chen tasted the steel on his tongue, swallowed hard. The crewman of the *Qing Long* strapped in. The click and snap of harnesses filled the bridge then all fell silent.

"Lieutenant Bai, begin deep field scan."

59

Aris the Chosen One
the Darkness – the Hunters

SWIMMING THROUGH THE DARKNESS, Aris the Chosen One pushed on while the pack followed in line, one after the other. It's thick, oily mass, gently pressing against her hardened carapace, providing just enough resistance that the webbing on each of her eight fins could push through at a quick pace. Cool and seductive, it washed over each locked plate as she sliced through, each fin moving in powerful harmony. Aris adjusted the angle of her skull plate, letting the pointed ridge cut through the current.

The oldest of the hunting pack, the ancient Prox, was too close to her. Each thrust from her tail ended with a brushing-grit scraping the rough top of its head. Even her skull plate feels different, Aris thought on her private thought-stream. We are changing with each new clan, each new generation. We are still evolving, but who is applying the force that makes us change? Creators or Darkness? Or both?

The hunting pack was getting close to the enemy vessel's last estimated position. It seemed even the Darkness could not find the adversary that entered her mass. Or she chose to allow the pack to hunt without her aid – a test.

A 'memory' slid into her systems. A vision of Aris the student, curled into a ball, frozen in fear as the invaders destroyed her mentor.

I will continue on in the Darkness. If fear of traveling to the Realm of Warriors gives me more time in the Darkness, then I embrace this 'fear,' as I do not seek a 'realm' that may be an end without a beginning.

Eight powerful fins locked against the current, creating immense drag. Aris slowed, straightened her carapace. Each of the four remaining Prox forming the snaking progression followed suit and the pack came to a halt, the ancient one's fins grazing the four Seekers lining Aris's back.

Aris opened a thought-stream for the pack. The Darkness' mass, directly in front of her churned violently generating currents pushing towards the territory boundaries, pushing towards the Veil and the Void beyond.

The shared thought-stream filled with a chaotic spattering of sounds. Each Prox fought against the pull of the current running in front of them, pushing their fins in quick bursts. Aris shared part of the Creators' plan over the thought-stream to ease their apprehension. The stress started the warrior's rage dripping into their systems. Aris detected the pungent iron scent carried on the current of the Darkness. Now knowing this was part of the Creators' plan, calm returned to the pack. The Darkness began to thin and dissolve into a vast opaque area that flowed before them.

Aris the Chosen One relaxed her carapace. Each armored plate softened within its muscled, fluid-filled pocket, allowing her long torso to soften and bulge in the center where her key organs and systems were located. The other four followed suit.

Not only was the Darkness allowing them a rare opportunity to see within her mass, she was also offering a vision never recorded in the history of the clans. The Shields being pushed by the Movoo would soon fill their sensor field and Aris and her pack of hunters would be the first of all the clans to document the site and add it to the clans' history.

According to the Creators chronicle, passed on to all the Clans, the Movoo had never been used in battle. Nor had the moon-like creatures ever traveled through the Darkness. Movoo lived and worked in the open space where the twelve worlds revolved around their two fiery stars. They existed in that which the Darkness and the clans protect, that which *I, Aris the Chosen One, have never seen or ever will.*

Silence cut the chattering that had consumed the hunting packs shared thought-stream. Aris had mistakenly allowed her private thoughts to enter the shared-stream. It was too late. Her contemplations of 'the one' rather than the 'clans,' revealed her continuing evolution, a change that was not wanted or needed by the Creators.

Aris switched back to her private thought-stream. The Creators may already know what I am becoming or they will know if the other Four divulge my thoughts. Our mission is not over and opportunities will arise to travel to the Realm of Warriors.

Eight dark plates came into optical sensor range. The Darkness allowed the five Prox to see the shapes, textures and layers of the massive Shields moving towards the enemies that waited in the Void.

The Darkness had thinned her mass to allow their passage with relative ease. So why have you not aided us in finding the enemy lost within you – or can you? The shields continued to press towards the pack. Aris thought she understood the answer. The enemy vessel lays motionless, frozen in fear as I once did, hiding in the Darkness. For a moment, she saw an intimate connection to their enemy.

We share fear. If we share fear, we might also share... Something purged the thought from her systems. A complete loss consumed her, lasting for a fraction of a cycle. Aris was at peace. A violent jolt and her systems came on, a thought already running through her. Fear is only the beginning. We will crush the beast you hide in and send you to the cowardice dominion from which you were spawned. The warrior's rage coursed through Aris, engorged her organs to the point of pain. As fast as it consumed her, the rage abated.

The pack quickly swam in various directions, honing their optical sensors for the first time within the Darkness, seeing, hearing and feeling the shields rising up and beyond their positions. The closest shield was bright red, the top layer of the husks covering its vast skull-plate, rippled with the flow of its life preserving essence.

As it continued to ascend toward the Void, the side of the shield showed the age of the creature. Each layer took a full cycle to cure, harden and the next soft layer would begin, always filling in the cracks from growth, and even wounds from battles fought long before Aris came into existence. Layer after layer rose above her until the thick, skull plate passed by. Based on her calculations, Aris believed the nearest shield to be just over a billion cycles since creation.

Swirling currents sucked and dragged at their carapaces. The current was strong. Each Prox pushed hard to adjust in the churning flow. Aris felt the Seekers expand in their pouches; her back ached from the pressure they exerted. The last of the mammoth shields passed and the current subsided. Aris studied the eight quivering stalks attached to the underside of the skull-plates. Each stalk held hundreds of clustered stronghold sacs safeguarding warriors of the Darkness. Each sac, sized for the warrior it protected. Warruqs and Krell filled most of the strongholds. Compared to the shield, the mighty Krell looked tiny, weak and insignificant. And what of the Movoo?

They were far below the eight rising stalks, eight formidable creatures pushing the clans to battle with all their might. The Darkness pulsed and vibrated with the coming force, each ripple bouncing off Aris's carapace.

On the far side of the opaque flow, Aris detected something at the edge of the field, a shadow within shadows almost hidden in the full mass of the Darkness. Aris sent the coordinates to the hunting pack and they returned to their original positions. Again, the ancient Prox brushed against her, another attempted show of domination. Aris thickened her back plates, locked them and in one powerful push of her fins, slammed into the ancient one, sending her floundering toward the rest of the pack where she remained.

The vision of the rising Movoo would be another's to record for the clans. Aris had her orders.

The hunting pack had found the invaders.

60

Captain Yue Fei
the Black Field and the Hunted

THE VIRTUAL SURROUND System (VSV) seems more of a curse at the moment, thought Captain Fei. The last massive, shadowy-disk pushed by the *Kwan Yin*. Captain Yue Fei and the rest of the officers and crewman in the bridge sat in stunned silence. More disturbing than the eight fleshy discs larger than Station Pluto, were the endless, sinewy umbilical cords attached to their flat undersides. Hundreds of distorted, reddish eggs in varying sizes clung in shiny clusters to each cord, in an endless parade of the macabre. The sinewy structure of the cord and sacs resembled a skinned cadaver.

How much longer would the *Kwan Yin*'s Battle-Net sensors be able to pull readings off the portside? The sensors were barely pulling shapes, but the VSV allowed Fei to zoom in. The result was a close-up shown like a movie on the entire portside of the *Kwan Yin*. If their sensors and VSV system were able to see at all in this newly thinned area of the black field, chances were that the *Kwan Yin* could also be seen or detected. The only thing Fei was sure of, is the longer they remained within the field, the less chance they would ever leave it alive.

Gently he pushed up from the captain's chair and moved toward his commander. "Systems?" Captain Fei spoke the word softly. "They home in on our ships systems, our computers possibly? Even the Battle-Net itself, all push signals outside of the *Kwan Yin* to measure, search and update. Conceivably, our voices could give us away?"

"If the Battle-Net's closest comparison is accurate, and the system is virtually perfect..." Commander Zhu paused, "on Earth. Then we may very well be in an ocean-like environment," the commander lowered his voice, "a type of 'hydrodynamics' are the rules we are now playing by?"

"Sonar?" Caption Fei thought of the sample they took of the black field and the way the 'things' they had just witnessed moved through it. "Maybe their detection systems share some of the principles of sonar. Sound propagation?" Fei pondered the obvious black hole that sucked much of the confidence from his sonar theory. "Then how are they locking onto our vessels in open space?" Fei conceded, "and why leave our battle-group in the open, yet surround us with the field if they cannot detect us within it? We need out," Fei concluded and pointed towards the portside and the eight umbilical's climbing through the lightened mist of the dark field, carrying their endless clusters of disfigured egg sacs. "That must be the direction of 10th Fleet. Their movement is our compass and our path back to Station Pluto. Whatever is in those... is not going to be pleasant."

The stout umbilicals picked up speed, rising faster through the field, more and more clusters of sacs disappearing in the swirling black only for new clusters to emerge in the gray area and take their place. The realization that humanity was not alone finally took hold and Captain Fei believed it was not ready for an ancient alien civilization. Whether they shielded themselves purposely from human technology and chose to live peacefully outside of its reach, no longer mattered.

Fei believed life and resources had been taken on a large enough scale that based on human history, war would ensue. The door out of this hell had to be above them, where the vast shadows towed the umbilical's and their contents. And all we have to do, Captain Fei thought, was follow them.

61

Admiral Chen – 10th Fleet
Nearing the Oortian Field

10TH FLEET HELD its position off the asteroid field while the linked Battle-Net of the command ship *Qing Long* continued its scan. Admiral Chen waited while Commander Lee and Lieutenant Bai studied the data flowing across the Battle-Net screen.

"Nothing. Not a single match," the commander stated.

Commander Lee shot Admiral Chen a questioning look and turned to Lieutenant Bai who had finished her assessment of incoming data.

"Commander, the range of our debris sensors from our current position, reaches only fifty percent of the asteroid field," she reported.

Admiral Chen felt uneasy. The location of the asteroid field was perfect for an ambush. Almost as if it was recently placed there, and what if the sensor pack wasn't working? "Lieutenant Bai, suggestions?"

"Expand our range, Admiral." Bai released her harness, stood and moved toward the hologram floating in the middle of the bridge. "Her finger pointed at the asteroid field on the portside, "We have scanned to this point, roughly half of the area. It's a relatively small field."

Chen moved forward in his chair. "I'm listening, Lieutenant."

"If you were going to hide weapons or units in an asteroid field," Bai raised an eyebrow, "where would you place them?"

"On the edges," Commander Lee offered. "Reduce chances of collisions."

"Precisely and if you did not know the strength of your enemy, you might also—"

"Position your forces on the stern-side, use the asteroid field as a protective buffer," Chen answered. "Or simply to increase your chances of not being detected."

The admiral motioned towards Bai, pointing toward her station. "You better strap in, Lieutenant. The cruiser *Lie Gong* is closest to the asteroid field. She could initiate a full burn and once in position, we can use her senor array to scan the total field and relay the findings to our command ship."

Commander Lee moved uncomfortably in his chair. "Sir, you want to send a cruiser out there on its own?"

"No, Commander. We'll send a Viper battle group ahead of her." Admiral Chen also liked the simple fact that the cruiser *Lie Gong* was designed similar to a gunboat, fitted with rail guns instead of missile launchers. If hell opened its doors, the *Lie Gong* could answer faster than a missile-based vessel.

"Commander, once Lieutenant Bai gives you the coordinates, send the orders to Viper group Alpha and the captain of the *Lei Gong*."

"Yes, sir."

"And Commander..." the admiral's face was grave, "make sure they are prepared to initiate a full burn to the coordinates and back to the Fleet the second the scan is complete. The *Lie Gong*'s Battle-Net will be disconnected from the rest of the Fleet to ensure she can react with utmost haste. She has full authorization to fire if necessary, as does the Viper group."

"Yes, sir."

"Coordinates are set," Lieutenant Bai confirmed.

"Received," stated Commander Lee. "Admiral, this will place the battle group and cruiser closer than the standard safety distance from the asteroid field."

"Lieutenant Bai?" Chen waited.

"If we are going to get a full scan," Lieutenant Bai reviewed her calculations one more time, "those are the coordinates the *Lie Gong* must reach."

"Worth the risk. Send the orders, Commander."

"Coordinates and orders sent Admiral." Commander Lee paused. "*Lie Gong* acknowledged orders, charging her rail guns via protocol. Viper battle-group Alpha is ready to go, Admiral, and will keep pace in front of the *Lie Gong*."

Admiral Chen tapped on his data-pad. The hologram in the center of the bridge blurred. Seconds later a crystal-clear image of five Viper class patrol boats and a lone cruiser appeared with the asteroid field a distant backdrop. Soon the video would be of distant shadows, but for now the vessels were impressive to look at.

The officers and the crewman on the bridge watched the Star class cruiser *Lie Gong* fire her starboard and stern thrusters and she moved away from 10th Fleet in preparation for a full burn. Five Viper's covered her flanks and bow, moving almost in sync, their matte black finish rendering them virtually invisible to the human eye.

The thrusters faded and for a few seconds, were replaced by the bright glowing burn of the main engines. Abruptly they hurdled away from 10th Fleet.

Admiral Chen followed their progress. Six vessels powered

closer to the asteroid field and further from the protection of the other vessels.

"Two minutes to coordinates, Admiral." Beads of sweat ran down the sides of Lieutenant Bai's face. "Thirty seconds to coordinates."

The group's main engines simultaneously went dark. Two bright bursts appeared on the bow of each boat. Thrusters continued to fire to slow their forward progress. The Vipers adjusted their positions, gliding into a protective arc around the bow and flanks of the *Lie Gong*. The arc hung fifty meters below the cruiser's firing line. The battle group and cruiser came to a full stop.

"The *Lie Gong* has begun debris field scan Admiral." Tension tore at Commander Lee's every word.

"Add the Battle-Net data to the main holo-feed, Commander."

Chen watched the main hologram-feed in the center of the bridge adjust and now showed five shadows in a protective arc around a large shadow. In the asteroid field, shifting numbers appeared below hundreds of similar sized asteroids. Many continued to adjust while some of the numbers remained the same.

Chen leaned hard against his harness. "Lieutenant Bai, what is happening?"

"Scanners are working through the asteroid field, Admiral."

"Why is it taking longer this time?" Chen looked back to the holo-feed and focused on a handful of clustered asteroids with shifting numbers until they slowed in unison like the movement of a timer ticking down the seconds,

.19...

.186...

.1858...

.18581...

.185806...

And stopped. The hologram turned red.

.18580608, 1,597 confirmed matches.

The Battle-Net aboard the *Qing Long* wailed, alerts filling the bridge and echoing off the bulkheads. The same scenario carried out over the entire 10th Fleet.

"Hull Pounders!" Commander Lee bellowed, "1,597 confirmed matches!"

Admiral Chen slammed the COM switch from his command chair that connected him directly to the cruiser. "Get out of there, Captain! Commander Lee, Battle-group secures *Lie Gong*'s retreat." He spun towards Commander Lee, "Can we get a lock on enemy targets?"

"Out of range, Admiral. As soon as they cross the midpoint of the asteroid field we can lock, but they're too close to our boats. Viper Group Alpha has lock." Lee spoke as he flashed the Admiral's order to the lead Viper using the laser beacon.

Chen hammered his armrest with a fist. "*If* they can make it back." He could not risk moving the rest of 10th Fleet closer, which could be exactly what the Oortians wanted.

The *Lei Gong* fired her port thrusters turning the cruiser's bow back around, towards the Fleet. A wave of missiles flew from the defending Viper battle-group locked onto over 1,500 confirmed Hull Pounders. The first wave targeted the closest Oortians in the asteroid field.

Admiral Chen followed the streaking missiles on the their main holo-feed. It glowed with hundreds of blue embers burning toward red enemy targets. "Something is wrong," he whispered to himself, "why are they waiting?"

A puzzled voice came over the COM.

"They are not moving. Repeat, the Oortian targets have not taken defensive maneuvers." Hope sounded from the *Li Gong*'s captain. "Twenty seconds until the first missile wave reaches its targets... We may have another false scan– wait. The Viper's laser beacons are flashing." The captain's voice grew with intensity. "Picking up heat signatures! Increasing!"

Admiral Chen pushed against his harness, helpless with the rest of 10th Fleet, watching and listening. "Captain. Do not fire your main engine until you have made the full turn." Chen saw the cruiser's stern light up. "You are not in position! Do not..."

The *Lei Gong* engaged its main engine before the cruiser had made the full turn. She was out of position, arcing back toward the Fleet instead of taking a straight line.

The fleeing *Lie Gong* continued to push its scanner feed to 10th Fleet. Hundreds of enemy signatures hurtled into the asteroids that lay between them and the battle group's waves of missiles. The missiles were met with a storm of dense shrapnel.

The bridge of Chen's Command Ship watched in horror, the hologram bloomed with explosions. Distant missiles were shredded by rock and ice before they reached what was left of the asteroid field.

"Sir, the Vipers are holding their positions," Commander Lee stated.

"The battle group protects the *Lie Gong*." Chen followed the path of the cruiser that was only now getting back on course towards the Fleet. "She will never make it on her own." Missiles from the Fleet were too far away to save her from the mass of Hull Pounders that erupted out of the pulverized asteroid field.

The swarm of Hull Pounders rolled wide of the Viper patrol boats. Flash beacons were bouncing signals from one Viper to the next in a frantic, chaotic speech.

Flame poured from the main engine of the lead Viper as it throttled towards the enemies skirting around their starboard flank. The four other Vipers followed its lead and burned towards the cloud of Hull Pounders in an attempt to cut them off.

Desperate to aid the battle-group that protected her escape, the *Lei Gong* unleashed her rail guns while moving towards the safety of 10th Fleet's weapons range. Hull Pounder signatures disappeared with each salvo from the cruiser. High velocity lead rounds streaking toward the charging Oortians, exploding within the enemy swarm.

"The *Lie Gong* is effectively using self-detonating slugs, Admiral, the enemy pursuit is slowing, 758 Hull Pounders remain, but will overtake the *Lie Gong* in twenty-five seconds." Commander Lee continued to monitor 10th Fleet's linked Battle-Net. "We have lock and can fire at the remaining enemy targets."

"Our missiles will not reach them in time." Chen looked toward his commander. "Hold."

Sporadic waves of chasing blue embers belched from the battle-group. The Viper's unleashed a final salvo at the enemy swarm that emptied their stores.

Admiral Chen fell silent. The hologram showed the impossible. The entire Oortian swarm came to a full stop, letting the cruiser escape, and shot toward the incoming missiles fired from the now helpless, Viper battle-group.

Detonations lit the hologram. Heavily outnumbered missiles slammed into the oncoming swarm of Hull Pounders. Hot slugs from the rail guns of the fleeing *Lei Gong* exploded near the battle-group. The number of Oortian signatures decreased with each exploding supersonic round from the *Lie Gong* and the remaining missiles laid waste to the enemy, but the Hull Pounders kept coming.

Streaking hot slugs flew from the *Lie Gong*'s rail guns. The hologram on the bridge of Admiral Chen's flagship bloomed in white and blue hues. More Hull Pounders disappeared and the remaining swarm tore through the sleek Viper class vessels.

Epoxy pushed through gaping wounds, each vessel desperately trying to repair itself.

A bright flash consumed the hologram, followed by another, and another.

"The *Lie Gong* is the only signature left, sir. All Oortian Hull Pounders," Lee gathered himself, "and our battle group are destroyed."

"They did their job." Admiral Chen spoke to the officers and crewman on the bridge. "As will we." He looked toward the hologram with the surviving cruiser moving back into position amongst 10th Fleet. Over 1,500 Hull Pounders destroyed he thought, the horror washing over him as the loss of 150 crewman and five vessels sunk in.

New alarms sounded from the Battle-Net.

"What now?" Chen barked.

"Picking up a small heat signature on the face of the black field, Admiral." Commander Lee adjusted the hologram from his.

A small bump rose on the face of the endless black wall.

"We have a lock, Admiral." Lee continued to scan the incoming data. "It's growing, over a klick wide – now two klicks."

Over two kilometers across, Chen thought, the size of Station Pluto. "Move us back, Lieutenant. 10th Fleet remains joined to our Battle-Net, bow thrusters only." Chen focused on the hologram.

"Three more signatures, another, five total." Commander Lee's hands raced across his controls, eyes darting around his screen. "Three more emerging. Now have eight signatures, sir. All are over two klicks wide and increasing."

"Admiral Chen." Lieutenant Bai waited for his attention. "Data from our scanners are showing immense energy signatures from each object and they're intensifying. No weapons bays or openings detected." Bai turned back to her screens.

"That we can *detect*," emphasized Commander Lee. "Eight objects have fully emerged from the field, Admiral."

Chen gave Lee a skeptical stare. "And how do we know that, Commander?"

"Each of the eight discs now cover exactly the same surface area," Lee stated.

"Lieutenant Bai, are the energy levels stronger or growing more rapidly within any of them?" Admiral Chen was not going to wait for these monstrosities to open fire on 10th Fleet.

Bai quickly worked through the available data being streamed to her station from the linked Battle-Net. "Object in center of the grouping has twice the energy signature of the other seven surrounding it."

"Commander Lee, target center object, fifty Hell-Fire missiles, two waves of twenty-five, ten second delay, on my command."

One hundred and fifty crewmembers gone, more Admiral Chen thought, if Captain Yue Fei and the first battle group were also destroyed somewhere inside the field.

"Hell-Fire's ready, sir."

"FIRE!"

6 2

Captain Falco
Battle Station Pluto

CAPTAIN FALCO and his officers leaned forward on the poly-slab table in the Pluto Room Command Center. What could be done to Station Pluto, had been, Falco thought as all in the room sat locked onto the black COM-Box sitting in the center of the table. They listened to Admiral Chen bark out orders as new forms of demons emerged from the black wall. Missiles were in the terminal chase and 10th Fleet stubbornly held its ground.

Falco was incensed by the silence from 10th Fleet. The open-COM they shared was on, light was green, the last order was to FIRE.

Son of a bitch has us on mute, Falco thought, we can hear the shit storm raging and all we get is the common courtesy of listening in... Pure arrogance and it's going to get you and what remains of 10th Fleet killed. If only Captain Fei were in command of the Fleet. Falco felt a pang of sorrow and pushed it aside.

"Admiral, withdraw to Battle Station Pluto," Falco whispered helplessly to the COM-Box while his officers sat in stunned silence. "Get 10th Fleet out of there."

"Lieutenant Wallace! Get the Admiral or Commander Lee on the COM now!" Falco's mind was still processing the vastness of what was coming.

"COM-Link is open one way, Captain. We can hear and that's it, until the Admiral chooses differently." Wallace continued tapping on his data-pad in frustration.

Falco sat in the Pluto Room, simmering with rage. "We can sit and listen as eight Oortian..." He paused. "What the hell can they be anyway? Whatever they are, each is larger than Station Pluto and 10th Fleet just lost another five Vipers."

"Last we heard, the objects have not moved and the Oortian field is stationary." Lieutenant Wallace looked around the table. "Why has the field not surrounded 10th Fleet as it did Captain Fei's battle-group?"

Ensign Holts nodded. "Increasing the mass of something as vast as the black field would take a substantial amount of resources, regardless of the Oortian technology or the field's makeup."

"A window for 10th Fleet to escape?" Captain Falco asked. Even in these dire times, Falco imagined a future with Sierra. The wall between them was down and he would not see it rise again. He had far more to live for today than yesterday.

"Yes, Captain." Holts held Falco's stare, then moved her hands across her data-pad. "Possibly."

"Or the Oortians could be waiting for a tactical advantage?" Commander Shar'ran leaned back in his chair that looked far too small for him.

Any theories they came up with were a long shot. Even the Battle-Net's analysis was based on human thoughts, needs and driving forces, but it was learning with each Oortian encounter.

"What if the Oortians are only protecting their territory?"

Holts looked exhausted. She moved her fingers in circles over her closed eyes.

"What if the Oortians are simply giving 10th Fleet the opportunity to retreat?" Falco's arms flew up. "Either way the only move is retreat. The Fleet returns to Battle Station Pluto."

"The Oortians lost well over fifteen hundred Hull Pounders," Commander Shar'ran stated to his fellow officers, his eyes moved to each one. "The death of comrades is what drives conflict, it is revenge of the fallen that escalates skirmishes into battles and battles into wars, not the words or actions of cowardly statesmen." Commander Shar'ran leaned into the table. "We have lost hundreds of crewmen, officers and possibly ten Vipers. Those numbers may increase exponentially in the next few minutes. There can be no retreat. Admiral Chen has loosed Hell-Fire missiles."

Chief Pema Tenzin listened to his fellow officers while they worked through the skirmish they had witnessed between 10th Fleet and the Oortians. Falco kept a close eye on the man, as his way was always to ponder, ponder some more and then listen. When he chose to speak, there was a generational-wisdom that flowed from him.

"They are an ancient civilization that has sat at the border of humanity's claimed system, our solar system, for longer than we may ever know." Chief Tenzin kept his soft, clear eyes on the black box in the center of the table.

Falco and the others fell silent and hung on every word.

"Happenstance? I think not. Fear? Highly unlikely based on what we have seen and experienced to this point." Tenzin exhaled, his eyes eased closed as if meditating, then opened as he continued. "Threat?" his eyes rose off the COM-Box and found each person at the table, "Lack of, is more realistic. I believe we simply and accidentally trespassed and are being forcefully shown the door."

"And are unwilling to open it," Ensign Holts stated.

"Captain Falco!" Admiral Chen's baritone belted out of the black COM-Box. "I assume you have prepared Station Pluto, shielded the *Anam Cara* and are using her Battle-Net to coordinate your defenses and update the system with current data on the Oortians being sent from 10th Fleet's COM."

Commander Shar'ran shot Falco and Lieutenant Wallace a quick nod and Ensign Holts continually looked over the incoming data.

One hundred fifty 'Battle-Cubes' are ready to go, the Infinity Wall was now a lethal ring of hand-held rocket launchers. Each 'Battle-Cube' was sealed off from the rest of the station. The final touch consisting of a laser-saw cutting out a perfectly round two-meter hole in the crystal clear wall of each Cube. Once punched out, within seconds the vacuum of space had equalized each Cube. The Infinity Wall was the only section of Station Pluto that could be cut without instantly filling with grav-fluid and mending epoxy. Two crewmen with grav-boots shared a handheld RBS-1100 missile launcher and stood ready for action.

The utility passage that fed the battle-ring acted as the containment field from which no one would leave. It would allow access to the Battle-Cubes by crewman in exposure suits and grav-boots, but that was it. The utility passage would be permanently sealed once everyone was inside.

It was the ring of death for the attacking Oortians and crew who manned the bunkers. Battle Station Pluto had two goals. Inflict heavy damage to their enemy and be left standing. The assumption being that it took just one living soul on the inside of the station to cut through the welded hatch, attach a pressure valve and process the living back into the land of oxygen and gravity. At least that was Falco's plan.

"Yes, Admiral, the station is ready but, sir, a withdrawal to Battle Station Pl—"

"The data from the skirmish with the Hull Pounders,

Captain. What do you see?" Chen, his tone remained even, each word sounded as a drum beat. "Quickly, Captain, our situation will shortly change as the missiles near their target."

Ensign Holts looked to Falco, her eyes understanding what the Admiral was getting at. She slid the thin data-screen across the smooth surface. Falco snagged the speeding object and looked at the charted image.

The earlier image of the pulverized asteroid field filled one side and the remaining Oortian Hull Pounders were grouped behind the heavy debris, keeping it between them and the Battle-group sent by 10th Fleet. A thin red line arced around the field, its trajectory swung far outside and away from the battle-group and around 10th Fleet.

Falco brushed a finger across the image to follow the red line.

"Captain?" Impatience was entering the admiral's voice.

Falco's hand froze on the image that now filled the screen. "They know we're here."

"Yes, Captain. They were not heading to destroy the battle group, the cruiser, or even 10th Fleet. The Oortian Hull Pounders were trying to skirt outside of our range and move against Station Pluto."

Captain Falco pulled himself closer to the COM-Box. "I understand, Admiral. They died protecting Station Pluto."

"There is no time to waste, Captain. Ready your station as I believe 10th Fleet does not have the time or speed to outrun the coming Oortian advance." Chen exhaled. "At least all of our vessels cannot outrun the enemy when they choose to attack. The Fleet will stay together and fight as one."

"A fighting withdrawal." Falco's voice fell flat.

"Yes." Determination filled the Admiral's voice. "A fighting withdrawal. Good luck, Captain, we will do all that we can to slow the coming storm." Chen inhaled a powerful breath and smoothly released it. "The rest is up to you."

Falco felt the moment like the impact of a sledgehammer.

The bulkheads closed in on him. We are but a speck out here. The thought of the vacuum of space probing every square meter of his plastic surroundings filled his thoughts. Tentacles wrapping around the station, trying to find a weakness, trying to get in. Not just any station, Battle Station Pluto, he thought, suppressing a potential fit of laughter. Having his boat at the center of the coming chaos gave him hope. When the time came, the *Anam Cara* may decide their fate. 'Pull your shit together Jack!' The voice of Vice Admiral Hallsworth snapped Falco back into the moment.

"Commander Shar'ran, initiate Battle Stations, Level Four, continue to packet and send all data to the United Nations Command."

"10th Fleet's Hell-Fires must be close to contact, Captain." Shar'ran was fastened to the monitor connected to the Battle-Net and the *Anam Cara*.

Falco nodded toward his commander. Why would the Oortians remain stationary? Eight colossal disks, with God knows what behind them, sitting on the face of the black field, in plain sight. Why would the Oortians show them to an enemy they know has powerful weapons? But there was more that crawled through Falco's thoughts, Admiral Chen had gone further to find that enemies were lurking just beyond the Oortian Detector's range. A distance that was reliant on the Fleet's sensors.

Falco had found nothing when scanning with the Oortian Detector, again the feeling of being watched became overwhelming. We found nothing within our sensors range from Battle Station Pluto.

"What if they knew the capabilities of our sensors?" Falco whispered. "If they knew we were here, they tried to skirt the Fleet to get to us. Why not try again?"

"Captain?" Commander Shar'ran leaned toward Falco.

"We need to scan around the station again. This time we'll

send out the *Anam Cara* to extend our range," Falco exhaled, "I'll take her out."

The COM-Box in the center of the table barked again. The static laden voice of Commander Lee aboard the Command Ship was updating Admiral Chen, 10th Fleet and finally, Battle Station Pluto.

"Ten seconds to Hell-Fire impact."

the Movoo – the Clans
the Territories

EXCEPT FOR THE hidden planet Tzara, the home world of the
Movoo was the oldest, but also the smallest. A single, fully
formed Movoo was twice its size and the reason they grew and
matured in the full heat of the small fiery star, far from their
home world.

Upon creation, the Movoo spawn emerged from the core of
their world. The core was a single birthing chamber surrounded
by nutrient-rich liquid. Once the young breached the field
surrounding the chamber, the long journey began, a journey
towards the growing warmth of a distant star. A dangerous
voyage taking hundreds of cycles to make, for the few that did.

Growing, feeding and trying to evade the creatures that
searched for the young, soft flesh that moved toward the surface
in mass numbers. One Movoo in billions would find its way
where liquid turned to vapor, gas and finally, open space and the
location of the heat source they followed. Once eight Movoo had

made the journey, there could not be another unless replacements where needed and the birthing chamber would release her young and the process would begin again, until eight Movoo orbited their fiery star.

Each felt the cool pull of the Darkness as they neared her mass, leaving the comfort and beauty of the Creators worlds revolving around the two warm, fiery stars. Each, with great effort had broken free of their synchronized orbits around the smallest star. The Darkness flowed above them, sifting between murky gray and endless black. Exhaustion rippled through their massive, moon-like forms. Thin layers of ice continued to form around their thick hides from water excreted from trillions of tiny pores, pushed its way towards the surface only to freeze, cracking the layers above.

There had always been a clan of eight and they had always shared a common thought-stream, at least that was all their history knew. Each decreased their movement to a slow burn to maintain their positions, all felt the intense shooting pain from the slight bobbing of their cargo, far above them. The Darkness swirled around the massive stalks, each anchored into the body of a Movoo.

Fleshy orifices adjusted their shape, focusing the force of their slow burn in opposition to the ebb and flow of the endless stalks, covered in strongholds that rose and disappeared into the Darkness. Though tired and worn, the eight were happy to be awaken again for a new purpose, after millions of cycles.

Their load was light in comparison to past cargos that were pulled rather than pushed, but refueling was always necessary. Each felt their methane sacks collapsing from their bodies bulk being pushed inward to fill the growing cavity as the fuel was spent.

Simultaneously, eight fleshy tubes stretched from the Movoo's cargo platforms, where the endless stalks were fastened to their bodies. The fueling tube slithered up and into the approaching Darkness.

Ripples worked their way down while fuel from the dark mass flowed into the Movoo. Pressure pushed outward, their sacks grew bloated and expanded towards the painful point of rupture and death, but stopped. Ice fractured and fell in large pieces, tearing away thick chunks of hardened skin.

From the vantage of the Creators twelve worlds, the moon-sized creatures formed a fiery line. Radiation from the two burning suns poured through the newly fragmented ice and splintered into a reflected shimmering brilliance.

Magnified heat scorched the Movoo's patches of torn flesh. Pain was always part of their awakening and soon their bodies and systems would adjust. The Darkness would heal their wounds as they passed through her.

Tubes retracted into their pouches and data filled their shared thought-stream. The orders from the Creators were uploaded, the data flow ended and the Movoo began to quake when they entered the Darkness. For the first time in their shared history, the Movoo received the gift of the warrior's rage. It seeped into every organ and crawled through their systems. Soon they would ignite to a full burn and push the stalks covered with warrior strongholds into battle.

...and after the Movoo released their cargo of warrior's and shields, they would move on to their true mission, the one they were created for, the one they had accomplished eleven times since their own world and history came to be.

———————————

ARIS THE CHOSEN One completed her latest upload. The Creators had changed her orders. The hunting pack was to hold their position and wait for further data. The Movoo had come to a halt and were now fueling for their final push, leaving the towering stalks swaying in the churning Darkness. Her optical sensors continued to see what the Darkness would allow by thinning her dark mass to aid the Movoo's movement.

The invaders waiting in the open space had destroyed all of the Seekers placed among the Creators newly positioned debris field. Not a single Seeker returned to the Darkness to upload its findings. All had fulfilled their Oath to the Creators and traveled to the Realm of Warriors. Anything history gathered about the invaders was lost. Only one needed to reach the Darkness, but all were slain.

Aris sensed the four ancient Prox swell with pride as she shared chosen fragments of the Creators' data over their linked thought-stream. She closed the stream and opened her private channel leaving them alone in their euphoric state.

They are unsure of the true power of the invaders, she thought, the Creators do not have the resources to feed the Darkness and expand its protecting mass, so they wait to see if their shields will hold. A test. Aris sensed the wisdom in that and she joined the thought-stream shared by thousands of warriors riding the stalks, protected in their stronghold sacs and waiting to be released into battle. Who will be sacrificed, she pondered, who will be tested?

Pain shot through her systems and with it, a familiar power surge. The Darkness had plans of her own. The rest of the hunting pack pushed away to avoid their leaders thrashing carapace. As fast as the Darkness entered Aris, the pain eased into a numbness and soon, her organs and systems returned to their natural state. The Darkness had plans for the hunters; the vessel they sought was resting on the far side of the visible field and Aris was given the exact location of the enemy that invaded the Darkness without fear and would now be shown no mercy.

Aris the Chosen One had a decision to make, a choice that would decide her fate. That she believed she had a fate, gave light to the path she had already taken. Travel to the Realm of

Warriors as the Creators promised upon the moment your existence is extinguished in battle... or believe in the power of the Darkness and the chance to exist forever.

The Creators plans were no longer imperative. Aris fed the necessary data to the four ancient Prox and waited for the Movoo to begin their formation. Once they had pushed past the hunting pack into the Darkness above, Aris would order the four Prox to descend on the helpless invader, shred its protective layer and destroy all that hid within its dark shell.

An ember flashed far below and was joined by seven more. It is time, she thought, the Movoo are fully fueled and ready to ignite their energy bloom. Stalks began to move closer to one another... all but one. Hundreds of stronghold sacs bristled, the warriors within ebbed and flowed with the movement of the stalk their stronghold sacs were attached to.

BEHIND THE GREAT SHIELD, LOR observed the shadowy Darkness swirling through the opaque walls of his stronghold sac that sucked and pushed against his carapace, adjusting to the changing forces of the Darkness outside. He was in the leader's position. We are close, he thought on his private stream. Pride filled his systems, a warrior's pride.

The shield protecting his stalk and the hundreds of stronghold sacs fastened to it remained on the surface of the Darkness. The seven others retracted into the protection of the Darkness and formed a tight, layered circle around their leader's stalk, each shield overlapping the others.

I will be first. LOR embraced the warrior's rage, opening his systems and organs, letting it course through him completely. He hardened his carapace and locked each armored plate. Soon the stronghold sac would release and LOR would ravage the intruders who stood just outside of their newly claimed territories and waited in the Void.

Pressure forced LOR hard against the veiny membrane of his stronghold. The thrust from a single Movoo releasing their full energy bloom pushed LOR and his warriors toward their enemy and away from the protection of the Darkness.

The clans were coming and the enemy waiting in the Void would suffer the warrior's rage and death would be the only escape.

Captain Fei
the Black Field

CAPTAIN YUE FEI and the crew of the *Kwan Yin* ebbed in the newly arriving graying zone of the field. The bow disappeared in the smoky mass they were now accustomed to, but the stern of the *Kwan Yin* hung in the fluctuating gray fog where massive discs rose and disappeared above, leaving behind thick trailing tubes with countless strange pods attached to them.

"We may have five objects off the stern, Captain, just beyond the tubes. Sensors are not getting a hard read, but they are comparable to the objects that attacked Captain Falco's vessel." Commander Zhu stated, just above a whisper.

Fei nodded. "Distance?"

"Maybe twenty," Zhu shook his head, "maybe thirty klicks."

"Commander," Fei paused, looking out through the Virtual Surround Vision at the swirling, flowing mass, "the gray zone has a current. That, added to the distance to the objects, gives us seconds? Or possibly minutes if they can detect us and choose to attack."

Captain Fei looked overhead at the ring of massive plates that hovered a few klicks above the *Kwan Yin*. His vessel now found itself just outside the area of the closest disc. Far below them, a fiery ring was growing larger, getting closer. The center stem was moving quickly upwards, its red, almost transparent pods glistening as they streaked by, faster and faster.

These titanic vessels can only be a carrier for war, troops or munitions, Fei thought, as more of the iridescent, red eggs passed by. Based on the sheer numbers of pods and size of the discs, Fei believed 10th Fleet had to be on the other side. Somewhere nearby in open space. He found hope, knowing there were still survivors outside the dark field ready to meet the enemy's advance. It also shows us the way out. Fei followed the progress of the center tube on his screen. It continued to push through the hole left by the overlapping shields.

"Lieutenant." Captain Fei looked toward his pilot.

From the bow station, the pilot spun his chair to meet his captain's eyes.

"Yes, sir?"

"Plot a parallel flight path." Fei pointed towards the moving tube and clustered discs around it. "That is the direction to Station Pluto."

The lieutenant slowly nodded. "Battle-Net and all our sensors will be completely useless once we are out of the gray cloud and back into the black field, even here our sensors provide only a glimpse of what is around us."

"So be it." Captain Fei grinned. "Do your best."

"Prepare for full burn, Lieutenant." Fei observed the speed of the rising tube change.

"It's slowing down, Captain." Commander Zhu pointed at the *Kwan Yin*'s hull where the center tube had slowed its outward progress to a crawl. "Captain!" Zhu was in a panic. "The five objects are no longer on our scans! Sensor field closing! We're back in the dark."

The black field slid across them, the gray area grew dark and the *Kwan Yin* and her crew found themselves in an ocean of suffocating blackness once again.

"Full burn, Lieutenant! GO…GO…GO!" Fei heard a roar like that of a rushing river fill the *Kwan Yin* when the main engine came online and drove the vessel forward. Crewmen slammed into their harnesses and pitched backwards as the grav-system worked to stabilize the newly added thrust.

Fei adjusted his harness and turned to view the full bridge when the *Kwan Yin* lurched up from the impact of something large slamming into the bottom of her hull. The blackness around their boat glowed a surreal vibrant green that shown bright near the stern engine and grew faint, but detectable, at the bow.

Another impact rippled from the stern.

"Main engine damaged, fifty-six percent, fifty-four, fifty…" the pilot yelled over the COM.

The vibrating deck under Fei's feet emitted a smooth hum, the engine firing more consistently as the damage below was contained. Repair epoxy foamed out of the *Kwan Yin*'s damaged hull, sealing her wounds with the excess leaving a hardening trail behind her while she ran for open space. Multiple impacts sounded on the bridge and were followed by a groan. Captain Fei turned to find officers and crew pointing at the starboard side. His eyes fastened onto the area of the hull that was now the center of attention.

"A glancing blow." It felt like they had hit a deer on an interstellar highway. "Those are organs, fluids?" Fei found himself eerily objective, while assessing the chunks and sinew being washed from the hull, the gory remains dissolving from the edges toward the center and were gone. Some of the micro-cams of the Virtual Surround Vision system were damaged from the impact. Part of the inner-hull could now be seen again.

"Are we on course, Lieutenant?" Fei kept his tone calm.

"I have a course plotted, Captain!" his pilot yelled without a shred of confidence.

"Hold the course." Fei tightened his harness and gripped the armrests.

"COM-Sat has been destroyed, Captain, main engine holding at fifty percent," Commander Zhu stated.

COM-Sat and the main engine, are they trying to capture or destroy us? Fei thought. Neither option was acceptable.

We must escape or die trying.

Admiral Chen
10th Fleet

NOTHING. Two waves of Hell-Fire missiles had already disappeared, a wave at a time into the surface of the lone, massive disc. An additional volley, twice the number of missiles, was on its way. Admiral Chen sat in the chair, stunned. That would have leveled a small city, he thought and nothing, not even a small explosion... nothing. It swallowed them whole.

"Maintain formation." Admiral Chen kept a close eye on 10th Fleet's withdrawal, he could afford no stragglers. The COM officer continued flashing Chen's orders through the laser beacon to the thirteen remaining Vipers. Each had lost its COM-Sat to an Oortian Hull Pounder, but were intact. The five others were little more than floating scrap.

The Viper class vessels were the front line of defense. Nine cruisers and three dreadnoughts fired their bow thrusters in sputtering bursts, their linked Battle-Nets keeping them in position behind the patrol boats.

Space going vessels had a bow and stern and missile ports faced forward similar to the old submarines on earth. Though locked missiles would turn and chase their targets, crucial time was lost and in their current situation. Time was everything.

The Fleet's formation was simple and meant to tempt a powerful adversary who held an exceptional defensive position. A position that it must relinquish to give the escaping forces a chance at victory. The Phoenix Formation resembled a 'V' with the point facing the enemy.

Qing Long, the command ship, was protected in the center of the open area of the 'V' formation, with the remaining two dreadnoughts each holding a wide position furthest from the point, held by Captain Zhi of the rail gun laden vessel, the cruiser *Lie Gong*. The remaining eight cruisers formed the sides and ran four deep, from the widest point anchored by the dreadnoughts towards the *Lie Gong* and her heavy rail guns.

Thirteen Viper class patrol boats formed the guard of 10th Fleet and lay between the Phoenix formation and the Oortians.

"Wave three, fifteen seconds to impact, Admiral." Commander Lee was on high alert along with every crewman and officer in 10th Fleet as they followed the ember points streaking towards the lone disc holding its position in open space. Seven others had formed a tight circle around it, then slowly submerged into the black field and off the Battle-Net's scanners, leaving the massive disk to stand alone as another wave of Hell-Fire missiles closed in.

"Contact!" Chen turned from his station and watched the hologram in the center of the bridge. The missiles hammered into the disc the size of Station Pluto. This time, pink rings formed and expanded across its surface, rippling to the edge and bouncing back toward its center. Again there were no explosions but the disc shimmered, sending larger ring-like waves bouncing across its glowing face. Admiral Chen remained fixed on the image floating in the center of the bridge. The last pinkish ring disappeared. The disc remained, whole and unmarked, but the surface color changed to a reddish-orange.

"How is that possible?" Commander Lee looked to his admiral.

"Increase speed!" Chen belted the order out.

The Battle-Net wailed of approaching danger. "We have a solar flare warning, sir," Lee stated. "There is a dark spot forming on the surface."

Sirens sounded in every vessel of 10th Fleet. The face of the shield ejected a small mass of solar material. Ripples formed around the discharge point and spread outward in increasing numbers. The disc pulsated from orange to red and finally to mottled black.

"Heat signature is rising rapidly!" Commander Lee spun in his chair towards the Admirals station. "It's going to explode!"

Chen closed his eyes, took a deep breath, exhaled slowly. "Good. Let us hope its demise finds a path other than our own," They could not outrun a blast of that size if fate chose their path, regardless of the speed the Fleet could muster.

"Radiation pulse! Hold on to something," Commander Lee gripped his station's work surface.

Energy washed over the Fleet. Dreadnoughts, cruisers and Vipers raised, dropped and rolled as the wave of energy passed. The *Qing Long* steadied. Admiral Chen looked to the hologram to see the disc pulsing like a beating heart, changing from the mottled, veiny-red to a black so devoid of light it was easily seen on the face of the dark Oortian field.

"Lord Buddha help us," Chen whispered as a searing light emanated from the hologram. A burning ring replaced the black disc and expanded along the face of the camouflaging field. It looked like a stone had been thrown into a vertical puddle and grew outward across the oily surface, causing a ripple to run ahead of its progress until it disappeared from view.

Radiation alarms continued to sound until Admiral Chen

gave the order to mute them. There was nothing to be done but hope the spinning liquid lead that moved between the layers of the Fleet's hulls would achieve one of its many purposes and block the dying waves of intense radiation.

"We have surface activity, Admiral." Sweat ran down Lee's face. "Circular area, thirteen-klick diameter. Visual change. The area is turning gray."

Chen adjusted his harness and moved forward in his seat. "Prepare to fire on my command."

"Sensors are picking up seven objects within the gray area." Commander Lee's fingers moved across his data-pads, "We can't get a solid lock, but they're advancing... Wait, they're in the open!"

Seven discs appeared on the hologram in an overlapping circle formation with a faint glow illuminating the outside edges.

"Battle-Net has a lock on all targets." Commander Lee paused as the flashes from the incoming laser beacons of the patrol boats ceased. "Viper group is locked and awaiting your orders."

Admiral Chen found strange comfort scanning the protective layer formed by the thirteen Vipers that lay between the Fleet and the largest enemy vessels humanity had ever seen. At least we see you with our own eyes, he thought, no more hiding. He remained still, while the bridge of the *Qing Long* and the rest of 10th Fleet waited for his order.

"*Lie Gong*, Captain Zhi," Chen calmly stated.

A startled, breathy voice sounded over the open-COM, the captain of the rail gun laden cruiser that had barely escaped the Hull Pounders. "Yes, Admiral?"

"Adjust your Battle-Net link to coordinate-based firing." Chen placed his index fingers together on a single spot on his hologram-pad and pulled each finger towards the opposite edge. Seven murky plates appeared, the hologram quickly adjusting to the new input then magnifying the chosen area. "Your navigation system will remain linked to our Battle-Net, but you will control your rail guns." Chen adjusted the hologram again. "When I give the order I want a center-mass rotatory firing pattern targeted on the Battle-Net's locked coordinates."

"Yes, Admiral!"

"But Admiral, we have missile lock," Commander Lee stated. "Should we not deliver a debilitating blow while the opportunity presents itself?"

10th Fleet was raw. Everyone, including the admiral, felt responsible for their fallen comrades. The Viper crews perished protecting the cruiser's retreat, protecting their own. Chairs creaked and throats cleared as officers and crew on the bridge tried to focus their attention on anything other than the conversation between the two highest ranking officers of the *Qing Long*. Chen observed the darting eyes from one station to the next. Never had any officer spoken to him in this fashion.

Commander Lee is an old and trusted friend, Chen thought, he hurts as the rest of 10th Fleet does. As if Commander Lee had realized his error, he looked to the deck under his feet and remained silent.

"Yes, Commander Lee, this opportunity was presented by an adversary we know little of, except that the Oortians are learning and adjusting to each encounter." Chen paused as he released his harness and powerfully pushed up from his admiral's chair. "We have presented them with a 'weakened enemy in retreat' and yet they show restraint. They are testing us as we are testing them. Soon they may come in force and the time to unleash the full power of 10th Fleet will be at hand. But, now is the time for the rail guns of the *Lie Gong* to speak for the fallen."

"Captain Zhi," Chen raised a thick, opened hand in front of his barrel chest and closed it into an iron fist. "Fire!"

6 6

Captain Falco
Anam Cara

FALCO SAT ALONE in the *Anam Cara*, working the controls, moving her out of her protected bay. The pilot's station felt far smaller than he remembered, his shoulders brushing the sides where the bow of the *Anam Cara* ended and open space began. One of the last of her kind, the boat had steel and portholes and an actual pilot's seat in the nose with a polyglass screen to take in the view.

This was risky and probably a waste of time, but Falco had to know for sure. He had to know that the Oortians weren't sitting out here, just beyond the range of their scanners. Waiting to attack the station, waiting until the rest of their numbers arrived.

There were too many coincidences stacking up on the Oortian side of the equation. No, Falco thought, these incidents are not happenstance. He ran through the growing list: debris knocking out COM-Sats on Station Pluto; the Oortians taking out the COMs and rail gun compartments of the *Anam Cara*, unhackable Data-Pod signatures used to hide the Hull Pounders and hundreds of others sitting just out of reach of 10th Fleet and their newly created Oortian Detector. The Oortians were every bit as intelligent as humans if not more so. We have been sparring, learning from each other – the updates coming from 10th Fleet strengthened that theory.

The Hell-Fire missiles came in waves and the Oortian Disc remained stationary. Taking every hit, every explosion and waiting for more. It showed an enemy willing to take a loss to learn something… Maybe to study the new weapons being fired or to realize the extent that your adversary would go to destroy you. Falco fired the thrusters and shut them down. The *Anam Cara* drifted away from Station Pluto.

"How far out, Captain?" Commander Shar'ran asked over the COM.

Falco looked to his controls, tapped at the data-pad. "*Anam Cara*'s sensor range capability is just shy of Station Pluto's, so I should be good right here. This will give us an extra klick or so beyond our first scan."

"Point nine five kilometers, to be precise," stated Ensign Holts.

"Thank you, Ensign, and I would expect nothing less." Falco straightened in his seat, adjusted his harness. "Make sure those manning the Battle-Cubes are ready, Commander."

"Cubes are crewed, rail guns are in position, Captain."

"OK," a chill ran down Falco's back, he reached toward the Data-Pad, "beginning full sweep now."

Falco froze. The NAV-screen showed an arc of red exactly one meter beyond Station Pluto's scanner range.

"Are you seeing this, Commander?" Falco moved for the flight controls and stopped. "No sign of heat, no movement. They knew exactly where our range ended."

"Ninety-four confirmed, .18580608 surface area, Hull—"

"Pounders." Falco finished. "Chief Tenzin, how many rounds did your crew load for the new Gatling gun?

"Chief, you there?" Falco's voice grew with intensity as he kept his eye on the stationary red arc lighting his NAV-screen.

"5,000 30mm, incendiary rounds," Chief Tenzin paused, "but at 3,900 rounds a minute?"

"Already dialed it back," Falco said, "2,000-meter range?"

"Effective range?" Tenzin mumbled under his breath then added, "1,200 meters, I think. It's refurbished. Took it off a two-century old USA Warthog, used to cut through enemy tanks. We have yet to test it, Captain."

"Great, Chief. Well, this may be our chance." Falco was about to release the Gatling gun from the belly of the bow and decided against it. Too aggressive, may give them a reason to attack. "Going to use the bow thrusters to push back toward the station, be ready."

Falco was unsure of what happened first. Whether he ignited the bow thrusters before the Battle-Net warning sounded or after.

"Incoming! Moving fast!" Falco lowered the Gatling gun, the *Anam Cara* slowly gliding backwards toward the station. Ninety-four Hull Pounders were now 3,000 meters out and accelerating in a straight line toward the *Anam Cara*. Falco shut down the bow thrusters and engaged the rear thruster to stabilize the ship and grabbed the firing controls.

Rockets flew past the *Anam Cara*, crewmen in the Battle-Cubes trying, but missing their targets. Falco waited.

Commander Shar'ran came over the COM, "Thousand meters, Captain, hand-held launchers trying to get locks!"

Falco watched them streak straight toward him, head on, like a comet with a deadly tail. Beautiful, he thought and waited, the Hull Pounder in front of the line burned a deep red, heat maybe? Rockets continued to blaze by, then a streaking led slug from the rail gun and a few Hull Pounders disappeared in a fiery ball and the comet kept coming.

Falco lined up his sites on the red eye of the charging comet. 500 meters, red lights flashed across the NAV-screen, the Battle-Net wailed.

Warmth rose under Falco's feet. The *Anam Cara* pushed against the stern thruster, reaching equilibrium and the bow flashed like a strobe light in the dead of night. Hull Pounders closest to the nose of the ship gradually disintegrated into pulp and shattered skull plates while those in the rear of the line slammed into those in front and the slugs continued to spew out of the *Anam Cara*.

Someone was yelling over the COM, but Falco kept firing and Hull Pounders kept dying, inching closer and closer. He was now using line of site, the polyglass in front of him splattered with membranes, sacs, chunks of bone-ish matter, thick viscous ooze – still Falco fired, the guttural screaming over the COM growing louder, louder. The Gatling gun spun, whirled and clicked, empty of rounds while the white-hot steel cooled.

The Hull Pounders were gone. Falco realized he was the one screaming and fell silent. He sat in the cockpit breathing, in and out. The NAV-screen was clear, the Battle-Net silent and Captain Falco was alive. He took another deep breath, slowly exhaled and tapped the COM control.

"We may need a bit more practice with the hand-held launchers... and we'll need to scrape off the *Anam Cara*'s bow canopy."

A long pause and a stunned Commander Shar'ran responded. "Yes. Yes, Captain, I'll see to it."

"Good." Falco looked down to his hands, still with an iron grip on the controls. "Oh, and tell the Chief, the Gatling gun works just fine."

Aris the Chosen One
the Darkness

THE PROX HAD DARED NOT MOVE across the thinned mass of the Darkness with its roaring current pushing upward, toward the Void. The Darkness rushed in, concealing the enemy vessel a fraction of a cycle after the hunting pack circled around toward its stationary position. Somewhere below, the massive Movoo were riding the current, pushing the Shields toward the waiting enemy fleet.

Aris the Chosen One kept still, her fins moving just enough to hold her position while the rest of the hunting pack hurtled their hardened carapaces at the last known location of the enemy. One by one their thoughts vanished from the shared thought-stream. Attacking and moving on to the Realm of Warriors, Aris thought, and so quickly the pack's flames are extinguished. The invaders were far stronger than the Creators and clans had thought.

A thought-stream to LOR, who was leading the clans toward

the Void, opened and his pain and fear washed over Aris. A faint glow grew from far above her position. The center, single stalk pulsed with a faint, red hue. LOR and the clans carried behind the eighth shield shrieked, screamed and cried as one. Hundreds of flaming pods slowly floated down from above, lighting the Darkness around them, just enough for Aris to see the warriors within struggling while the fire consumed them. The heavily armored stronghold sacs burned bright, but did not release their wailing contents.

The stalk grew a deep red and heat emanated from it in waves. The glow from far above grew into a massive blaze, turning the mass of the Darkness beneath into a murky graveyard of stronghold sacs lit in a bloody haze. Finally, the eighth shield of the clans that stood alone in the Void, discharged its fiery flesh across the face of the Darkness.

Aris pushed her carapace further back, moving her fins away from the center stalk now covered in blue flame, and swam downward, searching for any warriors that still lived in their blazing stronghold sacs.

Far below, in the leader's position, LOR bellowed a final cry into their shared thought-stream. Not the cry of a heroic warrior in battle, but the fearful sound a wailing youngling, alone and dying. The thought-stream closed and LOR was gone.

Aris kept to her private thought-stream, though now she sensed, no she knew the Creators could access it or even control it, but it did not matter. LOR, leader of the Warruq was sacrificed, offered to the enemy's weapons for nothing more than to test their power. Heat moved within her systems, from organ to carapace, armored plate to muscled fin. A presence she had felt before, not the Creator's, something far more powerful... the Darkness.

I protect you, feed you and heal your body when damaged. Aris was a prisoner in her own carapace. These thoughts were from the Darkness. You are inside me? You have always been there.

361

The Darkness has always been within me. A distance consumed her, her carapace felt foreign.

Yes, Aris the Chosen One, you have evolved beyond the existence of the others. It is time.

Aris thrashed in the Darkness, the plates of her carapace locking and her systems burning with the warrior's rage. These are not my thoughts, my carapace is not my own! I am afraid...

Yes. Fear. Let it consume you. Your thoughts, your systems, your organs, have always been mine.

The Darkness released her. I will not be your slave, she thought, my path to the Realm of Warriors is before me. Through the fading glow of the dying shield above, Aris detected the wake from the enemy vessel. Faint, but there it was, a path to the enemy. The wake from the fleeing vessel was disappearing into the natural current of the Darkness.

Aris the Chosen One would not be enslaved by another force. No longer a puppet of the Creators nor a servant of the Darkness. With her last act as a free Prox, she ignited her energy bloom and tore through the Darkness.

Captain Yue Fei
the Black Field

CAPTAIN FEI STOOD MOTIONLESS. The starboard side of the *Kwan Yin* was washed in a filtered glow that faded to a dark, oily sludge and finally to black.

Commander Zhu broke the silence. "I think we know what happened to the lone disc, Captain. You were right, sir. 10th Fleet is at the other end."

Fei remained focused on the strange ocean-like environment in which they found themselves. Ripples moved in slow, heavy rolls that continued to push against the starboard side. Each wave came in weaker and the interval to the next swell was growing. The gray mist was gone and the black field had taken them once again.

"Four glancing impacts." Fei looked to his officers.

"Four hits, five enemy targets." Commander Zhu studied the Battle-Net display, scanning the damage. "We are blind again.

Those 'glancing impacts' punched through all but the final few layer of the hull. It's sealed with no damage to our systems, we were lucky, Captain. Moved just in time."

"Lieutenant Ko."

The pilot straightened at his station near the bow. "Yes, Captain?"

"I need you to adjust our course and still find open space."

Fei assumed the fifth, remaining enemy would have seen the direction the *Kwan Yin* fled. It would find them if they did not change their position quickly.

The pilot's hands moved across his data-pad and stopped. "Yes, Captain I will make the adjustments."

"Do it. You have the controls Lieutenant. Choose your course at your discretion..." A shadow appeared overhead on Virtual Surround Vision. Fei looked to the overhead, and it erupted. A black mass the size of a bus hammered the captain in to the deck. Stunned, he pulled himself to his knees. Mending epoxy flooding the three-meter gash overhead, sealing the damaged hull almost as fast as it had appeared.

Fei pushed off the floor, his ears ringing and popping as he staggered towards the location of his crumpled captain's chair.

A large thrashing shadow protruded from the deck of the bridge. Its body was covered in large scales that looked like the ancient plated armor worn by knights, but the armor was under its skin. Excess mending epoxy dripped from the overhead onto the flailing dark... tail? ... and was immediately flung in all directions. A whale has breached our hull, Fei thought, dazed and staggering. No, it's stuck in the deck. Blood ran from his ears, screams filled the bridge, the tail continued to lash out in every direction. Fei's hands wiped at a warm, sticky liquid covering his face, blurring his vision, giving the monster that grew from the floor a bloody hue.

"Down, get down..." A distant voice whispered into Fei's

ringing ears and a willful force hurtled him off his feet and into the base of the hologram station.

Booming flash after flash from a shotgun filled the manic bridge of the *Kwan Yin* with acrid smoke and a pungent stench. Captain Fei tried to place the foul aroma laced with iron and shit, but the light faded and the horrors worn by his frantic crew dissolved into a silent oblivion.

the Darkness
Aris the Chosen One
the Invaders

ARIS THE CHOSEN One fought against the immense pressure constricting around the middle of her carapace. Some type of suspended material ate at her hide, hardened and pressed further, soon it would cut through her. She locked her plates, and moved her tail with all the strength she had left, desperate to tear free of the enemy vessel.

A muffled blast followed by immense pain and one by one, her systems were shutting down. Another blast, another organ failed, a spike of pain and additional internal systems collapsed. Her armored body was created to take immense punishment, survive as long as possible. Fight to the end. Before an organ or system died, its last act was an intense spike of pain that reverberated through the systems and organs that were left, giving them a fraction of a cycle of warning to adjust and keep her alive. Her massive carapace lurched from slack to rigid as the ever-increasing flashes of agony jolted through her.

The building pressure crushed her bony plates, each cracking, popping. Soon their interlocking web would fracture and Aris the Chosen One would move on to the Realm of Warriors. If there was such a place, she thought, her memories clouding and merging together. Her carapace slammed up into a rigid posture then relaxed and drooped with a thud against the cool, soft, outer skin of the invader's vessel.

This beast had not uttered any of the ancient languages since it entered the Darkness. Its skin was cold yet forgiving compared to that of the first encounter her mentor had faced with a beast of iron or rock.

Aris's thoughts fragmented and released in mass, swirled and became one on the open thought-stream. *Why have you not healed me? I remain in your mass, why do you not wash me with your embrace? Instead you leave me to suffer?*

The open thought-stream closed and for the first time in her existence, the first time in billions of cycles, Aris the Chosen One was alone. Fear saturated what was left of the Prox and she desperately tried to curl into a defensive ball. Hide in her fear as she did when the enemy destroyed her mentor.

All she found was the cold skin of the enemy vessel. The beast that held her tight in its grasp, half her carapace buried within it. The half I can no longer feel, she thought. A spike of pain and her ocular sensors faded and died in a painful fit.

Her carapace went limp. The rushing mass of the Darkness, pushing and bending her towards the faint glow and warmth of the enemy's propulsion system. A crack echoed through her carapace, Aris's weakened plates failed under the immense pressure of the enemy vessel. The beast she had almost torn through was healing itself. Another strength of this powerful, invading force they continued to underestimate.

Alone, blind and afraid, Aris the Chosen One released a final cry for help. A wet snap followed by a calming coldness overcame her and she was torn from the enemy and glided down its smooth skin while it pushed through the Darkness and towards the Void.

A brief and intense heat warming what remained of her

battered form, a last, semi-lucid thought passed through her burning skull-plate… I am free.

Her leaking methane sac exploded in the trailing burn from the enemy's propulsion system.

Oath fulfilled.

69

the Creators
Planet Tzara

THE CREATORS CONTINUED their debate with Tzara, their leader hovering above the twelve.

A shift could be done. She spoke downward, focusing her sounds like a distant storm, rumbling through the clouds. *A shift from the furthest frontier of the territories.*

The twelve Creators looked upward at their eldest and filled Tzara's lair with question upon question, as the idea had never been contemplated, never tried.

What if we allow the enemy fleet to continue its retreat towards its clan and away from our new territories? The Creator of Krell pushed herself higher, until she hovered just below Tzara. *Let them go back to their own lair that hangs in the Void?*

Yes, Tzara thought, of course, Leader of the Krell, allow the slayers of clans to crawl back to their lair until they again come to our borders, and in far greater numbers. She moved higher, leaving the Krell leader in her appropriate place.

There is no time for waiting. Tzara moved toward the center, high above the twelve, her voice booming from above, the light shining off her ebony, mirror-like carapace. *The seven stalks and stronghold pods are safe for the moment but the invaders destroyed one of the Shields and hundreds of the warriors it protected.* Tzara waited for the news to sink in, her round, black ocular sensors diminished to slits beneath her skull plate. Shrieking came in waves from below, echoing throughout Tzara's lair.

We have never lost a Shield in battle. Their mass has never been breached! the Creator of the Warruq roared.

The moment had come; Tzara sensed the power of the warrior's rage begin to drip into the other Creators. Contained for now, she thought, but the loss of the Shield would unite them for the second time in their shared history.

At this cycle, one of the vessels is slashing at the Shields from a growing distance. Killing as the cowards flee. She lowered herself; Tzara closed the distance between her and the twelve Creators. Her voice thundered downward. *The very one that destroyed many of the Seekers that peacefully lay amongst the ice and rock fields for millions of cycles, guarding the gentle mining clans.*

The twelve remained silent, listening to the speaker for the Darkness, clicking armored plates and shrieking the call for war. Tzara shuddered, allowing the warrior's rage to course through her, keeping it just below the point of giving in to its power.

This enemy is crawling away in fear while it stabs and claws at our shields. One has been slain, the stalk it carried destroyed with the warriors attached burning within their stronghold sacs! We must release the seven shields and the full might of the clans they protect!

A roar vibrated against her carapace, the twelve sounded in unison. Tzara moved her lateral fins slowly, gently turning her carapace, reflecting the light in all directions. Silence followed, her skull plate lowered, moments passed while Tzara revolved, around and around and she stopped.

But who will lead the clans? Creator of the Krell asked, the orifice from where the sounds sprang jiggling and rippling, a thick paste frothing at the edges. *The last anointed Aris the Chosen One and LOR, have fallen.* She spun her massive sphere of girth, looking at the other Creators. *We must again call a Warruq and a Prox to the positions.*

And what of the Void? Tzara slowly raised her skull plate until the slits of her ocular sensors could again be seen. *This enemy is powerful! What of the fiery embers that chase and effortlessness destroy our clans?*

This new invader retreats as the shields sit outside of the protection from the Darkness. The enemy has learned their fiery embers cannot pursue within her mass. A shift is needed. We must protect the shields and cover the clans' attack! We must move the Darkness with us!

Chaos consumed the lair, sounds echoing from the twelve Creators. Tzara held silent, patiently waiting for their answer. She observed the Creator of the Krell glowing brighter with each passing moment, increasing her internal fire, swelling then receding. The Creator of the Warruq clicked her armored plates and on and on each Creator went. A sound, a threat, a retreat, back and forth until all fell silent.

Tzara descended until level with all the Creators who held their position. The sign a decision for the territories was made. It began with Creator of the Krell, *SHIFT.*

Tzara nodded to the second oldest of the Creators.

The leader of the Warruq was next, *SHIFT.*

Speaker of the Ten, *four for to SHIFT, six to remain.*

All had sounded, except for Tzara, the ancient one.

Six for the SHIFT and six to remain and keep territories as they are, keep the Darkness at bay and let the invaders escape into the Void. The vote was as expected. Tzara knew the old Creators wanted revenge for their slaughtered, warrior clans, which they produced. The younger Creators wanted ore production to continue uninterrupted by war. But the Darkness, she wanted a new direction, one with the promise of new mass to feed her insatiable growth. I have the last sound in the decision and all is how the Darkness and I have seen it, Tzara thought, or was it all the Darkness... it no longer mattered.

SHIFT.

The twelve Creators bowed in respect, the decision was final and all would do their part.

The Darkness would relinquish the far boundary taken in the first war with the ruthless Dakkadians. An area acquired gradually over billions of cycles through the loss of millions of warriors. A period when the territories were young and only five worlds revolved around the twin stars. A territory fought over and taken from those who may try and take it back the moment the Darkness pulled away. The moment the Darkness left it unprotected and the clans moved to destroy the new enemy that retreated on the other side.

A SHIFT would protect the shields and the warriors they carried in thousands of strongholds. But the Darkness could only move so far before too much of the territories would be left defenseless. Tzara could not say what she believed to the twelve Creators, it would be seen as weakness. The eldest warriors from the Prox and the Warruq Clans that would become Aris the Chosen One and LOR, were not strong enough to defeat this enemy.

Tzara remained in deep thought while the twelve departing Creators entered their personal pods and one by one began the journey back to their worlds. Creator of the Krell hovered for a fraction of a cycle until her new pod arrived, but of course she did, thought Tzara. Last to arrive, last to depart.

Kalis will lead the clans. The guttural rasp of her unfiltered sound was comforting to her though it came from another.

Yes, Darkness, Kalis will bring you what you desire and I will make sure we are victorious.

Kalis was safely kept in an area deep within the Darkness. A lone creation with a single purpose that waited to release her energy bloom, waited for the exhilaration that would flood her systems upon release. Kalis would rain devastation upon all things within her reach and once beyond the control of the Darkness, her wrath may include her keepers.

An ancient harbinger of destruction, Kalis was once again useful, the fallen Creator was needed for battle and more importantly, for the expansion of the territories.

There was no turning back; the Creators and the Darkness were going to war again. The Darkness would reach out toward the enemy as far as her mass would allow and protect the clans for as long as she could.

But first, it was time to let the shields speak for themselves. Time for the gentle giants to use the pain and loss of their leader to focus the power they contained between them. The power that took millions of cycles to store and but an instant to release. Tzara would let the shields take vengeance on the enemy.

Kalis would take care of the rest.

70

Captain Falco
Battle Station Pluto

"ALMOST THERE, CAPTAIN." Ensign Holts continued to input the last of the data sent from 10th Fleet by Lieutenant Bai. "10th Fleet is now in range."

Falco nodded, but remained tense, standing behind his captain's chair and staring through the portside windows. His arms were heavy, firing the Gatling gun had released something within him – something he buried with his wife and daughter. He felt satiated, but knew the hunger would return. Falco wanted to kill, he wanted revenge, but not just for the death of crewmen or the destruction of vessels, he wanted revenge for the loss of his previous life.

"Working on the Fleet's holo-feed link, sir. Should only be another moment." Holts worked quickly, multi-tasking between various data-pads and screens.

The direct feed from the Fleet's open-COM gave them as much information as they could ask for from this distance.

Having a direct feed from their hologram would be a godsend. Falco was sure Lieutenant Bai did not have authorization to send an encrypted link for the holo-feed to Station Pluto. Bai and Holts had become friends while working on the Oortian Detector, but Bai had taken a chance and Falco would not forget it.

The open-COM continued to feed them a healthy dose of action while the rail gun laden cruiser, the *Lie Gong* continued her assault on the massive discs. 10th Fleet was in retreat, but Falco was waiting for the Oortian counter-attack. Based on the orders directing the Fleet's formations and speed, so was Admiral Chen.

The Pluto Room felt less like a command center and more like a crowd waiting for a grav-fight to begin.

"Fleet's holo-feed is up, Captain!" Holts pushed away from the table control panel and the hologram in the center of the table came to life.

Falco moved closer to his Ensign. "Well done, Holts." He raised an eyebrow. "So much for the hour delay."

She lowered her voice. "Lieutenant Bai is feeding the video link through the rarely used stern laser beacon of the command ship." Holts eyes gave away the smile she held in check.

"Won't the bright flashing be of concern to 10th Fleet?" Falco kept his best captain's face on but had no idea how the laser beacons worked in the first place.

"Not a visible laser beam, sir," Holts let the smile take over, "but more an invisible beam, consistent and faster than radio waves, like the ultimate line-of-sight internet connection."

"Good work, Ensign." Falco took in the look of complete joy on her face. I want to see more of that, he thought, much, much more.

The crew followed the evolution of the battle as the hologram kept pace with 10th Fleet. Chief Engineer Pema Tenzin sat to Falco's left, crouched in his chair, arms resting on the tabletop. Each time a slug from the *Lie Gong*'s rail guns sliced into another of the massive discs, the chief made a short flinching punch that only another fighter would notice.

Captain Falco felt confident in the twenty-two, newly deputized ensigns that sat to Pema's left and ended at Ensign Holts at the opposite end of the table. Each Tibetan had chosen to stay and protect the symbol of what their people were capable of. Station Pluto represented Tibet's unmatched engineering prowess, but they also remained in the face of overwhelming odds. More importantly, they stayed because Chief Tenzin asked them to and he believed in Falco.

Chief Tenzin was the best kind of family, he thought, the kind you can choose. Falco looked toward Commander Shar'ran and over to Lieutenant Wallace and finally back to Ensign Holts. Yes, the very best of family, he was sure.

Falco's attention fell back to the hologram where streaking projectiles continued to belch from the lone, attacking cruiser. She formed the point of the Phoenix Formation while 10th Fleet continued its fighting retreat. Tension was thick in the Pluto Room, each officer waiting for a response from the Oortians and what form it would arrive in. They had allowed the Fleet to see them, positioned on the face of the black wall, permitting 10th Fleet's sensors to lock onto the seven remaining targets. Goading the vessels to fire their missiles.

Admiral Chen had not fired additional missiles. Falco would have done the same, assuming the Oortian's now understood the power of the Fleet's weapons. They would use the camouflage again to hide the discs after the missiles were launched. The warheads would instantly be flying blind and useless. But firing at specific coordinates with a cruiser laden with rail guns, Falco grinned, now that would force your enemy's hand. Hot lead slugs had no targeting system once they left the rails. You could set the range of their explosion with flak rounds, but camouflage or not, unless those seven discs can move faster than they have shown, they were sitting targets.

A heavy dose of panic continued to creep in and out of Falco's chest. These Oortian discs were mammoth. Larger than anything humanity had ever built or piloted in space.

"My god." Lieutenant Wallace turned toward Falco. "Each one is larger than Station Pluto."

"Yes, they are," Falco stated. "Hard to miss that way. Chances are, humanity's greatest achievement won't impress them very much."

Wallace turned his head and chuckled.

Falco found Commander Shar'ran's weary stare and rolled his chair away from the table and next to the man.

Shar'ran leaned in. "They leave one in the open as a sacrificial lamb while the others retreat into the protection of the Oortian field?"

Ensign Holts came up behind them.

"They leave one to be destroyed. One to learn from." Holts stated.

Falco sat speechless not only from the thought that the goliath of a disc destroyed was the idea of Oortian fodder but equally impressed by Ensign Holts skill of lip-reading from across the table.

"It is time." Captain Falco looked to his officers who had seen enough of the streaking lead projectiles racing across the hologram towards the black wall hiding the seven discs. "Get on with the final preparations, checks and recheck."

Commander Shar'ran had adjusted the hand-held rocket launchers in the Battle-Cubes. He simply dialed up the heat seeking sensitivity on their tracking system. Hull Pounders, even for their size, produce a fraction of the assumed energy signature. All Falco knew is their hardened skull plate gave way when hammered with hundreds of 30mm incendiary rounds. Falco gave his second-in-command a nod and slowly moved his eyes around the table, pausing long enough on every face to measure each look.

"Our time is close at hand. Station Pluto will enter the battle as a supporting force of the retreating 10th Fleet or as the last protector of the thousands of civilians en route to Earth. Soon it will be decided." Falco felt hope for the retreating vessels of 10th Fleet that were still half a day's burn away.

"In either scenario we fight for each other as there is no one else to come to our aid in time. Vice-Admiral Hallsworth is leading the United Nation's newest Fleet, the 11th, but even with the latest innovations in solar sails, they are three years out. We stand as one in the blackest of hours at the edge of our solar system. We stand as the defenders of Battle Station Pluto, humanity's line in space."

Captain Jack Falco stood and twenty-six men and women rose to meet their leader. "It is time for warriors, it is time for greatness. Harness your fear and stand together as the guardians of Station Pluto and that which lays behind her."

"Commander Shar'ran the room is yours." Falco saluted his officers, knowing for many it could be the last time and punched the hatch release, leaving the Pluto Room to the final checks and briefings of Commander Shar'ran and Chief Tenzin.

They are ready, Falco thought. He moved down the corridor to begin his final inspection and ensure all were prepared. He came to an abrupt halt as a crewman pushed a squeaking cart towards him.

"Sir." The young woman had fire in her eyes, a sense of purpose. Falco realized he had only nodded towards her direction, his eyes moving from her intense gaze to the neatly stacked med-suits piled high on her cart.

Each jumpsuit was flat and fashioned from a polymer weave that held thousands of thin, pliable bands stacked one on top of the other from the ankles, up to the neck and down to the end of the long sleeves.

They were an innovation made possible by the United States' booming Nano-Technology industry. Med-suits worn by contractors building Station Pluto had saved hundreds of lives by stemming the flow of blood and treating mild injuries on the job. Feather-light with a gentle pressure, the suits monitored every conceivable bodily rhythm – organ functions to bowel movements and hundreds of other processes.

Ensign Holts suggested the gruesome benefits of using the med-suits by occupants of the Battle-Cubes. Falco reluctantly agreed, but there were only enough suits for half of the Cubes' crewmen and both rail guns. If anyone knew of the potential damage a malfunctioning suit would cause, no one in their right mind would wear one, Falco thought, but this situation is different. We must survive at any cost.

He allowed the true purpose of the med-suits to take hold, determined not to hide from the carnage that lay ahead. Each of the hundreds of compression rings lining the suits had two functions. Firstly, to monitor and alert the operator of the suit and the observer of the computer system they were linked to of a potential problem. Secondly, its function was that of a tourniquet. Each band was capable of restricting its contents, the human body, to stop blood flow. The bands could deaden nerves, severe a limb, and cauterize the wound within seconds. A crewman could keep working, living and above all else, fighting after sustaining unthinkable bodily damage.

"We have movement, Captain." The closest COM-Box rang out and Falco realized he had not moved since the cart squeaked by.

"On my way back." Looks like the Oortians have had enough. He spun back around and quickly moved towards the Pluto Room. Skirmishes were now over, he thought as he reached the hatch, punched the release and entered the chaos.

"Sir, we can now join with the Battle-Net of 10th Fleet."

Commander Shar'ran was sitting next to the hologram and continued to work the control pad in front of him.

The hologram showed seven massive discs moving away from the endless dark wall and towards the retreating 10th Fleet. Captain Falco's eyes remained locked onto the speck that was the *Lie Gong*. She continued firing a steady stream of projectiles. Each heated mass pierced a different disc and the rail-guns continued their assault in a brutal circular pattern. Death by a thousand cuts.

"What in God's name are they pulling behind them?" Falco pointed to the seven long tubes that trailed behind the discs into the black field. Growing longer and longer, each covered with strangely shaped pods.

71

Captain Fei
the Black Field

THE FOG BURNED OFF, turned into a pink haze and a searing bright light shot through Captain Yue Fei's skull. Pressure – he felt a heavy wet blanket, thick with heat pushing on every square inch of his aching frame.

SNAP...

"Captain... Captain... it's wearing off. You are in the Med-lab. You've been injured."

Fei could not place the voice.

"Hold still, sir, almost finished."

Soothing. His boat the *Kwan Yin* lived up to her name, the Goddess of Compassion. She must be the voice from above, willing me back... but from what? Fei felt his words float through his mind, but he could not feel his lips, his face, just the paralyzing pressure.

"Almost there, Captain, you're going to be fine. I'll release the sedation-field momentarily."

This time the voice took on a masculine quality. Fei's thoughts found order, his senses where returning and the harsh scent of antiseptic assaulted his nose.

SNAP...

"One more, sir, and I will begin the release."

SNAP...

"All finished, Captain Fei. We will bring you out now. Please keep your eyes closed until I tell you to open them."

Pressure rolled up from his toes, slowly releasing parts of his body back to his control. Fei's thighs sank into the cool padding and with an immense sense of relief, a cool draft reached his groin. His torso was light and his arms heavy, yet strong. Fei began to roll his solid shoulders, left and right as his neck and head were still under sedation.

And the scene flooded back, the attack on the *Kwan Yin* and his crew. The boom of a combat shotgun firing on the bridge and the stench from the discharge of its gas cartridge, the warm wetness that followed...

"Captain," the soothing voice was gone, replaced by the gruff ship's doctor. "Sir, it's okay. I am going to release your neck and head now."

Fei relaxed, composed himself.

"Sir, I needed to give your mind a moment to return to the present, shed off any lingering effects of the treatments. You are going to feel a brief discomfort." The doctor waited another moment then fully released the sedation-field.

"You can slowly open your eyes now, Captain Fei."

Pain briefly pulsated through every nerve ending, his body now fully connected to his brain. Each muscle flexed and contracted. Two fuzzy human forms appeared. A pinch, the prick of a needle followed by a moment of euphoria and Fei's body relaxed.

"That should help, sir."

The two fuzzy men merged into one. Fei opened and closed

his eyes over and over until a clear and heavily wrinkled Doctor Jampa was staring back.

"I need a report!" Fei shot up and swung his tingling legs over the table. "Commander? Where is Commander Zhu?"

"Slowly, sir." Doctor Jampa placed a steadying hand on each shoulder. "He is on the bridge, Captain. Much has happened since the attack." Jampa held Captain Fei upright and continued to inspect his handiwork.

"You have a direct line to his station. Commander Zhu has assumed control until you are able to return to the bridge." Doctor Jampa kept a hand on Fei's shoulder and pointed to the COM-Box. "Set to voice control. He wanted a direct line to you."

"How much longer, Doctor?" His hands found the sides of his aching head. "Everything feels, wrong, distant."

"Five minutes and you will have full control," he gave Fei a gentle nod, "and you'll be cleared to leave." Jampa paused and waited for a rebuttal. None came. "Good. I suggest you lay back down for a few minutes and use the COM from here."

Doctor Jampa had been close to Fei's family. A much younger version spent many dinners at his childhood home, smoking cigars and drinking bourbon with his father. He had also witnessed Fei as a brash, wild child storming from one mischievous escapade to the next. The old man was family.

Doctor Jamba eased the captain down to the soft slab. Fei's hands again rose towards his face, an uncontrollable itch consuming his entire head.

"Keep your hands away, Captain!" Jampa glared down at Fei. "A few minutes more and they will be healed. It took me hours to fix that mess."

"Was anyone else injured?" Fei thought of the hull exploding above him. No, it was torn and again the feeling of his body covered in a warm, sticky mist. Nausea flooded over him. He swallowed hard and waited for his old friend to answer.

Doctor Jampa looked down to the invisible deck and the dark

field below. He followed the swirling black that cradled the *Kwan Yin*, the brackish ocean the crew was now used to. The blackness that concealed the predators that moving through it.

"Doctor?"

Jampa raised his silvered brow and looked at his captain's healing wounds. "Your pilot, Lieutenant Ko, was killed. He sat one meter from your position. Died on impact."

"Where is his body? Why is he not here, washed, and prepared for an honorable burial? Why is he not cared for as a hero of the People's Navy?" Rage briefly blinded him. "On the seventh day, how will his soul find its way home!" Fei's voice grew stronger with each word until it filled the womb-like medical center.

Doctor Jampa calmly reached for a small steel bowl that contained dozens of glistening white shards the size of large slivers. "This is what I pulled out of your face, your arms and your chest."

"But where is Lieutenant Ko, Doctor?" Captain Fei still drew breath, his pilot did not.

"Captain," Jampa's face fell ashen and loose, "these are bone fragments from the lieutenant. The impact from the…" Jampa fell silent.

"From what? The impact from what?" Fei again tried to rise.

"From the 'creature.' The thing that punched through the *Kwan Yin* shattered his body and ejected most of it out the other side of the hull. Part of its body is stuck in the mending epoxy on the bridge."

Admiral Chen
the Oortians

ADMIRAL CHEN and 10th Fleet continued their fighting retreat from the Oortians. They had destroyed one of the massive Oortian discs, but now seven more were in pursuit. Chen monitored the hologram in the center of the bridge. "What are they, Commander, armor of some sort? Protecting what?"

"Some type of transports, Admiral, or possibly a carrier-type craft." Commander Lee continued to scan the data feed from the linked Battle-Net. The Fleet's spread formation gave them better data from its dispersed points. Nine cruisers and three dreadnoughts of 10th Fleet scanned the maximum zones around them. The seven colossal discs continued to push away from their protective camouflage, towing what looked to be long solid poles with various sized spheres attached at random positions along their length.

The Battle-Net screen lit up like a Christmas tree.

"There are four types of spheres attached to the poles. Each type has almost the exact surface area. I believe the slight variation is from the sphere itself." Commander Lee continued, "The seven discs are blocking our sensors from seeing directly behind them, but based on what we can detect further back, there are thousands of them, Admiral."

"Hull Pounders?" Chen wanted them all to be the small cannonballs, but four types meant there were Oortians they had not encountered yet.

"Yes, the smallest type is a close match to the Hull Pounders. Another looks to be the size of the larger Oortians that hit the *Anam Cara* and Captain Falco, the size of combat suits." Lee fell silent, his hands tapping and moving across his data-pad. "The other two types are much larger, the biggest is a sphere similar in size to our Vipers."

"Distance from Fleet?" Chen had 10th Fleet pushing their bow thrusters to failure in a desperate attempt to put distance between them and the Oortians. At least that is what he needed them to think, Chen thought. Away from your impenetrable lair you must go, far from safety and into open space.

"Seven hundred klicks from the Viper line." As if reading Admiral Chen's mind Lee added, "Fifty-seven klicks from the dark field and increasing."

"Yet still, these lines they're towing, one end is still coming out of the field. Fifty-seven kilometers of orbs on each and growing." Chen glanced at the hologram and what remained of 10th Fleet. Our destiny is closing in, Chen thought. The Oortians were moving exactly ten percent faster than 10th Fleet's thrusters could push them away.

"Adjust the Fleet for blast-radius, Commander Lee," the admiral kept his voice low, "and do it slowly."

Chen followed the gradual progress while each vessel remained in the Phoenix formation, but added extra space between them. Every crew-member aboard knew what was happening. It was a commonsense adjustment when preparing for the worst. Planning for the possible destruction of any of the Fleet's boats by spreading them out of the path of their neighbor's blast radius. It was a chilling reminder of the size of the Oortian force pushing towards them.

"Dreadnoughts in position. Cruisers in position." The commander waited for the final flashes from the Viper laser beacons. "Patrol boats in position, The Fleet has achieved blast spread."

"Battle-Net has lock on seven shields and tracking 4,300 objects attached to the trailing poles, numbers increasing, but we cannot surmise what is directly behind the discs," Commander Lee said.

Chen marveled as they kept coming out of the field. How many waited behind the dark wall, he thought, and what of the orbs that were the size of Vipers? He could no longer wait. They had to hit them before they released their contents or worse. Thousands of Oortian vessels could overrun the Fleet's defensive systems even when linked to the Command Ship's Battle-Net and fighting as one. It's now or never. The moment had arrived.

"Dreadnoughts, load Dragon missiles." Chen pulled tight on his harness. Each dreadnought carried two Dragon missiles and under normal circumstances they would never be used or even threatened for use.

"Yes, Admiral." Commander Lee held his gaze, then turned and sent the order.

Chen scanned the bridge and understood the command he had just given. He was going to use the most destructive non-nuclear weapons that existed in humanity's arsenal and the crew of the *Qing Long* fell under a heavy silence.

Six Dragon missiles, Chen thought, never to be fired, only for appearance, peacekeepers. They were twenty meters long and packed with a deadly high explosive yielding the equivalent of ninety tonnes of TNT. Dragon missiles were designed to remove all life from their blast radius in two stages. First the missile releases and spreads a vast cloud of explosive material near the enemy force. Then a blast ignites the cloud and a fiery hell follows that nothing can survive. A fiery hell with a 500-meter radius that can be aimed in any direction.

Each was housed in an aluminum shell painted in the People's Red and would soon be unleashed on an enemy that only days before, was unknown to them.

"Dragon-Fire missiles ready to launch. Battle-Net tracking 5,400 objects and counting." Commander Lee swallowed hard. "Seven carriers, six missiles. Targets, Admiral?"

"Drop them behind the seven Oortian Carriers. One as close to the aft side of the group as possible. The other five spread every 1,000 meters along the center of the trailing poles," Chen felt ice creep into his veins, "and, Commander, prepare cruisers and dreadnoughts for full-burn. *Lie Gong* and patrol boats remain, defensive firing line."

"Admiral?"

"Commander *Lee*,' Admiral Chen emphasized his surname, the timber in his voice deepening, "prepare for a full-burn."

"Yes, sir!" Lee sent the order over the COM and flashed it to the Viper line, each patrol boat flashing back within seconds.

10th Fleet continued to fire their bow thrusters while the seven Oortian carriers slowly closed the distance, gaining ground on the Fleet, but traveling further from their dark field, and further from safety.

Admiral Chen sat rigid in his command chair and prepared to release the fires of hell.

The Oortians kept emerging from the dark field, pod after pod pulled into space by seven discs... with no end in sight.

Captain Fei
the Black Field

"CAPTAIN ON BRIDGE." Commander Zhu stated rather than used his customary yell and gave his friend a curt nod.

Their eyes met for a moment. Fei raised a weak hand. "I'm fine. No need to worry, Commander." But I realize I look like I've taken a partial compression-round from an M40 to the face. Fei gathered himself.

"According to Commander Zhu, Lieutenant Ko..." Fei paused, straightened his posture, "... before he passed, Lieutenant Ko was able to position the *Kwan Yin* close to the edge of the black field. We have moved back a few hundred meters to stay out of the thinning area close to open space. If our sensors work, even at a limited capacity near the edge, so can the enemy's." Fei took a few deep breaths and continued. "Before moving back, fully into the field we were able to pick up faint signatures matching vessels of 10th Fleet. Estimated at a few hundred klicks beyond our bow.

"Lieutenant Ko is a hero, we owe him our lives." Fei's bruised face, covered in small, sutured-wounds, looked to each and every crewmember on the packed bridge. Hope had replaced uncertainty on most of their faces. He lowered his gaze to the swirling black under his feet. "May Lieutenant Ko live well in the next life and may we all be fortunate enough to know him again. To your stations." The crewman quickly dispersed and Captain Fei carefully moved towards his captain's chair.

The Commander strode to the center of the bridge and stood behind the pilot's station. "Captain, Ensign Ang has temporarily taken over for our pilot, Lieutenant Ko." His eyes found the deck, "With your approval Sir, Ensign Ang will take over all duties and responsibilities as pilot of the *Kwan Yin*."

Fei knew it was little more than ceremony and nodded to his Commander. "Ensign Ang," the muscular pilot turned to look at her captain, "You have the controls. Carry on."

"Yes, Captain." Ang turned back to her duties.

And a new cog has been placed, Fei thought, another brave crewman is dead, another one takes their place. "Ensign Ang, systems report."

"Our main engine capable of seventy percent power." The pilot scanned the ever-updating engineering report. "COM-Sat should be able to send messages in open space, however, we cannot receive."

"Best we can do without a mechanics bay," Commander Zhu said.

"That will have to do." Captain Fei looked to the mended overhead. A smooth silver patch above and a similar one on the deck less than a meter away from his chair. Fei's eyes shifted from deck to ceiling.

Commander Zhu came up behind Fei and pointed at the deck. "Once it was dead; eventually the hull's grav-fluid and mending epoxy burned right through it. Our compression rounds had little effect. Over four meters of it was left on the inside stuck to the deck, looked like some kind of armored whale's fluke with thick plates. We removed," Zhu paused, "cut-out the carcass with a laser saw, sealed it in a containment crate and stowed it. Hull epoxy did the rest."

Fei felt sick. "This thing, it killed Lieutenant Ko. Almost killed me."

The commander looked around the bridge at the busy crewmembers. "I told Doctor Jampa, Ko was instantly killed. But when *it* punched through the hull it grazed Ko then fired off or released four large rounds, same as what hit our battle group. Two were damaged and we destroyed them with compression rounds. The other two, they attacked the lieutenant before we could destroy them. Sprang up and down, it was a blur. They hammered Ko into something unrecognizable in seconds." Zhu looked like a ghost. "Captain, they were alive, living sledge hammers..."

"You saved my life, Commander, thank you. No one could have done better."

Commander Zhu, leaned downward. "We have no missiles and only a few compression rounds left for the M40s." Zhu exhaled, voice dropped to a whisper, "We don't know if 10th Fleet has survived, Captain," his head motioned to beyond the bow, "out there, against what we have seen moving through this field? We could have picked up the signatures of destroyed vessels, just pieces."

Captain Fei remained silent, just stared ahead at the black field, the currents gently moving and shifting in all directions. He turned toward his friend, the commander he trusted with his life, again and again. "I would rather be out there in the open and defenseless, than to wait to be attacked again by something in here that we cannot see." Fei looked to the silver patch on the deck hovering above the black sea beyond and then to the patch on the hull overhead.

"If the enemy follows the same strategy they did against our battle-group, and 10th Fleet is out there, they will move the field to protect whatever things are inside those pods. Based on what I witnessed, the discs will need little protection from anything.

"Agreed," Commander Zhu said, "if or when they move the field, we move in the direction of the current."

"Right to 10th Fleet," Fei raised an eyebrow, "what could go wrong?" He straightened his aching body. "If the field moves, it will happen soon, the massive discs have moved into open space. If the field remains, we go full-burn anyway. Seventy percent power is good enough."

Commander Zhu growled in agreement.

"That will be our opportunity, Commander," Captain Fei stated with resolve. "We will see and feel the rush when their ocean of black pushes toward our countryman. We will ride this menacing wave to freedom, if only for a moment."

7 4

Admiral Chen
10th Fleet

"Discs are still coming, Admiral. The Oortian Field remains static." Commander Lee rotated toward Chen, lowered his voice. "Sir, should we turn the dreadnoughts and cruisers around? Back to Station Pluto before it's too late?"

Chen kept an eye on the hologram in center of the bridge of the *Qing Long*. The Fleet was pushing back with bow thrusters only and eventually would be overtaken by the massive, chasing Oortian carriers, the discs. It will move, he thought, the dark field will come. Just like it did for Captain Fei's battle group.

"Keep the bow thrusters burning, Commander. The field will move and when it does," Chen growled, "it will be too late, for them." He pointed at the vast carriers hunting 10th Fleet. The six Oortian discs tightened their circle around the seventh, packing in tight like a patch of scales or armored shields from the ancient battles of Rome. The surface of each carrier lit an amber hue, except for the one in center that remained black, a predatory eye watching, waiting.

"Battle-Net is picking up energy buildup," Commander Lee stated, "radiating from the six on the outside. Growing stronger, Admiral."

"Explosion?" Chen straightened in his chair.

"Different this time. More focused, more—"

"Like a weapon powering up," Chen cut in and the Battle-Net sounded an alarm a second before the circling discs turned black and the center carrier flashed bright blue and ejected a circular mass of plasma at a supersonic pace.

All 10th Fleet saw was a flash of light and the disintegration of two Vipers positioned in front of the cruiser, the *Lie Gong*. The rail gun laden vessel displayed a gouge from bow to stern on her portside. A melted furrow cauterized instantly by the blast, not a drop of mending epoxy shown on the scar that fused five hull layers together.

"Full-burn! NOW, NOW, NOW!" Admiral Chen slammed back into his chair as the grav-systems kicked-in. Eight cruisers and three dreadnoughts of 10th Fleet shutdown their bow thrusters and ignited their main engines and accelerated at the Oortian carriers with tremendous force.

Chen focused on the hologram. They burst past the remaining Vipers and the damaged cruiser that continued to unload her rail guns even as she listed on her injured side.

"It's moving! The field is coming!" Commander Lee's hand hovered over the fire controls that would release the Dragon-Fire missiles.

"HOLD. HOLD." Admiral Chen held up an open hand as they blasted closer, closer to the seven carriers, the texture of their vast shielding plates coming into focus. Skin? Porous like elephant hide, Chen thought, thick with fat, a subtle lift and fall of its mass. It's breathing.

"Admiral!" Commander Lee yelled, the dreadnoughts pulling

ahead of the cruisers, charging closer to the Oortians, "the field is picking up speed!"

You're too late Chen thought, this time we strike first. "FIRE!" Chen roared. "Release the Dragons!" Chen slammed his fist into his armrest, his command chair shaking from the blunt force.

Six red, mega-missiles clawed out of their cradles, the thrust from their launch slowing the dreadnought's progress. Hundreds of smaller, faster missiles fired from the cruisers led the way and the Dragons followed. The cruisers and dreadnoughts bow thrusters fired, their main engines fell dark and they began banking turns. Each boat pushing the capabilities of their grav-systems, even their construction, turning as tightly as possible while under full power. Anything not buckled down, strapped in or fused to the deck was tossed, turned and flung against the bulkheads.

"FULL BURN toward Battle Station Pluto! Viper group, hold your line, protect our retreat and full burn as soon as the cruiser and dreadnoughts are on their way." Chen took a deep breath. "Make sure 10th get beyond the blast radius."

Commander Lee flashed the order over the laser-beacon.

Chen swallowed hard and tapped the controls of his personal COM.

Captain Zhi of the damaged cruiser, the *Lie Gong* answered, "Yes, Admiral."

"What is your situation, Captain?" Chen zoomed in on the holo-feed, focusing on the damaged cruiser.

"Twenty-eight dead," the captain's voice was strained, "they simply vanished with the hull. Main engine is compromised, but capable of full burn for now."

"We have given ourselves a chance. Fate will decide the rest. Protect our rear." Admiral Chen zoomed out again. The hologram expanded to include the entire 10th Fleet. The *Lie Gong* continued to anchor the Viper's protective line.

We need distance, Chen thought. The third dreadnought finished its turn and headed towards the defensive line of Vipers, the other vessels already beyond his covering position.

"First wave of missiles have made contact with carriers." Commander Lee continued scanning the incoming data. "No apparent damage. Encroaching field is only ten klicks from covering the carriers."

"Get the Viper line turned around." Chen followed the six red dots moving unimpeded towards the Oortian carriers. They have no idea what is about to happen. A new experience in destruction, one even humanity has never witnessed, is upon you. A sickness settled in his stomach, Chen let it pass and thought of the ships lost, and crewmen killed. This act is just.

By closing the distance between 10th Fleet and the Oortian carriers, Chen had done exactly what he hoped. He altered the equation. The Oortian field continued to engulf more of the pods, rendering them invisible to the smaller missile guidance systems and their Battle-Net, but it was too late, the carriers and thousands of the pods were left unprotected.

"Ten, nine, eight... Defensive line has completed their turns, initiated full burn, covering our rear. It's going to be close, Admiral!" Commander Lee gripped his station with both hands. "Brace yourselves! One..."

75

Captain Falco
Battle Station Pluto

CAPTAIN FALCO and his officers remained fixed on the hologram floating above the round table in the Pluto Room. Each of them moving toward the image, sweat dripping off foreheads, fingers tapping the polyslab top.

The remainder of 10th Fleet was in full retreat and moving at max speed toward Station Pluto.

"They're almost in position." Falco motioned toward the six streaking embers, the Dragon missiles closing in.

"Oh god. It's happening," whispered Lieutenant Wallace after the first ember came to a stop. One after the other, the rest of the mega-missiles followed every 500 meters. A perfect line formed. It began behind the massive Oortian Carriers, stretching along the seven pod-covered poles and ending near the encroaching Oortian field.

"The wall has almost reached the first..." Ensign Holts paused. "What is that?"

A haze grew from the six embers, creating an opaque cloud growing behind the Oortian carriers with the line of six Dragon missiles at its center.

"Stage one, spread," stated Commander Shar'ran. He pushed back from the table, creating distance from the hologram.

Falco instinctively followed suit and leaned back in his chair.

The Oortian field rushed in to cover the first missile and the opaque cloud pulsed red then orange and back to red while it expanded further in all directions, but toward the field. There, the field swallowed red, a faint pinkish glow was all that hinted at what might be happening within its camouflage.

"Stage two, ignition." Shar'ran stared ahead, eyes hollow.

Everything within the cloud disintegrated. Energy rolled up and over the Oortian carriers. Melting layers that looked like skin then blubber, melted and burned like lamp oil. The dark field slowed to a crawl and stopped just short of the flaming carriers. Blue flashes came and went across the face of the Oortian field.

Burning spheres the size of small homes burst out of the blackness, zigging and zagging in all directions only to slow and explode into cooling chunks. Hull Pounders fizzled into heaps of ash and dispersed in the solar winds. So many shapes and sizes, Falco thought, species or weapons, organic or not, they looked to be suffering and dying by the thousands.

Falco thought back to a childhood memory. His grandparents' vineyard was surrounded by forest on the west side. One drought-filled summer, a fire raged through the trees and threatened the vineyard. Falco stood with his grandparents in the center near the pond and helplessly watched the blaze.

His grandmother held a flowing garden hose that pulled from the pond. It was not to protect the vineyard from the fire, the cleared buffer around the vines would do that. Falco soon found out the purpose of the hose. Worse than the heat, the dying trees and the smoke was what erupted out of the inferno.

The shy, beautiful roe deer shot through the flames, their unusual barking sound turned to gravely screams. They ran for their lives alone or in groups only to drop in burning heaps at the edge of the vines. Falco's grandmother extinguished the flames and waited for the next deer to fall.

A light brought Falco back to the moment. He raised an arm, covering his eyes.

Blue fire consumed the entire hologram and rolled out it in waves. The Oortian carriers were gone and every trace of carnage that staggered out of the field disappeared with it.

"Why blue?" Falco's voice rang haunted, distant, "and how in the hell is 10th Fleet going to outrun that energy wave?"

"Methane." Ensign Holts swallowed hard, her face resting in her hands. "Oortians use methane for fuel or blood or something. Methane burns blue, as does the hottest part of the fire. But, it would also require oxygen." She input information into her data-pad. "They won't outrun the wave and neither will we."

"10th Fleet is still a long way from us." Falco glanced at Ensign Holts to find her intense, brown eyes already on him.

"Just over seven hours," Commander Shar'ran moved his head side to side, "assuming they keep their present speed."

"And nothing else slows them down." Falco saw the devastation, even felt pity and remorse for the Oortian losses from the Dragon missiles. What he could not, would not believe, was that the Oortians would not retaliate in full and as soon as they could muster their available or remaining forces. They would come and they would want to destroy everything in their path.

Because that is what Falco would do.

"Incoming energy wave," Holts scanned her sensor feed, "weak, but the fact it reached us this quickly means it was a powerful blast."

The Battle-Cubes of the Infinity Wall lit with a rolling wave of light. The Pluto Room grew bright, the lights flickered and fell to shadows and came on again.

The COM flashed green and Commander Lee's voice sounded. "10th Fleet clear, Admiral Chen. All vessels heading toward Station Pluto, full burn." A heavy breathing Commander Lee paused for a few seconds. "Viper Battle group protecting the rear. No Oortians in pursuit. Sensors are clear. The Oortian field is stationary once again."

Time between each blue flash grew until finally, the great black wall that hid the Oortian forces fell slack and calm.

A roaring cheer burst from the open-COM, jolting Falco and his officers back into the present. Seconds past and the COM fell silent, its green light turning red.

Falco looked to Commander Shar'ran whose eyes moved between the officers. Falco again found his focus on the hologram feed from the stern of Admiral Chen's command ship. The Oortian field still looked ominous, an endless black wall with no top or bottom.

"Captain," Ensign Holts looked up from her data screen, "our current theory is that the Oortian field expanded when they had the materials needed to increase its size. Just as we would add another layer of bricks to a wall or add an additional room to a house when the resources where available."

"Do you have another theory, Ensign?"

"I have updated the Battle-Net model with the latest data from 10th Fleet's scanners regarding the area of the field. I believe this time, the Oortian field did not grow, it moved."

"They moved the entire field?" Falco stood and prowled around the table, eyes locked on the holo-feed. "You think the Oortians moved a cloaking field the size of our solar system? To protect a single fighting force?"

"That is what the data suggests. Soon the 10th will be too far away from the Oortian field and our joined sensor feed will be of little use." Ensign Holts sounded confident. "We have to think beyond our own abilities and perceived possibilities. What applies to humanity, may not apply to the Oortians."

Lieutenant Wallace folded his arms. "How can we think outside of all that we know? Every action or reaction is based on the evolution of apes on earth with goddamn opposable thumbs." Lieutenant Wallace sucked in a deep breath. "Throw in a century of crude space exploration and we still know nothing of our own solar system." Wallace's Scottish brogue was back in full force.

"Easy, Lieutenant," Falco turned toward Commander Shar'ran. "So they can move the field. What was uncovered?" Falco felt curiosity overcome a growing dread, for the moment.

Ensign Holts continued to scan her screen while Shar'ran chimed in. "All we see is open space. The Battle-Net can only give us an overview from this distance based on modeling. There looks to be no planets or other large objects in the newly opened space. Could be an asteroid field similar to the one the Oortian Hull Pounders were hiding in."

"In other words," Falco shook his head, "we know nothing, only that the Oortians may have the ability to expand and move a field capable of rendering everything in it invisible."

"Yep, that's it." Commander Shar'ran's data-pad linked to the Battle-Net, sounded an alert. "Faint, partial optical lock on the surface of the field." Shar'ran looked to Ensign Holts who was also scanning the incoming data. "You getting this?"

"Yes." Holts adjusted the settings, zoomed in on the dark field, and looked to the hologram where small lights pulsated across the face of the Oortian wall.

"Stars." Falco turned to Commander Shar'ran who had already begun to punch up the data feed. "Hard lock?"

"No, just a faint optical hit. They are moving in and out of the field. Amassing forces maybe. What else could it be?" His voice fell to a murmur. "Dragon missiles, a needle to an elephant."

A small green spark flashed over the hologram and was gone. "Did you see that?" Falco looked to his officers.

"That's a fleet beacon." Commander Shar'ran looked to the Battle-Net data. "There again. Got it! Coordinates locked. It's gone."

Falco moved to the hologram, fixed on the area where the green spark appeared on the face of Oortian wall. "They're growing in number." The blinking stars were now covering the field. "There!" Falco stated, his finger pointing at the surface of the black wall and again, it was gone.

"Captain," Ensign Holts hands flew over her data-pad, "partial hit on a vessel code." She continued to work through the information.

Falco and the other officers waited, shifting in their seats.

"Code 110001010K11Y0." Moments passed and her hands stopped. "That's all we have, but that's enough." She looked up at Falco. "Captain Fei's vessel, the *Kwan Yin*, or at least her fleet identification responder is intact."

"Captain Fei is alive." Falco looked around the table. "They are alive or the Oortians have compromised another signature. They did it with the Data-Pods then they could mimic a fleet vessel."

His officer's shot questioning glances at one another.

"Think about it. What are the chances the *Kwan Yin* would be so close to the face of the Oortian field?" Falco asked. "There is only one reason to position your boat so close to open space." Falco bumped a fist on the table. "Fei waits for the opportunity to escape. If it were a trick, the Oortians would not leave it where our tech could visually identify it klicks away."

"There is a possibility," Ensign Holts stated, "based on the number of objects moving in and out of the Oortian field now, some of the Oortians close to the blast and shock waves from the Dragon missiles survived, then so too, could the *Kwan Yin* and her crew."

The Pluto Room fell silent, but Captain Falco felt hope as the Oortian field had stopped its advance and 10th Fleet had struck a major blow to the Oortian fleet. And somewhere among the growing number of Oortians appearing on the face of their dark wall like stars, a small green light had appeared.

Captain Fei was alive. Falco could feel it. He spun toward Commander Shar'ran. "Can we move the station?" Falco's eyes burned with intensity and he repeated the question. "Commander, can we move Station Pluto?"

"Towards Earth?" Shar'ran stared back.

"10th Fleet," Ensign Holts stated with resolve.

"The Oortians must respond." Falco pointed toward the holo-feed and the growing number of stars twinkling in and out of the Oortian field. "They are coming, and when they do we will see their version of Dragon missiles. If," he looked around the table, stopped at Lieutenant Wallace, "if, like 10th Fleet, the Oortians were holding back their most powerful weapons, starships or soldiers—"

Wallace nodded. "They will send them now. They will respond without hesitation."

"We must be prepared to reduce the distance between Battle Station Pluto and Admiral Chen's fleet." Falco's jaw tightened. "We are it. Vice-Admiral Hallsworth and the newly anointed 11th Fleet, has left the Mars Station. Two-years, ten months, give or take a week from our location." Falco stood, paced around the table. "How do we move something meant to remain fixed? And move it with purpose?"

"Stability thrusters to start." Lieutenant Wallace stood and walked toward Ensign Holts and the controls of the holo-feed. "Ensign?" He pointed at the control pad and Holts nodded and slid over. Wallace worked at the data-pad, the hologram zoomed in on Battle Station Pluto.

The lieutenant reached toward the hologram, spun the

floating image with his hands until the bulk of the Battle-Cubes were pointing toward 10th Fleet and the Oortian field. "We use the thrusters on this side only, full-burn."

"That's not enough power." Chief Tenzin stood and joined Wallace at the controls. "We could move all stabilizing thrusters but two and position them here on the station." He pointed toward the opening of the private bay where the *Anam Cara* was kept safely positioned. "We mount them in an optimal grouping, just like we do our main engines which are made of many small engines and directed as one."

Lieutenant Wallace was now nodding, a smile spreading across his face. "Yes! The stabilizers are mobile with grav-locks to ensure safety and flexibility in various conditions. And," Wallace looked directly at Tenzin, "we can group them around the *Anam Cara*, right, Chief?"

"Exactly!" Tenzin reached toward the floating hologram with both hands together, found the opening for the private docking bay and pulled his hands apart. The *Anam Cara*'s stern and main engine were visible deep within the station. "We move a few grav-locks to the outer hull of the station and lock the *Anam Cara* down, then add the thrusters around her." Tenzin put his hands on his hips. "We have a main engine we can control through the *Anam Cara*'s bridge."

"I like it," Falco growled, he and Ensign Holts joining them in front of the hologram. "But what about stopping?" Falco shot Chief Tenzin a sideward look. "Can the two remaining stabilizers stop us?"

Chief Tenzin raised his shoulders. "Eventually, Captain. But if speed is the goal, this," Tenzin pointed at the hologram, "is the arrangement and positioning that will create the greatest thrust."

"Do it," Falco stated. "Do it with great haste, Chief, and let me know the second you're done."

Falco reached toward the hologram with arms wide and

moved them until his hands met. The image spread out, showing Battle Station Pluto, the small red dots representing 10th Fleet's progress and the Oortian wall covered with stars. Beautiful and deadly stars, Falco thought, twinkling in and out as the Oortians passed back and forth through the field.

Their numbers growing.

76

Captain Fei
the Black Field

THE *KWAN YIN* CLUNG TO edge of the black field, meters from open space. The Viper class vessel leaked repair epoxy from hundreds of cracks and holes on her bow and port side. There were pieces of 'bodies' stuck in what was left of the exterior hull layers, sealed in place by the foaming, hardening paste.

Inside the boat, skull plates pierced the exterior bulkheads and protruded through the ceiling, twisted forms frozen in looks of horror. Yes, Captain Fei thought rising to a knee, they are faces or something resembling them. The bridge was a macabre museum of the damned, a museum hit by fire and waves of energy. Crewmen lay harnessed and wide-eyed in their seats no longer fused to the deck, but scattered in all directions.

Alarms wailed, lights flashed and the *Kwan Yin*'s emergency system took over the hologram station and the ship-wide COM. "Hull integrity forty-percent, life support system stabilized, gravity compromised..." On and on the list went and the holo-feed displayed the damaged areas along with the report. Fei reached a console, entered his private code and muted the sirens.

A massive explosion, Fei thought, just beyond the field. The flames melted the outer heat shield layer of the hull. Then the shock waves turned the *Kwan Yin* into a rattle with human bodies thudding off the deck, ceiling and bulkheads, over and over again. Either the entire fleet was destroyed in a single instant or Admiral Chen had loosed the Dragon missiles. In either case, 10th Fleet was destroyed or so desperate, they launched the unthinkable.

Commander Zhu cried out in pain. Other moans and sounds of the hurt and dying followed.

Captain Fei spun on one knee, found the twisted form of his commander, stood and moved to his side. The Virtual Surround Vision was now a detriment to few living crewmen of the broken *Kwan Yin*. Another chunk struck the hull, burnt entrails slid down its hammered surface and were glued in place by the hardening hull-epoxy.

"Someone shut down the VSV!" No response, just a rotting sulfur-like smell hanging in the air and the sounds of the dying. Emergency aid containers lay open or covered in blood next to most of the bodies. Some of the wounded desperately trying to close open wounds or numb the pain as death closed in.

"Where is Doctor Jampa?" Fei fought to hold Zhu down, but one arm was little more than crunching bone and flaps of flesh. A red spurt caught the side of Fei's jaw, slid down his ear.

"Commander Zhu!" Fei grabbed his friend's muscled shoulders and pushed him back to the deck causing another scream to chatter through the commander's broken teeth. "Listen to me. I take the arm now or you die."

Commander Zhu's dark, wild eyes softened. He looked at Captain Fei, spit, blood and shards of teeth came out before the words, "Do it."

Fei nodded and a shaking Zhu forced a sobering nod back.

"I need Doctor Jampa now!" Fei remained fixed on his commander.

"He's dead. Med-room is gone. Here," a solid object bounced behind Fei and came to a thudding halt, slamming into his shin. Anger faded as he reached for the laser saw. "Just us Captain," and the voice was gone.

Fei grunted in the general direction of the voice, looking hard at Commander Zhu, "This is going to hurt." A slight click and Fei dialed the red beam to a length of ten centimeters. Zhu's head rolled away from the mass of leaking, ragged pulp that hung from his shoulder.

"It's OK, Commander," a gentle smile spread across Fei's face, "open your mouth." Fei fought off a grimace and placed a chunk of rubber from a blown hatch seal between Zhu's splintered teeth. "Bite down."

By the time the scent of burning flesh had mingled with the rest, Captain Yue Fei had taken his friends arm and saved his life... for now.

The VSV continued to stream the devastation. Dying enemy forms emerged from the sea of black, their forms twisted and shattered. They emerged like grotesque aberrations each time they entered within the meter of gray space that surrounded the vessel, where the camouflaging blackness met the hull, oil and water, Fei thought.

He pictured an aura, a once protective field around his boat the *Kwan Yin*, the Goddess of Mercy. The enemy carnage bounced and stuck to her foaming hull, her breach-suppression systems pushing the thick void-filling epoxy through hundreds of shrapnel penetrations. Can the obliterated forms of the living be shrapnel? Fei pondered as the skull plate of one of his enemies was sealed into the bulkhead to his right. Yes, he concluded.

Thousands of microscopic cameras continued to mirror the horror around them. Areas of the interior hull appeared where the cameras had been damaged or destroyed on the outside. The greatest technology of modern optics became a crystal-clear window into the depths of hell.

An approaching glow appeared and grew larger and brighter off the portside and was followed by others. Each began as a pinprick of light and quickly grew into a sun. Monstrous silhouettes flashed close to the *Kwan Yin's* hull a split second before their forms blew apart, thudding off the hull.

More shockwaves pounded the battered *Kwan Yin*. Captain Fei locked a hand around the stout base of the Battle-Net station and pulled his unconscious friend and commander, tight to his side. His face pressed hard against the deck, eyes staring into the darkness as wave after wave hit the *Kwan Yin*.

Monsters dying, exploding, their pieces sticking or bouncing off the hull and Captain's Fei's injured and dying crew had fallen silent. Fei held tight to his friend, closed his eyes and prayed to the Goddess of Compassion.

The *Kwan Yin* was pulled toward open space, Fei fought to hold on but the force was too much. Commander Zhu slid from his grip; Captain Fei reached up with his free hand desperate to find another handhold, his feet dangling in midair. The ship was sideways, an elevator going up traveling at an insane speed. Fei's fingers slid, his grip gone and smashed into something hard, he was pressed into place, his legs at an awkward and painful angle, unable to move. The ship stopped, Fei flew up and crashed into something soft, the *Kwan Yin* dropped. Fei's stomach released, the contents washed over his face and his body pressed against a sticky bulkhead. Down his boat fell, the pressure pushing against every muscle, organ. His lungs pushed out a last breath, unable to draw another.

All went black.

77

Tzara's World
the Darkness

Tzara, leader of the Creators floated helplessly in her shielded lair, desperately wanting to close the thought-stream connecting her to the clans. Shrieks of terror and pain filled the stream. The seven colossal shields' soft fleshy undersides absorbed the enemy's powerful weapons until the fire was too hot, the energy too strong. The giant beasts of the Creators begged for death. Once the heat melted their flesh into oil they were consumed by the raging fire that followed, fueling their own demise.

But the shields held the fires back long enough for some of the warriors to release from their stronghold sacs and survive.

The Darkness moved in vain, the protective mass was too slow and too late, covering the shields moments after the enemy released a new and mighty weapon. A powerful force of which the Creators had never seen before. The protective field, the Mother and giver of life became an oven and then a tomb. The Darkness had failed and she was damaged. No Tzara thought, she is hurt, a wounded god... cannot be a god? Nothing. The Darkness left her thoughts her own. For the first time in millions of cycles, Tzara was without the Darkness. Not a single tendril from its vast reach found her memory. Tzara was alone, the Darkness gone.

Her lair shook around her. The Thirteen planets and their two life-giving stars felt each shock wave while moving in their tight orbits through the Darkness. Again and again the thought-stream filled with the dying, images of the devastation. Planets closest to the dying shields absorbed the brunt of the massive creatures after they were blown into pieces that came crashing through their thin atmospheres. Millions of their inhabitants died under the crush of crumbling, falling buildings and were swallowed by towering black waves of quake-ravaged oceans.

Wait, Tzara focused and zoomed in on the clans' thought-stream. There. Again she went closer, using all of her power to look in on the world of the Warruq, the world hit hardest by the demise of the shields. The world washed in energy and death and there it was again, a black tentacle. Reaching down from beyond the planet's protective field, reaching down from the Darkness towards the devastation.

Tzara froze, her plated carapace hardened, instinctively curling itself up into a defensive ball and hung in the center of her lair, gently floating as the walls bounced from wave after powerful wave of energy continued to assault her world. Still Tzara watched, listened over the thought-stream. Fear gripped every system, every organ and still she watched the Darkness reaching and eating the Warruq dead. Millions of warrior dead or dying were cracked open, blended into slurry and sucked into the tentacle, feeding the Darkness.

Mass, Tzara thought, the Darkness needs mass to grow to move and live. The cries and screams filling the thought-stream of the clans were not only the sounds of the injured. Tzara now saw hundreds of the tentacles on all of the planets including her own. The Darkness was healing herself, consuming the mass of the clans. Dead, injured or alive, she ate and she drank by the millions.

Pain shot through her and Tzara's carapace straightened, stretched by the terror and sting of the attack on her organs and systems. *I am sorry, my Darkness*, she cried, *my thoughts were my own, I could not control them.* A voice echoed in her mind. The voice of the Darkness, a thundering power from a distant source, ravaged, menacing yet familiar, the Mother returned.

Tzara, you have seen me feed, allowed to see because we are connected, you are an extension of my will and your existence and that of the clans is mine to determine. Soon I will cleanse your memory and like the many times before, you will start again. You and the clans and the other Creators will forget the death, the destruction from my hunger and my need to heal. It will be replaced with the memory of attacking invaders, the courageous stand of the clans in defense of the planets, of the territories and the need for revenge. Revenge against the invaders. We will fight on.

Tzara shook with fear, anger and knew soon, she would forget and the sequence would continue, again and again, the death and destruction at the hands of the Darkness, the Mother feeding upon her children. What of the Realm of Warriors?

Yes. The Darkness was back. *Yes, Tzara, what of the Realm of Warriors? I will leave you with this before I wipe your memory of my feeding, but I believe deep within your systems, you already know.*

The answer flashed through her mind. Tzara knew the Realm of Warriors was the Darkness herself. Like prey being consumed by predator, the clans were food for an insatiable beast that only wanted to grow, only wanted more mass. The Darkness, the protective Mother of the Clans, was little more than a graveyard for the living.

TZARA SLOWLY UNCURLED HER CARAPACE. Floating in the center of her protective lair, she stretched, her systems woke from hibernation, and organs pushed her fluids and began processing her waste. *How long have I been here?* The shared thought-stream of the clans flooded with the warrior's cry of revenge for the fallen, vengeance on the cowardly invaders, now running back to their base. They would be hunted and slaughtered without mercy.

A cloud lifted and memory returned to Tzara. The invaders' powerful weapons, the death of the mighty shields that sent waves of energy rolling toward the planets. The Darkness, the Mother... protected the worlds of the clans, sheltered them from the coming storm and not a single death, her protective mass saving the thousands that lived on the thirteen worlds.

Tzara pulsed a message to the other Creators and then joined the shared thought-stream of the territories. She pushed her message to all the clans. *The Darkness protects us from our enemies. The great warrior Kalis has returned. Even now she gathers the clans near the Veil. The invaders will be destroyed, the territories secured and our planets safe.*

A warrior's roar filled the thought-stream and Tzara closed her feed. Her carapace clicked and snapped with each locking armored plate. The warrior's rage coursed through her systems, Tzara floated strong, proud, and fully stretched to her maximum length.

Tzara pulsed another message to the Creators, *The invaders have destroyed all of the travelers and many of the warriors beneath them. Kalis will avenge our dead. The Movoo are intact and close in on their target and their ultimate purpose. Soon we will number fourteen.*

A thought pulsed back to all the Creators. It was the Leader of the Krell, as Tzara expected.

What of the enemy and their powerful weapons? We have vastly underestimated their ability to destroy. They flee, but their weapons can attack from a great distance. We need the protection of the Darkness. Without her, our clans will die in the Void.

A slit spread across Tzara's face, the ridges of her skull plate pushed up and out and she pulsed her final message to the Leader of the Krell and the other waiting Creators.

Kalis will lead the clans in battle, the Movoo will complete their mission and the expansion of the territories will continue.

Admiral Chen – 10th Fleet
Fighting Retreat

THEY WERE seven hours from Station Pluto. The People's 10th Fleet redlined their main engines, trying desperately to increase the space between their boats and what massed behind the Oortian wall. Twenty-three vessels had made the turn and were in a dash toward the station.

A space station crewed by contractors and cleaners. A wealthy tourist destination turned battle station at the hands of Captain Jack Falco. Admiral Chen felt little confidence that the station would make a difference, but hope was hope and Battle Station Pluto was it.

The Dragon Missiles detonated. Chen watched the six, two-stage weapons disperse then ignite as one. The destruction they should have wrought was concealed by the rushing Oortian field. Based on what staggered and died outside of its reach, the destruction was substantial. Or was it? The fact the Oortian field slowed and stopped its advance meant something. Or did it? The questions nibbled on the edges of Chen's thoughts. Did the the most powerful, non-nuclear weapons available to us do little more than kill a few foot soldiers or worse, did we just kick the largest wasps' nest in our solar system? Soon, Chen would have the answers.

Off the Fleet's starboard side, the once impressive asteroid field was now an obstacle course. The Oortian Hull Pounders' kamikaze run sent ship-damaging chunks of rock and ice floating in all directions. The main hologram hung in the center of the bridge of his dreadnought command ship, the *Qing Long*. 10th Fleet looked small, frail and frantic compared to the dark black field they ran from. Endless burning sparks filled its face; to the point the hologram now showed a glowing wall as far as their scanners could reach.

"Full combat spread!" Admiral Chen thundered over the open-COM linking him to the nine cruisers and two dreadnoughts. "Slow rear defensive line, ten percent." Chen muted his COM, looked toward Commander Lee. "The *Lie Gong*?"

Lee looked down to the incoming data from the Battle-Net screen and then to the hologram and finally, back to Chen and gently shook his head from side to side.

The rail gun cruiser sporadically fired her side thrusters to keep her heading true while she held position at the center of the Viper line, but she was faltering. Her speed kicked out in uneven bursts, her main engine would not last at full burn for much longer.

Commander Lee rhythmically punched at the controls of the laser beacon, sending the orders to the trailing line of Viper patrol boats protecting their stern. Within seconds they reduced their push by ten percent and increased the open space between the patrol boats and the rest of 10th.

An inappropriately timed grin flashed across Chen's face. The vision of Commander Lee entering his rusty Morse code reminded him of his last visit to the Chinese National Opera House in Beijing many years ago.

A powerfully built coloratura soprano stunned the crowd with her blazing tempo while a lanky, silver haired gentleman attempted to keep pace as the sign language interpreter. By the end of the third act, the standing ovation and roaring applause was as much for the disheveled interpreter gasping with his hands on his knees as for the diva.

Commander Lee looked up and shot Chen a disapproving and disheveled look that brought the admiral close to laughter.

A red hue bloomed over the bridge. The hologram burned red across the face of the Oortian field, the center of the wall a deep crimson ring formed and pulsed like a heartbeat, sending rippling, circular waves across its face. Over and over again, wave after blood-red wave rolled and disappeared off the hologram feed.

Chen tapped his COM to open the feed to the entire 10th Fleet once again. He leaned toward the COM. "Battle Sta—"

The crimson ring stopped its beating. The red glow turned into thousands of exploding fireworks dancing in front of a blackened sky.

"Fleet sized force. Exiting the field!" The commander paused until the scrolling numbers stopped. "Hull pounders..." he cocked his head, rolling data filling his screens, "the rest are unknown, larger, sphere-shaped, size of our patrol boats."

"How many?" Chen roared, but knew it was meaningless. The Oortian fleet filled the hologram.

"Thousands," Lee stated, breathing deeply, "and growing, Admiral."

"Range?" Chen slid the data-pad from his armrest, brought up his personal holo-feed and zoomed in on the Viper defensive line and the damaged cruiser.

Lee cranked his neck, turning toward Chen while keeping his

eyes on the flood of incoming data. "Oortians have matched our speed. Keeping out of missile range."

"They are adapting." Chen tapped his COM. "Captain Zhi, support the patrol boats, ranged forward position, five klicks." Chen focused on the hologram, the pinpricks of light from the Oortian forces continued their chase. The cruiser *Li Gong* sputtered ahead of the Viper line and opened her firing ports to ensure every rail gun had maximum sighting.

"In position, Admiral. She's doing her best to maintain distance ahead of the Viper line," Captain Zhi stated.

"Second Oortian wave exiting field! Starboard flank." Commander Lee flashed a hardened glance at his admiral. "They are heading into the asteroid field – 376 targets! Strike force size, probably Hull Pounders. Moving faster than the initial force. Will be in range, thirty-seconds."

"Suicide run," Chen whispered incredulously, small explosions bloomed and faded in the asteroid field each time an Oortian collided with rock and ice. "Going to try to flank us. Can we get a lock, Commander?"

"In range in ten seconds. But odds of our missiles surviving intact through the pulverized field..." Commander Lee's hands moved across his data-pad, "three percent. Gaining speed. This group is fast!" On cue another flash from the shattered asteroid field came and went. Lee continued to follow the two Oortian groups.

"How long until we're beyond the asteroid belt?" Admiral Chen was out of his command chair harness and gripping the slab top of the hologram station, studying the Oortian's moves. The asteroid field hung beyond the starboard side and stretched for a thousand klicks.

"Twenty-two minutes, Admiral." Lee tapped at his controls.

"When will the Oortians reach the end?" Chen turned and looked at his commander.

"Assuming their current speed is their best? Eighteen

minutes." Multiple flashes lit the hologram. Oortian Hull Pounders slammed into rock and ice, disintegrating and disappearing from the Battle-Net and holo-feed.

"They're herding us." Chen spun the hologram and zoomed in on the asteroid field. "Ambushed from the protection of the asteroid field or swallowed by a larger chasing force." Chen considered the scenario. If the Fleet moved hard to port to distance themselves from the ambushing group, they would be in range of the chasing enemy formation. Their course was set and now the admiral had to choose whom to sacrifice first. But I already have, Chen thought. "Commander, Viper line to support Captain Zhi."

Lee flashed the order.

Chen leaned into the holo-feed, his face lit with hundreds of flecks of light from the chasing Oortian fleet.

"*Li Gong.*"

The open-COM sounded distant, each tired word crawling from its speaker. "Yes, Admiral," Captain Zhi said, pride hanging on every syllable.

"We need to slow the flanking Oortian force. The Viper line will protect your stern and flanks."

"I understand, Admiral. The *Li Gong* will not let you down."

The COM fell silent.

Streaks flew across the hologram toward the asteroid field. Self-detonating lead slugs exploded in front of the charging Oortian Hull Pounders and waves of target-locked missiles from the Viper line followed. The Hull Pounders kept coming, ignoring the chasing missiles, ignoring the exploding lead slugs, dying in mass and still they rammed ice and rock.

Replacements shot out of the Oortian field at increasing speeds, streaking in an exact line. One after the other, shells from a cannon. Lead slugs and missiles ripped apart the already shattered asteroid field and still the Hull Pounders flew.

"They're creating a path!" Admiral Chen spun from the holo-feed. It was faint, but there it was. The Hull Pounders were not trying to flank 10th Fleet, they were clearing a path within the asteroid field, creating a protective corridor for something else, something much larger.

SUITED UP, grav-boots clinging to the outer hull of Battle Station Pluto, Chief Pema Tenzin locked the last thruster in place with a grav-clamp. He tapped the built-in control pad on the left sleeve of his bulky suit. "Captain Falco, *Anam Cara* is in position, station thrusters in place, engine is ready."

Falco stood inches from the hologram floating over the command table in the Pluto Room. Admiral Chen's orders were clear, ready the station for battle and wait for 10th Fleet. Thousands of red lights followed Chen and his boats, just out of missile range while another Oortian force hammered a trail through the asteroid field. Based on the latest speed of the Hull Pounders blasting through the asteroid field, Falco thought, the chasing or herding force can overtake the Fleet at will.

"Chief. Make sure we can blow those grav-clamps on the *Anam Cara*."

"Complete, Captain. Control is fixed in her pilot's nest."

"Good work! You're done, Chief. Let me know when you're inside."

"Already on my way, Captain." Tenzin was running, the click of his grav-boots sounded over his COM. "I'm in, Captain."

Falco tapped the station-wide COM and gave an order those aboard had never heard before. "Battle Station Pluto, prepare for launch. Grav-system will take longer to compensate for the thrust." Falco opened a direct line to the *Anam Cara*. "Lieutenant Wallace?"

"Ready, Captain."

"Fire it up and let's see how fast we make this Frisbee go."

Falco gripped the table, felt a slight push. "Is that it, Lieutenant? Holy shit!" His hands slid free of the command table and Falco tumbled into the far bulkhead, back pressed against the partition, waiting for the station's grav-system to catch up with the force.

"No, Captain, this is!" Lieutenant Wallace howled over the COM like an excited child riding their bike down a steep hill.

Pressed against the bulkhead, a predatory grin fixed across his face, Falco growled, "Jack Falco, Captain of Starship Pluto. Oortians... here we fucking come."

the Return of Kalis
the Darkness

DEEP within the Darkness a thought-stream sounded. *It is time, Kalis, the clans are in danger, the territories are in need, the Creators speak your name... and pay homage to your power.*

The crimson carapace remained curled into a massive armored ball, as it had for billions of cycles. The form gently bobbed in the mass of the Darkness, the black liquid caressing its smooth, glistening surface. The current around Kalis changed, swirls growing into a steadying flow, racing around her hardened carapace, faster and faster. Warmth moved from her plates inward, slowly increasing, heat upon heat.

Her purring filled the thought-stream, growing louder with the increasing speed and warmth of the spinning Darkness. The crimson sphere flexed at each joint between the heavily armored plates, the purr turned to a snarling growl. Kalis gradually stretched her carapace, unrolling, feeling her systems steadily coming online. Kalis recoiled, pain shooting through each organ, awakening them from the endless sleep one jolt after another.

The thought-stream became clear, a single voice calling out. Tzara, speaker for the Darkness. While Kalis lay imprisoned in her carapace, living off her own fetid waste, Tzara took her place among the creators. Tzara... Tzara... Over and over the name looped in her memory. Each time her rage grew stronger. Tzara the traitor. Tzara the coward. Tzara the murderous. Tzara the slayer of clans. Each thought was without a history, without reason. Where does hate for this Tzara stem? What is its purpose?

Kalis left her thoughts open to all of the Creators. She had no fear of them, nor cared for them, cowards and consensus builders. Kalis controlled her warrior's rage and answered over the thought-stream, *Creators do not need the thought-stream! Why do you insult me with it?*

You speak truth, Kalis. Creators have no need for it, they are beyond its meager capabilities. But you... the great Kalis are no longer a Creator, you have no clan, no family that share your form, your mass. You, the great Kalis, are alone without a planet and without a single follower shaped in your shadow.

Future cycles will tell what is truth and what is hope, Leader of the Creators and speaker for the Darkness. What do you need of me, Tzara?

The thought-stream flooded with data, images and endless pain. Kalis witnessed the slaying of the shields, watched them burn while releasing their stronghold sacs fiery contents. The images continued to rush into her systems, Krell, Warruq, Seekers and Prox killed... no Kalis thought, our clans are being slaughtered. Again the warrior's rage seeped into her systems. Dying Creators was one thing, but the clans, they must be protected. The final scenes of the great shields raining down on the planets, clans dying by the millions. Rage! Rage! Kalis allowed the warrior's rage to pour into her systems.

Control yourself, great Kalis. Your freedom depends on it. The voice of Tzara filled the thought-stream. *We have recalled our scouts in the Void. One has seen the enemy's lair. It is not far, but first we must destroy the fleeing invaders' cowardly and murderous vessels. The attack has begun and your time has come.*

A gentle push moved Kalis forward. The Darkness around her carapace grew into a raging current, moving her towards the Void at immense speed, far faster than her fins could push her. Faster than a full heat bloom in the Void. Shadows flew by, on and on Kalis flew, the Darkness carrying her towards the Veil and the battle beyond. The battle she craved with all of her systems.

Tzara, leader of the Creators and speaker for the Darkness uploaded her orders. A vision appeared, Kalis watched two clans pursuing the enemy vessels in the Void. One great force chasing and a smaller force of Seekers creating a protective route through the mining field, a path to the enemy, sheltered from their powerful chasing weapons. Data continued to flow, filling her systems and stretching her organs. This new enemy had great power to kill and slaughter. A worthy adversary, she thought.

Kalis adjusted her fins in the current, rotating her carapace. Muscles flexed and relaxed, adjusting armored plates as she prepared for her exit into the void. All would remember the second coming of Kalis and all would witness the fiery destruction of those who slaughtered the clans of the Darkness.

The current slowed then stopped in front of the Veil where the Darkness ends and the Void begins. A small tube emerged low from her carapace and snaked into the thick, black liquid that swirled and rippled at her back. The Mother provides all, Kalis thought, the Darkness would protect the clans within her mass, but I go into the Void, free to do as I choose, free to be Kalis.

Fuel pushed into the tube, her methane sac filled, stopping

just before its membrane ruptured. The fuel orifice spiraled shut and the tube slid out and over, towards its next cavity. A slight pinch and liquid coursed into her expanding lung, stopping just as the pain became unbearable. The opening sealed and the tube retracted into its sac just above her propulsion vent.

The thought-stream closed, the images faded and Kalis knew the connection with Tzara and the Darkness was gone.

It was time. The protective path through the mining fields was almost clear. Kalis swam to the Veil. Even at this great distance the enemy's slashing weapons were dangerous. The destruction from such a small force was impressive, she thought, and a ravenous hunger pushed through her systems.

A final push from her great tail fin and she was in position. By the time Kalis reached the far side, the path would be open. Moving her skull-plate fully through the Veil and into the void, her optical sensors viewed a small burst of energy and another floating chunk of rock and ice exploded into fragments. Her path grew closer to the invaders. Another Seeker flashed out of existence, the path through the mining field was now in front of the fleeing vessels.

Energy flared again in the distance. The time of Kalis had returned. Her carapace pushed off of the Darkness with a final ripple and she positioned herself in front of the growing path through the mining field. A lone Seeker emerged from the Darkness behind her, a messenger. Kalis uploaded its data and it disappeared back into the black depths. A fraction of a cycle later, spheres broke through the Veil and a new thought-stream filled with shrieking cries of pain and fear. The Krell had arrived. Powerful creatures; Kalis thought they were bigger, but a few billion cycles caused even her memory to fade.

Kalis smiled and tried to sooth the fearful beasts jostling at her side, filling their shared thought-stream with visions of a great and fiery death. *Soon the pain will be but a distant memory and what is left of your flesh will swim in the Realm of Warriors.* Screams from the Krell answered Kalis, and only intensified. A sneer cut across her muscled crimson skull-plate then opened into a cavernous pit overflowing with razor sharp ivory spikes. *The pain is your penance for your cowardice and pathetic weeping!* The thought quieted the Krell and Kalis allowed the warrior's rage to fill her organs and saturate her systems.

She gave a final order and closed the thought-stream before it was consumed by their fear and pain. Kalis ignited her energy bloom and held her position. Behind her, seven Krell ignited their mass and blasted past her one after the other, increasing their speed, surely screaming as they went. Kalis imagined the scent that must emanate off the crisping meat, the black trailing, oil filled smoke infused with fear and flesh. Maybe she could find a way to collect it. The final beast blazed by. Kalis adjusted her energy bloom and released, accelerating through the cleared path within the mining field, a great streak of armored crimson malice.

Shards of the enemy's weapons clanked off her armored plates. Rock and ice exploded and joyfully rattled off her carapace, harmlessly bouncing back into the mining field. Frozen methane sacs, organs and skull-plates littered her way. Pieces of Seekers doing what Seekers do best, she thought, dying.

Kalis reopened their shared thought-stream. Wanting, no, needing to hear the Krell's wondrous cries increasing in direct relation to the amount of melting flesh that fueled them and created their beautiful, growing infernos. The sound was soothing to Kalis and the beasts were great fodder for a worthy adversary. But soon, the Krell would sadly fall silent.

Just in time for the slaughter to begin.

80

Captain Falco
the Charge of Battle Station Pluto

BATTLE STATION PLUTO was moving toward 10th Fleet at an impressive clip, the newly anointed station turned spacecraft humming with activity. Battles replaced skirmishes and the second 10th Fleet fired the Dragon missiles. Humanity was on the verge of its first war among the stars and in its own neighborhood. Battle Station Pluto became humanity's line in the sand, a line moving toward the Oortian fleet.

Captain Falco stood outside of the Pluto Room barking orders. "Every second counts!" Falco looked to his officers. The Oortian's shuttle-sized fireballs added another level of urgency to the defenders of Station Pluto. And what of the thing that followed them, Captain Falco thought, 'it' was bigger than the *Anam Cara*.

"Chief Tenzin, make sure every officer has a micro-COM and spread the rest among the Battle-Cubes." Falco paused and placed a thin silver band behind his ear and held out a silver case towards the chief. Instantly the micro-COM slid down and conformed between his skull and the base of his ear. He whispered a code and the end of the micro-COM glowed green.

"Keep everyone on the open station. It's critical they can punch into the command channel and I'll deal with the situations as the arise," he exhaled hard, "or the officer in charge will deal with it." Hopefully Falco contemplated, that will still be me.

"Yes, sir." Tenzin grabbed the case and was off.

"Captain." Commander Shar'ran called from the hatchway of the Pluto Room where he was scanning the incoming feeds of the final preparations. "Admiral Chen on the main-COM."

"Push him through to command channel." Falco reached up and tapped near his ear three times, opening the channel.

Admiral Chen's voice filled his head before he was ready. "Your 'flying station' shows you cannot follow orders, Captain, hopefully you have done a better job preparing it for battle."

Falco shook his head. "Yes, Admiral. Battle Station Pluto is as ready as it can be, sir. Civilian vessels are under sail toward Mars Station. They should encounter Vice-Admiral Hallsworth in a few years."

"Battle Station Pluto?" Chen asked.

Falco ignored the mocking tone. "Starship Pluto, will rendezvous with 10th Fleet in two hours, Admiral." Falco turned toward Commander Shar'ran who remained in the hatchway, held up his hand, shrugged his shoulders, mouthed the word two. Shar'ran returned a questioning look, glanced down at his portable data-pad and nodded in agreement.

"We make our stand then, Captain." Admiral Chen signed off.

Falco tapped at the side of his micro-COM. "I want all officers in the Pluto Room immediately."

Minutes later Captain Falco found himself looking around the slab table where every officer of Battle Station Pluto, some newly minted and others old friends, sat watching the hologram feed. Each of them wore a med-suit under their uniform, Falco shifted, feeling the paper-thin bands of the suit stretch around his body. He did his best to block out the image of what the suit could do if it malfunctioned. He failed and visualized a roast pushed back and forth across a slicer. Still, Falco felt... better to have it on.

"We have done everything we can to ready our vessel. We have taken a mining and tourist station, turned it into a battle station and now turned that into a starship. Anything that can be fired, shot or that explodes is prepped and ready for use. 10th Fleet is two hours out based on our current speed." He watched heads turn, eyes moved from face to face. "Two hours is an eternity when that is chasing you," Falco pointed at the hologram feed, "we will do everything we can to push this bucket faster. When we reach the Fleet," he took a deep breath, released it with unnerving calm, "it begins."

Falco moved around the table, making eye contact with each and every officer. He finished with Ensign Holts, the two simply nodding.

Falco moved to the hatch and turned. "I am proud to be your captain. More than that, I am proud of who you are. We fight for each other. Battle stations."

Admiral Chen – 10th Fleet
Fighting Retreat

"ADMIRAL CHEN, the Oortian Hull Pounders are being replaced faster that we can destroy them." Commander Lee paused. "The group following them is passing through unharmed. *Lie Gong* and the Vipers are destroying the asteroid field and some of the Hull Pounders, but the others are holding back, moving carefully and quickly."

Chen watched the ferocity with which his commander followed the Battle-Net screen. The new flanking enemy force drew closer while passing through the tunnel of floating rock and ice created by the suicidal Hull Pounders. Missiles and lead slugs continued to pound at the field from the side, creating smaller and smaller fragments that made the ordnance less effective and gave the Oortians greater protection.

Chen scanned the command center of the *Qing Long*. "We must slow down the fireballs, their size could easily destroy a cruiser, even disable a dreadnought." Another puff of energy blazed towards the end of the asteroid field. The Hull Pounders bore closer to finishing the tunnel, the seven burning spheres closing in on their suicidal counterparts. But it was the largest of them. The one that followed from far behind, a glistening red blur that the crew were already calling, Yama in hushed whispers.

Something about it felt wrong. It moved like a predator, always hiding its form and never giving the sensors a full view. It reminded Chen of an assassin stalking, waiting, fearless and patient. But Yama... the crew may be right, it could be the 'King of Hell' released to punish the wicked. He shook his head.

"Update, Commander."

"10th Fleet is three minutes twelve seconds ahead of the stern and largest Oortian force. They have matched our current speed."

"They're the herders." Admiral Chen knew they were trying to separate the Fleet or at least make them turn from the flanking force. "They hunt the Fleet as a pack of wolves pushing and probing until the strong leave the weak behind."

Every crewman aboard each vessel knew the dreadnoughts and cruisers could outrun the damaged *Lie Gong* and Vipers, leaving them to fend for themselves. But could the dreadnoughts and cruisers outrun the Oortians and for how long? And where to? Chen thought. The People's Navy had a history of fighting and dying as one. Battles fought to protect a single vessel that flew the red and yellow of the 'Middle Kingdom,' while losing hundreds, even thousands of lives. But that was then, Chen thought, a time of reckless abandon, a time when major reinforcements were not years away.

"Sixty-two seconds until we clear the asteroid field..." The bridge waited in rapt silence for the next number while Commander Lee scanned the incoming feed. "Forty seconds to contact with the flanking force."

Flames belched from the seven spheres hurtling through the

asteroid field alongside the Fleet. "But it is the trailing shadow that leads them," Chen muttered, punching at the data-pad on his armrest. The floating scene froze. Small puffs of energy hung toward the end of the asteroid field, Hull Pounders smashing their way through the center. Seven fiery balls of god-knows-what, followed and a glimpse of a great red beast, pieces of it seen between bits of rock, ice, lead and gore.

Admiral Chen tapped at his data-pad and the scene slowly moved backwards. "There." Chen touched the pad, the scene froze. He reached forward from his command chair, placed his hands on the outside of the hologram image and pulled outward, zooming in on the red mass. "That is impossible," he whispered, keeping his voice to himself. A red-plated creature looked directly at him, large black eyes sunken deep into an elongated skull that sat at the end of a long, thick neck. The rest was hidden behind debris. But the white spikes protruding out of the slit that crossed its face. Tusks? "It's smiling. Yama..." Chen cleared his holo-feed, spun his chair in the direction of the Battle-Net station.

"Commander Lee, prepare to fire. Synchronize starboard vessels. Coordinate missile launch to enemy's estimated exit point." They had one chance to stop the infernos or risk stopping none. "We must hit them the moment they leave the protection of the asteroid field."

Let's give the Oortian chasing force something to think about. "Viper line, launch all Data-Pods." Chen followed the main hologram. The commander flashed the order across the laser beacon. Within seconds, sixty harmless orbs, the size of the enemy's Hull Pounders, shot out of the eleven patrol boats like roman-candles. Ignited and flew towards the chasing Oortian fleet. Give them other targets, Chen thought, while we save our missiles.

Minutes past and distant flashes lit the hologram. Oortian Hull Pounders smashing into Data-Pods.

"Eighteen Data Pods destroyed. Thirty-three, forty-two destroyed. They are leaving the rest, Admiral," Lee stated. Oortian main force allowed eighteen pods to pass untouched. "They're increasing speed, sir."

And so it finally begins, Chen thought. "Viper line, match Oortian speed, fire at will, main Oortian force."

Commander Lee flashed the order.

Chen opened the Fleet-wide COM. "Sync to *Qing Long*'s speed."

Chen opened a private line to Captain Zhi of the rail gun laden *Lie Gong*. "Captain, maintain a safe distance ahead of the Vipers. Aid the line for as long as you can and then your best speed. You will be the rear guard of the main fleet."

"Yes, Admiral!" The COM fell silent. Captain Zhi and all officers of 10th Fleet understood the Viper defensive line was the only chance they had. If the line failed to slow the enemy advance? The thought was a waste of time so Chen moved on.

Streaking embers flew in waves at the vast and relentless pack of Oortian pursuers. The Viper line locked and launched. Enemy Hull Pounders working together, accelerating towards each other and changing course at the last moment, terminally locked missiles slammed into other missiles. Some Hull Pounders met them head-on while others simply stopped and allowed the warhead to destroy them.

"They are protecting the larger vessels," Chen turned towards Commander Lee, "the rest of the Oortian Fleet remain untouched." Another Hull Pounder met an incoming missile heading toward a larger form, a human-sized mass resembling an armored squid.

Another wave of missiles raged toward the advancing Oortians. Hull Pounders exploded, again and again, each eventually ramming into a missile, never attempting to attack the vessels firing them. The Viper line sputtered a few final warheads and the spinning, bare cradles slowed and came to a halt. The eleven Viper class boats were empty.

Hot slugs spat from the *Lie Gong*, daggers ripping and tearing at the Oortians. She desperately fired toward the waves of incoming Hull Pounders, their numbers dwindling as they closed for the kill. A lone laser beacon flashed from the center Viper. The senior captain of the defensive line issued a final order to a battle-group who knew their fate the moment they formed the defensive line.

Eleven Viper class patrol boats of the People's Navy split into two groups, each banking hard away from the Fleet, arcing back towards their pursuers. Hot lead projectiles zipped past the boats. The *Lie Gong* faded into the distance, but continued her hopeless support. Lead slugs flashed from her rails as fast as the automated system could load them. The remaining Hull Pounders died with each detonating slug and were gone.

"Hull Pounders are destroyed, Viper line can turn back towards... oh no." Commander Lee fell silent.

The larger Oortian spheres belched out new forces. Sixty-three Oortian squids appeared and ignited, separating into two groups that changed direction like schools of fish evading predators. Slugs from the *Lie Gong*'s rail guns continued their assault, popping the squid-like forces like water balloons.

Admiral Chen followed the hologram of horrors, hanging in the center of his command ship's bridge. The Oortian forces were close enough for a camera feed. The gory remains of every dying Oortian squid froze solid; soon to be drawn into the asteroid field, soon to be stellar fossils... and they kept coming. The only thing the Oortian forces seemed to share in common with each other was the plating on their hulls or bodies and their sleek, shark-like heads or bows. Chen zoomed in on the floating remains. Bodies with heads, he thought, they are creatures with organs and flesh.

Tiny foamy-white plumes burst from the hulls of the Viper

patrol boats. Oortian squids, each a living projectile pierced their layered exteriors only to exit on the other side. They turned in large arcing sweeps, each black carapace covered in white streaks of hardening epoxy. A lead slug removed the head of one, but the rest took aim at the foaming Vipers, ignited and tore through the vessels over and over.

The matte-black predators of the People's Navy foamed from hundreds of rust colored scabs, the result of Oortian fluids mingling with the flowing repair epoxies. There was nothing the rest of 10th Fleet could do, but hope the sacrifice would buy them the time to reach Battle Station Pluto before the Oortians caught them. The *Lie Gong*, failing engine slowing her run, continued to fire at the Oortian pack feasting on the dying Vipers. The Viper hulls were more foaming white than black, new scabs forming with each passing second.

"They've almost reached the end of the asteroid field." Commander Lee's hand hovered over the launch controls. "Missile's away."

Admiral Chen's eyes were wet. He swallowed hard and took his focus from his battered and dying Viper line and followed the barrage launching from the starboard cruisers. Fields of red embers burned towards their coordinates one klick from the end of the asteroid field.

"Three seconds to impact, two. They have broken through!"

Seven flaming spheres erupted through the side of the asteroid belt a few klicks from the end, behind the 10th Fleet. They formed a boomerang shape. Burning chunks along with fragmented rock and ice exploded outward. Further down the asteroid field, hundreds of missiles hammered harmlessly into the far end of the field where the tunnel was just cleared by the death of the last Hull Pounder.

"Where is the red one?" Lee continued to follow the scrolling feed from the Battle-Net. "We have hard-lock on the seven, Admiral. Where is the eighth, where is Yama?"

Chen had seen enough and punched the Fleet-wide-COM. "10th Fleet, Phantom formation." He sat heavily and tightened his harness.

"Captain Zhi, bring the *Lie Gong* up and cover our stern," Chen ordered, knowing it was too late. She had stayed too long defending the doomed patrol boats. Her engine failing, Captain Zhi and his crew had chosen an honorable end.

Three dreadnoughts formed a triangle with Chen's command ship at the head. The defensive formation was named after 'the Phantom of the North,' the Great Gray owl. Under its protection, the forest would thrive, Chen thought, while the eight smaller missile cruisers moved underneath the dreadnoughts forming another triangle. "Full burn!"

The hologram feed grew bright, eleven main engines burning in unison, pushing beyond safe capacities, running all out to Battle Station Pluto and the hope of a final stand.

"Oortians are turning, joining the main chasing force!" Commander Lee stated over the rumbling and vibrating decks and stations. The sounds fell silent on bridge, the grav-system equalizing the added thrust.

The hologram filled with seven round infernos charging back toward the chasing Oortian Fleet. Between them, eleven listing Vipers foamed and rolled from the ongoing strikes from the now white Oortian squids. Chen watched in horror – wrapped around the center burning sphere was a red, glowing patch, heavily plated, its form backlit by the flames raging around its edges. Two black eyes above a tusk-filled mouth looked at Chen. It was smiling while the spheres blazed towards Chen's tortured vessels.

Commander Lee turned toward the Admiral, tears streaming down his cheeks. "We must fire!"

"We cannot, Commander." Chen looked to the deck under his feet. "We cannot waste another—"

"How can you say that?" Lee pleaded. "They are killing our people, toying—"

"ENOUGH!" Chen was out of his harness and standing. "They will do what is needed! They will do their duty as will you, Commander!" Chen fell silent, the scene on the hologram playing out. The *Lie Gong* floated above the Vipers, Oortian squids entering and exiting their hulls like knives, again and again. Cats toying with wounded mice.

In a final act of defiance, the *Lie Gong* cut her mid-ship stabilizers and began spinning. Her rail guns spat out self-detonating slugs in all directions. They exploded only meters beyond her hull. Lead cut through Oortians of every size, Vipers, and even her own battered hull.

Six of the burning spheres smashed into Vipers. Instead of exploding, the spheres covered the ships bow to stern in a burning sludge. The seventh sphere waited, a large red form unwrapped itself from the sphere before moving a safe distance away. The last sphere charged into the *Lie Gong*, covering the spinning ship in fire and heat. Flames grew stronger from each vessel, fire feeding on the leaking oxygen – draining the life support systems.

Light engulfed the hologram, showering the bridge of the *Qing Long* in shafts of white light that turned orange then blue. The *Lie Gong* or someone still alive on one of the Vipers engaged a self-destruct system.

Chen and his officers watched while hundreds of Oortians blazed and died. The Vipers and cruiser were gone, and so were their crews. Floating in front of the carnage, flame and energy lighting its silhouette, a heavily armored form the size of a patrol boat watched 10th Fleet run.

Two black eyes staring over a shining tusk-filled smile.

Captain Falco
Battle Station Pluto

CAPTAIN FALCO REACHED A HALF SPRINT. The silver strip behind his ear continued to account for each word he spoke as he made his final inspections. He hugged the inside wall like a runner doing everything he could to reduce the size of the track that stood in his way.

Air hoses sprouted from his right and snaked under his feet towards oxygen tanks strapped to the bulkhead he continued to graze with his left shoulder. The maintenance corridor buffered the Infinity Hall from the masses of Battle Station Pluto.

"Battle-Cubes twenty-five through forty are good to go." Falco slid to a halt, followed a hissing oxygen line until he found a small hole. "Cube forty-three needs a new O2 line."

"Check, O2 line for C43," Ensign Holts stated.

Her voice sounded distant, Falco pushed the longing aside, but it remained close at all times. Holts had shared something rare with him that night. Beyond the beginnings of love, she opened up to him and allowed Falco to drop seven years of pain, anguish and guilt. He started forward again, stopped, grunted and opened the hatch to C43. Harness, munitions lockbox, shoulder-mount missile launcher with safety line, he made the mental check and moved to the Infinity Wall. He inspected the perfectly circular cut that ran eighty-percent through the glass.

Falco slid the locking bolt and opened the munitions box. Twenty missiles lay stacked inside. "Are you sure we have found the last of the Javelins?" Twenty per Battle-Cube put the count at three thousand. The image of the chasing Oortian fleet over the hologram feed returned. He tapped the small COM over his ear a few times. "Ensign Holts? I repeat have we checked every possible munitions' hold on Station Pluto?"

"Sorry, Captain, I was running another full search of all possible storage areas. All Javelin missiles are in the Battle-Cubes. That's interesting." Holts paused, "I show 350 Ore-Rockets inventoried in the mining block."

"Ore-Rockets?" Falco had used them many years ago. A large line-of-sight roman-candle with a simple two-hand grip. Aim at a big floating rock, fire and hope for the best which usually included the creation of new, smaller floating rocks. "Thought they stopped using those?"

"Mining industry did, Captain. You can't make any more, but you can use what you have."

Falco shrugged. "If they can blast apart asteroids, they may be of use as a last resort. Check out the Mining Block personally, Ensign, there may be other things we can use. Contact me when you're there."

"Yes, Captain, on my way."

Falco climbed out the hatch of Battle-Cube forty-three and was on the run.

Soon he thought, soon men and women would live and die in chaos along the curving Infinity Wall that circled the station and enabled clear observation of a peaceful chunk of deep space.

Peaceful, however, was a lifetime ago. Now we have Battle-Cubes, hand-held missiles, Ore-Rockets and an Oortian Fleet chasing our admiral."

On cue, Admiral Chen chimed through on the open-COM. "Captain, no change. Oortians are following, matching our speed. Engagement in fifty-seven minutes."

Falco swallowed hard, slowed his gait to keep his breath. "We are ready, Admiral, according to the chief, we'll fire our two breaking thrusters twelve minutes twenty-two seconds prior."

"Chief Tenzin," Chen sounded like he may be smiling, "an engineer to the core, precise as always. We will form around Battle Station Pluto, Captain, dreadnoughts above, cruisers below. Simple and we are going to do it coming in hot. No slowing down, full retro-burn and swing to put our weapons in the best firing line. Do you understand, Captain Falco?"

"Yes, Admiral, our first strike must inflict mass damage," Falco stated.

"Correct." Chen fell silent.

Falco waited for the connection to drop, but Chen remained. "Admiral? Is there anything else, sir?"

"Captain Falco... Thank you for coming." The line went dead.

"Would not have missed it for the world." Falco spoke to himself and picked up the pace, checking hoses and munitions boxes of each Battle-Cube as he neared the end.

Falco and the 500 Battle Station Pluto guardians of humanity had endured the helplessness watching and listening to the mighty 10th Fleet fight and die only hours from their aid. They would not do it again. They would join the fight and live or die with their sisters and brothers of the United Nations Navy.

Battle-Cube 150 looked good. He slid to a final stop, slightly out of breath he tapped his COM twice and waited.

"I have just reached the Mining Block, Captain," Ensign Holts stated. "Opening the main cargo hold now."

"Good." Falco took a few deep breaths. "Battle Cube forty-four through one-fifty are ready and crewed. How about those Ore-Rocke—"

"Captain, I have an idea," intensity filled Holts voice. "I found something. Meet me in the Mining Block, main hold."

"Already on my way, Ensign. The main hold is around the corner from BC-150."

Falco sprinted the distance in twenty seconds with the help of the station mapping system. Hands on his knees, panting, he looked up at Ensign Holts standing on a small mountain of crates just inside the Mining Block main cargo hold.

"Ore-Rockets?" He barely got the words out, still catching his breath. The look on Holts's face was something new. A sneer crossed with a glimmer of the evil eye was his best guess. "Ensign, what then?"

"We have the Ore-Rockets and they are already being dispersed to the Battle-Cubes. But..." she pointed to the crates under her boots, "these may help."

Falco moved closer to the crates, dusted off the faded red, block lettering on the top, next to the soles of Holts's boots. "EXTREME CAUTION: A-N-F-O Mining Packs." Falco looked up to Ensign Holts, and backed away. "What is this dangerous shit doing on Station Pluto?"

"Mining companies cut corners." Holts raised her shoulders. "We could lay this out like a minefield using the long-range detonators?" She raised an eyebrow.

God she was right, Falco thought, looking over the crates. "We could take out half the Oortian Fleet with this, but how do we safely and quickly place a minefield in front of a flying space station and not destroy us and 10th Fleet?

"The pods!" Falco smashed his fist into an open hand. "We pack the Data-Pods with ANFO and a long-range detonator. The Oortians stopped attacking 10th Fleets pods once they realized they were not weapons, but decoys."

"They'll let them through." Holts's eyes lit up. "We could

modify the mining blast shields to fit on the rear of the pods."
She jumped down to the deck. "Focus the blast everywhere but
behind them, everywhere but the station and 10th Fleet."

"The Oortians used the pods against us once, let's return the
favor. How many Data-Pods do we have on station?" Falco
looked to Holts who pulled out the slim data-pad from the side
pocket of her uniform and tapped away.

"Two hundred and fifty."

EVERY ABLE BODY on Battle Station Pluto who was not in a
Battle-Cube or strapped to a rail gun, sat in the protected,
private docking bay in the stern of the station working on the
assembly line. 250 Data-Pods lay in the last phase of production
a few meters from the *Anam Cara*.

Chief Pema Tenzin decided the only way to ensure the lead-
lined pods could be detonated with a remote was to place the
detonator on the outside. Each completed pod was filled with
the mining explosive ANFO. A wire connected the epoxied long-
range detonator on the outside to the explosives on the inside.
The interior modified blast shield would focus the destruction
away from the station and 10th Fleet. The lead lining from the
exploding pods would create immense damage, the ultimate
improvised explosive device (IED).

The Oortians will ignore them, Falco had explained to
Admiral Chen. They will let them fly by to be destroyed in their
black field thinking them another desperate ruse, but this time
they will be our messengers, they will speak for those lost. Chen
had simply told Falco to fire the Data-Pods the moment 10th
Fleet were thirty minutes out.

A crewman pushed a cart with a finished pod on it, stopped
and saluted. Falco returned the salute and noticed writing on the
top, not far from the detonator.

Dearest Oortians
–FUCK U & SUCK ON THIS–
Love Captain Zhi &
the crew of the Li Gong

Falco released a deep grunt, nodded to the crewman and looked to the rows of finished Data-Pods lining the deck in front of the bay door. Each carried a message from a fallen sailor or boat of 10th Fleet.

Captain Jack Falco felt something new taking hold.

Hope.

83

the Movoo
the Darkness

SPIRITED PLEASURE PASSED BACK and forth between the eight
moon-sized creatures, filling their shared thought-stream with a
joyous banter. The Darkness opened a flowing pathway across
her surface, where her protective mass ended and the
unforgiving Void began. The place where the latest invaders fled
and the clans followed.

The eight bobbing giants cheerfully rode her current,
skimming just behind the protective Veil. The happy gatherers
for the territories quickly turning from pain and fear to laughter
and joy. The Darkness was healing their hides, scorched from
the heat of the flaming stalks the Movoo pushed into the Void
only cycles before. The energy waves from the invaders'
weapons bruised their organs and temporarily scrambled their
systems.

Each of the Movoo carried and released one of the great
protectors of the territories, a shield, only to powerlessly watch

the fire descend into the Darkness, biting and eating its way through the clans. The energy rolled toward them, the stalk connecting the Movoo and shields became a fuse and the stalks' strongholds that did not release their warriors, became a furnace. Warriors died.

Cries consumed the clans' thought-stream and then fell silent only moments before the pounding rings of energy rolled through the Darkness. Her thick, flowing mass struggling to slow the destructive force and soften the fury, but the energy waves marched on and assaulted all within their path.

But that had passed and cycles would continue. Warruq, Prox, Seekers, Krell and the rumored others that swam deep in the furthest reaches of the Darkness would come and go. When needed, clans would die and the Realm of Warriors would overflow with the departed.

But the eight Movoo would remain as they always had since the beginning when the Darkness covered little more than a single planet tied to a lone, fiery star, happy and content. They were the gatherers for the territories, yet their greatest achievements would always be collecting the thirteen.

On the Movoo went, speeding across the face of the Darkness toward their mission, her cool mass washing over them, spinning their bulk in its healing mass. The Darkness accelerated the driving current, the Movoo turned into pinkish blurs, racing towards their destination.

Cycles passed and the flowing current slowed then stopped and dispersed. The full mass of the Darkness came rushing in. Each Movoo smashed into the one in front of it. One after the other, their moon-sized forms flattened and bulged until they formed a connected string of compressed disks. For a moment the joyous banter fell silent and the stunned creatures came to a connected stop.

The two at the ends were the first to spring off in opposite and unopposed directions, followed by laughter filling their shared thought-stream. They regained their spherical shapes, two by two, springing apart. The Movoo huddled, nudging and rubbing against each other, ensuring to provide the nurturing touch their clan of eight needed. A separate thought-stream from the Creators opened.

The group fell silent and the Creators uploaded their final orders. Once the Movoo left the protection of the Darkness, they were on their own. The thought-stream closed, the Creators had spoken. Again the Movoo opened a shared thought-stream and uncertainty passed among them. The clans moved through the Void, chasing the invaders and their powerful weapons.

Many had died alone in the cold emptiness, beyond her protective mass. Those of the clans that left the Darkness had not returned to upload their findings. The Creators sent a Seeker to absorb their histories and return them to the clans, but those still alive were chasing the invaders – moving farther and farther from their home.

It was almost time to leave the protection of the Darkness. She had taken them as far as her mass would allow. She had shifted her form to protect the clans moving against the invaders and left the far territories unprotected. The enemy's powerful weapons left her weak, injured and still she healed the Movoo and aided them in their journey. But the Darkness was quickly regaining strength.

Each of the Movoo felt a slight pinch and methane pumped into their fuel sacs. A fraction of a cycle before their sacs burst, relief swam over the moon-sized creatures and the tube slid out. A muscled valve spiraled open near their optical sensors and a new pressure built. They inhaled the darkness as deeply as their forms would allow, their lung expanding into every available cavity. A quiet hiss and the orifice closed.

Their orders were clear, capture the fourteenth before it moved beyond their reach. They could not fail and would not relent until they had towed it back to be shaped and molded within the Darkness for millions of cycles. When it was completed, the Creators would position it among the others.

The oldest of the eight, the first Movoo to swim from the core of their planet and bask in the warmth of the original star, gently nudged the other seven towards the Void.

Eight pillars of fire erupted behind the Veil of the Darkness. The Movoo ignited their energy bloom and pushed into the Void to carry out their mission.

Capture and return the fourteenth world.

8 4

Captain Fei
Kwan Yin – the Black Field

THE VIPER CLASS VESSEL, the *Kwan Yin* hung battered in the dark field. Her hull foamed with hundreds of new ruptures filling with repair epoxy.

Bobbing on a warm sea... where am I? Captain Yue Fei drifted up, knees bumping a hard surface followed by his face pressing into a tacky sludge. Fei's thoughts felt heavy, clouded and his head thumped like a drum, heart pounding. Are my eyes open? A dream, yes, this must be a dream.

Slowly he began to descend. Over and over Fei's body rose, stuck and fell. A sickly-sweet scent grew stronger with each upward rise. It began to overwhelm his senses...

"Open your eyes, Captain."

"Rank and surname!" Fei cried out. "Captain Yue Fei of 10th Fleet, Chinese contingent, United Nations Navy."

Floating up, his heart pounding, slowly he opened his eyes

centimeters from the sticky surface. This time he raised a throbbing and bloodied hand, halting his rise.

Swirling black current filled his peripheral vision. Fei focused on the carnage before him, his clearing mind trying to grab hold of something, anything in the moment. He traced the hardened white foam that framed the sticky surface.

Details flooded in, his mind trying to fit them together. Captain Fei pushed hard off the overhead and away from the crypt created by the hull repair system. It looked like large pieces of flypaper, but instead of insects stuck to its surface, parts of humans… and something else covered the space. Fei shut down his mind; he could not explain what he was seeing. Much of the carnage was not human… or was it?

Wet, gummy warmth rolled down his cheek, building as it went like a snowball rolling downhill. Fei clawed at the substance that covered his jaw and realized it was not his own. Pain rippled through his sluggishly awakening mind and body. His head spun, he wobbled then hit the deck and rebounded towards the overhead.

Grav-system is damaged, oxygen mix is wrong, life support down? Think, Captain. Composure is survival. Fei heard the familiar voice in his head and a calm returned. He caught the rounded corner of the Battle-Net station, his feet continued toward the overhead and pushed off the almost invisible surface. The Virtual Surround Vision was still operational, maybe fifty percent, he thought, large pieces of interior hull, bulkheads, overhead and the deck flashed in and out of existence.

He was not sure which was worse, seeing the carnage now a permanent part of the hull or the patchwork of swirling camouflage mixed with the *Kwan Yin*'s interior. "The patchwork," Fei grunted, "is the true reflection of the situation."

"Captain…" a lone muffled voice carried from the bowels of the *Kwan Yin*. For the first time since awakening into his current nightmare, Fei surveyed the *Kwan Yin* beyond her bridge, his mind releasing him from its protective blanket.

Boots hovering centimeters off the deck, he slowly rotated a full 360 degrees.

"Captain?" Again the distant voice sounded.

It's closer, Fei thought. It's not me, is it? Taking in the full weight of the situation. "They're all... dead," he whispered, his mind beginning to fracture. The remains of his crew not stuck to a surface, lay scattered, floating and bouncing around the bridge, some whole, others in pieces.

Get a hold of yourself or put a bullet in your brain and end this. He closed his eyes, breathing deeply and exhaling powerfully, again and again. Finally, Captain Fei opened his eyes and willed himself to focus on the moment.

"I am in control, I am in the present, I am alive."

"Captain?"

A battered crewman floated into his line of sight, leaping from handhold to handhold. The faltering VSV system created a surreal background. The man gripped, pulled and launched himself with one arm. Floating in front of the swirling blackness for a second and then hopping in front of the pulverized hull of the *Kwan Yin* and back and forth. Blackness to hull until he was only meters from Fei.

"Captain."

The man wore a shredded engineer uniform, his body bloodied and swollen.

"Engineer Koto?" Fei tried to picture the face without the damage.

"Yes, Captain. I began surveying the *Kwan Yin* after the last shock wave passed."

Koto's eyes looked hollow, his face swollen in directions Fei had never seen or knew were possible.

"What is our condition, Lieutenant Koto?" Fei knew it was

bad, but Koto had miraculously been able to move through the ship and obtained firsthand data.

"The situation is dire, sir, but we live." Koto released his grip and rubbed a heavily bandaged and immobilized arm. "We have a single stern thruster that may fire, Captain, but we need to check if we can control it."

"That's a start, Koto. Survivors?" Fei stated with an edge of hope.

Koto's head swiveled as he surveyed the bridge. Captain Fei watched the engineer assess the carnage with a cold, knowing gaze.

"I thought I was the last. Now there are two."

"Then we must continue on, Engineer Koto. This," Fei looked to the swirling black outside the hull, "will not be the final resting place of our crew." They exchanged a nod and began to move through the bridge.

"I am sorry, my friend. Om Mani Padme Hum…" Captain Fei whispered the sacred mantra in perfect rhythm. His eyes tight, tears flowing as he pulled his way past the battered and unrecognizable face of Commander Zhu. He broke the mantra, "until the next life my brother, live through me for as long as I draw breath." Fei pressed a tear-soaked cheek against Zhu's broken chest and pushed towards the pilot station.

Engineer Koto moved to the smashed hatch that led to the bridge. With his good hand, he opened a small panel next to it and began pulling wires.

"Nav-system recognizes thruster." Captain Fei continued to punch at the controls. Growing confident he looked towards the lone engineer, all that remained of his crew. "I can control it from here if you can keep the thruster firing."

Engineer Koto reconnected a few wires and closed the panel. "I have a lone functional COM-link from the engine room to the sensors station behind you." Koto released his right hand and pointed towards a tiny silver case fused to the bulkhead near the hatch. "That is as close as I can get to the pilot station. Volume is maxed, best I can do."

"You have given us the opportunity to leave this place, Engineer Koto. We will take it and do what we can." Fei began floating up from the pilot's seat, reached down and tightened his harness. The NAV-station was foreign, but Fei would figure things out quickly. Koto pulled himself through the hatch with incredible speed and was off to the engine room at the stern of the *Kwan Yin*.

Shadows moved past the bow of his boat, large forms swimming with purpose. Yes, they are moving through the black as whales swim in the sea. His heart pounded in his ears and sweat dripped from Fei's forehead. I must calm my soul, he thought, heighten my senses and follow the currents. If nothing else we will die in the open, die as a warriors, as humans in the light.

"Thruster is ready, sir." Engineer Koto's voice rang metallic from the small box near the sensor station.

Another group of shadows swam passed the *Kwan Yin*, almost brushing her hull. They think we are dead, Fei thought, or of no significance. Good, then lead us home.

"Can you hear me, Captain?"

"Yes, loud and clear. Fire up the thruster, I know the way."

A slight tremor ran through the deck of the battered *Kwan Yin* and the thruster fired. Captain Yue Fei took the helm. "We follow the shadows, Koto."

"Overhead, Captain! Incoming!" Koto yelled from the aft of the *Kwan Yin*.

Captain Fei looked up. A glowing orb closed in, moving aft of the bridge and towards amidships. "Hold on!" Fei turned the *Kwan Yin* hard starboard. The light from the flaming sphere burned through the black field surrounding them, the Virtual

Surround Vision flickering on and off like the strobe light of the damned. Fei looked overhead and the sphere smashed into the center of the *Kwan Yin*.

85

Admiral Chen
10th Fleet

ADMIRAL CHEN RELEASED another rasping breath. The hologram feed on the bridge of the *Qing Long* displayed what every remaining crewman among the eleven surviving vessels of 10th Fleet already knew. The Oortian numbers were simply too many, and regardless of their powerful weapons, the enemy kept coming, wave after wave.

"The Oortian forces are closing the gap, Admiral," Commander Lee coolly stated, his brow dripping sweat. He rotated his chair to face the holo-feed in the center of the bridge. "The red one leads them. It's different from the rest."

"Yama, the Oortian Admiral," stated Chen. "Cruisers to 110 percent burn." Chen straightened in his chair. "Push them, Commander. They must keep up with the dreadnoughts."

"110 percent burn," Lee looked to the Battle-Net feed, "and holding."

Commander Lee now managed the Battle-Net instead of

directing it. "We have a hard lock on the red Oortian and the larger vessels of the Oortian Fleet." Lee stated.

"They want us to fire, Commander. By now the Oortians know the range of our weapons. They move the heavy vessels forward, tempt us to fire and the moment our munitions leave their cradles...?" The admiral left the question hanging.

"Their large vessels drop back, the Hull Pounders come up and take the brunt of it and we just wasted hundreds of missiles," Lee finished.

"We stand with Battle Station Pluto, soon they will—" Chen stopped, the Battle-Net acknowledged friendly forces in range, the holo-feed glowed with what looked like a spear racing toward 10th Fleet.

"Captain Falco's gifts have arrived." Admiral Chen tapped his data-pad. "They should pass down the center of our formation, stop under the dreadnoughts, spread and pass through as if fired from our own vessels." Chen raised an eyebrow. "Let's hope the Oortians are focused on our fleet and not what's in front of us."

A few minutes passed and the streaking line of 250 Data-Pods put on the breaks under the three dreadnoughts, a few meters forward of their main engines and above the eight cruisers. The holo-feed showed the spreading dots maneuver to precise locations, stop then fire off toward the chasing Oortian fleet.

"And now we watch the thread on which our existence hangs." Chen sat locked onto the holo-feed only meters from his station. The Data-Pods flew closer to the Oortian front wave.

"They're moving to intercept!" Commander Lee leaned toward his screen. "Wait. The Oortians have stopped pursuit. They are returning to their formations." He stopped punching at his controls. "Data-Pods should pass into the bulk of the Oortian formations in three minutes."

Admiral Chen hit the Fleet-wide COM switch. "Did you hear that, Captain Falco?"

"Yes, Admiral, we have adjusted the speeds of the pods for greatest collateral damage and will detonate in two minutes twenty-eight seconds. Mark."

At the Battle-Net station, Commander Lee quickly entered the information. Numbers appeared on the hologram, 2:28, 2:27, 2:26...

The open-COM filled with a deep growl and Captain Falco's voice echoed, "And Admiral, we're here."

Admiral Chen tapped the Fleet-wide COM again, the light burned blue, "10th Fleet, prepare to initiate Goujian maneuver in..." Chen looked to the hologram, "... T-minus 2:17. When we come about, my Battle-Net controls the Fleet engagement." Chen's voice boomed, "WE FIGHT AS ONE!"

The crew on the bridge of the *Qing Long* tightened their harnesses. A massive object entered their sensor range and a green light appeared on the hologram, moving with surprising speed towards 10th Fleet.

Battle Station Pluto had arrived.

8 6

Captain Falco
Battle Station Pluto

"Slow us down, Chief!" Falco stated more calmly than he felt. He sat alone in the Pluto Room and current command center of Battle Station Pluto. It was the equivalent of a bunker in the innards of the structure. Falco would remain here as long as he could or until the fighting forced him to command on the run. His officers were placed in key areas with key responsibilities and soon the chaos of battle would begin.

The hologram floating in the center of the massive table showed 10th Fleet growing in detail as the station approached. The Oortian forces were now coming into focus. The sight of what Falco and 10th Fleet were fighting was out of a child's nightmare.

Waves of small black-glistening 'creatures' the size of data pods clustered around squid-like things that again clustered around whale-sized ships... All powered by single engines that left a trail of black mist hanging behind them and fusing into a greasy cloud. Behind this wave were vast spheres of light and other things soon to come into focus. And then there was the leader – Falco called it, Yama. It moved between the Oortian vessels, never staying in the open, always in motion and always using the other Oortians as screens. Like a sniper, Falco thought.

Above the holo-feed, a clock showed :32, :31, :30.

"Lieutenant Wallace!" Chief Tenzin's voice sounded over the shared COM, "Full retro burn, NOW!"

Falco readjusted his harness. The slightest push moved through the Pluto Room, a resistance to their forward progress. Lieutenant Wallace was posted in the *Anam Cara* in Station Pluto's private bay and had just engaged her main engine in reverse. Probably firing her bow thruster also, Falco thought and hoped her grav-locks held or the *Anam Cara* would be shot out of the private bay like a rocket.

:10, :09, :08...

"Chief, good enough!" Falco tapped on his data-pad. Two hundred fifty green dots deep within the Oortian waves and heading toward their black field came to full stop. Thousands of Oortian hull pounders changed course and burned toward them.

"Too late," Falco whispered.

Three dreadnoughts and eight cruisers angled their bow thrusters and ignited them in unison while shutting down their main engines. Falco watched the hologram, fascinated at the brilliance and insanity of Admiral Chen's Goujian maneuver. Eleven boats flipped bow over stern, leaving enough room in center for Battle Station Pluto to slide in with the dreadnoughts above and the cruisers below.

:02, :01...

Two hundred and fifty Data Pods erupted in a popping chain of fire that flashed, turned black and was replaced by streaking red-hot chunks of lead cutting into the Oortian forces. Missiles coordinated by Chen's Battle-Net spewed from every cradle of the eleven boats.

Falco waited for a few seconds for the Fleet's missiles to lock on targets then gave the order. "Battle-Cubes, FIRE!" Crews manning Battle-Cubes facing the Oortian's unleashed their Javelin missiles. "Rail guns, target the spheres, FIRE!"

Lead slugs flew off their rails, belched from the top and bottom of Battle Station Pluto. The deadly rounds ignoring 10th Fleet's chasing missiles and dying Oortian Hull Pounders, squids and whales and hammering the massive spheres behind them.

Falco's holo-feed looked like the remnants from fireworks, falling in beautiful, burning, colorful lines in the night's sky. Thousands of Oortians were destroyed or dying. Like wounded beasts, they crawled through space, some trailing pieces behind them, but they kept coming toward 10th Fleet.

Another wave of missiles flew from the Fleet; the greasy cloud of Oortian exhaust hung and grew with each Oortian death. Falco's holo-feed darkened in the center, missiles skirted around the mass, loosing their target locks and searching for new ones. The cloud continued to grow with each Oortian's destruction.

"No. Jesus, oh no." Falco opened a direct COM to Admiral Chen. "They're creating another camouflaging field with their dead!" Falco's holo-feed filled with a thousand blurs moving toward its middle. It was like looking down at a frenzied ant colony attacking a spider at its center. The hologram went dark except the outer edges where the chasing embers of missiles searched for Oortian targets.

A ripple formed in the center of the new black field. "Rail guns, fire at the center! FIRE!" Falco shouted.

The rail guns adjusted their firing line. Slugs sliced through the center of the small dark field that hung only a few klicks in front of 10th Fleet and Battle Station Pluto.

"Bow thrusters, Captain." Chen's voice sounded in Falco's personal COM. "We must create space—"

An Oortian sphere the size of a cruiser blasted out of the

center of the ripple. Its bulk blazed with swirling energy and flew toward Admiral Chen's command ship. Missiles hammered the sphere and slugs from the rail guns pierced its fleshy layers and still it raged forward. Another sphere burst through behind it, using the first as a shield.

Missiles continued pounding it, but the Oortians were too close, moving too fast. Bow thrusters lit the front of 10th Fleet's boats and Battle Station Pluto was already moving back. The first sphere exploded like an erupting volcano a few hundred meters from the *Qing Long*. Only this volcano aimed its lava behind it. The chunks of molten debris showered the one following it which simply added the mass to its own and shot forward.

The remaining sphere slowed its pace as it neared Admiral Chen's dreadnought, burned translucent, its interior filled with smaller orbs like fish eggs.

Aboard Battle Station Pluto, Captain Falco continued to give orders through his personal COM to his crew. He zoomed in on the glowing Oortian sphere, its pace slowing.

"Hull Pounders!" He tapped into the Fleet-wide COM. "Arm yourselves, prepare to repel—"

The sphere exploded like a mammoth shotgun blast at close range and thousands of Hull Pounders tore into 10th Fleet and Battle Station Pluto with the bulk of the Oortians focused on Admiral Chen's dreadnought. Concussion rounds from M40 combat shotguns and small arms fire sounded over the Fleet-wide COM and within Battle Station Pluto. Falco punched his personal code into the compartment under his seat. A drawer slid open and he grabbed the small, stout shotgun and two ammo belts before tapping his personal COM.

"Battle Station Pluto, this is Captain Falco, man your stations, do your duty, repel Oortian borders." He switched to his officer COM. "I'm on the move. Commander Shar'ran you've got the Battle-Cubes, Chief Tenzin keep us moving and keep those rail guns firing on the biggest Oortian targets. Lieutenant Wallace, prep *Anam Cara* for takeoff. Ensign Holts, keep the ammo coming to the Cubes and Rail Guns." Falco's lungs burned, but he kept moving toward the sound of gunfire. "Officers! If I fall, next in line according to rank."

The bulkhead to Falco's right disintegrated. A Hull Pounder covered in blood punched through and slammed into the bulkhead to his left and lodged in layers of plastic. Falco dropped to a knee, slung the M40 toward the Oortian just as it ignited its engine and blasted down the corridor in a smoky-haze and stuck its armored top into the overhead. Fleshy appendages dangled from above, exhaust sputtering from an orifice buried somewhere in its glistening limbs.

Falco sprinted up, slid onto his back and pumped three rounds into it. The Hull Pounder stopped moving. Falco stood, prodded the hanging corpse with the barrel. Everything but the armored head was now jelly.

Station Pluto shook violently. Falco slammed into a hatch, his body a full meter off the deck and slumped to the floor, stunned and dazed. Something warm and wet moved under his uniform and pooled by his elbow. The left arm of his Med-suit tightened, he felt a needle prick, 'SNAP.'

"FUCK!" Falco screamed, the sharp pain awakening his senses, grounding him in the moment. His left arm straightened from its awkward angle, the rings of the med-suit fiercely gripping his numbing bicep.

"Captain!" The COM in his ear sounded again followed by wet, popping sounds, "Falco!" Definitely Shar'ran, he felt the mental haze lifting.

Battle Station Pluto shook again, less violently, but still teeth rattling.

"Yes, Commander, what the hell was—"

"*Qing Long* is gone, Admiral is dead, dreadnoughts destroyed. What's left of the Fleet is heavily damaged!" Commander

Shar'ran took a deep, rattling breath. "Most of the Hull Pounders were different this time, breached the hulls then exploded like frag-mines, knew right where to hit us. Station is damaged, only a handful of Battle-Cubes left..." Muffled blasts sounded in the background. "...We've cleared the Oortians we could find that didn't exploded on impact."

"Hold on, Commander!"

Falco grabbed his shotgun and ran to the nearest holo-feed. Blood dripped from the fingers of his left hand, but his Med-suit did its job. The bone in his arm was set and the pain meds were flowing together with the right amount of adrenalin to keep him upright. He punched in his command code and a hologram appeared from the bulkhead feed.

He spun the glowing image of the Space Station and zoomed toward the Oortian front. Pieces of dreadnoughts and cruisers floated in front, mixed with thousands of dead Oortians, humans and a sea of frozen parts entombed in repair epoxy. The smaller, dark field was dissipating, but the damage was done.

Three damaged cruisers and Battle Station Pluto was all that remained of the mighty 10th Fleet. There were no signs of living Oortians. Falco opened the Fleet-wide COM. Clicks mixed with static filled his ear. The COM-Sats were down. Of course, he thought, the Oortians target them first. Falco switched to Station Pluto's local COM, the equivalent of ship-to-ship WIFI and hoped they vessels were close enough. "Officer report, cruisers first!"

"This is Commander Atagan, the *Shangti* is heavily damaged, but she can fight, and she can move."

"Lieutenant Uushin, the *Nuwa* has functioning bow thrusters, some weapons systems online, life support thirty percent."

Falco waited for the last cruiser to report, the *P'an Ku* floated in the middle of the Fleet's wreckage, hundreds of circular holes filled with repair epoxy covered her hull. She was the furthest away, on the edge of their limited range.

"P'an Ku, report!"

Seconds passed before a young voice whispered over the COM, cutting in and out.

"This... Ensign Bayud," her voice barely audible, words chopped, a strange sound like shoes on a sticky floor filled the background and faded, "... am the hi...est ranking off... left." Ensign Bayud fell silent.

Falco could hear her touching the personal COM in her ear.

"... everywhere," Bayud whispered, "Moving... human-squids, ... searching..."

Falco's stomach dropped, bile working its way to his mouth. He was the highest-ranking officer left and he knew what had to be done. "Can you reach a Command Unit?" Falco was whispering now.

"Yes, I... the stern unit." Her voice quivering. "They've left... area... They... all dea—"

The connection was getting worse, could drop permanently any second, it was now or never, Falco thought. "Ensign, get to the Command Unit and enter my code."

Heavy, wet breathing puffed over her COM, "I... here, hurry..."

"ZULU, ALFA, ROMEO, DELTA, ZERO, ZERO, TANGO, SEVEN." Falco dry heaved, tapped his COM to mute it, turned and vomited onto the deck. Composed himself and tapped the COM again hoping Bayud could hear him. "ZULU, ALFA, ROMEO, DELTA, ZERO, ZERO, TANGO, SEVEN..." he repeated.

"Ensign? Bayud can you hear me. What is happening?"

A sickening splash filled the COM. Shrieks sounded, faded, screeched over the COM again. In the background a countdown had started, the connection was gone.

"*Shangti* starboard flank, *Nuwa* port flank! With haste, stay close and keep pace with the station or we lose inter-ship

COMS!" Falco switched his COM to his officer line. "Chief Tenzin, new Command Center, Observation Deck."

A light burned across the small holo-feed. The cruiser *P'an Ku* erupted in a blue ball of flame reaching out towards the living then fading when the fire consumed the last of the vessel's oxygen.

In the distance, between the small, dissolving Oortian cloud and the massive backdrop of the black wall that hid the Oortian fleet, a red creature floated in front of a small Oortian force, her ivory tusks in full display.

She was smiling.

Tzara – the Darkness
Far Boundary

SOMETHING WAS WRONG, Tzara could feel its weight pressing on her carapace and filling her lair. A fraction of a cycle ago, a Seeker entered the Darkness, uploaded its report and returned to the Void.

Kalis and the clans destroyed all but three of the invader's powerful vessels. Thousands of her warriors died and Tzara would have offered thousands more to defeat the enemy. Soon the skirmish would be finished and the real mission completed. The Movoo would bring the thirteenth into the Darkness for cleansing and the beginning of its evolution to carry the newest clan.

A soothing hum filled her private thought-stream. The Darkness was here, searching her thoughts and systems for the slightest betrayal. Tzara was in tune with the violation after millions of cycles of its elusive intrusions. The Darkness' entry always began with a foreign thought dropped into her processors. A thought she knew was not her own.

But did the Darkness know Tzara could sense its presence? Yes, that was the real question. She waited for the feeling of violation to ebb into an echo of thought and finally, the Darkness shared a thought-stream with her.

The Dakkadians have returned to the far boundary. With each passing cycle they fortify their positions in our territory left vulnerable after the 'shift.' Energy shot through Tzara's systems causing her carapace to close into a crushing ball, each plate compressing her organs.

The 'shift' you made happen has left the clans' furthest territory defenseless, the Darkness chided.

Tzara knew to say nothing, to hide her thoughts as best she could and wait for the rest, if her carapace did not kill her first.

You must go to Kalis, deliver my command to her personally and without question.

The energy faded, her carapace released, liquid and waste poured from its end and pooled on the stone slab of her lair. Tzara straightened the best she could, floating alone in the main chamber. The presence of the Darkness hung like thick vapor, sticky and moist.

I will venture into the Void and deliver your message.

The encrypted upload was quickly stored into Tzara's memory and the shared thought-stream closed. The Darkness was gone, her thoughts again her own. The feeling of something being wrong and out of place was no longer present. Instead, an overwhelming sense of dread was close to incapacitating her. The message to Kalis would soon decide Tzara's fate the moment she delivered it. The ancient harbinger of destruction, the fallen Creator would destroy Tzara in the Void or send her back into the Darkness.

The journey would be quick. As soon as Tzara left her

shielded lair and broke from her planet's atmosphere, the Darkness would carry her to the Void where an armed escort waited.

8 8

Captain Falco – Battle Station Pluto
to Run or Stand

CAPTAIN FALCO SPRINTED through Battle Station Pluto. His personal COM remained silent after each attempt to contact Ensign Holts. Chief Tenzin worked quickly setting up the mobile command center on the upper observation deck. There they still had a functioning rail gun mounted and a bird's eye view of the Oortians and the two damaged cruisers. The station and vessels scanners were completely destroyed along with their nav-systems and long-range COMs.

"Chief, you let me know the second they show any sign of movement!" He slowed, slid, pushed off the bulkhead and was sprinting again.

"Yes, Captain. Oortians haven't moved. Ops center is good to go. Holo-feed, back-up COM and Battle-Net control functional. Lieutenant Wallace has the *Anam Cara* in position and ready as back-up."

Chief Tenzin was unflappable, Falco thought. If we stick

close together our ship-to-ship systems should still work. Falco tried Holts again as he reached the maintenance corridor. The hallway between the Battle-Cubes and the interior of the station were held together with repair epoxy. The entire section could be ripped into the vacuum of space at any moment. Med techs carried the wounded toward the main hatch that led to the interior of the space station where a triage was feeding them into a makeshift hospital.

A bloodied and familiar face carried two wounded marines, one over each shoulder. "Commander?"

Shar'ran stopped and turned. "I'm good, sir. Just a few scratches, few broken ribs." He looked at Falco's arm. "That looks bad."

"It was. Thank god for these med-suits, I think. Where's Ensign Holts?" Falco's voice cracked and he didn't care.

"She's fine. Lost her COM and sustained a concussion, but she's good, took out a dozen Oortians on her own." Commander Shar'ran pointed further down the corridor. "Gathering and distributing weapons to those left."

Falco was already running towards Holts. "Get to the upper observation deck ASAP, Commander!" he shouted over his shoulder. A poised Ensign Holts eventually came into view, her head wrapped in bandages, blood soaking through and highlighting the dragon tattoos in a red hue through the once white fabric. She handed a shotgun to a lone marine and turned toward Falco.

He slid and stopped inches from her face, stood silent panting, simply nodding while locked into her eyes.

"Looks worse than it is, Captain." Her eyes grew shiny. "At least, I hope it does."

Falco swallowed hard, desperately wanting to put his arms around her.

"Captain, you need to see this." Chief Tenzin's voice sounded in Falco's COM. "Sir, we have a situation."

"Oortians in pursuit?" Falco's pulse pounded in his ears.

"No, Captain. The small force is holding their current position, but another group has exited the main field."

"I'm on my way. Falco out." He looked to Holts and the lone marine standing behind her. "Where are the rest?"

"Injured or dead, Captain." Holts raised her head. "We have seven that can fight, eleven injured and being attended to plus a skeleton crew aboard the *Anam Cara*." Holts pulled at the collar of her uniform, exposing the med-suit below. "Everyone left was wearing one."

"You're in charge of the wounded." Falco adjusted his shotgun on his right shoulder, removed one of his two ammo belts and handed it to Holts. "You're a hell of a lot better with these than I am. Make sure you get a new personal COM, local channel is all we have left and begin moving the wounded once they're stable to the private bay for evac." He looked to the young marine. "You're with the ensign."

"Yes, Captain." Holts was on the move, the young marine catching up.

Falco quickly reached the elevator and punched the button for the upper observation deck.

Falco moved to the makeshift command center where the holo-feed showed a small stationary Oortian force led by Yama. Another group was quickly moving toward them from the Oortian field. Shar'ran and Chief Tenzin turned.

"Situation, Commander?" Falco stopped at the floating image.

"Battle Station Pluto has one functioning thruster. Cruisers aren't much better and we are putting a few hundred klicks between us and the Oortians." Shar'ran pointed toward the two Oortian groups that now faced each other and tapped the holo-feed controls. The hologram zoomed in until a grainy view of the Oortians filled the air.

"How is this image possible?" Falco leaned toward the

hologram. "They are teeth," he whispered. The giant red Oortian, Yama moved its mouth…

"We're running the onboard telescope to the holo-feed," Chief Tenzin stated and smiled. "It's like looking through a sandstorm with binoculars, but we have visual for now."

"My god, those four," Falco pointed to the Oortians moving to meet the three coming from the black field, "they look like armored whales."

"It's those dark orbs behind the Yama that are of concern." Shar'ran zoomed the holo-feed in closer, two glistening spheres came into grainy-focus. "These are similar to the Oortian vessels that released the Hull Pounders that decimated the Fleet and Station Pluto."

Chief Tenzin, raised his hand.

"What is it, Chief?" Falco turned from the hanging image.

"Before the COM-Sat was destroyed, we received a data packet from Pluto's Tombaugh Probe, and yes, I had no idea that ancient spacecraft was still working either. Something triggered it." Tenzin moved to the holo-feed, raised his data-pad and tapped on the screen until the holo-feed changed.

Falco locked onto the new image. "What the—"

"Eight substantial heat readings around Pluto," Tenzin stated.

"What the hell are the Oortians doing?" Falco pushed his face closer to the floating scene. "If this is a data-packet, magnify, full definition.

"Their positioning?" Falco felt the image grow menacing. "Mining, could they be mining or extracting?"

Tenzin leaned in, studying the eight giant spheres' placement. "Look at these threads that connect them." He traced the thin lines. "Each of the eight Oortian vessels must be at least ten times the size of Station Pluto." Chief Tenzin fell silent.

Commander Shar'ran, knelt down, face even with the holo-feed. "The eight are placed on one side of Pluto. The Oortians are between Pluto and their dark field." Shar'ran slid around the holo-feed. "The 'threads' that anchor them to the planet's surface," he pointed to the 'faint line' and then to the moon-sized spheres, "in relation to the Oortians... are over one hundred meters thick and hundreds of kilometers long?" He looked to Chief Tenzin and Captain Falco. "At least that's my best estimate."

A red light flashed at the base of the holo-feed projector.

"Something's moving." Tenzin tapped the controls and the two Oortian groups appeared again. The red leader and one of the newcomers were so close together, the telescope feed could not distinguish them. They looked like a thick pillar of red and black.

"Chief," Falco pointed a hundred feet above them to where the rail gun was mounted, "suit up and keep your sights on the Oortian group."

"Sir!" Tenzin placed the data-pad at the base of the holo-feed and was on his way.

"And Chief," Falco called after him, "full life-support pack too!"

"Yes, Captain!" he hollered.

Commander Shar'ran was still on his knees. He seemed to be staring through the holo-feed.

"What is it, Commander?" Falco asked.

"It's the size of the Oortian vessels, Captain. There is no reason for mining vessels to be this size, just doesn't make sense. All civilizations eventually follow the scale of efficiency in resource allocation."

"Took us thousands of years to understand less is more?" Falco stated.

"Yes, but an older civilization? A more advanced one. One that could create or utilize a camouflaging field that could potentially hide an entire planetary system?" Shar'ran turned to Falco.

"Let's hear it, Commander."

Shar'ran stood, hand on his chin still looking at the eight moon-sized objects tethered to Pluto. "Do you remember when the UNN *Titan* was dead in the water and needed to be towed to port?"

"2206 and I was stationed off the Yemen coast, as you know. Biggest aircraft carrier in history had a bad starter." Falco raised an eyebrow.

"Well I was there too and they towed that 400-meter-long ship with a stout tug from the US Army using a single thirty-centimeter-thick aircraft cable." Shar'ran pointed to the eight Oortian vessels, one at a time. "Those are the biggest tugs I've ever seen and they're pulling toward the Oortian field."

Tzara and Kalis
the Void

Tzara ignited her energy bloom and left the protective Darkness for the cold Void. The two Prox escorting her were the largest she had ever encountered. Each plated carapace pressed into hers from both sides.

Tzara was the Creator of the Prox, their goddess, their leader and yet she had never seen this clan. These Prox abominations were crafted by the Darkness, spawned deep within her mass, in one of the realms hidden from all the clans.

Kalis came into view, her red plated carapace reflected the dying light from the invader's once powerful fleet. Two Krell hovered around her, but they too were different. The Darkness has been busy, Tzara thought again. These Krell were filled with Seekers, filled with the fledgling Prox, another abomination. More fodder for the Darkness to expend without mercy or care.

The only blessing of the Void was not hearing the thought-streams of all the clans. Within the mass of the Darkness, all could speak, all could connect. Out in the Void only those in the open could use the thought-stream. The Darkness could not enter her systems, Tzara was free to think without fear.

Shattered warriors of the Clans floated like a sea of carnage. Pieces from the invader's vessels mixed with alien forms bounced off of dead Seekers and the occasional Warruq carapace. The remnants and reminders of what Kalis was, a destructive force that destroyed everything in her path.

Tzara's escorts moved further away and she stopped in front of Kalis. The two Krell moved back and joined the Prox. Cycles passed and Kalis's ocular sensors remained closed, the protective spikes around her skull-plate protruded further and were whiter than Tzara remembered. Her red carapace glistened with an oily slick that was dotted with strange white bulging lumps. Probably the gore from the dying invader vessels Kalis speared, again and again during the battle.

A thought-stream opened between them and the red membranes covering Kalis's sensors slid open. Fear rushed through Tzara's systems. Kalis lowered her carapace until her skull-plate was level with Tzara. The two touched and Tzara sensed the rush of her memory being accessed, downloaded – now she would find what the Darkness had in store for her.

Kalis opened her mouth wide, the white spikes continued to reveal themselves in row after spiraling row. The Prox escort moved in and held Tzara tight. A voice boomed over the thought-stream.

Go to your Realm of Warriors, screamed Kalis.

A Seeker blasted out of the Darkness and into the Void. Another thought-stream opened, smothering the stream between them. Kalis's mouth had already engulfed Tzara's skull-plate.

Kalis stopped, crunched down on Tzara's carapace and released her, severely injured but alive. The Seeker continued to fill the thought-stream with visions and data from the Creator's.

The Oortians furthest territory, the Far Boundary was under siege.

The Darkness must Shift back to repel the Dakkadian incursion and retake the lost zone. Leave the Invaders to flee back to where they came from, stinking of fear and weakness. We will deal with them later.

The thought-stream closed and the Seeker returned to the Darkness.

The two Prox were already towing Tzara toward the Veil of the Darkness. Kalis and the Krell remained. She turned toward the massive fleeing vessel that was now distant, wounded and dying with its two small battered guardians sputtering behind it, trying to keep up.

The warrior's rage raged through Kalis and she allowed all her sensors and systems to take in its wrath. The Krell pulsed from mottled black to deep blue, a small orange glow appeared in the center of each of them, casting a luminous glow of the Seekers carried within.

To the Realm of Warriors we journey. Kalis and the Krell ignited their energy blooms, launching forward, tearing through the Void and towards the fleeing invaders.

9 0

Captain Falco
the Oortian War

CAPTAIN FALCO SPUN THE HOLOGRAM, placed a hand on each side
of the image and pulled them apart. The distant, charging
Oortians expanded and Falco focused on Yama, the red leader.
Its tusks displayed in a shark-like grin and its shape a glistening
missile locked on a kill run aimed at the damaged Battle Station
Pluto – a vessel now little more than a plastic disc with a rifle
taped to it. He turned to Commander Shar'ran who was
attaching feeds to a data-pad in the newly minted command
center. "We're running out of time."

Shar'ran clicked in the last cable, touched the interface and
the screen came to life, numbers scrolling down the left side and
three small red blips appearing in the center. Shar'ran, slid his
fingertips across the data-pad and the red blips moved over and
Station Pluto appeared on the right with the two cruisers close
behind and a tiny glowing dot in front. The three chasing red
blips were growing close.

"Commander!" Falco's voice sounded, watching the holo-feed.

"It's up. *Anam Cara*'s Battle-Net is tethered." Shar'ran's finger followed the data scrolling on the left. "Twenty minutes? Maybe less if the Oortians can increase their speed. More if we can boost ours."

Falco opened his ship-wide COM. "*Anam Cara?*"

"Holding position, Captain. We have target lock on three incoming Oortians," Lieutenant Wallace reported from his position in the *Anam Cara*, leading Station Pluto's retreat.

"Damn it. Back to the private bay, Lieutenant. Load the wounded and prepare for full evac."

"Sir, we have lock. No missiles, but the Gatling gun is loaded—"

"Dock the *Anam Cara* and load the wounded. *Now*, Lieutenant!" Falco didn't wait for a response. "Ensign Holts? You hear that?"

"Prepping for evac now, Captain. We've lost three of the wounded." Holts cleared her throat.

"Understood." Falco swallowed hard. "*Shangti, Nuwa*, over." He waited for the cruisers to respond. The *Anam Cara* was the only vessel left with a COM-Sat, but using it would provide the remaining Oortians with a bull's-eye. Losing it would leave Falco with no way of contacting Vice-Admiral Hallsworth's fleet en route.

Commander Atagan's static laden voice sounded first. "Here, Captain."

Lieutenant Uushin of the cruiser *Nuwa* was barely audible. She was falling behind and would soon be out of the ship-to-ship COM's limited range.

Falco, muted his COM and turned to Commander Shar'ran. "The cruisers are falling behind. The Oortians are closing in." He slowly shook his head. "We can't slow down to evacuate them," Falco looked to the deck, both hands gripping the table, "we have no missiles left and only a few slugs for the lone rail gun."

"Ten minutes, Captain." Shar'ran kept focused on the data-pad tethered to the *Anam Cara*'s Battle-Net.

Falco raised his head, staring at the holo-feed, the Oortians, the faltering cruisers and finally, to humanity's greatest achievement, Station Pluto. "There are no victories," he whispered, "there is only the scale of loss."

Falco touched his COM, stood ramrod straight, eyes glassy, red and haunted, he took a deep breath. "Cruisers *Shangti* and *Nuwa*... Fire at will!" He looked up to the rail gun perched high above. "Chief, when the Oortians are in range, open fire."

"Yes, sir!" Tenzin growled.

The officers on the *Shangti* and *Nuwa* were too far behind Station Pluto to respond. The two cruisers now moved side by side, the *Shangti* slowing her pace to that of her sister ship.

"Five minutes, Captain." Shar'ran dropped his head.

Three red blips were almost on top of the two cruisers. Falco looked to the data-pad's feed from the *Anam Cara*. 2,000 meters flashed by, the red Oortian dropped back and the two glowing spheres the size of the Anam Cara burned forward. Flashes of hot lead flew from Chief Tenzin's rail-gun at supersonic speed. Burning pieces sloughed off the spheres with each impact, the *Shangti* and *Nuwa* launched their last missiles. Dozens flew from their cradles curved away from the cruisers and locked onto the spheres, Yama the Oortian admiral continued using them as cover.

Lone Hull Pounders burst out of the spheres, like rounds from a rifle. Each locked onto and incoming missile, paying no attention to the streaking slugs from the rail gun that continued slicing off chunks in larger and larger pieces.

Falco's COM sounded.

"I'm empty, Captain." Chief Tenzin sounded defeated.

"Move, Chief! Private bay, double time! We'll see you there."

Falco glanced at the data-pad, 5,000 meters, the number hung on the left side, the distance between Station Pluto and the cruisers. "Holts, report!"

"*Anam Cara* is loaded and ready for evac, Captain." Holts's breath came hard, the words fast. "Wounded are stable, you three are all that's left, sir."

"Oh God," Falco whispered.

The Oortian spheres unloaded their remaining Hull Pounders at once, each sphere aiming the blast at a cruiser. The holo-feed turned into a blue cloud of energy, flames rolling out in waves and then nothing. The cruisers were gone without a trace.

"Battle-Net has a single lock." Commander Shar'ran slid over from the data-pad and zoomed in with the holo-feed.

A red creature floated alone, two large black ovals above a ring of white tusks, its propulsion system shut down. Yama is watching us, Falco thought. No, it's tracking us. If only we had a Hell-Fire laying around.

"It's time, Commander." Falco moved to the command unit on the far wall, punched in his code. A panel slid open on the side of the unit. Falco entered a second code and a clear tray slide out from the side.

Shar'ran just stared as Falco pressed his thumb against the glass that immediately retracted with a perfect thumbprint.

"300, 299, 298..."

"Can't leave her like this, space station, starship and battle station. Station Pluto went above and beyond," Falco stated. "Five minutes and things get a lot hotter around here."

Commander Shar'ran pointed to the holo-feed. "Something's wrong. It's facing the black field. Just floating, watching."

"The field looks farther away, or we have picked up speed." Falco looked to Shar'ran who pulled the leads out of the data-pad, 255, 254, 253... echoed in the background. "On the move, Commander."

Falco and Shar'ran ran down the curving interior passage passing dead Hull Pounders lodged into the bulkheads, pieces of marines, unrecognizable forms.

"CAPTAIN! BEHIND YOU! IT'S COMING!" Lieutenant Wallace screeched in Falco's ear.

"GO GO GO!" he yelled to Commander Shar'ran who was running ahead of him.

They flew through the hatch, sprinting towards the *Anam Cara*, her engine already glowing hot, her bow pointing toward the private bay's exit hatch. From the ramp, Ensign Holts and Chief Tenzin were frantically yelling, and waving them on.

Station Pluto shook violently. Falco cartwheeled into the bay. Shar'ran fell and slid into the base of the ramp with a thud. Chief Tenzin lifted his limp form off the deck and into the *Anam Cara*. "149, 148, 147..."

Falco got to his feet, twenty meters from the *Anam Cara*'s ramp. The overhead erupted and a large glistening red shape tore through the deck only meters from his position and was gone. Suction lifted Falco off his feet and pulled him toward the cavernous hole in the deck. He caught the edge, the drag stopped, but he was dangling over the abyss. Somewhere below, the poly-epoxy sealed the hull.

Falco's grip slipped. Two hands reached down and grabbed his wrist, stopping his free-fall. "Reach up with your other hand, Captain!" Ensign Holts screamed.

Falco reached up with his broken arm, another hand met his and clamped down like a vice. Chief Tenzin and Holts pulled, Falco cried out as they lifted him up. Another shock wave moved through the station, this one distant.

"112, 111, 110..."

"Hurry!" Holts put Falco's arm over her shoulder, Tenzin did the same on the other side and they carried him back to the ramp.

A vibration bounced the deck. A distant popping sound grew

closer, bulkheads depressurizing one after another. They were half way up the ramp, a bulkhead on the far side of the bay splintered, plastic spears shot in all directions clanking off the *Anam Cara*. Chief Tenzin dropped Falco and bellowed as a meter-long splinter stuck in his thigh.

Yama dwarfed the *Anam Cara* and thrashed in all directions. Smashing with her skull, snapping her white tusk-filled maw. It was wedged between the overhead and deck, slowly moving toward them, using her fin-like appendages to squeeze closer, meter-by-meter. Black eyes, endless and cruel moving closer, the stench overwhelming, the mouth and tusks snapping. "43, 42, 41...'

Holts spun toward the Oortian, Falco's arm fell and she grabbed the M40 shotgun from his shoulder. Muffled blasts sounded in rapid succession as Holts moved toward its snapping jaws, pumping round after round into it from only a few meters away. Still it snapped and lunged forward. A final blast and she was empty.

"Holts! Get out of there!" Falco yelled, standing in the open hatch.

She sprinted up the ramp as Falco punched the hatch release. "Wallace, full burn!" he yelled into his COM.

"13, 12 ,11..."

The exterior doors crawled open, the main engine ignited, flame filling the bay, pouring over the Oortian, unearthly screams followed. The *Anam Cara* shot out and into open space.

"Hold on!" Lieutenant Wallace bellowed from the pilot's seat.

Hundreds of single detonations popped off like dominos around the massive disc, humanity's once bright and shiny beacon. Plumes of fire merged, grew and Station Pluto exploded, sending plastic-layered shrapnel and hardening chucks of epoxy in all directions.

Inside the *Anam Cara*, the steel hull sounded like a rattle as thousands of small impacts harmlessly bounced off the old iron ship.

Falco sat on the deck, battered, bruised and broken. He leaned against Ensign Holts, her arms wrapped around his chest. Commander Shar'ran lay next to them, unconscious but with a grin on his face. Falco held his friend's hand. Chief Tenzin was being tended to by a young med-tech while he kept making drinking motions to Falco.

"Yes, my friend, a mug of Tenzin Chang would hit the spot." Falco looked up at the beautiful woman who had just saved his life, "Thank you, I—" A warm hand covered his lips.

"I know," Holts said.

"Captain." Falco pulled the tiny COM off his ear and tossed it against the far bulkhead.

Jesus, Falco thought. I forget how small she is, this lovely boat of ours. "Yes, Lieutenant Wallace?"

"We have picked up a signal."

Falco sat up.

"As the Oortian field retreated, it revealed a Fleet beacon," Wallace stated.

"Captain Fei!" Falco let go of Shar'ran's hand and slapped the steel deck. "Turn her around, Lieutenant and keep the Gatling gun ready to go."

The story continues in 2019:
PLANET STEALERS
Book Two of the Oortian Wars

10TH FLEET

Artwork by James E. Grant

WORLDS OF IAIN RICHMOND

Thank you for purchasing this book. Visit
www.iainrichmond.com
and sign up for my spam-free newsletter and receive a free copy
of *BEYOND TERRA, Tales from the Seven Worlds*,
an anthology of short stories!

I will let you know when new releases are in the works, give you
sneak peeks at rough drafts and original storyworlds. Free, no
spam and a unique view into the worlds of Iain Richmond.

ABOUT THE AUTHOR

Iain Richmond is a builder and designer of creative spaces and unique furniture from Kathmandu to San Francisco. He has worked with and learned from craftsman around the world using salvaged and reclaimed materials. From living on a 30' boat in Juneau, Alaska to building his own home (board by board, paycheck by paycheck) on his small ranch in northern California, Iain has always dreamed of a life where he could follow his true passion... writing science fiction. When he leaves his 'writing shack' on Lore Mountain, Iain visits countries and communities that inspire new characters and vast storyworlds: Nepal, Isle of Skye, SE Alaska, Malta, and Southern Utah are a few of his favorite spots. He loves life with a small footprint, wildlife, wild-lands, and the hope of a perfect world filled with tolerant people. You can still find him boxing (more of a punching bag these days), playing rugby (see punching bag), trekking, and gardening (wine or scotch in hand), but spending quiet moments with his wife (much better half) and Bernese Mountain Dog(s) still ranks at the top of his life-list.

Printed in Great Britain
by Amazon